Post Captain

'*Master and Commander* raised almost danger-ously high expectations; *Post Captain* trium-phantly surpasses them. Mr O'Brian is a master of his period, in which his characters are firmly placed, while remaining three-dimensional, in-tensely human beings. This book sets him at the very top of his genre; he does not just have the chief qualifications of a first-class historical novelist, he has them all. The action scenes are superb; towards the end, far from being aware that one is reading what, physically, is a fairly long book, one notes with dismay that there is not much more to come. It is a brilliant book.'
Mary Renault

The complete Aubrey/Maturin tales
are available in Fontana

PATRICK O'BRIAN

Post Captain

FONTANA/Collins

First published in 1972 by William Collins Sons & Co. Ltd
First issued in Fontana Paperbacks 1974
Eighth impression February 1989

© Patrick O'Brian 1972

Made and printed in Great Britain by
William Collins Sons & Co. Ltd, Glasgow

FOR MARY, WITH LOVE

CHAPTER ONE

At first dawn the swathes of rain drifting eastwards across the Channel parted long enough to show that the chase had altered course. The *Charwell* had been in her wake most of the night, running seven knots in spite of her foul bottom, and now they were not much above a mile and a half apart. The ship ahead was turning, turning, coming up into the wind; and the silence along the frigate's decks took on a new quality as every man aboard saw her two rows of gun-ports come into view. This was the first clear sight they had had of her since the look-out hailed the deck in the growing darkness to report a ship hull-down on the horizon, one point on the larboard bow. She was then steering north-north-east, and it was the general opinion aboard the *Charwell* that she was either one of a scattered French convoy or an American blockade-runner hoping to reach Brest under cover of the moonless night.

Two minutes after that first hail the *Charwell* set her fore and main topgallants – no great spread of canvas, but then the frigate had had a long, wearing voyage from the West Indies: nine weeks out of sight of land, the equinoctial gales to strain her tired rigging to the breaking-point, three days of lying-to in the Bay of Biscay at its worst, and it was understandable that Captain Griffiths should wish to husband her a little. No cloud of sail, but even so she fetched the stranger's wake within a couple of hours, and at four bells in the morning watch the *Charwell* cleared for action. The drum beat to quarters, the hammocks came racing up, piling into the nettings to form bulwarks, the guns were run out; and the warm, pink, sleepy watch below had been standing to them in the cold rain ever since – an hour and more to chill them to the bone.

Now in the silence of this discovery one of the crew of a gun in the waist could be heard explaining to a weak-eyed staring little man beside him, 'She's a French two-decker, mate. A seventy-four or an eighty: we've caught a tartar, mate.'

'Silence there, God damn you,' cried Captain Griffiths. 'Mr Quarles, take that man's name.'

Then the grey rain closed in. But at present everyone on the crowded quarterdeck knew what lay behind that drifting, formless veil: a French ship of the line, with both her rows of gun-ports open. And there was not one who had missed the slight movement of the yard that meant she was about to lay her foresail to the mast, heave to and wait for them.

The *Charwell* was a 32-gun 12-pounder frigate, and if she got close enough to use the squat carronades on her quarterdeck and forecastle as well as her long guns she could throw a broadside weight of metal of 238 pounds. A French line-of-battle ship could not throw less than 960. No question of a match, therefore, and no discredit in bearing up and running for it, but for the fact that somewhere in the dim sea behind them there was their consort, the powerful 38-gun 18-pounder *Dee*. She had lost a topmast in the last blow, which slowed her down, but she had been well in sight at nightfall, and she had responded to Captain Griffiths's signal to chase: for Captain Griffiths was the senior captain. The two frigates would still be heavily outgunned by the ship of the line, but there was no doubt that they could take her on: she would certainly try to keep her broadside to one of the frigates and maul her terribly, but the other could lie on her bow or her stern and rake her – a murderous fire right along the length of her decks to which she could make almost no reply. It could be done: it had been done. In '97, for example, the *Indefatigable* and the *Amazon* had destroyed a French seventy-four. But then the *Indefatigable* and the *Amazon* carried eighty long guns between them, and the *Droits de*

8

l'Homme had not been able to open her lower-deck ports – the sea was running too high. There was no more than a moderate swell now; and to engage the stranger the *Charwell* would have to cut her off from Brest and fight her for – for how long?

'Mr – Mr Howell,' said the captain. 'Take a glass to the masthead and see what you can make of the *Dee*.'

The long-legged midshipman was half-way to the mizen-top before the captain had finished speaking, and his 'Aye-aye, sir' came down through the sloping rain. A black squall swept across the ship, pelting down so thick that for a while the men on the quarterdeck could scarcely see the forecastle, and the water ran spouting from the lee-scuppers. Then it was gone, and in the pale gleam of day that followed there came the hail. 'On deck, sir. She's hull-up on the leeward beam. She's fished her . . . '

'Report,' said the captain, in a loud, toneless voice. 'Pass the word for Mr Barr.'

The third lieutenant came hurrying aft from his station. The wind took his rain-soaked cloak as he stepped on to the quarterdeck, and he made a convulsive gesture, one hand going towards the flapping cloth and the other towards his hat.

'Take it off, sir,' cried Captain Griffiths, flushing dark red. 'Take it right off your head. You know Lord St Vincent's order – you have all of you read it – you know how to salute . . . ' He snapped his mouth shut; and after a moment he said, 'When does the tide turn?'

'I beg your pardon, sir,' said Barr. 'At ten minutes after eight o'clock, sir. It is almost the end of slack-water now, sir, if you please.'

The captain grunted, and said, 'Mr Howell?'

'She has fished her main topmast, sir,' said the midshipman, standing bareheaded, tall above his captain. 'And has just hauled to the wind.'

The captain levelled his glass at the *Dee*, whose top-gallant-sails were now clear above the jagged edge of the sea: her top-sails too, when the swell raised both the frigates high. He wiped the streaming objective-glass, stared again, swung round to look at the Frenchman, snapped the telescope shut and gazed back at the distant frigate. He was alone there, leaning on the rail, alone there on the holy starboard side of the quarterdeck; and from time to time, when they were not looking at the Frenchman or the *Dee*, the officers glanced thoughtfully at his back.

The situation was still fluid; it was more a potentiality than a situation. But any decision now would crystallize it, and the moment it began to take shape all the succeeding events would follow of themselves, moving at first with slow inevitability and then faster and faster, never to be undone. And a decision must be made, made quickly – at the *Charwell*'s present rate of sailing they would be within range of the two-decker in less than ten minutes. Yet there were so many factors . . . The *Dee* was no great sailer close-hauled on a wind; and the turning tide would hold her back – it was right across her course; she might have to make another tack. In half an hour the French 36-pounders could rip the guts out of the *Charwell*, dismast her and carry her into Brest – the wind stood fair for Brest. Why had they seen not a single ship of the blockading squadron? They could not have been blown off, not with this wind. It was damned odd. Everything was damned odd, from this Frenchman's conduct onwards. The sound of gunfire would bring the squadron up . . . Delaying tactics . . .

The feeling of those eyes on his back filled Captain Griffiths with rage. An unusual number of eyes, for the *Charwell* had several officers and a couple of civilians as passengers, one set from Gibraltar and another from Port of Spain. The fire-eating General Paget was one of them, an influential man; and another was Captain Aubrey, Lucky Jack Aubrey, who had set about a Spanish 36-gun xebec-frigate not long ago with the *Sophie*, a 14-gun brig, and had taken her. The *Cacafuego*. It had been the talk of

10

the fleet some months back; and it made the decision no less difficult.

Captain Aubrey was standing by the aftermost larboard carronade, with a completely abstracted, non-committal look upon his face. From that place, being tall, he could see the whole situation, the rapidly, smoothly changing triangle of three ships; and close beside him stood two shorter figures, the one Dr Maturin, formerly his surgeon in the *Sophie*, and the other a man in black – black clothes, black hat and a streaming black cloak – who might have had *intelligence agent* written on his narrow forehead. Or just the word *spy*, there being so little room. They were talking in a language thought by some to be Latin. They were talking eagerly, and Jack Aubrey, intercepting a furious glance across the deck, leant down to whisper in his friend's ear, 'Stephen, will you not go below? They will be wanting you in the cockpit any moment now.'

Captain Griffiths turned from the rail, and with laboured calmness he said, 'Mr Berry, make this signal. *I am about to . . .* '

At this moment the ship of the line fired a gun, followed by three blue lights that soared and burst with a ghostly effulgence in the dawn: before the last dropping trail of sparks had drifted away downwind she sent up a succession of rockets, a pale, isolated Guy Fawkes' night far out in the sea.

'What the devil can she mean by that?' thought Jack Aubrey, narrowing his eyes, and the wondering murmur along the frigate's decks echoed his amazement.

'On deck,' roared the look-out in the foretop, 'there's a cutter pulling from under her lee.'

Captain Griffiths's telescope swivelled round. 'Duck up,' he called, and as the clewlines plucked at the main and foresails to give him a clear view he saw the cutter, an English cutter, sway up its yard, fill, gather speed, and come racing over the grey sea, towards the frigate.

'Close the cutter,' he said. 'Mr Bowes, give her a gun.'

At last, after all these hours of frozen waiting, there came the quick orders, the careful laying of the gun, the crash of the twelve-pounder, the swirl of acrid smoke eddying briefly on the wind, and the cheer of the crew as the ball skipped across the cutter's bows. An answering cheer from the cutter, a waving of hats, and the two vessels neared one another at a combined speed of fifteen miles an hour.

The cutter, fast and beautifully handled – certainly a smuggling craft – came to under the *Charwell*'s lee, lost her way, and lay there as trim as a gull, rising and falling on the swell. A row of brown, knowing faces grinned up at the frigate's guns.

'I'd press half a dozen prime seamen out of her in the next two minutes,' reflected Jack, while Captain Griffiths hailed her master over the lane of sea.

'Come aboard,' said Captain Griffiths suspiciously, and after a few moments of backing and filling, of fending-off and cries of 'Handsomely now, God damn your soul,' the master came up the stern ladder with a bundle under his arm. He swung easily over the taffrail, held out his hand and said, 'Wish you joy of the peace, Captain.'

'Peace?' cried Captain Griffiths.

'Yes, sir. I thought I should surprise you. They signed not three days since. There's not a foreign-going ship has heard yet. I've got the cutter filled with the newspapers, London, Paris and country towns – all the articles, gentlemen, all the latest details,' he said, looking round the quarterdeck. 'Half a crown a go.'

There was no disbelieving him. The quarterdeck looked utterly blank. But the whispered word had flown along the deck from the radiant carronade-crews, and now cheering broke out on the forecastle. In spite of the captain's automatic 'Take that man's name, Mr Quarles,' it flowed back to the mainmast and spread throughout the ship, a full-throated howl of joy – liberty, wives and sweethearts, safety, the delights of land.

And in any case there was little real ferocity in Captain Griffiths's voice: anyone looking into his close-set eyes would have seen ecstasy in their depths. His occupation was gone, vanished in a puff of smoke; but now no one on God's earth could ever know what signal he had been about to make, and in spite of the severe control that he imposed upon his face there was an unusual urbanity in his tone as he invited his passengers, his first lieutenant, the officer and the midshipman of the watch to dine with him that afternoon.

'It is charming to see how sensible the men are – how sensible of the blessings of peace,' said Stephen Maturin to the Reverend Mr Hake, by way of civility.

'Aye. The blessings of peace. Oh, certainly,' said the chaplain, who had no living to retire to, no private means, and who knew that the *Charwell* would be paid off as soon as she reached Portsmouth. He walked deliberately out of the wardroom, to pace the quarterdeck in a thoughtful silence, leaving Captain Aubrey and Dr Maturin alone.

'I thought he would have shown more pleasure,' observed Stephen Maturin.

'It's an odd thing about you, Stephen,' said Jack Aubrey, looking at him with affection. 'You have been at sea quite some time now, and no one could call you a fool, but you have no more notion of a sailor's life than a babe unborn. Surely you must have noticed how glum Quarles and Rodgers and all the rest were at dinner? And how blue everyone has always looked this war, when there was any danger of peace?'

'I put it down to the anxieties of the night – the long strain, the watchfulness, the lack of sleep: I must not say the apprehension of danger. Captain Griffiths was in a fine flow of spirits, however.'

'Oh,' said Jack, closing one eye. 'That was reyther different; and in any case he is a post-captain, of course.

13

He has his ten shillings a day, and whatever happens he goes up the captains' list as the old ones die off or get their flag. He's quite old – forty, I dare say, or even more – but with any luck he'll die an admiral. No. It's the others I'm sorry for, the lieutenants with their half-pay and very little chance of a ship – none at all of promotion; the poor wretched midshipmen who have not been made and who never will be made now – no hope of a commission. And of course, no half-pay at all. It's the merchant service for them, or blacking shoes outside St James's Park. Haven't you heard the old song? I'll tip you a stave.' He hummed the tune, and in a discreet rumble he sang.

> 'Says Jack, "There is very good news, there is peace
>   both by land and by sea;
> Great guns no more shall be used, for we all dis-
>   banded be,"
> Says the Admiral, "That's very bad news;" says
>   the captain, "My heart will break;"
> The lieutenant cries, "What shall I do? For I know
>   not what course for to take."
> Says the doctor, "I'm a gentleman too, I'm a gentle-
>   man of the first rank;
> I will go to some country fair, and there I'll set
>   up mountebank."

Ha, ha, that's for you, Stephen – ha, ha, ha –

> Says the midshipman, "I have no trade; I have
>   got my trade for to choose,
> I will go to St James's Park gate, and there I'll
>   set black of shoes;
> And there I will set all day, at everybody's call,
> And everyone that comes by, 'Do you want my
>   nice shining balls?' " '

Mr Quarles looked in at the door, recognized the tune

14

and drew in a sharp breath; but Jack was a guest, a superior officer – a master and commander, no less, with an epaulette on his shoulder – and he was broad as well as tall. Mr Quarles let his breath out in a sigh and closed the door.

'I should have sung softer,' said Jack, and drawing his chair closer to the table he went on in a low voice, 'No, those are the chaps I am sorry for. I'm sorry for myself too, naturally – no great likelihood of a ship, and of course no enemy to cruise against if I do get one. But it's nothing in comparison of them. We've had luck with prize-money, and if only it were not for this infernal delay over making me post I should be perfectly happy to have a six months' run ashore. Hunting. Hearing some decent music. The opera – we might even go to Vienna! Eh? What do you say, Stephen? Though I must confess this slowness irks my heart and soul. However, it's nothing in comparison of them, and I make no doubt it will be settled directly.' He picked up *The Times* and ran through the *London Gazette*, in case he should have missed his own name in the first three readings. 'Toss me the one on the locker, will you?' he said, throwing it down. 'The *Sussex Courier*.'

'This is more like it, Stephen,' he said, five minutes later. '*Mr Savile's hounds will meet at ten o'clock on Wednesday, the sixth of November* 1802, *at Champflower Cross*. I had such a run with them when I was a boy: my father's regiment was in camp at Rainsford. A seven-mile point – prodigious fine country if you have a horse that can really go. Or listen to this: *a neat gentleman's residence, standing upon gravel, is to be let by the year, at moderate terms*. Stabling for ten, it says.'

'Are there any rooms?'

'Why, of course there are. It couldn't be called a *neat* gentleman's residence, without there were rooms. What a fellow you are, Stephen. Ten bedrooms. By God, there's a lot to be said for a house, not too far from the sea, in that sort of country.'

'Had you not thought of going to Woolhampton – of going to your father's house?'

'Yes . . . yes. I mean to give him a visit, of course. But there's my new mother-in-law, you know. And to tell you the truth, I don't think it would exactly answer.' He paused, trying to remember the name of the person, the classical person, who had had such a trying time with his father's second wife; for General Aubrey had recently married his dairy-maid, a fine black-eyed young woman with a moist palm whom Jack knew very well. Actaeon, Ajax, Aristides? He felt that their cases were much alike and that by naming him he would give a subtle hint of the position: but the name would not come, and after a while he reverted to the advertisements. 'There's a great deal to be said for somewhere in the neighbourhood of Rainsford – three or four packs within reach, London only a day's ride away, and neat gentlemen's residences by the dozen, all standing upon gravel. You'll go snacks with me, Stephen? We'll take Bonden, Killick, Lewis and perhaps one or two other old Sophies, and ask some of the youngsters to come and stay. We'll lay in beer and skittles – it will be Fiddler's Green!'

'I should like it of all things,' said Stephen. 'Whatever the advertisements may say, it is a chalk soil, and there are some very curious plants and beetles on the downs. I am with child to see a dew-pond.'

Polcary Down and the cold sky over it; a searching air from the north breathing over the water-meadows, up across the plough, up and up to this great sweep of open turf, the down, with the covert called Rumbold's Gorse sprawling on the lower edge of it. A score of red-coated figures dotted round the Gorse, and far away below them on the middle slope a ploughman standing at the end of his furrow, motionless behind his team of Sussex oxen, gazing up as Mr Savile's hounds worked their way through the furze and the brown remnants of the bracken.

Slow work; uncertain, patchy scent; and the foxhunters had plenty of time to drink from their flasks, blow on their hands, and look out over the landscape below them – the river winding through its patchwork of fields, the towers or steeples of Hither, Middle, Nether and Savile Champflower, the six or seven big houses scattered along the valley, the whale-backed downs one behind the other, and far away the lead-coloured sea.

It was a small field, and almost everyone there knew everyone else: half a dozen farmers, some private gentlemen from the Champflowers and the outlying parishes, two militia officers from the dwindling camp at Rainsford, Mr Burton, who had come out in spite of his streaming cold in the hope of catching a glimpse of Mrs St John, and Dr Vining, with his hat pinned to his wig and both tied under his chin with a handkerchief. He had been led astray early in his rounds – he could not resist the sound of the horn – and his conscience had been troubling him ever since the scent had faded and died. From time to time he looked over the miles of frigid air between the covert and Mapes Court, where Mrs Williams was waiting for him. 'There is nothing wrong with her,' he observed. 'My physic will do no good; but in Christian decency I should call. And indeed I shall, unless they find again before I can tell a hundred.' He put his finger upon his pulse and began to count. At ninety he paused, looking about for some reprieve, and on the far side of the covert he saw a figure he did not know. 'That is the medical man they have been telling me about, no doubt,' he said. 'It would be the civil thing to go over and say a word to him. A rum-looking cove. Dear me, a very rum-looking cove.'

The rum-looking cove was sprawling upon a mule, an unusual sight in an English hunting-field; and quite apart from the mule there was a strange air about him – his slate-coloured small-clothes, his pale face, his pale

17

eyes and even paler close-cropped skull (*his* hat and wig were tied to his saddle), and the way he bit into a hunk of bread rubbed with garlic. He was calling out in a loud tone to his companion, in whom Dr Vining recognized the new tenant of Melbury Lodge. 'I tell you what it is, Jack,' he was saying, 'I tell you what it is . . .'

'You sir – you on the mule,' cried old Mr Savile's furious voice. 'Will you let the God-damned dogs get on with their work? Hey? Hey? Is this a God-damned coffee-house? I appeal to you, is this an infernal debating society?'

Captain Aubrey pursed his lips demurely and pushed his horse over the twenty yards that separated them. 'Tell me later, Stephen,' he said in a low voice, leading his friend round the covert out of the master's sight. 'Tell me later, when they have found their fox.'

The demure look did not sit naturally upon Jack Aubrey's face, which in this weather was as red as his coat, and as soon as they were round the corner, under the lee of a wind-blown thorn, his usual expectant cheerfulness returned, and he looked eagerly up into the furze, where an occasional heave and rustle showed the pack in motion.

'Looking for a *fox*, are they?' said Stephen Maturin, as though hippogriffs were the more usual quarry in England, and he relapsed into a brown study, munching slowly upon his bread.

The wind breathed up the long hillside; remote clouds passed evenly across the sky. Now and then Jack's big hunter brought his ears to bear; this was a recent purchase, a strongly-built bay, quite up to Jack's sixteen stone. But it did not much care for hunting, and then like so many geldings it spent much of its time mourning for its lost stones: a discontented horse. If the moods that succeeded one another in its head had taken the form of words they would have run, 'Too heavy – sits too far forward when we go over a fence – have carried him far enough for one day – shall have him off presently, see if I don't. I smell a mare! A mare! Oh!' Its flaring nostrils quivered, and it stamped.

Looking round Jack saw that there were newcomers in the field. A young woman and a groom came hurrying up the side of the plough, the groom mounted on a cob and the young woman on a pretty little high-bred chestnut mare. When they reached the post and rail dividing the field from the down the groom cantered on to open a gate, but the girl set her horse at the rail and skipped neatly over it, just as a whimpering and then a bellowing roar inside the covert gave promise of great things.

The noise died away: a young hound came out and stared into the open. Stephen Maturin moved from behind the close-woven thorn to follow the flight of a falcon overhead, and at the sight of the mule the chestnut mare began to caper, flashing her white stockings and tossing her head.

'Get over, you – ,' said the girl, in her pure clear young voice. Jack had never heard a girl say – before, and he turned to look at her with a particular interest. She was busy coping with the mare's excitement, but after a moment she caught his eye and frowned. He looked away, smiling, for she was the prettiest thing – indeed, beautiful, with her heightened colour and her fine straight back, sitting her horse with the unconscious grace of a midshipman at the tiller in a lively sea. She had black hair and blue eyes; a certain ram-you-damn-you air that was slightly comic and more than a little touching in so slim a creature. She was wearing a shabby blue habit with white cuffs and lapels, like a naval lieutenant's coat, and on top of it all a dashing tricorne with a tight curl of ostrich-feather. In some ingenious way, probably by the use of combs, she had drawn up her hair under this hat so as to leave one ear exposed; and this perfect ear, as Jack observed when the mare came crabwise towards him, was as pink as . . .

'There is that fox of theirs,' remarked Stephen, in a

conversational tone. 'There is that fox we hear so much about. Though indeed, it is a vixen, sure.'

Slipping quickly along a fold in the ground the leaf-coloured fox went slanting down across them towards the plough. The horses' ears and the mule's followed it, cocked like so many semaphores. When the fox was well clear Jack rose in his stirrups, held up his hat and holla'd it away in a high-seas roar that brought the huntsman tearing round, his horn going twang-twang-twang, and hounds racing from the furze at all points. They hit the scent in the sheltered hollow and they were away with a splendid cry. They poured through the fence; they were half-way across the unploughed stubble, a close-packed body – such music – and the huntsman was right up there with them. The field came thundering round the covert: someone had the gate open and in a moment there was an eager crowd jostling to get through, for it was a devilish unpleasant downhill leap just here. Jack held hard, not choosing to thrust his first time out in a strange country, but his heart was beating to quarters, double-time, and he had already worked out the line he would follow once the press had thinned.

Jack was the keenest of fox-hunters: he loved everything about the chase, from the first sound of the horn to the rancid smell of the torn fox, but in spite of a few unwelcome spells without a ship, he had spent two thirds of his life at sea – his skill was not all he thought it was.

The gate was still jammed – there would be no chance of getting through it before the pack was in the next field. Jack wheeled his horse, called out, 'Come on, Stephen,' and put it at the rail. Out of the corner of his eye he saw the chestnut flash between his friend and the crowd in the gate. As his horse rose Jack screwed round to see how the girl would get over, and the gelding instantly felt this change of balance. It took the rail flying high and fast, landed with its head low, and with a cunning twist of its shoulder and an upward thrust from behind it unseated its rider.

He did not fall at once. It was a slow, ignominious glide down that slippery near shoulder, with a fistful of mane in his right hand; but the horse was the master of the situation now, and in twenty yards the saddle was empty.

The horse's satisfaction did not last, however. Jack's boot was wedged in his near stirrup; it would not come free, and here was his heavy person jerking and thumping along at the gelding's side, roaring and swearing horribly. The horse began to grow alarmed – to lose its head – to snort – to stare wildly – and to run faster and faster across those dark, flint-strewn, unforgiving furrows.

The ploughman left his oxen and came lumbering up the hill, waving his goad; a tall young man in a green coat, a foot-follower, called out 'Whoa there, whoa there,' and ran towards the horse with his arms spread wide; the mule, the last of the vanishing field, turned and raced back to cut the gelding off, swarming along in its inhuman way, very close to the ground. It outran the men, crossed the gelding's path, stood firm and took the shock: like a hero Stephen flung himself off, seized the reins and clung there until Green Coat and the ploughman came pounding up.

The oxen, left staring half-way along their furrow, were so moved by all this excitement that they came very nearly to the point of cutting a caper on their own. But before they had made up their minds it was over. The ploughman was leading the shamefaced horse to the side of the field, while the other two propped raw bones and bloody head between them, listening gravely to his explanations. The mule walked behind.

Mapes Court was an entirely feminine household – not a man in it, apart from the butler and the groom. Mrs Williams was a woman, in the natural course of things; but she was a woman so emphatically, so totally a woman,

21

that she was almost devoid of any private character. A vulgar woman, too, although her family, which was of some importance in the neighbourhood, had been settled there since Dutch William's time.

It was difficult to see any connection, any family likeness, between her and her daughters and her niece, who made up the rest of the family. Indeed, it was not much of a house for family likeness: the dim portraits might have been bought at various auctions, and although the three daughters had been brought up together, with the same people around them, in the same atmosphere of genteel money-worship, position-worship and suffused indignation – an indignation that did not require any object for its existence, but that could always find one in a short space of time; a housemaid wearing silver buckles on Sunday would bring on a full week's flow – they were as different in their minds as they were in their looks.

Sophia, the eldest, was a tall girl with wide-set grey eyes, a broad, smooth forehead, and a wonderful sweetness of expression – soft fair hair, inclining to gold: an exquisite skin. She was a reserved creature, living much in an inward dream whose nature she did not communicate to anyone. Perhaps it was her mother's unprincipled rectitude that had given her this early disgust for adult life; but whether or no, she seemed very young for her twenty-seven years. There was nothing in the least degree affected or kittenish about this: rather a kind of ethereal quality – the quality of a sacrificial object. Iphigeneia before the letter. Her looks were very much admired; she was always elegant, and when she was in looks she was quite lovely. She spoke little, in company or out, but she was capable of a sudden dart of sharpness, of a remark that showed much more intelligence and reflection than would have been expected from her rudimentary education and her very quiet provincial life. These remarks had a much greater force, coming from an amiable, pliant, and as it were sleepy reserve, and before now they had startled men who did not know her well – men who had been prating away happily with the conscious superiority of their sex. They dimly grasped an underlying strength, and they connected it with her occasional expression of secret amusement, the relish of something that she did not choose to share.

Cecilia was more nearly her mother's daughter: a little goose with a round face and china-blue eyes, devoted to ornament and to crimping her yellow hair, shallow and foolish almost to simplicity, but happy, full of cheerful noise, and not yet at all ill-natured. She dearly loved the company of men, men of any size or shape. Her younger sister Frances did not: she was indifferent to their admiration – a long-legged nymph, still given to whistling and shying stones at the squirrels in the walnut-tree. Here was all the pitilessness of youth intact; and she was perfectly entrancing, as a spectacle. She had her cousin Diana's black hair and great dark blue misty pools of eyes, but she was as unlike her sisters as though they belonged to another sex. All they had in common was youthful grace, a good deal of gaiety, splendid health, and ten thousand pounds apiece.

With these attractions it was strange that none of them should have married, particularly as the marriage-bed was never far from Mrs Williams's mind. But the paucity of men, of eligible bachelors, in the neighbourhood, the disrupting effects of ten years of war, and Sophia's reluctance (she had had several offers) explained a great deal; the rest could be accounted for by Mrs Williams's avidity for a good marriage settlement, and by an unwillingness on the part of the local gentlemen to have her as a mother-in-law.

Whether Mrs Williams liked her daughters at all was doubtful: she loved them, of course, and had 'sacrificed everything for them', but there was not much room in her composition for liking – it was too much taken up with being right (*Hast thou considered my servant Mrs Williams, that there is none like her in the earth, a perfect and an upright woman?*), with being tired, and with being ill-used. Dr Vining, who had known her all her life and who had seen her children into the world, said that she did not; but even he, who cordially disliked her, admitted that she truly, whole-heartedly loved their interest. She might damp all their enthusiasms, drizzle grey disapproval from one year's end to another, and spoil even birthdays with bravely-supported headaches, but she would fight parents, trustees and lawyers like a tigress for 'an adequate provision'. Yet still she had three unmarried daughters, and it was something of a comfort to her to be able to attribute this to their being overshadowed by her niece. Indeed, this niece, Diana Villiers, was as good-looking in her way as Sophia. But how unlike these two ways were: Diana with her straight back and high-held head seemed quite tall, but when she stood next to her cousin, she came no higher than her ear, they both had natural grace in an eminent degree, but whereas Sophia's was a willowy, almost languorous flowing perfection of movement, Diana's had a quick, flashing rhythm – on those rare occasions when there was a ball within twenty miles of Mapes she danced superbly; and by candlelight her complexion was almost as good as Sophia's.

Mrs Villiers was a widow: she had been born in the same year as Sophia, but what a different life she had led; at fifteen, after her mother's death, she had gone out to India to keep house for her expensive, raffish father, and she had lived there in splendid style even after her marriage to a penniless young man, her father's aide-de-camp, for he had moved into their rambling great palace, where the addition of a husband and an extra score of servants passed unnoticed. It had been a foolish marriage on the emotional plane – both too passionate, strong, self-willed, and opposed in every way to do anything but tear one another to pieces – but from the worldly point of view there was a great deal to be said for it. It did bring her a handsome husband, and it might have brought her

24

a deer-park and ten thousand a year as well, for not only was Charles Villiers well-connected (one sickly life between him and a great estate) but he was intelligent, cultivated, unscrupulous and active – particularly gifted on the political side: the very man to make a brilliant career in India. A second Clive, maybe, and wealthy by the age of thirty-odd. But they were both killed in the same engagement against Tippoo Sahib, her father owing three lakhs of rupees and her husband nearly half that sum.

The Company allowed Diana her passage home and fifty pounds a year until she should remarry. She came back to England with a wardrobe of tropical clothes, a certain knowledge of the world, and almost nothing else. She came back, in effect, to the schoolroom, or something very like it. For she at once realized that her aunt meant to clamp down on her, to allow her no chance of queering her daughters' pitch; and as she had no money and nowhere else to go she determined to fit into this small slow world of the English countryside, with its fixed notions and its strange morality.

She was willing, she was obliged, to accept a protectorate, and from the beginning she resolved to be meek, cautious and retiring; she knew that other women would regard her as a menace, and she meant to give them no provocation. But her theory and her practice were sometimes at odds, and in any case Mrs Williams's idea of a protectorate was much more like a total annexation. She was afraid of Diana, and dared not push her too far, but she never gave up trying to gain a moral superiority, and it was striking to see how this essentially stupid woman, unhampered by any principle or by any sense of honour, managed to plant her needle where it hurt most.

This had been going on for years, and Diana's clandestine or at least unavowed excursions with Mr Savile's hounds had a purpose beyond satisfying her delight in riding. Returning now she met her cousin Cecilia in the hall, hurrying to look at her new bonnet in the pier-glass between the breakfast-room windows.

'Thou looks't like Antichrist in that lewd hat,' she said in a sombre voice, for the hounds had lost their fox and the only tolerable-looking man had vanished.

'Oh! Oh!' cried Cecilia, 'what a shocking thing to say! It's blasphemy, I'm sure. I declare I've never had such a shocking thing said to me since Jemmy Blagrove called me that rude word. I shall tell Mama.'

'Don't be a fool, Cissy. It's a quotation – literature – the Bible.'

'Oh. Well, I think it's very shocking. You are covered with mud, Di. Oh, you took my tricorne. Oh, what an ill-natured thing you are – I am sure you spoilt the feather. I shall tell Mama.' She snatched the hat, but finding it unhurt she softened and went on, 'Well: and so you had a dirty ride. You went along Gallipot Lane, I suppose. Did you see anything of the hunt? They were over there on Polcary all the morning with their horrid howling and yowling.'

'I saw them in the distance,' said Diana.

'You frightened me so with that dreadful thing you said about Jesus,' said Cecilia, blowing on the ostrich-feather, 'that I almost forgot the news. The Admiral is back!'

'Back already?'

'Yes. And he will be over this very afternoon. He sent Ned with his compliments and might he come with Mama's Berlin wool after dinner. Such fun! He will tell us all about these beautiful young men! Men, Diana!'

The family had scarcely gathered about their tea before Admiral Haddock walked in. He was only a yellow admiral, retired without hoisting his flag, and he had not been afloat since 1794, but he was their one authority on naval matters and he had been sadly missed ever since the unexpected arrival of a Captain Aubrey of the Navy – a captain who had taken Melbury Lodge and who was therefore within their sphere of influence, but about whom they knew nothing and upon whom (he being a bachelor) they, as ladies, could not call.

'Pray, Admiral,' said Mrs Williams, as soon as the Berlin wool had been faintly praised, peered at with narrowed eyes and pursed lips, and privately condemned as useless – nothing like a match, in quality, colour or price. 'Pray, Admiral, tell us about this Captain Aubrey, who they say has taken Melbury Lodge.'

'Aubrey? Oh, yes,' said the Admiral, running his dry tongue over his dry lips, like a parrot, 'I know all about him. I have not met him, but I talked about him to people at the club and in the Admiralty, and when I came home I looked him up in the Navy List. He is a young fellow, only a master and commander, you know – '

'Do you mean he is *pretending* to be a captain?' cried Mrs Williams, perfectly willing to believe it.

'No, no,' said Admiral Haddock impatiently. 'We always call commanders Captain So-and-So in the Navy. Real captains, full captains, we call *post*-captains – we say a man is made post when he is appointed to a sixth-rate or better, an eight-and-twenty, say, or a thirty-two-gun frigate. A *post*-ship, my dear Madam.'

'Oh, indeed,' said Mrs Williams, nodding her head and looking wise.

'Only a commander: but he did most uncommon well in the Mediterranean. Lord Keith gave him cruise after cruise in that little old quarter-decked brig we took from the Spaniards in ninety-five, and he played Old Harry with the shipping up and down the coast. There were times when he well-nigh filled the Lazaretto Reach in Mahon with his prizes – Lucky Jack Aubrey, they called him. He must have cleared a pretty penny – a most elegant penny indeed. And he it was who took the *Cacafuego*! The very man,' said the Admiral with some triumph, gazing round the circle of blank faces. After a moment's pause of unbroken stupidity on their part he shook his head, saying, 'You never even heard of the engagement, I collect?'

No, they had not. They were sorry to say that they had not heard of the *Cacafuego* – was it the same as the Battle of St Vincent? Perhaps it had happened when they were so busy with the strawberries. They had put up two hundred pots.

'Well, the *Cacafuego* was a Spanish xebec-frigate of two and thirty guns, and he went for her in this little fourteen-gun sloop, fought her to a standstill, and carried her into Minorca. Such an action! The service rang with it. And if it had not been for some legal quirk about her papers, she being lent to the Barcelona merchants and not commanded by her regular captain, which meant that technically she was not for the moment a king's ship but a privateer, he would have been made post and given command of her. Perhaps knighted too. But as it was – there being wheels within wheels, as I will explain at another time, for it is not really suitable for young ladies – she was not bought into the service; and so far he has not been given his step. What is more, I do not think he ever will be. He is a vile ranting dog of a Tory, to be sure – or at least his father is – but even so, it was shameful. He may not be quite the thing, but I intend to take particular notice of him – shall call tomorrow – to mark my sense of the action: and of the injustice.'

'So he is not quite the thing, sir?' asked Cecilia.

'Why no, my dear, he is not. Not at all the thing, they tell me. Dashing he may be! indeed, he is; but disciplined – pah! That is the trouble with so many of your young fellows, and it will never do in the service – will never do for St Vincent. Many complaints about his lack of discipline – independence – disobeying orders. No future in the service for that kind of officer, above all with St Vincent at the Admiralty. And then I fear he may not attend to the fifth commandment quite as he should.' The girls' faces took on an inward look as they privately ran over the Decalogue: in order of intelligence a little frown appeared on each as its owner reached the part about

28

Sunday travelling, and then cleared as they carried on to the commandment the Admiral had certainly intended. 'There was a great deal of talk about Mrs – about a superior officer's wife, and they say that was at the bottom of the matter. A sad rake, I fear; and undisciplined, which is far worse. You may say what you please about old Jarvie, but he will not brook undisciplined conduct. And he does not love a Tory, either.'

'Is Old Jarvie a naval word for the Evil One, sir?' asked Cecilia.

The admiral rubbed his hands. 'He is Earl St Vincent, my dear, the First Lord of the Admiralty.'

At the mention of authority Mrs Williams looked grave and respectful; and after a reverent pause she said, 'I believe you mentioned Captain Aubrey's father, Admiral?'

'Yes. He is that General Aubrey who made such a din by flogging the Whig candidate at Hinton.'

'How very disgraceful. But surely, to flog a member of parliament he must be a man of considerable estate?'

'Only moderate, ma'am. A moderate little place the other side of Woolhampton; and much encumbered, they tell me. My cousin Hanmer knows him well.'

'And is Captain Aubrey the only son?'

'Yes, ma'am. Though by the bye he has a new mother-in-law: the general married a girl from the village some months ago. She is said to be a fine sprightly young woman.'

'Good heavens, how wicked!' said Mrs Williams. 'But I presume there is no danger? I presume the general is of a certain age?'

'Not at all, ma'am,' said the admiral. 'He cannot be much more than sixty-five. Were I in Captain Aubrey's shoes, I should be most uneasy.'

Mrs Williams brightened. 'Poor young man,' she said placidly. 'I quite feel for him, I protest.'

The butler carried away the tea-tray, mended the fire and began to light the candles. 'How the evenings are

29

drawing in,' said Mrs Williams. 'Never mind the sconces by the door. Pull the curtains by the cord, John. Touching the cloth wears it so, and it is bad for the rings. And now, Admiral, what have you to tell us of the other gentleman at Melbury Lodge, Captain Aubrey's particular friend?'

'Oh, him,' said Admiral Haddock. 'I do not know much about him. He was Captain Aubrey's surgeon in this sloop. And I believe I heard he was someone's natural son. His name is Maturin.'

'If you please, sir,' said Frances, 'what is a natural son?'

'Why . . . ' said the admiral, looking from side to side. 'Are sons more natural than daughters, pray?'

'Hush, my dear,' said Mrs Williams.

'Mr Lever called at Melbury,' said Cecilia. 'Captain Aubrey had gone to London – he is always going to London, it appears – but he saw Dr Maturin, and says that he is quite strange, quite like a foreign gentleman. He was cutting up a horse in the winter drawing-room.'

'How very undesirable,' said Mrs Williams. 'They will have to use cold water for the blood. Cold water is the only thing for the marks of blood. Do not you think, Admiral, that they should be told they must use cold water for the marks of blood?'

'I dare say they are tolerably used to getting rid of stains of that kind, ma'am,' said the admiral. 'But now I come to think of it,' he went on, gazing round the room 'what a capital thing it is for you girls, to have a couple of sailors with their pockets full of guineas, turned ashore and pitched down on your very doorstep. Anyone in want of a husband has but to whistle, and they will come running, ha, ha, ha!'

The admiral's sally had a wretched reception; not one of the young ladies joined in his mirth. Sophia and Diana looked grave, Cecilia tossed her head, Frances scowled, and Mrs Williams pursed up her mouth, looked down her nose and meditated a sharp retort.

'However,' he continued, wondering at the sudden chill

in the room 'it is no go, no go at all, now that I recollect. He told Trimble, who suggested a match with his sister-in-law, that he had *quite given up women*. It seems that he was so unfortunate in his last attachment, that he has quite given up women. And indeed he is an unlucky wight, whatever they may call him: there is not only this wretched business of his promotion and his father's cursed untimely marriage, but he also has a couple of neutral prizes in the Admiralty court, on appeal. I dare say that is why he is perpetually fagging up and down to London. He is an unlucky man, no doubt; and no doubt he has come to understand it. So he has very rightly given up all thoughts of marriage, in which luck is everything – has quite given up women.'

'It is perfectly true,' cried Cecilia. 'There is not a single woman in the house! Mrs Burdett, who *just happened to be passing by*, and our Molly, whose father's cottage is directly behind and can see everything, say there is not a woman in the house! There they live together, with a parcel of sailors to look after them. La, how strange! And yet Mrs Burdett, who had a good look, you may be sure, says the window-panes were shining like diamonds, and all the frames and doors had been new-painted white.'

'How can they hope to manage?' asked Mrs Williams. 'Surely, it is very wrong-headed and unnatural. Dear me, I should not fancy sitting down in that house. I should wipe my chair with my handkerchief, I can tell you.'

'Why, ma'am,' cried the admiral, 'we manage tolerably well at sea, you know.'

'Oh, at sea . . . ' said Mrs Williams with a smile.

'What can they do for mending, poor things?' asked Sophia. 'I suppose they buy new.'

'I can just see them with their stockings out at heel,' cried Frances, with a coarse whoop, 'pegging away with their needles – "Doctor, may I trouble you for the blue

31

worsted? After you with the thimble, if you please." Ha, ha, ha, ha!'

'I dare say they can cook,' said Diana. 'Men can broil a steak; and there are always eggs and bread-and-butter.'

'But how wonderfully strange,' cried Cecilia. 'How romantic! As good as a ruin. Oh, how I long to see 'em.'

CHAPTER TWO

The acquaintance was not slow in coming. With naval promptness Admiral Haddock invited the ladies of Mapes to dine with the newcomers, and presently Captain Aubrey and Dr Maturin were asked to dinner at Mapes; they were pronounced excellent young men, most agreeable company, perfectly well-bred, and a great addition to the neighbourhood. It was clear to Sophia, however, that poor Dr Maturin needed feeding properly: 'he was quite pale and silent,' she said. But even the tenderest heart, the most given to pity, could not have said the same for Jack. He was in great form from even the beginning of the party, when his laugh was to be heard coming up the drive, until the last repeated farewells under the freezing portico. His fine open battle-scarred countenance had worn either a smile or a look of lively pleasure from the first to the last, and although his blue eye had dwelt a little wistfully upon the stationary decanter and the disappearing remains of the pudding, his cheerful flow of small but perfectly amiable talk had never faltered. He had eaten everything set before him with grateful voracity, and even Mrs Williams felt something like an affectionate leaning towards him.

'Well,' she said, as their hoof-beats died away in the night, 'I believe that was as successful a dinner-party as I have ever given. Captain Aubrey managed a second partridge – but then they were so very tender. And the floating island looked particularly well in the silver bowl: there will be enough for tomorrow. And the rest of the pork will be delicious, hashed. How well they ate, to be sure: I do not suppose they often have a dinner like that. I wonder at the admiral, saying that Captain Aubrey was not quite the thing. I think he is *very much* the thing. Sophie, my love, pray tell John to put the port the gentlemen left into a small bottle at once, before he locks up: it is bad for the decanter to leave port-wine in it.'

'Yes, Mama.'

'Now, my dears,' whispered Mrs Williams, having left a significant pause after the closing of the door, 'I dare say you all noticed Captain Aubrey's great interest in Sophia – he was quite particular. I have little doubt that – I think it would be very nice if we were all to leave them alone together as much as possible. Are you attending, Diana?'

'Oh, yes, ma'am. I understand you perfectly well,' said Diana, turning back from the window. Far over in the moonlit night the pale road wound between Polcary and Beacon Down, and the horsemen were walking briskly up it.

'I wonder, I wonder,' said Jack, 'whether there is any goose left at home, or whether those infernal brutes have eaten it up. At all events, we can have an omelet and a bottle of claret. Claret. Have you ever known a woman that had any notion of wine?'

'I have not.'

'And damned near with the pudding, too. But what charming girls they are! Did you notice the eldest one, Miss Williams, holding up her wine-glass and looking at the candle through it? Such grace . . . The taper of her wrist and hand – long, long fingers.' Stephen Maturin was scratching himself with a dogged perseverance; he was not attending. But Jack went on, 'And that Mrs Villiers, how beautifully she held her head: lovely colouring. Perhaps not such a perfect complexion as her cousin – she has been in India, I believe – but what deep blue eyes! How old would she be, Stephen?'

'Not thirty.'

'I remember how well she sat her horse . . . By God, a year or two back I should have – . How a man changes. But even so, I do love being surrounded by girls – so very different from men. She said several handsome things about the service – spoke very sensibly – thoroughly understood the importance of the weather-gage. She must have naval connections. I do hope we see her again. I hope we see them all again.'

They saw her again, and sooner than they had expected. Mrs Williams too just happened to be passing by Melbury, and she directed Thomas to turn up the well-known drive. A deep and powerful voice the other side of the door was singing

> *You ladies of lubricity*
> *That dwell in the bordello*
> *Ha-ha ha-ha, ha-ha ha-hee*
> *For I am that kind of fellow,*

but the ladies walked into the hall quite unmoved, since not one of them except Diana understood the words, and she was not easily upset. With great satisfaction they noticed that the servant who let them in had a pigtail half-way down his back, but the parlour into which he showed them was disappointingly trim – it might have been spring-cleaned that morning, reflected Mrs Williams, drawing her finger along the top of the wainscot. The only thing that distinguished it from an ordinary Christian parlour was the rigid formation of the chairs, squared to one another like the yards of a ship, and the bell-pull, which was three fathoms of cable, wormed and served, and ending in a brass-bound top-block.

The powerful voice stopped, and it occurred to Diana that someone's face must be going red; it was indeed highly coloured when Captain Aubrey came hurrying in, but he did not falter as he cried, 'Why, this is most neighbourly – truly kind – a very good afternoon to you, ma'am. Mrs Villiers, Miss Williams, your servant – Miss Cecilia, Miss Frances, how happy I am to see you. Pray step into the . . .'

'We just happened to be passing by,' said Mrs Williams,

'and I thought we might just stop for a moment, to ask how the jasmin is thriving.'

'Jasmin?' cried Jack.

'Yes,' said Mrs Williams, avoiding her daughters' eyes.

'Ah, the jasmin. Pray step into the drawing-room. Dr Maturin and I have a fire in there: and he is the fellow to tell you all about jasmin.'

The winter drawing-room at Melbury Lodge was a handsome five-sided room with two walls opening on to the garden, and at the far end there stood a light-coloured pianoforte, surrounded by sheets of music and covered by many more. Stephen Maturin rose from behind the piano, bowed, and stood silently watching the visitors. He was wearing a black coat so old that it was green in places, and he had not shaved for three days: from time to time he passed his hand over his rasping jaw.

'Why, you are musicians, I declare!' cried Mrs Williams. 'Violins – a 'cello! How I love music. Symphonies, cantatas! Do you touch the instrument, sir?' she asked Stephen. She did not usually notice him, for Dr Vining had explained that naval surgeons were often poorly qualified and always badly paid; but she was feeling well-disposed today.

'I have just been picking out this piece, ma'am,' said Stephen. 'But the piano is sadly out of tune.'

'I think not, sir,' said Mrs Williams. 'It was the most expensive instrument to be had – a Clementi. I remember its coming by the waggon as though it were yesterday.'

'Pianos do go out of tune, Mama,' murmured Sophia.

'Not Clementi's pianos, my dear,' said Mrs Williams with a smile. 'They are the most expensive in London. Clementi supplies the Court,' she added, looking reproachful, as though they had been wanting in loyalty. 'Besides, sir,' she said, turning to Jack, 'it was my eldest daughter who painted the case! The pictures are in the Chinese taste.'

'That clinches it, ma'am,' cried Jack. 'It would be an ungrateful instrument that fell off, having been decorated by Miss Williams. We were admiring the landscape with the pagoda this morning, were we not, Stephen?'

'Yes,' said Stephen, lifting the adagio of Hummel's D major sonata off the lid. 'This was the bridge and tree and pagoda that we liked so much.' It was a charming thing, the size of a tea-tray – pure, sweet lines, muted, gentle colours that might have been lit by an innocent moon.

Embarrassed, as she so often was, by her mother's strident voice, and confused by all this attention, Sophia hung her head: with a self-possession that she neither felt nor seemed to feel she said, 'Was this the piece you was playing, sir? Mr Tindall has made me practise it over and over again.'

She moved away from the piano, carrying the sheets, and at this point the drawing-room was filled with activity. Mrs Williams protested that she would neither sit down nor take any refreshment whatsoever; Preserved Killick and John Witsoever, able seamen, brought in tables, trays, urns, more coal; Frances whispered 'What ho, for ship's biscuit and a swig of rum,' to make Cecilia giggle; and Jack slowly began shepherding Mrs Williams and Stephen out of the room through the french windows in the direction of what he took to be the jasmin.

The true jasmin, however, proved to be on the library wall; and so it was from outside the library windows that Jack and Stephen heard the familiar notes of the adagio, as silvery and remote as a musical-box. It was absurd how the playing resembled the painting: light, ethereal, tenuous. Stephen Maturin winced at the flat A and the shrill C; and at the beginning of the first variation he glanced uneasily at Jack to see whether he too was jarred by the mistaken phrasing. But Jack seemed wholly taken up with Mrs Williams's account of the planting of the shrub, a minute and circumstantial history.

Now there was another hand on the keyboard. The adagio came out over the sparse wintery lawn with a fine ringing tone, inaccurate, but strong and free; there was harshness in the tragic first variation – a real understanding of what it meant.

'How well dear Sophia plays,' said Mrs Williams, leaning her head to one side. 'Such a sweetly pretty tune, too.'

'Surely that is not Miss Williams, ma'am?' cried Stephen.

'Indeed it is, sir,' cried Mrs Williams. 'Neither of her sisters can go beyond the scales, and I know for a fact that Mrs Villiers cannot read a note. She would not apply herself to the drudgery.' And as they walked back to the house through the mud Mrs Williams told them what they should know about drudgery, taste, and application.

Mrs Villiers started up from the piano, but not so quickly as to escape Mrs Williams's indignant eye – an eye so indignant that it did not lose its expression for the rest of the visit. It even outlasted Jack's announcement of a ball in commemoration of the Battle of Saint Vincent, and the gratification of being the first guests to be bespoke.

'You recall Sir John Jervis's action, ma'am, off Cape Saint Vincent? The fourteenth of February, ninety-seven. Saint Valentine's day.'

'Certainly I do, sir: but' – with an affected simper – 'of course my girls are too young to remember anything about it. Pray, did we win?'

'Of course we did, Mama,' hissed the girls.

'Of course we did,' said Mrs Williams. 'Pray sir, was you there – was you present?'

'Yes, ma'am,' said Jack. 'I was third of the *Orion*. And so I always like to celebrate the anniversary of the battle with all the friends and shipmates I can bring together. And seeing there is a ballroom here – '

'You may depend upon it, my dears,' said Mrs Williams, on the way home, 'that this ball is being given in compliment to us – to me and my daughters – and I have no doubt that Sophie will open it with Captain Aubrey. Saint

38

Valentine's day, la! Frankie, you have dribbled chocolate all down your front; and if you eat so many rich pastries you will come out in spots, and then where will you be? No man will look at you. There must have been a dozen eggs and half a pound of butter in that smaller cake: I have never been so surprised in my life.'

Diana Villiers had been taken, after some hesitation, partly because it would have been indecent to leave her behind and partly because Mrs Williams thought there was no possible comparison between a woman with ten thousand pounds and one without ten thousand pounds; but further consideration, the pondering of certain intercepted looks, led Mrs Williams to think that the gentlemen of the Navy might not be so reliable as the local squires and their hard-faced offspring.

Diana was aware of most of the motions of her aunt's mind, and after breakfast the next day she was quite prepared to follow her into her room for 'a little chat, my dear'. But she was quite unprepared for the bright smile and the repeated mention of the word 'horse'. Hitherto it had always meant Sophia's little chestnut mare. 'How good-natured of Sophie to lend you her horse again. I hope it is not too tired this time, poor thing.' But now the suggestion, the downright offer, wrapped in many words, was of a horse for herself. It was a clear bribe to leave the field clear: it was also meant to overcome Sophia's reluctance to deprive her cousin of the mare, and thus to go riding with Captain Aubrey or Dr Maturin herself. Diana accepted the bait, spat out the hook with contempt, and hurried away to the stables to consult with Thomas, for the great horse-fair at Marston was just at hand.

On the way she saw Sophia coming along the path that led through the park to Grope, Admiral Haddock's house. Sophia was walking fast, swinging her arms and muttering 'Larboard, starboard,' as she came.

'Yo ho, shipmate,' called Diana over the hedge, and

she was surprised to see her cousin blush cherry-pink. The chance shot had gone straight home, for Sophia had been browsing in the admiral's library, looking at Navy Lists, naval memoirs, Falconer's *Dictionary of the Marine*, and the *Naval Chronicle*; and the admiral, coming up behind her in his list slippers had said, 'Oh, the *Naval Chronicle*, is it? Ha, ha! This is the one you want,' – pulling out the volume for 1801. 'Though Miss Di has been before you – forestalled you long ago – made me explain the weather-gage and the difference between a xebec and a brig. There is a little cut of the action, but the fellow did not know what he was about, so he put in a great quantity of smoke to hide the rigging, which is most particular in a xebec. Come, let me find it for you.'

'Oh no, no, no,' said Sophia in great distress. 'I only wanted to know a little about – ' Her voice died away.

The acquaintance ripened; but it did not mature, it did not progress as fast as Mrs Williams would have liked. Captain Aubrey could not have been more friendly – perhaps too friendly; there was none of that languishing she longed to see, no pallor, nor even any marked particularity. He seemed to be as happy with Frances as he was with Sophia, and sometimes Mrs Williams wondered whether he really were quite the thing – whether those strange tales about sea-officers might possibly be true in his case. Was it not very odd that he should live with Dr Maturin? Another thing that troubled her was Diana's horse, for from what she heard and from what little she could understand, it seemed that Diana rode better than Sophia. Mrs Williams could hardly credit this, but even so she was heartily sorry that she had ever made the present. She was in a state of anxious doubt: she was certain that Sophia was moved, but she was equally certain that Sophia would never speak to her of her feelings, just as she was certain that Sophia would never follow her advice about making herself attractive to the gentlemen – putting herself forward a little, doing herself justice, reddening her lips before she came into the room.

Had she seen them out one day with young Mr Edward Savile's pack she would have been more anxious still. Sophia did not really care for hunting: she liked the gallops, but she found the waiting about dull and she minded terribly about the poor fox. Her mare had spirit but no great stamina, whereas Diana's powerful, short-coupled bay gelding had a barrel like a vault of a church and an unconquerable heart; he could carry Diana's eight stone from morning till night, and he loved to be in at the kill.

They had been hunting since half past ten, and now the sun was low. They had killed two foxes, and the third, a barren vixen, had led them a rare old dance, right away into the heavy country beyond Plimpton with its wet plough, double oxers, and wide ditches. She was now only one field ahead, failing fast and heading for a drain she knew. At the last check Jack had a lucky inspiration to bear away right-handed, a short-cut that brought him and Sophia closer to hounds than anyone in the field; but now there was a bank, a towering fence, mud in front of it and the gleam of broad water beyond. Sophia looked at the jump with dismay, put her tired horse at it without any real wish to reach the other side, and felt thankful when the mare refused it. She and her mount were quite done up; Sophia had never felt so tired in her life; she dreaded the sight of the fox being torn to pieces, and the pack had just hit off the line again. There was a deadly implacable triumph in the voice of the old bitch that led them. 'The gate, the gate,' called Jack, wheeling his horse and cantering to the corner of the field. He had it half open – an awkward, sagging, left-handed gate – when Stephen arrived. Jack heard Sophia say 'should like to go home – pray, pray go on – know the way perfectly.' The piteous face wiped away his look of frustration; he lost his fixed 'boarders away' expression, and smiling very kindly he said, 'I think I will turn back too: we have had enough for today.'

'I will see Miss Williams home,' said Stephen.

'No, no, please go on,' begged Sophia, with tears brimming in her eyes. 'Please, please – I am perfectly – '

A quick drumming of hooves and Diana came into the field. Her whole being was concentrated on the fence and what lay beyond it, and she saw them only a vague group muddling in a gate. She was sitting as straight and supple as if she had been riding for no more than half an hour: she was part of her horse, completely unaware of herself. She went straight at the fence, gathered her horse just so, and with a crash and a spray of mud they were over. Her form, her high-held head, her contained joy, competent, fierce gravity, were as beautiful as anything Jack or Stephen had ever seen. She had not the slightest notion of it, but she had never looked so well in her life. The men's faces as she flew over, high and true, would have made Mrs Williams more uneasy by far.

Mrs Williams longed for the day of the ball; she made almost as many preparations as Jack, and Mapes Court was filled with gauze, muslins and taffeta. Her mind was filled with stratagems, one of which was to get Diana out of the way for the intervening days. Mrs Williams had no defined suspicions, but she smelt danger, and by means of half a dozen intermediaries and as many letters she managed to have a mad cousin left unattended by his family. She could not do away with the invitation, publicly given and accepted, however, and Diana was to be brought back to Champflower by one of Captain Aubrey's guests on the morning of February the fourteenth.

'Dr Maturin is waiting for you, Di,' said Cecilia. 'He is walking his horse up and down in a fine new bottle-green coat with a black collar. And he has a new tie-wig. I suppose that is why he went up to London. You have made

42

another conquest, Di: he used to be quite horrid, and all unshaved.'

'Stop peering from behind that curtain like a housemaid, Cissy. And lend me your hat, will you?'

'Why, he is quite splendid now,' said Cecilia, peering still and puckering the gauze. 'He has a spotted waistcoat too. Do you remember when he came to dinner in carpet slippers? He really would be almost handsome if he held himself up.'

'A fine conquest,' said Mrs Williams, peering too. 'A penniless naval surgeon, somebody's natural son, and a Papist. Fie upon you, Cissy, to say such things.'

'Good morning, Maturin,' said Diana, coming down the steps. 'I hope I have not kept you waiting. What a neat cob you have there, upon my word! You never found him in this part of the world.'

'Good morning, Villiers. You are late. You are very late.'

'It is the one advantage there is in being a woman. You do know I am a woman, Maturin?'

'I am obliged to suppose it, since you affect to have no notion of time – cannot tell what o'clock it is. Though why the trifling accident of sex should induce a sentient being, let alone such an intelligent being as you, to waste half this beautiful clear morning, I cannot conceive. Come, let me help you to mount. Sex – sex . . . '

'Hush, Maturin. You must not use words like that here. It was bad enough yesterday.'

'Yesterday? Oh, yes. But I am not the first man to say that wit is the unexpected copulation of ideas. Far from it. It is a commonplace.'

'As far as my aunt is concerned you are certainly the first man who ever used such an expression in public.'

They rode up Heberden Down: a still, brilliant morning with a little frost; the creak of leather, the smell of horse, steaming breath. 'I am not in the least degree interested in women as such,' said Stephen. 'Only in persons. There is

Polcary,' he added, nodding over the valley. 'That is where I first saw you, on your cousin's chestnut. Let us ride over there tomorrow. I can show you a remarkable family of particoloured stoats, a congregation of stoats.'

'I must cry off for tomorrow,' said Diana. 'I am so sorry, I have to go to Dover to look after an old gentleman who is not quite right in the head, a sort of cousin.'

'But you will be back for the ball, sure?' cried Stephen.

'Oh, yes. It is all arranged. A Mr Babbington is to take me up on his way. Did not Captain Aubrey tell you?'

'I was back very late last night, and we hardly spoke this morning. But I must go to Dover myself next week. May I come and beg for a cup of tea?'

'Indeed you may. Mr Lowndes imagines he is a teapot; he crooks one arm like this for the handle, holds out the other for the spout, and says, "May I have the pleasure of pouring you a cup of tea?" You could not come to a better address. But you also have to go to town again, do you not?'

'I do. From Monday till Thursday.'

She reined in her horse to a walk, and with a hesitation and a shyness that changed her face entirely, giving it a resemblance to Sophia's, she said, 'Maturin, may I beg you to do me a kindness?'

'Certainly,' said Stephen, looking straight into her eyes and then quickly away at the sight of the painful emotion in them.

'You know something of my position here, I believe . . . Would you sell this bit of jewellery for me? I must have something to wear at the ball.'

'What must I ask for it?'

'Would they not make an offer, do you think? If I could get ten pounds, I should be happy. And if they should give so much, then would you be even kinder and tell Harrison in the Royal Exchange to send me this list immediately? Here is a pattern of the stuff. It could come by the mail-coach as far as Lewes, and the carrier could pick it up. I must have something to wear.'

Something to wear. Unpicked, taken in, let out, and folded in tissue-paper, it lay in the trunk that stood waiting in Mr Lowndes's hall on the morning of the fourteenth.

'Mr Babbington to see you, ma'am,' said the servant.

Diana hurried into the parlour – her smile faded – she looked again, and lower than she would have thought possible she saw a figure in a three-caped coat that piped, 'Mrs Villiers, ma'am? Babbington reporting, if you please, ma'am.'

'Oh, Mr Babbington, good morning. How do you do? Captain Aubrey tells me you will be so very kind as to take me with you to Melbury Lodge. When do you please to start? We must not let your horse take cold. I have only a little trunk – it is ready by the front door. You will take a glass of wine before we leave, sir? Or I believe you sea-officers like rum?'

'A tot of rum to keep out the cold would be prime. You will join me, ma'am? It's uncommon parky, out.'

'A very little glass of rum, and put a great deal of water in it,' whispered Diana to the servant. But the girl was too flustered by the presence of a strange dogcart in the court-yard to understand the word 'water', and she brought a dark-brown brimming tumbler that Mr Babbington drank off with great composure. Diana's alarm increased at the sight of the tall, dashing dogcart and the nervous horse, all white of eye and laid-back ears. 'Where is your groom, sir?' she asked. 'Is he in the kitchen?'

'There ain't a groom in this crew, ma'am,' said Babbington, now looking at her with open admiration. 'I navigate myself. May I give you a leg up? Your foot on this little step and heave away. Now this rug – we make it fast aft, with these beckets. All a-tanto? Let go by the head,' he called to the gardener, and they dashed out of the forecourt, giving the white-painted post a shrewd knock as they passed.

Mr Babbington's handling of the whip and the reins raised Diana's dismay to a new pitch; she had been brought up among horse-soldiers, and she had never seen anything like this in her life. She wondered how he could possibly have come all the way from Arundel without a spill. She thought of her trunk behind and when they left the main road, winding along the lanes, sometimes mounting the bank and sometimes shaving the ditch's edge, she said, 'It will never do. This young man will have to be taken down.'

The lane ran straight up hill, rising higher and higher, with God knows what breakneck descent the other side. The horse slowed to a walk – the bean-fed horse, as it proved by a thunderous, long, long fart.

'I beg your pardon,' said the midshipman in the silence.

'Oh, that's all right,' said Diana coldly. 'I thought it was the horse.' A sideways glance showed that this had settled Babbington's hash for the moment. 'Let me show you how we do it in India,' she said, gathering the reins and taking his whip away from him. But once she had established contact with the horse and had him going steadily along the path he should follow, Diana turned her mind to winning back Mr Babbington's kindness and good will. Would he explain the blue, the red, and the white squadrons to her? The weather-gage? Tell her about life at sea in general? Surely it must be a very dangerous, demanding service, though of course so highly and so rightly honoured – the country's safeguard. Could it be true that he had taken part in the famous action with the *Cacafuego*? Diana could not remember a more striking disparity of forces. Captain Aubrey must be very like Lord Nelson.

'Oh yes, ma'am!' cried Babbington. 'Though I doubt even Nelson could have brought it off so handsome. He is a prodigious man. Though by land, you know, he is quite different. You would take him for an ordinary person – not the least coldness or distance. He came down to our place to help my uncle in the election, and he was as jolly as a grig – knocked down a couple of Whigs with his stick. They went down like ninepins – both of them poachers and Methodies, of course. Oh, it was such fun, and at Melbury he let me and old Pullings choose our horses and ride a race with him. Three times round the paddock and the horse to be ridden upstairs into the library for a guinea a side and a bottle of wine. Oh, we all love him, ma'am, although he's so taut at sea.'

'Who won?'

'Oh, well,' said Babbington, 'we all fell off, more or less, at different times. Though I dare say he did it on purpose, not to take our money.'

They stopped to bait at an inn, and with a meal and a pint of ale inside him Babbington said, 'I think you are the prettiest girl I have ever seen. You are to change in my room, which I am very glad of, now; and if I had known it was you, I should have bought a pincushion and a large bottle of scent.'

'You are a very fine figure of a man, too, sir,' said Diana. 'I am so happy to be travelling under your protection.'

Babbington's spirits mounted to an alarming degree; he had been brought up in a service where enterprise counted for everything, and presently it became necessary to occupy his attention with the horse. She had meant to allow him only the dash up the drive, but in the event he held the reins all the way from Newton Priors to the door of Melbury Lodge, where he handed her down in state, to the admiration of two dozen naval eyes.

There was something about Diana, a certain piratical dash and openness, that was very attractive to sea-officers; but they were also much attracted by the two Miss Simmonses' doll-like prettiness, by Frances dancing down the middle with the tip of her tongue showing as she kept the measure, by Cecilia's commonplace, healthy good looks, and by all the other charms that were displayed under the blaze of candles in the long handsome ballroom. And they were moon-struck by Sophia's grace as she and Captain

Aubrey opened the ball: Sophia had on a pink dress with a gold sash, and Diana said to Stephen Maturin, 'She is lovely. There is not another woman in the room to touch her. That is the most dangerous colour in the world, but with her complexion it is perfect. I would give my eye-teeth for such a skin.'

'The gold and the pearls help,' said Stephen. 'The one echoes her hair and the other her teeth. I will tell you a thing about women. They are superior to men in this, that they have an unfeigned, objective, candid admiration for good looks in other women – a real pleasure in their beauty. Yours, too, is a most elegant dress: other women admire it. I have remarked this. Not only from their glances, but most positively, by standing behind them and listening to their conversation.'

It was a good dress, a light, flimsy version of the naval blue, with white about it – no black, no concessions to Mrs Williams, for it was understood that at a ball any woman was allowed to make the best of herself; but where taste, figure and carriage are equal, a woman who can spend fifty guineas on her dress will look better than one who can only spend ten pounds.

'We must take our places,' said Diana a little louder as the second violins struck in and the ballroom filled with sound. It was a fine sight, hung with bunting in the naval way – the signal *engage the enemy more closely*, among other messages understood by the sailors alone – shining with bees-wax and candlelight, crowded to the doors, and the lane of dancing figures: pretty dresses, fine coats, white gloves, all reflected in the french windows and in the tall looking-glass behind the band. The whole neighbourhood was there, together with a score of new faces from Portsmouth, Chatham, London, or wherever the peace had cast them on shore; they were all in their best clothes; they were all determined to enjoy themselves; and so far they were succeeding to admiration. Everyone was pleased, not only by the rarity of a ball (not above three in

48

the season in those parts, apart from the Assembly), but by the handsome, unusual way in which it was done, by the seamen in their blue jackets and pigtails, so very unlike the greasy hired waiters generally to be seen, and by the fact that for once there were more men than women – men in large numbers, all of them eager to dance.

Mrs Williams was sitting with the other parents and chaperons by the double doors into the supper-room, where she could rake the whole line of dancers, and her red face was nodding and smiling – significant smiles, emphatic nods – as she told her cousin Simmons that she had encouraged the whole thing from the beginning. Crossing over in the dance, Diana saw her triumphant face: and the next face she saw, immediately in front of her, was Jack's as he advanced to hand her about. 'Such a lovely ball, Aubrey,' she said, with a flashing smile. He was in gold-laced scarlet, a big, commanding figure: his forehead was sweating and his eyes shone with excitement and pleasure. He took her in with benevolent approval, said something meaningless but kind, and whirled her about.

'Come and sit down,' said Stephen, at the end of the second dance. 'You are looking pale.'

'Am I?' she cried, looking intently into a mirror. 'Do I look horrible?'

'You do not. But you must not get over-tired. Come and sit down in a fresher air. Come into the orangery.'

'I have promised to stand up with Admiral James. I will come after supper.'

Deserting the supper-table, three sailors, including Admiral James, pursued Diana into the orangery; but they withdrew when they saw Stephen waiting for her there with her shawl.

'I did not think the doctor had it in him,' said Mowett. 'In the *Sophie* we always looked on him as a sort of monk.'

'Damn him,' said Pullings. 'I thought I was getting on so well.'

'You are not cold?' asked Stephen, tucking the shawl

round her shoulders; and as though the physical contact between his hand and her bare flesh established a contact, sending a message that had no need of words, he felt the change of current. But in spite of the intuition he said, 'Diana . . .'

'Tell me,' she said in a hard voice, cutting right across him, 'is that Admiral James married?'

'He is.'

'I thought so. You can smell the enemy a great way off.'

'Enemy?'

'Of course. Don't be a fool, Maturin. You must know that married men are the worst enemies women can have. Get me something to drink, will you? I am quite faint with all that fug.'

'This is Sillery; this iced punch.'

'Thank you. They offer what they call friendship or some stuff of that kind – the name don't matter – and all they want in return for this great favour is your heart, your life, your future, your – I will not be coarse, but you know very well what I mean. There is no friendship in men: I know what I am talking about, believe me. There is not one round here, from old Admiral Haddock to that young puppy of a curate, who has not tried it: to say nothing of India. Who the devil do they think I am?' she exclaimed, drumming on the arm of her chair. 'The only honest one was Southampton, who sent an old woman from Madras to say he would be happy to take me into keeping; and upon my honour, if I had known what my life in England, in this muddy hole with nothing but beer-swilling rustics, was going to be, I should have been tempted to accept. What do you think my life is like, without a sou and under the thumb of a vulgar, pretentious, ignorant woman who detests me? What do you think it is like, looking into this sort of a future, with my looks going, the only thing I have? Listen, Maturin, I speak openly to you, because I like you; I like you very much, and I believe you have a kindness for me – you are almost the only man I have met in England I can treat as a friend – trust as a friend.'

'You have my friendship, sure,' said Stephen heavily. After a long pause he said with a fair attempt at lightness, 'You are not altogether just. You look as desirable as you can – that dress, particularly the bosom of that dress, would inflame Saint Anthony, as you know very well. It is unjust to provoke a man and then to complain he is a satyr if the provocation succeeds. You are not a miss upon her promotion, moved by unconscious instinctive . . .'

'Do you tell me I am provocative?' cried Diana.

'Certainly I do. That is exactly what I am saying. But I do not suppose you know how much you make men suffer. In any case, you are arguing from the particular to the general: you have met some men who wish to take advantage of you, and you go too far. Not all French waiters have red hair.'

'They all have red hair somewhere about them, and it shows sooner or later. But I do believe you are an exception, Maturin, and that is why I confide in you: I cannot tell you what a comfort it is. I was brought up among intelligent men – they were a loose lot on the Madras side and worse in Bombay, but they *were* intelligent, and oh how I miss them. And what a relief it is to be able to speak freely, after all this swimming in namby-pamby.'

'Your cousin Sophia is intelligent.'

'Do you really think so? Well, there is a sort of quickness, if you like; but she is a girl – we do not speak the same language. I grant you she is beautiful. She is really beautiful, but she knows nothing – how could she? – and I cannot forgive her her fortune. It is so unjust. Life is so unjust.' Stephen made no reply, but fetched her an ice. 'The only thing a man can offer a woman is marriage,' she went on. 'An equal marriage. I have about four or five years, and if I cannot find a husband by then, I shall . . . And where can one be found in this howling wilderness? Do I disgust you very much? I mean to put you off, you know.'

'Yes, I am aware of your motions, Villiers. You do not disgust me at all – you speak as a friend. You hunt; and your chase has a beast in view.'

'Well done, Maturin.'

'You insist upon an equal marriage?'

'At the very least. I shall despise a woman so poor-spirited, so wanting in courage, as to make a mésalliance. There was a smart little whippersnapper of an attorney in Dover that had the infernal confidence to make me an offer. I have never been so mortified in my life. I had rather go to the stake, or look after the Teapot for the rest of my days.'

'Define your beast.'

'I am not difficult. He must have some money, of course – love in a cottage be damned. He must have some sense; he must not be actually deformed, nor too ancient. Admiral Haddock, for example, is beyond my limit, I do not insist upon it, but I should like him to be able to sit a horse and not fall off too often; and I should like him to be able to hold his wine. You do not get drunk, Maturin; that is one of the things I like about you. Captain Aubrey and half the other men here will have to be carried to bed.'

'No, I love wine, but I do not find it often affects my judgment: not often. I drank a good deal this evening, however. As far as Jack Aubrey is concerned, do you not think you may be a little late in the field? I have the impression that tonight may be decisive.'

'Has he told you anything? Has he confided in you?'

'You do not speak as you have just spoken to a tattle-tale of a man, I believe. As far as your knowledge of me goes, it is accurate.'

'In any case, you are wrong. I know Sophie. He may make a declaration, but she will need a longer time than this. She need never fear being left on the shelf – it never

52

occurs to her at all, I dare say – and she is afraid of marriage. How she cried when I told her men had hair on their chests! And she hates being managed – that is not the word I want. What is it, Maturin?'

'Manipulated.'

'Exactly. She is a dutiful girl – a great sense of duty: I think it rather stupid, but there it is – but still she finds the way her mother has been arranging and pushing and managing and angling in all this perfectly odious. You two must have had hogsheads of that grocer's claret forced down your throats. Perfectly odious: and she is obstinate – strong, if you like – under that bread-and-butter way of hers. It will take a great deal to move her; much more than the excitement of a ball.'

'She is not attached?'

'Attached to Aubrey? I do not know; I do not suppose she knows herself. She likes him; she is flattered by his attentions; and to be sure he is a husband any woman would be glad to have – well-off, good-looking, distinguished in his profession and with a future before him, unexceptionable family, cheerful, good-natured. But she is entirely unsuited to him – I am persuaded she is, with her secretive, closed, stubborn nature. He needs someone much more awake, much more alive: they would never be happy.'

'She may have a passionate side, a side you know nothing about, or do not choose to see.'

'Stuff, Maturin. In any case, he needs a different woman and she needs a different man: in a way you might be much more suited to her, if you could stand her ignorance.'

'So Jack Aubrey might answer?'

'Yes, I like him well enough. I should prefer a man more – what shall I say? More grown up, less of a boy – less of a huge boy.'

'He is highly considered in his profession, as you said yourself, just now.'

'That is neither here nor there. A man may be brilliant

53

in his calling and a mere child outside it. I remember a mathematician – they say he was one of the best in the world – who came out to India, to do something about Venus; and when his telescope was taken away from him, he was unfit for civilized life. A blundering schoolboy! He clung to my hand all through one tedious, tedious evening, sweating and stammering. No: give me the politicoes – they know how to live; and they are all reading men, more or less. I wish Aubrey were something of a reading man. More like you – I mean what I say. You are very good company: I like being with you. But he is a handsome fellow. Look,' she said, turning to the window, 'there he is, figuring away. He dances quite well, does he not? It is a pity he wants decision.'

'You would not say that if you saw him taking his ship into action.'

'I mean in his relations with women. He is sentimental. But still, he would do. Shall I tell you something that will really shock you, although you are a medical man? I was married, you know – I am not a girl – and intrigues were as common in India as they are in Paris. There are times when I am tempted to play the fool, terribly tempted. I dare say I should, too, if I lived in London and not in this dreary hole.'

'Tell me, have you reason to suppose that Jack is to your way of thinking?'

'About our suitability? Yes. There are signs that mean a lot to a woman. I wonder he ever looked seriously at Sophie. He is not interested, I suppose? Her fortune would not mean a great deal to him? Have you known him long? But I suppose all you naval people have known one another, or of one another, for ever.'

'Oh, I am no seaman, at all. I first met him in Minorca, in the year one, in the spring of the year one. I had taken a patient there, for the Mediterranean climate – he died – and I met Jack at a concert. We took a liking to one another, and he asked me to sail with him as his surgeon. I agreed, being quite penniless at the time, and we have been together ever since. I know him well enough to say that as for being interested, concerned for a woman's fortune, there never was a man more unworldly than Jack Aubrey. Maybe I will tell you a thing about him.'

'Go on, Stephen.'

'Some time ago he had an unhappy affair with another officer's wife. She had the dash, the style and the courage he loves, but she was a hard, false woman, and she wounded him very deeply. So virginal modesty, rectitude, principle, you know? have a greater charm for him than they might otherwise have had.'

'Ah? Yes, *I see*. I see now. And you have a béguin for her too? It is no use, I warn you. She would never do a thing without her mother's consent, and that is nothing to do with her mother's being in control of her fortune: it is all duty. And you would never bring my aunt Williams round in a thousand years. Still, you may feel on Sophie's side.'

'I have the greatest liking and admiration for her.'

'But no *tendre*?'

'Not as you would define it. But I am averse to giving pain, Villiers, which you are not.'

She stood up, as straight as a wand. 'We must go in. I have to dance this next bout with Captain Aubrey,' she said, kissing him. 'I am truly sorry if I hurt you, Maturin.'

CHAPTER THREE

For many years Stephen Maturin had kept a diary in a crabbed and characteristically secret shorthand of his own. It was scattered with anatomical drawings, descriptions of plants, birds, moving creatures, and if it had been deciphered the scientific part would have been found to be in Latin; but the personal observations were all in Catalan, the language he had spoken most of his youth. The most recent entries were in that tongue.

'*February 15* . . . then when she suddenly kissed me, the strength left my knees, quite ludicrously, and I could scarcely follow her into the ball-room with any countenance. I had sworn to allow no such thing again, no strong dolorous emotion ever again: my whole conduct of late proves how I lie. I have done everything in my power to get my heart under the harrow.

'*February 21*. I reflect upon Jack Aubrey. How helpless a man is, against direct attack by a woman. As soon as she leaves the schoolroom a girl learns to fend off, ward off wild love; it becomes second nature; it offends no code; it is commended not only by the world but even by those very men who are thus repulsed. How different for a man! He has no such accumulated depth of armour; and the more delicate, the more gallant, the more "honourable" he is the less he is able to withstand even a remote advance. He must not wound: and in this case there is little inclination to wound.

'When a face you have never seen without pleasure, that has never looked at you without a spontaneous smile, remains cold, unmoving, even inimical, at your approach, you are strangely cast down: you see another being and you are another being yourself. Yet life with Mrs W can be no party of pleasure; and magnanimity calls for understanding. For the moment it calls in vain. There are depths of barbarity, possibilities I did not suspect. Plain common sense calls for a disengagement.

'JA is uneasy, discontented with himself, discontented with Sophia's *reluctance* – coyness is no word to use for that dear sweet pure affectionate young woman's hesitation. Speaks of wincing fillies and their nonsense: he has never been able to bear frustration. This in part is what Diana Villiers means by his immaturity. If he did but know it the evident mutual liking between him and DV is in fact good for his suit. Sophia is perhaps the most respectable girl I have known, but she is after all a woman. JA is not percipient in these matters. Yet on the other hand he is beginning to look at me with some doubt. This is the first time there has been any reserve in our friendship; it is painful to me and I believe to him. I cannot bring myself to look upon him with anything but affection; but when I think of the possibilities, the physical possibilities I say, why then –

'DV insists upon my inviting her to Melbury to play billiards: she plays well, of course – can give either of us twenty in a hundred. Her insistence is accompanied by an ignoble bullying and an ignoble pretty pretty cajolery, to which I yield, both of us knowing exactly what we are about. This talk of friendship deceives neither of us; and yet it does exist, even on her side, I believe. My position would be the most humiliating in the world but for the fact that she is not so clever as she thinks: her theory is excellent, but she has not the control of her pride or her other passions to carry it into effect. She is cynical, but not nearly cynical enough, whatever she may *say*. If she were, I should not be obsessed. Quo me rapis? Quo indeed. My whole conduct, meekness, mansuetude, voluntary abasement, astonishes me.

'Quaere: is the passionate intensity of my feeling for Catalan independence the cause of my virile resurrection or its effect? There is a direct relationship, I am sure. Bartolomeu's report should reach England in three days if the wind holds.'

'Stephen, Stephen, Stephen!' Jack's voice came along the corridor, growing louder and ending in a roar as he thrust his head into the room. 'Oh, there you are. I was afraid you had gone off to your stoats again. The carrier has brought you an ape.'

'What sort of an ape?' asked Stephen.

'A damned ill-conditioned sort of an ape. It had a can of ale at every pot-house on the road, and it is reeling drunk. It has been offering itself to Babbington.'

'Then it is Dr Lloyd's lewd mangabey. He believes it to be suffering from the furor uterinus, and we are to open it together when I return.'

Jack looked at his watch. 'What do you say to a hand of cards before we go?'

'With all my heart.'

Piquet was their game. The cards flew fast, shuffled, cut, and dealt again: they had played together so long that each knew the other's style through and through. Jack's was a cunning alternation of risking everything for the triumphant point of eight, and of a steady, orthodox defence, fighting for every last trick. Stephen's was based upon Hoyle, Laplace, the theory of probabilities, and his knowledge of Jack's character.

'A point of five,' said Jack.

'Not good.'

'A quart.'

'To what?'

'The knave.'

'Not good.'

'Three queens.'

'Not good.'

They played. 'The rest are mine,' said Stephen, as the

singleton king fell to his ace. 'Ten for cards, and capot. We must stop. Five guineas, if you please; you shall have your revenge in London.'

'If I had not thrown away my hearts,' said Jack, 'I should have had you on toast. What amazing cards you have held these last few weeks, Stephen.'

'Skill enters into this game.'

'It is luck, all luck! You have the most amazing luck with cards. I should be sorry, was you in love with anyone.'

The pause lasted no more than a second before the door opened and the horses were reported alongside, but its effect hung about them for miles as they trotted through the cold drizzle along the London road.

However, the rain stopped while they were eating their dinner at the Bleeding Heart, their half-way point, a cheerful sun came out, and they saw the first swallow of the year, a blue curve skimming over the horse-pond at Edenbridge. Long before they walked into Thacker's, the naval coffee-house, they were far back in their old easy ways, talking without the least constraint about the sea, the service, the possibility of migrant birds navigating by the stars at night, of an Italian violin that Jack was tempted to buy, and of the renewal of teeth in elephants.

'Aubrey, so it is!' cried Captain Fowler, rising from his shadowy box in the far end of the room. 'We were just talking about you. Andrews was here until five minutes ago, telling us about your ball in the country – in Sussex. He said it was the finest thing – girls by the dozen, fine women, such a ball! He told us all about it. Pray,' he said, looking arch, 'are we to congratulate you?'

'Not – not exactly, sir, thank you very much however. Perhaps a little later, if all goes well.'

'Clap on, clap on! Else you will regret it when you are old – damnably mouldy a hundred years hence. Am not I right, Doctor? How do you do? Am I not right? If only he will clap on, we may see him a grandfather yet. My grandson has six teeth! Six teeth in his head already!'

* * *

'I shall not spend long with Jackson, I just want a little ready money – you have stripped me with your infernal run of luck – and the latest news from the prize-court,' said Jack, referring to his prize-agent and man of business. 'And then I shall go to Bond Street. It is a prodigious sum to pay for a fiddle, and I do not think I could square it with my conscience. I am not really a good enough player. But I should just like to handle it again, and tuck it under my chin.'

'A good fiddle would bring you into bloom, and you earned an Amati by every minute you spent on the deck of the *Cacafuego*. Certainly you must have your fiddle. Any innocent pleasure is a real good: there are not so many of them.'

'Must I? I have a great respect for your judgment, Stephen. If you are not long at the Admiralty, perhaps you would step round and give me your opinion of its tone.'

Stephen walked into the Admiralty, gave his name to the porter, and was shown straight past the notorious waiting-room, where an anxious, disconsolate and often shabby crowd of shipless officers were waiting for an interview, an almost certainly hopeless interview.

He was received by an elderly man in a black coat – received with marked consideration and begged to take a seat. Sir Joseph would be with them as soon as the Board rose; they had been sitting an hour longer than had been expected; and in the mean time Black Coat would be happy to deal with certain main heads. They had received Bartolomeu's report.

'Before we begin, sir,' said Stephen, 'may I suggest that I should use another entrance or that our meetings should take place in another house? There was a fellow lounging about by the hazard on the other side of Whitehall whom I have seen in the company of Spaniards from the embassy. I may be mistaken; it may be mere chance; but – '

Sir Joseph hurried in. 'Dr Maturin, I do apologize for keeping you. Nothing but the Board would have prevented me from . . . How do you do, sir? It is most exceedingly good of you to come up at such short notice. We have received Bartolomeu's report, and we urgently wish to consult you upon several points that arise. May we go through it, head by head? His lordship particularly desired me to let him have the results of our conversation by tonight.'

The British government was well aware that Catalonia, the Spanish province or rather collection of provinces that contained most of the wealth and the industry of the kingdom, was animated by a desire to regain its independence; the government knew that the peace might not last – Bonaparte was building ships as fast as he could – and that a divided Spain would greatly weaken any coalition he might bring into an eventual war. The various groups of Catalan autonomists who had approached the government had made this plain, though it was obvious before: this was not the first time England had been concerned with Catalonia nor with dividing her potential enemies. The Admiralty, of course, was interested in the Catalan ports, shipyards, docks, naval supplies and industries; Barcelona itself would be of incalculable value, and there were many other harbours, including Port Mahon in Minorca, the British possession, so strangely given up by the politicians when they negotiated the recent peace-treaty. The Admiralty, following the English tradition of independent intelligence agencies with little or no communication between them, had their own people dealing with this question. But few of them could speak the language, few knew much about the history of the nation, and none could evaluate the claims of the different bodies that put themselves forward as the true representatives of the country's resistance. There were some Barcelona merchants, and a few from Valencia; but they were limited men, and the long war had kept them out of touch with their friends; Dr Maturin was the Admiralty's most esteemed adviser. He was known to have had revolutionary contacts in his younger days, but his integrity, his complete disinterestedness were never called into question. The Admiralty also had a touching respect for scientific eminence, and no less a person than the Physician of the Fleet vouched for Stephen Maturin's. 'Dr Maturin's *Tar-Water Reconsidered* and his remarks on suprapubic cystotomy should be in every naval surgeon's chest: such acuity of practical observation . . . ' Whitehall had a higher opinion of him than Champflower: Whitehall knew that he was a physician, no mere surgeon; that he was a man of some estate in Lérida; and that his Irish father had been connected with the first families of that kingdom. Black Coat and his colleagues also knew that in his character as a physician, a learned man of standing perfectly at home in both Catalan and Spanish, he could move about the country as freely as any native – an incomparable agent, sure, discreet, deeply covered: a man of their own kind. And from their point of view his remaining tinge of Catholicism was but one advantage more. They would have wrung and squeezed their secret funds to retain him, and he would take nothing: the most delicate sounding produced no hint of an echo, no gleam in his purse's eye.

He left the Admiralty by a side door, walked through the park and up across Piccadilly to Bond Street, where he found Jack still undecided. 'I tell you what it is, Stephen,' he said. 'I do not know that I really like its tone. Listen – '

'If the day were a little warmer, sir,' said the shopman, 'it would bring out its fruitiness. You should have heard Mr Galignani playing it when we still had the fire going, last week.'

'Well, I don't know,' said Jack. 'I think I shall leave it for today. Just put up these strings in a paper for me, will you, together with the rosin. Keep the fiddle, and I will let you know one way or the other by the end of the week. Stephen,' he said, taking his friend's arm and guiding him across the busy street, 'I must have been playing that fiddle a good hour and more, and I still don't know my own mind. Jackson was not in the way, nor his partner, so I came straight here. It was odd, damned vexing and odd, for we had appointed to meet. But he was not at home: just this fool of a clerk, who said he was out of town – they expected him, but could not tell when. I shall pay my respects to Old Jarvie, just to keep myself in mind, and then we can go home. I shall not wait for Jackson.'

They rode back, and where they had left the rain there they found it again, rain, and a fierce wind from the east. Jack's horse lost a shoe, and they wasted the best part of the afternoon finding a smith, a surly, awkward brute who sent his nails in too deep. It was dark when they reached Ashdown Forest; by this time Jack's horse was lame, and they still had a long ride before them.

'Let me look to your pistols,' said Jack, as the trees came closer to the road. 'You have no notion of hammering your flints.'

'They are very well,' said Stephen, unwilling to open his holsters (a teratoma in one, a bottled Arabian dormouse in the other). 'Do you apprehend any danger?'

'This is an ugly stretch of road, with all these disbanded soldiers turned loose. They made an attempt upon the mail not far from Aker's Cross. Come, let me have your pistols. I thought as much: what is this?'

'A teratoma,' said Stephen sulkily.

'What is a teratoma?' asked Jack, holding the object in his hand. 'A kind of grenado?'

'It is an inward wen, a tumour: we find them, occasionally, in the abdominal cavity. Sometimes they contain long black hair, sometimes a set of teeth: this has both hair *and* teeth. It belonged to a Mr Elkins of the City, an eminent cheese-monger. I prize it much.'

'By God,' cried Jack, thrusting it back into the holster and wiping his hand vehemently upon the horse, 'I do wish you would leave people's bellies alone. So you have no pistols at all, I collect?'

'If you wish to be so absolute, no, I have not.'

'You will never make old bones, brother,' said Jack, dismounting and feeling the horse's leg. 'There is an inn, not a bad inn, half a mile off the side-road: what do you say to lying there tonight?'

'Your mind is much disturbed by the thought of these robbers, highwaymen, footpads?'

'I tremble so that I can hardly sit on my horse. It would be stupid to get knocked on the head, to be sure, but I am thinking more of my horse's legs. And then again,' he said, after a pause, 'I have a damned odd feeling: I do not much care to be home tonight. Strange, because I had looked forward to it – lively as a libertyman this morning – and now I do not care for it so much. Sometimes at sea you have that feeling of a lee-shore. Dirty weather, close-reefed top-sails, not a sight of the sun, not an observation for days, no idea of where you are to within a hundred miles or so, and at night you feel the loom of the shore under your lee: you can see nothing, but you can almost hear the rocks grinding out your bottom.'

Stephen made no reply, but wound his cloak higher against the biting wind.

Mrs Williams never came down to breakfast; and quite apart from this the breakfast-room at Mapes was the most cheerful in the house; it looked south-east, and the gauze curtains waved gently in the sun, letting in the smell of spring. It could not have been a more feminine room – pretty white furniture, a green sprigged carpet, delicate china, little rolls and honey, a quantity of freshly-washed young women drinking tea.

One of these, Sophie Bentinck, was giving an account of a dinner at the White Hart which Mr George Simpson, to whom she was engaged to be married, had attended. 'So then the toasts went round, and when George gave "Sophia" up starts your Captain Aubrey. "Oh," cries he,

"I will drink that with three times three. Sophie is a name very dear to my heart." And it could not have been me, you know, for we have never met.' She gazed about her with the benevolence of a good-natured girl who has a ring on her finger and who wishes everybody to be as happy as herself.

'And did he drink it with three times three?' asked Sophia, looking amused, pleased and conscious.

'It was the name of his ship, you know, his first command,' said Diana quickly.

'Of course I know it,' said Sophia with an unusual flush. 'We all know it.'

'The post!' shrieked Frances, rushing out of the room. An expectant pause, a temporary truce. 'Two for my mother, one for Sophie Bentinck with a sweet blue seal of a cupid – no, it's a goat with wings – and one for Di, franked. I can't make out the frank. Who's it from, Di?'

'Frankie, you must try to behave more like a Christian, sweetheart,' said her eldest sister. 'You must not take notice of people's letters: you must pretend to know nothing about 'em.'

'Mama always opens ours, whenever we get any, which isn't often.'

'I had one from Jemmy Blagrove's sister after the ball,' said Cecilia, 'and she said he said she was to say I danced like a swan. Mama was in a horrid wax – correspondence most improper, and anyhow swans did not dance, because of their webbed feet: they sang. But I knew what he meant. So your Mama allows you to correspond?' she said, turning to Sophie Bentinck.

'Oh, yes. But we are engaged, you know, which is quite different,' said Sophie, looking complacently at her hand.

'Tom Postman does not pretend to know nothing about people's letters,' said Frances. 'He said he could not make out Di's frank either. But the letters he is taking to Melbury are from London, Ireland and Spain. A double letter from Spain, with a vast sum to be paid!'

The breakfast-room at Melbury was cheerful too, but in a different way. Sombre mahogany, Turkey carpet, ponderous chairs, the smell of coffee, bacon and tobacco and wet men: they had been fishing since dawn and now they were half-way through the breakfast to which they were entitled, a breakfast that reached all over the broad white table-cloth: chafing dishes, coffee-pots, toast-racks, a Westphalian ham, a raised pie as yet untouched, the trout they had caught that morning.

'This was the one from under the bridge,' said Jack.

'Post, sir, if you please,' said his servant, Preserved Killick.

'From Jackson,' said Jack. 'And the other from the proctor. Forgive me, Stephen. I will just see what they have to say – what excuse . . .'

'My God,' he cried, a moment later. 'It can *not* be true.'

Stephen looked up sharply. Jack passed him the letter. Mr Jackson, his prize-agent, one of the most respectable men in the profession, had failed. He had bolted, run off to Boulogne with what remained of the firm's cash, and his partner had filed his petition in bankruptcy, with no hope of paying sixpence in the pound.

'What makes it so very bad,' said Jack in a low, troubled voice, 'is that I told him to put all *Sophie*'s prize-money into the funds as it came in. Some ships take years to be finally condemned, if the owners appeal. He did not do it. He gave me sums he said were interest from funds, but it was not true. He took it all as it came in, kept it in his own hands. It is gone, every last farthing.' He stared out of the window for some time, poising the other letter in his hand.

'This one is from the proctor. It will be about the two neutrals that were on appeal,' he said, breaking the seal at last. 'I am almost afraid to open it. Yes: just so. Here is my lee-shore. The verdict is reversed: I am to pay back eleven thousand pounds. I do not possess eleven thousand pence. A lee-shore . . . how can I claw off? There is only one thing for it: I will give up my claim to be made post

66

and beg for a sloop as a commander. A ship I must have. Stephen, lend me twenty pounds, will you? I have no ready money. I shall go up to the Admiralty today. There is not a moment to lose. Oh, I have promised to ride with Sophia: but I can still do it in the day.'

'Take a post-chaise. You must not arrive fagged out.'

'That is what I shall do – you are quite right, Stephen. Thank you. Killick!'

'Sir?'

'Cut along to the Goat and tell them to have a chaise here at eleven. Pack my valise for a couple of nights: no, a week.'

'Jack,' said Stephen urgently, when the servant had left the room, 'do not speak of this to anyone yet, I beg you.'

'You are looking terribly pale, Captain Aubrey,' said Sophia. 'I do hope you have not had another fall? Come in; please come in and sit down on a chair. Oh dear, I am sure you ought to sit down.'

'No, no, I promise you I have not fallen off my horse this last week,' said Jack, laughing. 'Let us make the most of this burst of sun; we shall get a ducking if we wait. Look at the clouds in the south-west. What a fine habit you are wearing.'

'Do you like it? It is the first time I have put it on. But,' she said, still looking anxiously into his face, which was now an unhealthy red, 'are you sure you would not like a cup of tea? It could be made in a moment.'

'Yes, yes, do step in and have a cup of tea,' cried Mrs Williams from the window, clutching a yellow garment to her throat. 'It will be ready directly, and there is a fire in the small sitting-room. You can drink it together – so cosy. I am sure Sophie is dying for a cup of tea. She would love a cup of tea with you, Captain Aubrey, would you not, Sophie?'

Jack smiled and bowed and kissed her hand, but his

iron determination not to stay prevailed, and in time they rode off along the Foxdene road to the edge of the downs.

'Are you quite sure you did not have a fall?' asked Sophie again, not so much from the idea that he had not noticed it and might recall it with application, as from a desire to express her real concern.

'No,' said Jack, looking at that lovely, usually remote face now gazing at him with such tenderness, such a worried and as it were proprietorial tenderness. 'But I did have a knock-down blow just now. A damned unlooked-for blow. Sophie – I may call you Sophie, mayn't I? I always think of you so – when I was in my *Sophie*, my sloop, I took a couple of neutrals sailing into Marseilles. Their papers said they were from Sicily for Copenhagen, laden with brimstone. But they were in the very act of running into Marseilles: I was within reach of that battery on the height. And the brimstone was meant for France.'

For Sophia brimstone was something to be mixed with treacle and given to children on Fridays: she could still feel the odious lumps between her teeth. This showed in her face, and Jack added, 'They have to have it to make gunpowder. So I sent both these ships into Port Mahon, where they were condemned as lawful prize out of hand, a glaring breach of neutrality; but now at length the owners have appealed, and the court has decided they were not lawful prize at all, that their masters' tale of merely taking shelter from the weather was true. Weather! There was no weather. Scarcely a riffle on the sea, and we stood in under our royals, stuns'ls either side, and the thirty-six-pounders up on the hill making rings in the still water a quarter of a mile wide.'

'Oh, how unjust!' cried Sophie in extreme indignation. 'What wicked men, to tell such lies! You must have risked your life to bring those ships out from under the battery. Of course the brimstone was meant for France. I am sure they will be punished. What can be done? Oh, what can be done?'

'As for the verdict, nothing at all. It is final, I am afraid. But I must go up and see what other measures – what I can wring out of the Admiralty. I must go today, and I may be away for some time. That is why I bore you with my affairs, to make it plain that I do not go away from Sussex of my own free will, nor with a light heart.'

'Oh, you do not bore – you could not bore me – everything to do with the Navy is – but did you say today? Surely you cannot go today. You must lie down and rest.'

'Today it must be, alas.'

'Then you must not ride. You must take a chaise and post up.'

'Yes. That is just what Stephen said. I will do it: I have ordered one from the Goat.'

'What a dear good man he is: he must be such a comfort to you. Such a good friend. But we must turn back at once, this minute. You must have all the rest you can before your journey.'

When they parted she gave him her hand and said, with an insistent pressure, 'I do pray you have the best of fortune, everything you deserve. I suppose there is nothing an ignorant girl in the country can do, but – '

'Why there you are, you two,' cried Mrs Williams. 'Chatting away like a couple of inseparables. Whatever can you be talking about all this time? But hush, I am indiscreet. La! And have you brought her back safe and sound, quite intact?'

Two secretaries, one sure if another failed, wrote as fast as their pens would drive.

'To the Marquis Cornwallis

My Lord,

With every disposition to pay the most prompt
attention to your Lordship's wishes in favour of
Captain Bull, I have greatly to lament that it is
not at present in my powers to comply with them.

I have the honour to be, etc.

are you there, Bates?'

'Yes, my lord.'

'To Mrs Paulett

Madam,

Although I cannot admit the force of your argument in favour of Captain Mainwaring, there is
something so amiable and laudable in a sister con-
tending for the promotion of her brother, that no
apology was needed for your letter of the twenty-
fourth, which I lose no time in acknowledging.

I am, Madam, etc.

'To Sir Charles Grey, KB.

My dear Sir Charles,

Lieutenant Beresford has been playing a game to
get to Ireland, which has lowered him much in my
opinion. He is grave and enterprising, but, like the
rest of the aristocracy, he thinks he has, from that
circumstance, a right to promotion, in prejudice of
men of better service and superior merit; which I
will never submit to.

Having refused the Prince of Wales, Duke of
Clarence, Duke of Kent, and Duke of Cumberland, you will not be surprised that I repeat the
impossibility of departing from my principle, which
would let in such an inundation upon me as would
tend to complete the ruin of the Navy.

Yours very sincerely

'To the Duchess of Kingston,
  Madam,
    Your Grace is largely correct in the character
of Captain Hallows of the *Frolic*; he has zeal and
conduct, and were it not for a certain independence
and want of willing submission to his superiors that
may be cured by the passage of time, as well as certain blemishes of a family nature, I should, exclusive
of the interest your Grace has taken in his fortunes,
be very glad to do justice to his merit, were I not
precluded from doing so by the incredible number
of meritorious commanders senior to him, upon half
pay, who have prior claims to any of the very few
ships that offer.
    I beg leave to assure your Grace that I shall be
happy in an occasion to mark the respect with which
I have the honour to be, Madam,
                    Your most obedient, humble servant

So much for the letters. Who is upon the list?'
    'Captains Saul, Cunningham, Aubrey and Small. Lieu-
tenants Roche, Hampole . . .'
    'I shall have time for the first three. '
    'Yes, my Lord.'
Jack heard the stentorian laughter as the First Lord
and his old shipmate Cunningham parted with a gun-
room joke, and he hoped he might find St Vincent in
a good mood.
    Lord St Vincent, deep in his attempts to reform the
dockyards, hamstrung by politics, politicians, and his
party's uncertain majority in the House, was not much
given to good moods however, and he looked up with an
unwelcoming, cold and piercing eye. 'Captain Aubrey, I
saw you here last week. I have very little time. General
Aubrey has written forty letters to me and other members
of the Board and he has been told that it is not in

71

contemplation to promote you for the action with the *Cacafuego*.'

'I have come here for another purpose, my Lord. To drop my claim to post rank in the hope of another sloop. My prize-agent has failed; two neutral owners have won their appeal against me; and I must have a ship.'

Lord St Vincent's hearing was not good, and in this innermost shrine of the Navy Jack had lowered his voice; the old gentleman did not quite catch his meaning. 'Must! What is this *must*?' he cried. 'Do commanders walk into the Admiralty nowadays and state that they *must* be given a ship? If you *must* be given a ship, sir, what the devil do you mean by parading Arundel with a cockade the size of a cabbage in your hat, at the head of Mr Babbington's supporters, knocking honest freeholders about with a bludgeon? If I had been there, sir, I should have committed you for a brawl, disorderly conduct, and we should have none of this talk of *must*. God damn your impudence, sir.'

'My Lord, I have expressed myself badly. With respect, my Lord, by that unhappy word I meant, that Jackson's failure puts me in the obligation of soliciting your Lordship for a command, sinking my other claim. He has ruined me.'

'Jackson? Yes. However,' said St Vincent coldly, 'if your own imprudence has lost you the fortune your command allowed you to win, you must not expect the Admiralty to feel responsible for finding you another. A fool and his money are soon parted, and in the end it is just as well. As for the neutrals, you know perfectly well, or you ought to know perfectly well, that it is a professional risk: you touch 'em at your peril, and you must make proper provision against an appeal. But what do you do in the event? You fling your money about – ducks and drakes – you talk about marriage, although you know, or ought to know, that it is death to a sea-officer's career, at least until he is made post – you lead drunken parties at a Tory by-election – you come here and say you *must* have a ship. And meanwhile your friends pepper us with letters to say that you *must* be made post. That was the very word the Duke of Kent thought fit to use, put up to it by Lady Keith. It was not an action that entitled you to post rank. What is all this talk about "giving up your claim"? There is no claim.'

'The *Cacafuego* was a thirty-two gun xebec-frigate, my Lord.'

'She was a privateer, sir.'

'Only by a damned lawyer's quibble,' said Jack, his voice rising.

'What the fucking hell is this language to me, sir? Do you know who you are talking to, sir? Do you know where you are?'

'I beg your pardon, my Lord.'

'You took a privateer commanded by God knows who, with a well-manned King's sloop at the loss of three men, and you come here prating about your *claim* to post rank.'

'And eight wounded. If an action is to be rated according to the casualty-list, my Lord, I beg leave to remind you that your flagship at the Battle of St Vincent had one killed and five wounded.'

'Do you presume to stand there and compare a great fleet action with a – '

'With a what, sir?' cried Jack, a red veil appearing in his eye.

The angry voices stopped abruptly. A door opened and closed, and the people in the corridor saw Captain Aubrey stride past, hurry down the stairs and vanish into the courtyard.

'*May 3.* I did beg him not to speak of all this: yet it is known throughout the countryside. He knows nothing about women except as objects of desire (oh quite honourable desire at times): no sisters, a mother who died when he was very young, and has no conception of the power and diabolical energy of a Mrs W. She certainly wrung her information out of Sophia with her customary lack of scruple, and has spread it abroad with malignant excitement and busyness – the same indecent busyness that she displayed in whirling the girls off to Bath. This transparent blackmail of her health: playing on Sophia's tender heart and sense of duty – what easier? All arrangements made in two days. None of her usual slow complaining muddle and whining vacillation for a month, nor yet a week, but two days' strong activity: packed and gone. If this had happened even a week later, with an understanding between them, it would not have mattered. Sophie would have held to her engagement "come Hell or high water". As it is, the circumstances could not be worse. Separation, inconstancy (JA's strong animal spirits, any young man's strong animal spirits), absence, the feeling of neglect.

'What a barbarous animal that Williams is. I should have known nothing of their unseemly departure but for Diana's notes and that sweet child's troubled, furtive visit. I call her child, although she is no younger than DV, whom I look upon in quite another light: though indeed she too must have been exquisite as a child – not unlike Frances, I believe: the same ruthless, innocent cruelty. Gone. What a silence. How am I to tell JA of all this? I am tormented by the thought of striking him in the face.'

Yet the telling was simple enough. He said, 'The girls have gone. Mrs Williams took them away to Bath last Tuesday sennight. Sophia came to see me and said she regretted it extremely.'

'Did she leave a message for me?' asked Jack, his sad face brightening.

'She did not. In direct terms, she did not. At times it was difficult to follow her in her agitation. Miss Anna Coluthon, overcome by her position – an unattended girl calling upon a single gentleman. Champflower has not seen such a thing. But I do not mistake when I state that in substance she told me you were to know that she did not leave Sussex of her own free will, nor with a light heart.'

'Do you think I might write to her, under cover to

Diana Villiers?' asked Jack.

'Diana Villiers is still here. She does not go to Bath: she stays at Mapes Court,' said Stephen coldly.

The news spread. The decision on the prizes was public knowledge, having been reported in the London papers; and there were enough naval officers in the neighbourhood, some of whom were affected by the agent's defection, to make the extent of the disaster clear. The announcement 'at Woolhampton, on the 19th instant, to the lady of General Aubrey, a son' merely rounded out the anecdote.

Bath was filled with Mrs Williams's triumph. 'It is certainly a divine retribution, my dears. We were told he was a sad rake, and you will remember I never liked him from the first: I said there was something wrong about his mouth. My instinct is never mistaken. I did not like his eye, neither.'

'Oh, Mama,' cried Frances, 'you said he was the most gentleman-like man you had ever seen, and so handsome.'

'Handsome is as handsome does,' cried Mrs Williams. 'And you may leave the room, Miss Pert. You shall have no pudding, for want of respect.'

It was soon found that other people had never liked Jack either: – his mouth, chin, eyes, lavish entertainment, horses, plans for a pack of hounds, all came in for adverse comment. Jack had seen this process before; he had an outsider's knowledge of it; but although his condemnation was neither gross nor universal, he found it more painful than he had expected – the first cautious reserve of the tradesmen, a certain easiness and assumption in the country gentlemen, an indefinible want of consideration.

He had taken Melbury for a year, the rent was paid, the house could not be sublet; there was no point in removing. He retrenched, sold his hunters, told his men that although it grieved him they must part as soon as they could find places, and stopped giving dinners. His horses were fine animals and he sold one for as much as he had given for it; this satisfied the immediate local duns, but it did not re-establish his credit, for although Champflower was willing to believe in any amount of cloudy wealth (and Jack's fortune had been reckoned very high), it had poverty weighed up to within a pound or two.

Invitations fell off, for not only was he much taken up with his affairs, but he had become prickly, over-sensitive to the least unintentional slight; and presently Mapes was the only place where he dined. Mrs Villiers, supported by the parson, his wife and sister, could perfectly well invite Melbury Lodge.

It was after one of these dinners that they rode back, stabled the cob and the mule and said good night to one another.

'You would not care for a hand of cards, I suppose?' said Jack, pausing on the stairs and looking down into the hall.

'I would not,' said Stephen. 'My mind is turned elsewhere.'

His person, too. He walked fast through the night over Polcary Down, carefully skirted a group of poachers in Gole's Hanger, giving them a wide berth, and paused under a clump of elms that stood, swaying and creaking in the wind, over against Mapes Court. The house was of some antiquity, irregular in spite of its modern alterations, and the oldest wing ended in a blunt square tower: one window lit. He passed quickly through the kitchen-garden, his heart beating, beating, so that when he stood at the little door deep in the base of the tower he could hear it, a sound like the hoarse panting of a dog. His face set in a steady, unmoved acceptance of defeat as he reached for the handle. 'I take my happiness in my hands every time I come to this door,' he said, not trying it for a moment. He felt the lock's silent response: turned it slowly.

He walked up the spiral staircase to the first floor, where Diana lived: a little sitting-room with her bedroom opening out of it, the whole communicating with the rest of the house by a long corridor that opened into the main staircase. There was no one in the sitting-room. He sat down on the sofa and looked attentively at the gold-thread embroidery of a sari that was being turned into a European dress. Under the golden light of the lamp gold tigers tore a Company's officer lying on the spotted ground with a brandy-bottle in his hand: sometimes in his right hand, sometimes in his left, for the pattern had many variations.

'How late you are, Maturin,' said Diana, coming in from her bedroom; she was wearing two shawls over her peignoir and her face was tired – no welcome. 'I was going to bed. However, sit down for five minutes. Eugh, your shoes are covered with filth.'

Stephen took them off and set them by the door. 'There was a gang with lurchers over by the warren. I stepped off the road. You have a singular gift for putting me at a disadvantage, Villiers.'

'So you walked again? Are you not allowed out at night? Anyone would think you were married to that man. How are his affairs, by the way? He seemed cheerful enough this evening, laughing away with that goose Annie Strode.'

'There is no improvement, I am afraid. The ship-owners' man of business is an avid brute, with no intelligence, sense, or bowels. Ignorant voracity – a wingless vulture – can soar only into the depths of ignominy.'

'But Lady Keith – ' She stopped. Lady Keith's letter had reached Melbury that morning, and it had not been mentioned at dinner. Stephen passed the sari through his hands, observing that sometimes the Company's officer looked gay, even ecstatic, sometimes agonized. 'If you suppose you have the right to ask me for explanations,' said Diana, 'you are mistaken. We happened to meet, riding. If you think that just because I have let you kiss me once or twice – if you think that just because you have come here when I have been ready to fling myself down the well or play the fool to get away from this odious daily round – nothing but a couple of toothless servants in the house –

that you are my lover and I am your mistress, you are wrong. I never have been your mistress.'

'I know,' said Stephen. 'I desire no explanation; I assume no rights. Compulsion is the death of friendship, joy.' A pause. 'Will you give me something to drink, Villiers my dear?'

'Oh, I *beg* your pardon,' she cried, with a ludicrous automatic return of civility. 'What may I offer you? Port? Brandy?'

'Brandy, if you please. Listen,' he said, 'did you ever see a tiger?'

'Oh yes,' said Diana vaguely, looking for the tray and the decanter. 'I shot a couple. There are no proper glasses here. Only from the safety of a howdah, of course. You often see them on the road from Maharinghee to Bania, or when you are crossing the mouths of the Ganges. Will this tumbler do? They swim about from island to island. Once I saw one take to the water as deliberately as a horse. They swim low, with their heads up and their tails long out behind. How cold it is in this damned tower. I have not been really warm right through since I came back to England. I am going to bed; it is the only warm place in the house. You may come and sit by me, when you have finished your brandy.'

The days dropped by, golden days, the smell of hay, a perfect early summer – wasted, as far as Jack was concerned. Or nine parts wasted; for although his naval and legal business grew steadily darker and more complex, he did go twice to Bath to see his old friend Lady Keith, calling up on Mrs Williams in the bosom of her family the first time and meeting Sophia – just happening to meet Sophia – in the Pump Room the second. He came back both elated and tormented, but still far more human, far more like the cheerful resilient creature Stephen had always known.

'I am resolved to break,' wrote Stephen. 'I give no

happiness; I receive none. This obsession is not happiness. I see a hardness that chills my heart, and not my heart alone. Hardness and a great deal else; a strong desire to rule, jealousy, pride, vanity; everything except a want of courage. Poor judgment, ignorance of course, bad faith, inconstancy; and I would add heartlessness if I could forget our farewells on Sunday night, unspeakably pathetic in so wild a creature. And then surely style and grace beyond a certain point take the place of virtue – *are* virtue, indeed? But it will not do. No, no, you get no more of me. If this wantonness with Jack continues I shall go away. And if he goes on he may find he has laboured to give himself a wound; so may she – he is not a man to be played with. Her levity grieves me more than I can express. It is contrary to what she terms her principles; even, I believe, to her real nature. She cannot want him as a husband now. Hatred of Sophia, of Mrs W? Some undefined revenge? Delight in playing with fire in a powder-magazine?'

The clock struck ten; in half an hour he was to meet Jack at Plimpton cockpit. He left the brown library for the brilliant courtyard, where his mule stood gleaming lead-coloured, waiting for him. It was gazing with a fixed, cunning expression down the alley beyond the stables, and following its eyes Stephen saw the postman stealing a pear from the kitchen-garden espalier.

'A double letter for you, sir,' said the postman, very stiff and official, with hurried pear-juice dribbling from the corner of his mouth. 'Two and eightpence, if you please. And two for the Captain, one franked, t'other Admiralty.' Had he been seen? The distance was very great, almost safe.

'Thankee, postman,' said Stephen, paying him. 'You have had a hot round.'

'Why, yes, sir,' said the postman, smiling with relief. 'Parsonage, Croker's, then Dr Vining's – one from his brother in Godmersham, so I'd suppose he'll be over this Sunday – and then right up to young Mr Savile's –

his young lady. Never was there such a young lady in the writing line; I shall be glad when they are married, and say it by word of mouth.'

'You are hot, thirsty: you must try a pear – it will keep the humours in motion.'

The main had started when Stephen walked in: a tight-packed ring of farmers, tradesmen, gipsies, horsecopers, country gentlemen, all too excited, the only tolerable thing the courage of the birds there in the pit.

'Evens on the speckled pie! Evens on the speckled pie!' cried a tall gipsy with a red scarf round his neck.

'Done with you,' said Jack. 'Five guineas at even odds on the speckled pie.'

'Done and done,' said the gipsy looking round. His eyes narrowed, and in a jocular, wheedling voice he went on, 'Five guineas, gentleman? Oh, such a purse for a poor travelling man and a half-pay captain! I lays my money down, eh?' He placed the five bright coins on the rim of the pit. Jack thrust out his jaw and matched the guineas one by one. The owners of the birds set them to the ring, clasping them just so and whispering close to their proud close-cropped heads. The cocks stalked out on their toes, darting glances sideways, circling before they closed. Both flew up at the same moment, the steel spurs flashing as they struck; up and up again, a whirlwind in the middle of the pit and a savage roaring all round it.

The speckled pie, staggering, one eye gone and the other streaming blood, stood his ground, peering through the mist for his enemy: saw his shadow and lurched in to get his death-wound. Still he would not die; he stood with the spurs labouring his back until the mere weight of his exhausted opponent bore him down – an opponent too cruelly lacerated to rise and crow.

'Let us go and sit outside,' said Stephen. 'Pot-boy, there, bring us a pint of sherry-wine on the bench outside. Do you mind me, now?'

'Sherry, for all love!' he said. 'The pretentious young

whore is wicked enough to call this sherry-wine. Here are letters for you, Jack.'

'The speckled pie did not really want to fight,' said Jack.

'He did not. Though he was a game bird, to be sure. Why did you bet on him?'

'I liked him; he had a rolling walk like a sailor. He was not what you would call a wicked bloody cock, but once he was in the ring, once he was challenged, he would fight. He was a rare plucked 'un, and he went on even when there was no hope at all. I am not sorry I backed him: should do it again. Did you say there were letters?'

'Two letters. Use no ceremony, I beg.'

'Thank you, Stephen. The Admiralty acknowledges Mr Aubrey's communication of the seventh ultimo. This is from Bath: I will just see what Queenie has to say . . . Oh my God.'

'What's amiss?'

'My God,' said Jack again, beating his clenched fist on his knee. 'Come, let's get out of this place. Sophie's to be married.'

They rode for a mile, Jack muttering broken sentences, ejaculations to himself, and then he said, 'Queenie writes from Bath. A fellow by the name of Adams – big estate in Dorset – has made Sophia an offer. Pretty brisk work, upon my soul. I should never have believed it of her.'

'Is this gossip Lady Keith has picked up?'

'No, no, no! She called on Mother Williams for my sake – my idea was she could not refuse to see me when I went down. Queenie knows everybody.'

'Certainly. Mrs Williams would be flattered by the acquaintance.'

'Yes. So she went, and Mrs Williams, tittering with joy, told her the whole thing, every last detail of the estate. Would you have believed it of Sophia, Stephen?'

'No. And I doubt the truth of the report, in so far as it assumes that the offer has been made directly and not through the mother, as a mere proposition.'

81

'By God, I wish I were in Bath,' said Jack in a low voice, his face dark with anger. 'Who would have believed it of her? That pure face – I should have sworn . . . Those sweet, kindest words so short a while ago; and now already things have gone as far as an offer of marriage! Think of the hand-holding, paddling . . . By God, and such a pure, pure face.'

Stephen said that this was no evidence, that Mrs Williams was capable of any invention; he was intelligent, comforting and wise, and he knew that he might as well have been talking to his mule. Jack's face had closed in a particular hard, determined set; he said he had thought for once he had found a perfectly straightforward girl – nothing hole-in-the-corner, nothing uneasy and complicated – but he would say no more about it; and when they came to the Newton Priors crossroads he said, 'Stephen, I know you mean very, very kindly, but I think I shall ride over the Downs to Wivenhoe. I'm not fit company for man or beast. You will not be wanting the cob? And don't wait supper – I shall get a bite somewhere on the road.'

'Killick,' said Stephen, 'put the ham and a pot of beer in the Captain's room. He may come home late. I am going out.'

He walked slowly at first, his heart and breathing quite undisturbed, but when the familiar miles had passed under him and he started to climb Polcary, the stronger rhythm had returned, increasing as all his resolution fell away, and by the time he reached the top of the hill his heart was keeping time with his brisk busy watch. 'Thump, thump, thump, you fool,' he said smiling as he timed it. 'It is true, of course, that I have never climbed the hill so fast – my legs are in training, ha, ha, ha. A pretty sight I should look. Kind night that covers me.'

More slowly now, his senses keen for the least movement in the wood, in Gole's Hanger or the lane beyond: far on his right hand the barking of a roe-buck in search of a doe, and on his left the distant screaming of a rabbit with a stoat at work upon it. An owl. Dim, fast asleep among its trees, the vague shape of the house, and at its far end the one square eye in the tower, shining out.

Down to the elms, silent and thick-leaved now: the house full-view. And under the elms his own cob tethered to a hazel-bush. He recognized the animal before it whinnied, and he stood stock-still. Creeping forward at its second neigh he stroked its velvet muzzle and its neck, patted it for a while, still staring over its withers at the light, and then turned. After perhaps a hundred yards, with the tower sunk in the trees behind him, he stopped dead and put his hand to his heart. Walked on: a heavy, lumpish pace, stumbling in the ruts, driving himself forward by brute force.

'Jack,' he said at breakfast next morning, 'I think I must leave you: I shall see whether I can find a place on the mail.'

'Leave me!' cried Jack, perfectly aghast. 'Oh, surely not?'

'I am not entirely well, and conceive that my native air might set me up.'

'You do look miserably hipped,' said Jack, gazing at him now with attention and deep concern. 'I have been so wrapped up in my own damned unhappy business – and now this – that I have not been watching you. I am so sorry, Stephen. You must be damned uncomfortable here, with only Killick, and no company. How I hope you are not really ill. Now I recollect, you have been low, out of spirits, these last weeks – no heart for a jig. Should you like to advise with Dr Vining? He might see your case from the outside, if you understand me. I am sure he is not so clever as you, but he might see it from the outside. Pray let me call him in. I shall step over at once, before he starts on his rounds.'

It took Stephen the interval between breakfast and the coming of the post to quiet his friend – 'he knew his disease perfectly – had suffered from it before – it was nothing a man could die of – he knew the cure – the malady was called solis deprivatio.'

'The taking away of the sun?' cried Jack. 'Are you making game of me, Stephen? You cannot be thinking of going to Ireland for the sun.'

'It was a kind of dismal little joke,' said Stephen. 'But I had meant Spain rather than Ireland. You know I have a house in the mountains behind Figueras: part of its roof has fallen in, the part where the sheep live – I must attend to it. Bats there are, free-tailed bats, that I have watched for generations. Here is the post,' he said, going to the window and reaching out. 'You have one letter. I have none.'

'A bill,' said Jack, putting it aside. 'Oh yes you have, though. I quite forgot. Here in my pocket. I happened to see Diana Villiers yesterday and she gave me this note to deliver – said such handsome things about you, Stephen. We said what a capital shipmate you were, and what a hand with a 'cello and a knife. She thinks the world of you . . . '

Perhaps: the note was kind, in its way.

My dear Stephen,

How shabbily you treat your friends – all these days without a sign of life. It is true I was horribly disagreeable when last you did me the pleasure of calling. Please forgive me. It was the east wind, or original sin, or the full moon, or something of that kind. But I have found some curious Indian butterflies – just their wings – in a book that belonged to my father. If you are not too tired, or bespoke, perhaps you might like to come and see them this evening.

D.V.

' . . . not that there is any virtue in that. I asked her

84

over to play with us on Thursday; she knows our trio well, although she only plays by ear. However since you must go, I will send Killick to make our excuses.'

'Perhaps I may not leave so soon. Lt us see what next week brings; the sheep are covered with wool, after all; and there is always the chapel for the bats.'

The road, pale in the darkness, Stephen riding deliberately along it, reciting an imagined dialogue. He rode up to the door, then tethered his mule to a ring, and he was about to knock when Diana opened to him.

'Good night, Villiers,' he said. 'I thank you for your note.'

'I love the way you say good night, Stephen,' she said, smiling. She was obviously in spirits, certainly in high good looks. 'Are you not amazed to see me here?'

'Moderately so.'

'All the servants are out. How formal you are, coming to the front door! I am so happy to see you. Come into my lair. I have spread out my butterflies for you.'

Stephen took off his shoes, sat deliberately on a small chair and said, 'I have come to pay my adieux. I leave the country very soon – next week, I believe.'

'Oh, Stephen . . . and will you abandon your friends? What will poor Aubrey do? Surely you cannot leave him now? He seems so very low. And what shall I do? I shall have no one to talk to, no one to misuse.'

'Will you not?'

'Have I made you very unhappy, Stephen?'

'You have treated me like a dog at times, Villiers.'

'Oh, my dear. I am so very sorry. I shall never be unkind again. And so you really mean to go? Oh, dear. But friends kiss when they say good-bye. Come and just pretend to look at my butterflies – I put them out so prettily – and give me a kiss, and then you shall go.'

'I am pitifully weak with you, Diana, as you know very well,' he said. 'I came slowly over Polcary, rehearsing the words in which I should tell you I had come to break, and that I was happy to do so in kindness and friendship, with no bitter words to remember. I cannot do so, I find.'

'Break? Oh dear me, that is a word *we* must never use.'

'Never.'

Yet the word appeared five days later in his diary. 'I am required to deceive JA, and although I am not unaccustomed to deception, this is painful to me. He endeavours to delude me too, of course, but out of a consideration for what he conceives to be my view of right conduct of his relationship with Sophia. He has a singularly open and truthful nature and his efforts are ineffectual, though persistent. She is right: I cannot go away with him in his present difficulties. Why does she increase them? Mere vice? In another age I should have said diabolic possession, and it is a persuasive answer even now – one day herself and none so charming, the next cold, cruel, full of hurt. Yet by force of repetition words that wounded me bitterly not long ago have lost their full effect; the closed door is no longer death; my determination to break grows stronger: it is becoming more than an intellectual determination. I have neither remarked this myself nor found it in any author, but a small temptation, almost an un-temptation, can be more dominant than a great one. I am not strongly tempted to go to Mapes; I am not strongly tempted to drink up the laudanum whose drops I count so superstitiously each night. Four hundred drops at present, my bottled tranquillity. Yet I do so. Killick,' he said, with the veiled dangerous look of a man interrupted at secret work, 'what have you to say to me? You are confused, disturbed in your mind. You have been drinking.'

Killick stepped closer, and leaning on Stephen's chair he whispered. 'There's some ugly articles below, sir, asking for the Captain. A blackbeetle in a scrub wig and a couple of milling coves, prize-fighters. Awkward buggers in little round hats, and I see one of 'em shove a staff under his coat. Bums. Sheriff's officers.'

Stephen nodded. 'I will deal with them in the kitchen. No, the breakfast-room: it looks on to the lawn. Pack the Captain's sea-chest and my small valise. Give me those letters of his. Put the mule to the little cart and drive to the end of Foxdene lane with our dunnage.'

'Aye aye, sir. Pack, mule and cart, and Foxdene it is.'

Leaving the bums grim and wooden in the breakfast-room, Stephen smiled with pleasure: here at last was a concrete situation. He knew where he should find them within a mile or two; but he did not know what it would cost him when, having toiled up the chalky slope in the sun, he met their expressions of cold anger, resentment, and hostility.

'Good morning, now,' he said, taking off his hat. Diana gave him a distant nod and a look that pierced him cruelly. 'You seem to have had a hot walk, Dr Maturin. How eager you must be to see – '

'You will forgive me if I say a word to Captain Aubrey, ma'am,' he said, with a look as cold as her own, and he led the cob aside. 'Jack, they have come to arrest you for debt. We must cross to France tonight and so to Spain. Your chest and the little cart will be at the end of Foxdene lane by now. You shall stay with me at my house: it falls out very well. We may catch the Folkestone packet if we drive hard.' He turned, bowed to Diana, and set off down the hill.

The drum of hooves, Diana's voice calling, 'Ride on, Aubrey. Ride on, I say. I must speak to Maturin,' and she reined in beside him. 'I must speak to you, Maturin. Stephen, would you leave and not say goodbye to me?'

'Will you not let me go, Diana?' he said, looking up, his eyes filling with tears.

'No, no, no,' she cried. 'You must not leave me – go, yes go to France – but write to me, write to me, and come back.' She gripped him hard with her small hand, and she was away, the turf flying behind her horse.

*　　*　　*

'Not Folkestone,' said Jack, guiding the mule through the grassy lanes. 'Dover. Seymour has the *Amethyst*; he carries the imperial ambassador across tonight. He will give us a passage – he and I were shipmates in the *Marlborough*. Once aboard a King's ship and we can tell the tipstaff to go to hell.'

Five miles later he said, 'Stephen, do you know what that letter was you brought me? The small one, wafered?'

'I do not.'

'It was from Sophie. A direct letter, sent straight to me, do you hear? She says there have been reports of this Adams fellow and his pretensions, that might have given her friends uneasiness. That there was nothing to it – all God-damned flummery – had scarcely seen him above a dozen times, though he was always closeted with Mama. She speaks of you. Sends you her very kind regards and would be so happy to see you in Bath; the weather there is charming. Christ, Stephen, I have never been so down. Fortune gone, career too maybe, and now this.'

'I cannot tell you what a relief it is,' he said, bending to see whether the *Amethyst*'s forestaysail were drawing, 'to be at sea. It is so clear and simple. I do not mean just escaping from the bums; I mean all the complications of life on shore. I do not think I am well suited to the land.'

They were standing on the quarterdeck amidst a crowd of wondering, staring attachés, secretaries, members of the suite, who staggered and lurched, clinging to ropes and to one another as the frigate began to feel the roll and the brisk cross-sea and Dover cliffs vanished in a swathe of summer rain. 'Yes,' said Stephen, 'I too have been walking a tightrope with no particular skill. I have the same sense of enlargement. A little while ago I should have welcomed it without reservation.'

CHAPTER FOUR

Toulon. The mistral had died away at last, and there was scarcely a fleck of white left on the sea; but the brilliant clarity of the air was still undimmed, so that a telescope from the hills behind the town could pick out even the names of the seven line-of-battle ships in the Petite Rade: the *Formidable* and *Indomptable*, both of eighty guns, and the *Atlas, Scipion, Intrépide, Mont-Blanc* and *Berwick* of seventy-four apiece. English pride might have been hurt at the sight of the last, for she belonged to the Royal Navy until some years before: and had English pride been able to look into the jealously guarded Arsenal it would have been mortified again by seeing two more British seventy-fours, the *Hannibal*, captured during Sir James Saumarez's action in the Gut of Gibraltar in 1801, and the *Swiftsure*, taken in the Mediterranean a few weeks earlier, both of them under active repair.

Indeed activity, extreme activity, was the word for Toulon. The silent, still-green hills, the great headlands, the enormous sweep of the Mediterranean beyond them and the islands, blue and motionless beyond expression, the flood of hot, oppressive light, and then in the middle this noisy little stirring concentrated town, filled with tiny figures – white shirts, blue trousers, the gleam of red sashes – all of them intensely busy. Even under this noonday sun they were toiling like ants – boats pulling from the Arsenal to the Petite Rade, from the Petite Rade to the Grande Rade, from the ships to the quays and back again, men swarming over the fine great ships on the stocks, plying their adzes, caulking-hammers, augers, beetles, harring-poles; gangs of convicts unloading oak from Ragusa, Stockholm tar, Hamburg tow, Riga spars and cordage, all in the din and the innumerable smells of a great port, the reek of open drains, old stagnant water, hot stone, frying garlic, grilling fish that wafted above the whole.

'Dinner,' said Captain Christy-Pallière, closing the file of Death Sentences, F-L. 'I shall start with a glass of Banyuls and some anchovies, a handful of olives, *black* olives; then I believe I may look at Hébert's fish soup, and follow it with a simple langouste in court-bouillon. Possibly his gigot en croûte: the lamb is exquisite now that the thyme is in flower. Then no more than cheese, strawberries, and some trifle with our coffee – a saucer of my English jam, for example. None of your architectural meals, Penhoët; my liver will not stand it in this heat, and we have a great deal of work to do if the *Annibale* is to be ready for sea by next week. There are all Dumanoir's dossiers to deal with – how I wish he would come back. I should have interrogated the Maltese this morning. If we have a good dinner they risk to escape unshot . . . '

'Let us drink Tavel with the lamb,' said Captain Penhoët, who knew that for his part he risked philosophical remarks about digestion – guilt – Pontius Pilate – the odious side of interrogating suspected spies, quite unfit for officers – if he did not interrupt. 'It is – '

'Two roast-beefs to see you, sir,' said an orderly.

'Oh no!' cried Captain Christy-Pallière, 'not at this hour, holy name. Tell them I am not here, Jeannot. I may be back at five. Who are they?'

'The first is Aubrey, Jacques. He claims to be a captain in their navy,' said the orderly, narrowing his eyes and scanning the official slip in his hand. 'Born 1 April 1066, at Bedlam, London. Father's profession, monk: mother's, nun. Mother's maiden name, Borgia, Lucrèce. The other pilgrim is Maturin, Etienne – '

'Quick, quick,' cried Captain Christy-Pallière. 'My breeches, Jeannot, my cravat – ' for ease and commodity he had been sitting in his drawers. 'Son of a whore, my shirt. Penhoët, we must have a real dinner today – find a clothes-brush, Jeannot – this is the English prisoner I was telling you about. Excellent seaman, charming company. You will not mind speaking English, of course. How do I look?'

'So pimping as possible,' said Captain Penhoët in that language. 'Camber the torso, and you will impose yourself of their attention.'

'Show them in, Jeannot,' said Christy-Pallière. 'My dear Aubrey,' he cried, folding Jack in his arms and kissing him on both cheeks, 'how very happy I am to see you! Dear Dr Maturin, be the very welcome. Allow me to present Captain of frigate Penhoët – Captain of frigate Aubrey, and Dr Maturin, at one time my guests aboard the *Desaix*.'

'Your servant, sir,' said Captain Penhoët.

'Domestique, monsieur,' said Jack, still blushing as far as his shirt. 'Penhoët? Je préserve – je ai – le plus vivid rémembrance de vos combatte à Ushant, à bord le *Pong*, en vingt-quatre neuf.' A second of attentive, polite but total blankness followed this, and turning to Christy-Pallière he said, 'How do you say I have the liveliest recollection of Captain Penhoët's gallant action off Ushant in '99?'

Captain Christy-Pallière said this in another kind of French – renewed, far warmer smiles, another British shake-hand – and observed, 'But we may all speak English. My colleague is one of our best translators. Come, let us go and have dinner in a trice – you are tired, dusty, quite fagged up – how far have you come today? How do you stand the heat? Extraordinary for the month of May. Have you seen my cousins in Bath? May we hope for your company for some time? How happy I am to see you!'

'We had hoped you would dine with us,' cried Jack. 'We have livré une table – booked it.'

'You are in my country,' said Christy-Pallière in a tone that allowed of no reply. 'After you, dear friends, I beg. A simple meal – a little inn just outside the town. But it has a muscat trellis – fresh air – and the man does the cooking himself.' Turning to Stephen as he shepherded them along the corridor he said, 'Dr Ramis is with us again! He came back from leave on Tuesday. I will ask him to come and sit with us after dinner – he could not bear to see us eat – and he will tell you all the news of our cholera outburst and the new Egyptian pox.'

'Captain Aubrey led us such a chase,' he said to Captain Penhoët, setting pieces of bread to represent the ships of Admiral Linois's squadron. 'He commanded that little quarter-decked brig the *Sophie* – '

'I remember myself of him.'

'And at first he had the weather-gage of us. But he was embayed – here is the headland, and the wind was so, a caprice wind.' He fought the battle over again, stage by stage. 'And then he put up his helm in a flash, set his studding-sails like a conjuring trick and ran through our line, close to the Admiral. The fox, he knew I dared not risk hitting the flagship! And he knew the *Desaix's* broadside would come rather slow! He ran through, and with a little luck – '

'What is luck?'

'Chance. He might have escaped. But the Admiral made my signal to chase, and the *Desaix* was only a week out of dock quite clean, and she loves a light breeze on the quarter: and in short . . . I should have blown you out of the sea with my last broadside, dear friend, if you had not jugged like an hare.'

'How well I remember it,' said Jack. 'My heart was in my boots as I saw you beginning to luff up. But it had gone down there much earlier, when I saw that you sailed two miles to my one, without troubling to set your stuns'ls.'

'It was an exploit of thunder, to run through the line,' said Captain Penhoët. 'I could almost to wish you had succeeded the blow. I should have struck as soon as the admiral had forereached my ship. But in principle you English carry too much guns, is it not? Too many for sail fast in a such breeze – too many to escape oneself.'

'I tossed mine all overboard,' said Jack. 'Though in principle you are right. Yet might we not say that in principle you carry far too many men, particularly soldiers? Remember the *Phoebe* and *Africaine* . . .'

The simple meal wound to its even simpler end – a bottle of brandy and two glasses. Captain Penhoët, exhausted by his efforts, had returned to his office; Stephen had been carried off to Dr Ramis's healthier table, to drink gaseous water from a sulphurous spring; and Cape Sicié had turned purple against the now violet sea. Crickets filled the air with a warm continuous omnipresent churr.

Both Jack and Christy-Pallière had drunk a great deal; they were now telling one another about their professional difficulties, and each was astonished that the other had reason to complain. Christy-Pallière too was caught on the promotion-ladder, for although he was a capitaine de vaisseau, very like a post-captain, there was 'no proper sense of seniority in the French navy – dirty, underhand intrigue everywhere – political adventurers succeeding – real seamen thrust to the wall.' He did not express himself directly, but Jack knew from their conversations a year ago and from the indiscretions of his English Christy cousins, that his friend was but a lukewarm republican, detested the upstart Bonaparte's vulgarity and total ignorance of the sea-service, would have liked a constitutional, liberal monarchy, and was uneasy in his skin – a man devoted to his navy and of course to France, but unhappy in his rulers. Long ago he had spoken in a remarkably informed and perceptive way, about the case of Irish officers in the Royal Navy and the moral dilemma of conflicting loyalties; but at this moment, although four sorts of wine and two of brandy had brought him handsomely into the area of indiscretion, he was solely concerned with his own immediate problems. 'For you it is perfectly simple,' he said. 'You will assemble your interest, your friends and the lords and sirs of your acquaintance; and eventually, with your parliamentary elections, there will be a change of ministry and your evident merits will be recognized. But what is the case with us? Republican interest, royalist influence, Catholic interest, Freemason interest, consular or what they tell me will soon be *imperial* interest, all cutting across one another – a foul hawse. We might as well finish this bottle. You know,' he said, after a pause, 'I am so tired of sitting on my arse in an office. The only hope, the only solution, is a – ' His voice died away.

'I suppose it would be wicked to pray for war,' said Jack, whose mind had followed exactly the same course. 'But oh to be afloat.'

'Oh, very wicked, no doubt.'

'Particularly as the only worth-while war would have to be against the nation we like best. For the Dutch and Spaniards are no match for us now. It makes me stare, every time I think of it, how well the Spaniards build – beautiful, beautiful great ships – and how strangely they handle them. At the Battle of St Vincent – '

'It is all the fault of their admiralty,' cried Christy-Pallière. 'All admiralties are the same. I swear, on the head of my mother, that our admiralty – ' A messenger brought him up short on the brink of high treason; he excused himself, stepped aside and read the note. He read it twice, clearing the fumes of brandy from his head, sobering fast. He was a massive, bear-like man, not as tall as Jack, but stouter, and he could stand his drink: broad, somewhat round-shouldered, with very kind brown eyes – kind, but not foolish; and when he came back to the table, carrying a pot of coffee, they were hard and piercing. He hesitated for some time, sipping the coffee, before he spoke. 'All navies have these problems,' he said slowly. 'My colleague who looks after them here is on leave: I take his place. Here I have a description of a man in a black coat with a telescope

94

on Mount Faron this morning, looking at our installations; medium height, slim, pale eyes, bob wig, grey breeches, speaks French with a southern accent. He has also been talking to a Barcelona merchant, a curious fellow with two feluccas in the darse.'

'Why,' cried Jack, 'that must certainly be Stephen Maturin. I have no doubt of it – he has a telescope. One of Dolland's very best glasses. I am sure he was up there on Faron this morning before I was out of bed, gazing about for his precious birds. He mentioned some monstrous rare pippit or titmouse that lives here. I wonder,' – laughing heartily – 'he did not go up to the fort and beg for the use of their big artillery instruments. Oh no, he is the simplest fellow in the world. I give you my word of honour – unspeakably learned, knows every bug and beetle in the universe, and will have your leg off in an instant – but he should not be allowed out alone. And as for naval installations, he really cannot tell port from starboard, a bonnet from a drabbler, though I have explained a thousand times, and he does try to apply himself, poor fellow. I am sure it must be he, from what you tell me about his speaking to the Barcelona merchant. And in that language, I dare say? He lived in those parts for years, and speaks their lingo like a – like a – why, like a native. We are on our way down there now, to a property he has; and as soon as he has been across to Porquerolles to see some curious shrub that grows on the island and nowhere else, we shall move on. Ha, ha, ha,' he laughed, his big voice full of intense amusement, 'to think of poor good old Stephen being laid by the heels for a spy! Oh, ha, ha, ha!'

There was no possibility of resisting his transparent good faith. Christy-Pallière's eyes softened; he smiled with relief and said, 'So you will vouch for him, then, upon your honour?'

'My hand upon my heart,' said Jack, placing it there. 'My dear sir, surely your men must be a very simple crew, to go round suspecting Stephen Maturin?'

'That is the trouble,' said Christy-Pallière. 'Many of them *are* stupid. But that is not the worst of it: there are other services, the gendarmerie, Fouché's men and all those land people, as you know, and some of them are no wiser. So pray tell your friend to be more discreet. And listen, my dear Aubrey,' he said in a low, significant voice, 'it might be as well if you did not cross to Porquerolles, but pressed on to Spain.'

'Because of the heat?' asked Jack.

Christy-Pallière shrugged. 'If you like,' he said. 'I say no more.' He took a turn up and down the terrace, ordered a fresh bottle, and returned to Jack.

'And so you saw my cousins in Bath?' he said, in quite another, conversational tone.

'Yes, yes! I did myself the honour of calling at Laura Place the first time I was there, and they very kindly asked me to drink tea with them. They were all at home – Mrs Christy, Miss Christy, Miss Susan, Madame des Aguillières and Tom. Charming people, so friendly and welcoming. We talked about you a great deal, and they hoped you might come over soon – sent everything proper, of course, kindest regards – kisses, I believe, from the girls. The second time they invited me to a ramble and a picnic, but unhappily I was bespoke. I was in Bath twice.'

'What did you think of Polly?'

'Oh, a dear girl – full of fun, and so kind to your old – aunt, I believe? And how she rattled away in French! I said several things myself, which she understood straight away, and relayed to the old lady, repeating my signals, as it were.'

'She *is* a dear child,' said her cousin. 'And believe me,' he said very seriously, 'that girl can *cook*. Her coq au vin –! Her sole normande – ! And she has a deep comprehension of the English pudding. That strawberries jam was hers. A wonderful housekeeper. She has a modest little fortune, too,' he added, looking abstractedly at a tartan working into the port.

'Ah, dear Lord,' cried Jack, with a vehemence that made Christy-Pallière look round with alarm. 'Dear Lord, for the moment I had almost forgot. Shall I tell you why I was in Bath?'

'Do, I beg.'

'It is between ourselves?' Christy-Pallière nodded. 'By God, I am so wretched about it: it was only that splendid dinner of yours that put it out of my mind these last two hours. Otherwise it has been with me ever since I left England. There was a girl, do you see, that I had met in Sussex – neighbours – and when I had a bad time in the Admiralty court with my neutrals, her mother took her down there, no longer approving of the connection. There was very nearly an understanding between us before then, but somehow I never quite clinched it. Christ, what a fool I was! So I saw her in Bath, but could never come to close quarters: I believe she did not quite like some little attentions I had paid her cousin.'

'Innocent attentions?'

'Well, yes, really; though I dare say they might have been misinterpreted. An astonishingly lovely girl, or rather woman – had been married once, husband knocked on the head in India – with a splendid dash and courage. And then, while I was eating my heart out between the Admiralty and the money-lenders in the City, I learnt that some fellow had made her an offer of marriage – it was spoken of everywhere as a settled thing. I cannot tell you how it hurt me. And this other girl, the one who stayed in Sussex, was so kind and sympathetic, and so very beautiful too, that I – well, you understand me. But, however, as soon as I thought things were going along capitally with her, and that we were very close friends, she pulled me up as though I had run into a boom, and asked me who the devil I thought I was? I had lost all my money by then, as you know; so upon my word, I could scarcely tell what to answer, particularly as I had begun to make out that maybe she was attached to my best friend, and perhaps the other way too, you follow me. I was not quite sure, but it looked damnably like it, above all when they parted. But I was so infernally hooked – could not sleep, could not eat – and sometimes she was charming to me again. So I committed myself pretty far, partly out of pique, do you see? Oh, God damn it all, if only – And then on top of it all there comes a letter from the first girl – '

'A letter to you?' cried Christy-Pallière. 'But this was not an intrigue, as I understand you?'

'As innocent as the day. Not so much as – well, hardly so much as a kiss. It was a surprising thing, was it not? But it was in England, you know, not in France, and things are rather different there: even so, it was astonishing. But such a sweet, modest letter, just to say that the whole thing about the marriage was so much God-damned stuff. It reached me the very day I left the country.'

'Why, then everything is perfect, surely? It is, in a serious young woman, an avowal – what more could you ask?'

'Why,' said Jack, with so wretched a look that Christy-Pallière, who had hitherto thought him a muff to mind having two young women at once, felt a wound in his heart. He patted Jack's arm to comfort him. 'Why, there is this other one, don't you see?' said Jack. 'In honour, I am pretty well committed to her, although it is not the same sort of feeling at all. To say nothing of my friend.'

Stephen and Dr Ramis were closeted in a book-lined study. The great herbal that had been one of the subjects of their correspondence for the past year and more lay open on the table, with a high-detailed map of the new Spanish defences of Port Mahon folded into it. Dr Ramis had just come back from Minorca, his native island, and he had brought several documents for Stephen, for he was his most important contact with the Catalan autonomists. These papers, read and committed to memory, were now crushed black ashes in the fireplace, and the two men had moved on to the subject of humanity at large – man's general unfitness for life as it is lived.

'This is particularly the case with sailors,' said Stephen. 'I have watched them attentively, and find that they are more unsuited for life as it is understood than men of any other calling whatsoever. I propose the following reason for this: the sailor, at sea (his proper element), lives in the present. There is nothing he can do about the past at all; and, having regard to the uncertainty of the omnipotent ocean and the weather, very little about the future. This, I may say in passing, accounts for the common tar's improvidence. The officers spend their lives fighting against this attitude on the part of the men – persuading them to tighten ropes, to belay and so on, against a vast series of contingencies; but the officers, being as sea-borne as the rest, do their task with a half conviction: from this arises uneasiness of mind, and hence the vagaries of those in authority. Sailors will provide against a storm tomorrow, or even in a fortnight's time; but for them the remoter possibilities are academic, unreal. They live in the present, I say; and basing itself upon this my mind offers a partially-formed conjecture – I should value your reflections upon it.'

'My lights are yours, for what they may be worth,' said Dr Ramis, leaning back and watching him with a dry, sharp, intelligent black eye. 'Though as you know, I am an enemy to speculation.'

'Let us take the whole range of disorders that have their origin in the mind, the disordered or the merely idle mind – false pregnancies, many hysterias, palpitations, dyspepsias, eczematous affections, some forms of impotence and many more that will occur to you at once. Now as far as my limited experience goes, these we do not find aboard ship. You agree, my dear colleague?'

Dr Ramis pursed his lips, and said, 'With reservations,

I believe I may venture to say that I am tempted to do so. I do not commit myself, however.'

'Now let us turn our honest tar ashore, where he is compelled to live not in the present but in the future, with reference to futurity – all joys, benefits, prosperities to be hoped for, looked forward to, the subject of anxious thought directed towards next month, next year, nay, the next generation; no slops provided by the purser, no food perpetually served out at stated intervals. And what do we find?'

'Pox, drunkenness, a bestial dissolution of all moral principle, gross over-eating: the liver ruined in ten days' time.'

'Certainly, certainly; but more than that, we find, not indeed false pregnancies, but everything short of them. Anxiety, hypochondria, displacency, melancholia, costive, delicate stomachs – the ills of the city merchant increased tenfold. I have a particularly interesting subject who was in the most robust health at sea – Hygeia's darling – in spite of every kind of excess and of the most untoward circumstances: a short while on land, with household cares, matrimonial fancies – always in the future, observe – and we have a loss of eleven pounds' weight; a retention of the urine; black, compact, meagre stools; an obstinate eczema.'

'And for you all this is the effect of solid earth beneath the subject's feet? No more?'

Stephen held up his hands. 'It is the foetus of a thought; but I cherish it.'

'You speak of loss of weight. But I find that you yourself are thin. Nay, cadaverous, if I may speak as one physician to another. You have a very ill breath; your hair, already meagre two years ago, is now extremely sparse; you belch frequently; your eyes are hollow and dim. This is not merely your ill-considered use of tobacco – a noxious substance that should be prohibited by government – and of laudanum. I should *very* much like to see your excrement.'

'You shall, my dear sir, you shall. But I must leave you now. You will not forget my tincture? I shall abandon it entirely once I am in Lérida, but until then it is necessary to me.'

'You shall have it. And,' said Dr Ramis, with a veiled look, 'it is possible that I may send you a note of the first importance at the same time: I shall not know for some hours yet. If I do, it will be in system three. But pray let me feel your pulse before you go. Reedy, intermittent, my friend, just as I thought.'

'What did he mean by that?' said Stephen, referring not to the pulse but to the hypothetical note, and thinking again with some regret of the simplicity of his dealings with plain mercenary agents. Their motives were so clear; their loyalties were to their persons and their purse. The complexities of the entirely honest men, their sudden reticences, the interplay of conflicting loyalties, the personal sense of humour, made him feel old and tired.

'Why, Stephen, here you are at last,' cried Jack, starting straight out of his sleep. 'I sat talking with Christy-Pallière; I hope you did not wait for me.' The subject of their conversation flooded his mind and put out its gaiety; but having gazed at the floor for a moment he looked up with at least an expression of cheerfulness and said, 'You were very nearly taken up for a spy this morning.'

Stephen stopped in his movement towards the desk and stood motionless, unnaturally poised.

'How I laughed when Christy-Pallière read me out your description, looking uncomfortable and prodigious grave; but I assured him on my sacred honour that you were looking for your double-headed eagles, and he was quite satisfied. He made an odd remark, by the way: said, was he in our shoes he should push on for Spain and not go to Porquerolles.'

'Aye, aye? Did he, so?' said Stephen mildly. 'Go back

to sleep now, my dear. I conceive he would not choose to traverse the street to see euphorbia praestans, let alone cross an arm of the sea. I have a few notes to write, but I shall not disturb you. Go to sleep: we have a long day head of us.'

Some hours later, in the first grey light, Jack awoke to a faint scratching on the door. His waking mind stated that this was a rat in the bread-room, but his body instantly contradicted it – sleeping or awake his body knew whether it was afloat or not; at no time was it ever unaware of the continual shift and heave of the sea, or of the unnatural stability of the land. He opened his eyes and saw Stephen rise from his guttering candle, open the door, receive a bottle and a folded note. He went back to his table, opened the note, slowly deciphered it, burnt both scraps of paper in the candle flame; without turning round he said, 'Jack, you are awake, I believe?'

'Yes. These last five minutes. A good morning to you, Stephen. Is it going to be hot?'

'It is. And a good morning to you, my dear. Listen,' he said, sinking his voice to no more than a whisper, 'and do not call out or agitate yourself. Do you hear me now?'

'Yes.'

'War will be declared tomorrow. Bonaparte is seizing all British subjects.'

In the narrow band of shade under the northern wall of Carcassonne a compassionate gendarme halted his convoy of English prisoners – seamen from detained and captured ships for the most part, a few officers who had been caught by the declaration of war, but some civilians too, travelling gentlemen, servants, grooms and tradesmen, since for the first time in civilized warfare Bonaparte had ordered the arrest of every British subject. They were hot, discon- solate and weary; their bundles had been soaked in a thunderstorm, and at first they had not even the spirit to spread them out in the sun, let alone to take notice of the dilapidated splendour of walls and turrets behind, the view of the new town and the river before them, or even the bear and its leader in the shadow of the next tower but one. But presently the word of the arrival of the convoy spread, and the crowd that had hurried out of the old town to stare was joined by market-women from over the bridge, bringing fruit, wine, bread, honey, sausages, pâté and goat cheeses wrapped in fresh green leaves. Most of the prisoners still had some money (this was only the beginning of their march to the far north-east) and when they had cooled a little, eaten and drunk, they put their clothes to dry and began to look about them.

'What o, the bear,' cried a sailor, quite happy now, with a quart of wine under his brass-buckled belt. 'Can he dance, mate?'

The bear-leader, an ill-looking brute with a patch over one eye and a fortnight's beard, took no notice. But the sailor was not to be put off by the sullenness of foreigners, and he was soon joined by an insistent group of friends, for he was the most popular and influential member of the crew of the pink *Chastity*, a merchantman that had had the unlucky idea of putting into Cette for water the day war was declared. One or two of them began shying stones at the great hairy mass to wake it up, or at least to have the pleasure of seeing it move. 'Avast the stone-throwing,' cried the sailor, his cheerful face clouding. 'You don't want to go a-teasing of bears, cully. Remember Elisha. There's nothing so unlucky as teasing of a bear.'

'You been a-bear-baiting, George, you know you have,' said a shipmate, tossing his stone up and down, not to have the air of abandoning it. 'We been to Hockley together.'

'Bear-baiting is different,' said George. 'The bears at Hockley is willing. This bear ain't. I dare say it's hot. Bears is Greenland creatures.'

The bear certainly looked hot. It was stretched out on what little grass it could find, strangely prostrate. But the clamour had spread; crews of other ships wanted to see it dance, and after some time the bear-leader came up and gave them to understand that the animal was indisposed – could only perform at night – 'im ave airy coat, mister; im ate up whole goat for im dinner; im belly ache.'

'Why, shipmates, there you are. Just as I said,' cried George. 'How would you like dancing in a – great fur pelisse, in this – sun?'

Events had escaped from George's control, however; an English sea-officer, wishing to impress the lady with whom he was travelling, had spoken to the sergeant of gendarmerie, and now the sergeant whistled to the master of the bear.

'Papers,' he said. 'A Spanish passport, eh? A very greasy passport too, my friend; do you sleep with your bear? Joan Margall, born in – what's this place?'

'Lérida, monsieur le sergent,' said the man, with the cringing humility of the poor.

'Lérida. Profession, bear-leader. Eh, bien: a led bear knows how to dance – that is logic. I have to have proof; it is my duty to see the bear perform.'

'Certainly, monsieur le sergent, at once. But the gentlemen will not expect too much from Flora; she is a female bear, and – ' He whispered in the gendarme's ear. 'Ah, ah? Just so,' said the gendarme. 'Well, just a pace or two, to satisfy my sense of duty.'

Dragged up by its chain and beaten by its leader till the dust flew from its shaggy side the bear shuffled forward. The man took a little pipe from his bosom, and playing it with one hand while he held the chain with the other, he hoisted the bear on to its hind legs, where it stood, swaying, amidst a murmur of disapprobation from the sailors. 'Crool buggers, these foringers,' said George. 'Look at his poor nose, with that – great ring.'

'English gents,' said the man, with an ingratiating leer. 'Ornpip.'

He played a recognizable hornpipe, and the bear staggered through a few of the steps, crossing its arms, before sitting down again. Trumpets sounded from the citadel behind the walls, the guard on the Narbonne gate changed, and the sergeant began to bawl 'En route, en route, les prisonniers.'

With avid and shamelessly persistent busyness, the bear-leader hurried up and down the line. 'Remember the bear, gents. Remember the bear. N'oubliez pas l'ours, messieurs-dames.'

Silence. The convoy's dust settled on the empty road. The inhabitants of Carcassonne all went to sleep; even the small boys who had been dropping mortar and clods of earth from the battlements on to the bear disappeared. Silence at last, and the chink of coins.

'Two livres four sous,' said the bear-leader. 'One maravedi, two Levantine coins of whose exact provenance I am uncertain, a Scotch groat.'

'When one sea-officer is to be roasted, there is always another at hand to turn the spit,' said the bear. 'It is an old service proverb. I hope to God I have that fornicating young sod under my command one day. I'll make him dance a hornpipe – oh, such a hornpipe. Stephen, prop my jaws open a little more, will you? I think I shall die in five minutes if you don't. Could we not creep into a field and take it off?'

'No,' said Stephen. 'But I shall lead you to an inn as soon as the market has cleared, and lodge you in a cool damp cellar for the afternoon. I will also get you a collar, to enable you to breathe. We must reach Couiza by dawn.'

* * *

The white road winding, winding, up and up the French side of the Pyrenees, the afternoon sun – the June sun now – beating straight down on the dusty slope: the bear and its leader plodding on. Scorned by carts, feared by horses, they had already walked three hundred and fifty miles, taking a zigzag route to avoid most large towns and the dangerous zone of the coast, and to stay two nights in houses belonging to sure friends. Stephen was leading the bear by the paw, for Jack could not see below his muzzle when his head was on, and in his other hand he had the broad spiked collar that covered the hole through which Jack breathed. He was obliged to put it on for the best part of the day, however, for although this was a remote valley there were houses every few hundred yards, hamlets not three or four miles apart, and fools that kept accompanying them on their way. 'Was it a wise bear? How much did it eat a week? Was it ever wicked? Could he buckle the two ends of his month by exhibiting it?' And the nearer they came to the mountains, the more anecdotes of the bears that had been heard of, actually seen, and even killed. Bears, wolves, smugglers and mountain bandits, the Trabucayres and the Migueletes. Communicative fools, cheerful villagers, all eager for a treat, and dogs. Every hamlet, every farmhouse had its swarm of dogs that came out, amazed, howling, yapping and barking, haunting the bear's heels sometimes as far as the next vile swarm; for the dogs, if not the men, knew that there was something unnatural in the bear.

'It will not be long now,' said Stephen. 'At the far end, beyond the trees, I can see the turning of the main Le Perthus road. You can lie in the wood while I walk to the village to find out what is afoot. Should you like to sit down for a moment on this milestone? There is water in the ditch, and you could soak your feet.'

'Oh, I do not mind it,' said Jack, staggering as Stephen altered the rhythm of his walk to peer into the ditch. 'And I dare not soak them again, in any case.' The massive, hairy shape writhed a little – a mechanical attempt at seeing its tattered buttocks, legs and lower paws, dog-lacerated. 'The wood is not very far off, I dare say?'

'Oh, not above an hour or so. It is a beech-wood with an old marle-pit; and you may – I do not assert it, but I say you *may* – see the purple helleborine growing there!'

Lying in the deep cool fern with his collar off Jack felt the sweat still coursing down his chest, and the movement of ants, ticks, unidentified insects invading him; he smelt his own unwashed reek and the moist stench of the skin, imperfectly preserved in turpentine; but he minded none of it. He was too far gone to do anything but lie in the complete relaxation of utter weariness. It had of course been impossible to disguise him: a six-foot, yellow-haired Englishman would have stood out like a steeple in the south of France – a France alive with people tracking fugitives of one kind or another, foreign and domestic; but the price for this attempt was beyond anything he had believed possible. The torment of the ill-fitting, chafing hide, the incessantly-repeated small rasping wounds, the ooze of blood, the flayed soles of his feet, attached to the fur by court-plaster, the heat, the suffocation, the vile uncleanliness, had reached what he had thought the unendurable point ten days, two hundred miles, ago, in the torrid waste of the Causse du Palan.

Was this attempt going to succeed? At the bottom of his heart he had never doubted it to begin with – so long as he did his part (barring some act of God or unaccountable misfortune) neither he nor Stephen Maturin would pass the rest of the war as prisoners, cut off from all possibility of service, promotion, a lucky cruise, cut off from Sophia; cut off, indeed, from Diana. A long war, he made no doubt, for Bonaparte was strong – Jack had been astonished by the state of forwardness of everything he had seen in Toulon: three ships of the line almost ready for launching, a huge quantity of stores, unexampled zeal. Any man bred to the sea, any born sailor, could tell within an hour of being aboard whether a ship was an efficient, happy co-ordinated whole; it was the same with a naval port, and in Toulon his quick, professional eye had seen a great machine running very fast, very smoothly. France was strong; France owned the fine Dutch navy, controlled huge areas of western Europe; England was weak and alone – no allies left at all, as far as he could tell from the fragmentary, partial news they had picked up. Certainly the Royal Navy was weak; he had no doubt of that at all. St Vincent had tried to reform the dockyards rather than build ships, and now there were fewer that could stand in the line of battle than there had been in '93, in spite of all the building and all the captures during the ten years of war: and that again was a reason – quite apart from the obligations of the treaty – why Spain should come in on the side of France – another reason why they should find the frontier closed and Stephen's refuge lost to them, the attempt a failure after all. Had Spain declared? For the last two or three days they had been in the Roussillon, in French Catalonia, and he had not been able to understand anything that Stephen and the peasants said to one another. Stephen was strangely reticent these days. Jack had supposed he knew him through and through in the old uncomplicated times, and he loved all he knew; but now there were new depths, an underlying hard ruthlessness, an unexpected Maturin; and Jack was quite out of his depth.

Stephen had gone on, leaving him. Stephen had a passport into Spain – could move about there, war or no . . . Jack's mind darkened still further and thoughts he dared not formulate came welling up, an ugly swarm.

'Dear God,' he said at last, twisting his head from side to side, 'could I have sweated all my courage out?' Courage gone, and generosity with it? He had seen courage go – men run down hatchways in battle, officers cower behind the capstan. He and Stephen had talked about it: was courage a fixed, permanent quality? An expendable substance, each man having just so much, with a possible end in sight? Stephen had put forward views on courage – varying and relative – dependent upon diet, circumstances, the functioning of the bowels – the costive frequently timid – upon use, upon physical and spiritual freshness or exhaustion – the aged proverbially cautious – courage not an entity, but to be regarded as belonging to different, though related, systems, moral, physical, sexual – courage in brutes, in the castrated – complete integrity, unqualified courage or puerile fiction-jealousy, its effect upon courage – Stoics – the *satietas vitae* and the supreme courage of indifference – indifference, indifference . . .

The tune that Stephen always played on his bear-leader's pipe began to run through his head, mingling with Stephen's voice and half-remembered instances of courage from Plutarch, Nicholas of Pisa and Boethius, a curious little air with archaic intervals, limited to what four fingers and overblowing could do, but subtle, complicated . . .

The roaring of a little girl in a white pinafore woke him; she and some unseen friend were looking for the summer mushrooms that were found in this wood, and she had come upon a fungoid growth.

'Ramón,' she bellowed, and the hollow echoed with the sound, 'Ramón, Ramón, Ramón. Come and see what I have found. Come and see what I have found. Come and see. . . '

On and on and on. She was turned three-quarters from him; but presently, since her companion did not answer, she pivoted, directing her strong voice to the different quarters of the wood.

Jack had already shrunk as far as he could, and now as the child's face veered towards him he closed his eyes, in case she should sense their savage glare. His mind was now all alive; no trace of indifference now, but a passionate desire to succeed in this immediate step, to carry the whole undertaking through, come Hell or high water. 'Frighten the little beast and you will have a band of armed peasants round the wood in five minutes – slip away and you lose Stephen – out of touch, and all our papers sewed inside the skin.' The possibilities came racing one after another; and no solution.

'Come, come, child,' said Stephen. 'You will spoil your voice if you call out so. What have you there? It is a satanic boletus; you must not eat the satanic boletus, my dear. See how it turns blue when I break it with a twig. That is the devil blushing. But here we have a parasol. You may certainly eat the parasol. Have you seen my bear? I left him in the wood when I went to see En Jaume; he was sadly fatigued. Bears cannot stand the sun.'

'En Jaume is my godfather's uncle,' said the child. 'My godfather is En Pere. What is the name of your bear?'

'Flora,' said Stephen; and called, 'Flora!'

'You said *him* just now,' said the child with a frown, and began to roar 'Flora, Flora, Flora, Flora! Oh, Mother of God, what a huge great bear.' She put her hand in Stephen's and murmured, 'Aie, my – in the face of God what a bear.' But her courage returned, and she set to bellowing 'Ramón, Ramón, Ramón! Come and see my bear.'

'Good-bye, poppets,' said Stephen, in time. 'May God go with you.' And waving still to the little figures he said, 'I have firm news at last; mixed news. Spain has not declared war: but the Mediterranean ports are closed to English ships. We must go down to Gibraltar.'

'What about the frontier?'

Stephen pursed his lips. 'The village is filled with police and soldiers: two intelligence men are in charge, searching everything. They have arrested one English agent.'

'How do you know?'

'The priest who confessed him told me. But sure I have never thought of the road itself. I know, I *did* know, another way. Stand over – stand over more this way. The pink roof, and behind it a peak? And to the right of that, beyond the forest, a bare mountain? That is the frontier, joy, and in the dip there is a pass, a path down to Recasens and Cantallops. We will slip across the road after dusk and be there at dawn.'

'May I take off the skin?'

'You may not. I regret it extremely, Jack; but I do not know the path well – there are patrols out, not only for the smugglers but for the fugitives, and we may blunder into one or even two. It is a smugglers' path, a dangerous path indeed, for while the French may shoot you for walking upon it as a man, the smugglers may do the same for looking like a bear. But the second is the proper choice; your smuggler is open to reason, and your patrol is not.'

Half an hour in the bushes by the road, waiting for the long slow train of a battery to pass by – guns, waggons, camp-followers – several coaches, one pulled by eight mules in crimson harness, some isolated horsemen; for now that they could see the frontier-line their caution grew to superstitious lengths.

Half an hour, and then across to the cart-track up to Saint-Jean de l'Albère. Up and up, the moon clearing the forest ahead of them after the first hour; and with the coming of the moon the first breaths of a sirocco from the Spanish plains, a waft from an opened oven-door.

Up and still up. After the last barn the track dwindled to a ribbon and they had to walk in single file; Jack saw Stephen's monstrous bundle – a dark shape, no more – moving steadily a pace or two in front of them, and something like hatred glowed around his stomach. He reasoned: 'The pack is heavy; it weighs fifty or sixty pounds – all our possessions; he too has been going on all these days, never a murmur; the straps wring his back and shoulders, a bloody welt on either side.' But the unwavering determination of that dim form, moving steadily on and on, effortlessly, it seemed, always too fast and never pausing – the impossibility of keeping up, of forcing himself another hundred yards, and the equal impossibility of calling for a rest, drowned his reason, leaving only the dull fire of resentment.

The path meandered, branching and sometimes disappearing among huge ancient widespread beeches, their trunks silver in the moon, and at last Stephen stopped. Jack blundered into him, stood still, and felt a hand gripping him hard through the skin: Stephen guided him into the black velvet shadow of a fallen tree. Over the soughing of the wind he heard a repeated metallic sound, and as he recognized the regular beat – a patrol making too much noise – all notion of the unbreathable air and the intolerable state of his body left him. Low voices now and then, a cough, still the clink-clink-clink of someone's musket against a buckle, and presently the soldiers passed within twenty yards of them, moving down the mountain-side.

The same strong hand pulling him, and they were on the path again. Always this eternal climb, sometimes across the leaf-filled bed of a stream, sometimes up an open slope so steep that it was hands and knees: and the sirocco. 'Can this be real?' he wondered. 'Must it go on for ever?'

The beech-trees gave way to pines: pine-needles under foot, oh the pain. Endless pines on an endless mountain, their roaring tops bowing northwards in the wind.

The shape in front had stopped, muttering 'It should be about here – the second fork – there was a charcoal burner's lay – an uprooted larch, bees in the hollow trunk.'

Jack closed his eyes for a great swimming pause, a respite, and when he opened them again he saw that the sky ahead was lightening. Behind them the moon had sunk into a haze, far down in the deep veiled complicated valleys.

The pines. Then suddenly no more pines – a few stunted bushes, heather, and the open turf. They were on the upper edge of the forest, a forest ruled off sharp, as though by a line; and they stood, silently looking out. After two or three minutes, right up there in the eye of the wind, Jack saw a movement. Leaning to Stephen he

112

said 'Dog?' Soldiers who had had the sense to bring a dog? Loss, dead failure after all this?

Stephen took his head, and whispering right into the hairy ear he said 'Wolf. A young – a young *female* wolf.'

Still Stephen waited, searching the bushes, the bare rocks, from the far left to the far right, before he walked out, paced over the short grass to a stone set on the very top of the slope, a squared stone with a red-painted cross cut into it.

'Jack,' said he, leading him beyond the boundary mark, 'I bid you welcome to my land. We are in Spain. That is my house below – we are at home. Come, let me get your head off. Now you can breathe, my poor friend. There are two springs under the brow of the hill, by those chestnuts, where you can wash and take off the skin. How I rejoice at the sight of that wolf. Look, here is her dung, quite fresh. No doubt this is a wolf's pissing-post: like all the dogs, they have their regular . . .'

Jack sat heavily on the stone, gasping inwards, filling his starved lungs. Some reality other than general suffering returned. 'Wolf's pissing-post: oh, yes.' In front of him the ground fell suddenly – almost a precipice – two thousand feet below there was Spanish Catalonia spread out in the morning light. A high-towered castle just below them on a jutting rock – a lobbed stone would reach it; the Pyrenees folded away and away in long fingers to the plain; square distant fields, vineyards green; a shining river winding left-handed towards the great sweep of the sea; the Bay of Rosas with Cap Creus at the far northern end – home water, and now the hot wind smelt of salt.

'I am happy you were pleased with your wolf,' he said at last in a sleep-walker's voice. 'There are – they are uncommon rare, I dare say.'

'Not at all, my dear. We have them by the score – can never leave the sheep by night. No. Her presence means we are alone. That is why I rejoice. I rejoice. Even so, I think we should go down to the spring: it is under the

113

chestnuts, those chestnuts not two minutes down. That wolfess may be a fool – see her now, moving among the junipers – and I should not wish to fail, just when we have succeeded. Some chance cross-patrol, douaniers rather than soldiers, some zealous sergeant with a carabine . . . Can you get up? God help me, I hardly can.'

The spring, Jack wallowing in it, cold water and grit sweeping off the crass, the stream running filthy, but coming fresh and fresh straight from the rock. Jack luxuriating, drying in the wind, plunging again and again. His body was dead white where it was not cruelly galled, bitten, rasped; his colourless face puffy, sweat-swollen, corpselike, a tangled yellow beard covering his mouth; his eyes were red and pustulent. But there was life in them, brilliant delight blazing through the physical distress.

'You have lost between three and four stone,' observed Stephen, appraising his loins and belly.

'I am sure you are right,' said Jack. 'And nine parts of it is in this vile skin, a good three stone of human grease.' He kicked the limp bear with his bleeding foot, damned it once or twice for a son of a bitch, and observed he must take the papers out before setting it alight. 'How it will stink – how it *does* stink, by God. Just hand me along the scissors, Stephen, pray.'

'The bear may serve again,' said Stephen. 'Let us roll it up and thrust it under the bush. I will send for it from the house.'

'Is the house a great way off?'

'Why no,' said Stephen, pointing to the castle. 'It is just there below us, a thousand feet or so – to the right of the white scar, the marble quarry. Though I am afraid it will take us an hour to get there – an hour to breakfast.'

'Is that castle yours, Stephen?'

'It is. And this is my sheepwalk. What is more,' he said, looking sharply at the cowpats, 'I believe those French dogs from La Vaill have been sending their cattle over to eat my grass.'

CHAPTER FIVE

Three days after crossing the tropic the *Lord Nelson*
East-Indiaman, Captain Spottiswood, homeward-bound
from Bombay, broached to in a westerly gale; the ship
survived, but she lost her maintopmast and its topgallant,
carried away her mizen just above the cap, sprang her fore
and main masts, and damaged her rigging to an extraordinary extent. She also lost her boats upon the booms and
most of the booms themselves; so, the wind being foul for
Madeira, the passengers in a state of panic and the crew
near mutiny after a very long and uniformly disagreeable
voyage, Mr Spottiswood bore away for Gibraltar, right
under his lee, although like all homeward-bound captains
he was very unwilling to put into a naval port. As he had
expected, he lost many of his English-born sailormen to
the press, all prime hands; but he did repair his ship,
and as some meagre consolation he did embark a few
passengers.

The first to come aboard were Jack Aubrey and Stephen
Maturin; they were received by the captain at the head of
his officers in some style, for the Company possessed, or
at least arrogated to itself, a particular status, and its ships
adopted many of the ways of the Royal Navy. There were
sensible reasons for some of these – the chequered gun-
ports, for instance, and the general appearance of regularity had persuaded many an enemy cruiser that he had to do
with a man-of-war and that he had better look elsewhere –
but there were many little pretensions that vexed the real
Navy, and King's officers aboard a Company ship were
apt to look about them with a carping eye. In this case
a critic could have found fault straight away: in spite of
the black side-boys in their white gloves, the reception

was incorrect – that vague huddle of figures would never have done aboard the *Superb*, for example, in which Jack had dined, and whose hospitality was still ringing in his head, although he could walk straight. Furthermore, he was conscious of a huge grin from the midst of that same huddle, a kind of half-determined nodding and becking, a bashfulness accompanied by familiarity that brought a hint of stiffness into his expression. He spoke with particular civility to Captain Spottiswood, who privately damned him for his condescension, and then turning he recognized the stare.

'Why, Pullings!' he cried, all his ill-humour – a very slight ill-humour in any case – vanishing at once and the hard lines of his face dissolving into a delighted smile. 'How happy I am to see you! How do you do? How are you coming along, eh? Eh?'

'And this is our supercargo, Mr Jennings,' said Captain Spottiswood, not best pleased at having his regular sequence changed. 'Mr Bates. Mr Wand. Mr Pullings you already know, I see.'

'We were shipmates,' said Jack, shaking Pullings's hand with a force in direct proportion to his affection for the young man, a former master's mate and acting-lieutenant in the *Sophie*, who was now beaming over his shoulder at Dr Maturin.

The *Lord Nelson* had never been a happy or a fortunate ship, but within an hour of taking her passengers on board a brisk Levanter sprang up to carry her right out through the strong current of the Gut and into the full Atlantic; and poor Captain Spottiswood, in the innocence of his heart, reckoned this a great stroke of luck – a good omen at last, perhaps. She was not a very comely ship, either, nor much of a sailer: comfortable for the passengers, roomy for her cargo, certainly; but crank, slow in stays, and near the end of her useful life. This was, in fact, to be her last voyage, and even for her trip in 1801 the underwriters had insisted upon an extra thirty shillings per cent.

It also happened that she was the first Indiaman Jack had ever sailed in, and as he walked about with Pullings during his watch below he gazed with astonishment at the general lumber of the deck and at the casks and water-butts lashed between the guns. Twenty eighteen-pounders and six twelves: an imposing show of force for a merchantman. 'And how many people have you aboard?' he asked.

'Just above a hundred now, sir. A hundred and two, to be exact.'

'Well, well, well,' said Jack. In the Navy they did not think nine men and a powder-boy too much for an eighteen-pounder, seven and a boy for the twelves: a hundred and twenty-four men to fight the guns one side – a hundred and twenty-four beef- and pork-fed Englishmen, and another hundred to trim the sails, work the ship, repel boarders, ply the small arms, and fight the other side on occasion. He glanced at the Lascars squatting around their heap of junk, working under the orders of their turbanned serang; they might be tolerably good seamen in their way, perhaps, but they were very slight, and he could not see five or six of them running out a two-ton gun against the Atlantic roll. This impression of smallness was increased by the fact that most of them were cold; the few European members of the crew were in their shirts, but several of the Lascars had pea-jackets on as well, and all had a blueish tinge in their dark complexions.

'Well, well, well,' said Jack again. He did not like to say more, for his opinion of the *Lord Nelson* was crystallizing fast, and any expression of it could not but give pain – Pullings must feel himself part of the ship. The young man certainly knew that Captain Spottiswood lacked all authority, and that the *Lord Nelson* moved like a log, and that she had twice missed stays off Cape Trafalgar, having to wear round at last: but there was certainly no point in putting this into words. He looked round for something that he could praise with at least an appearance of candour. The gleam of the brass larboard bow-gun caught his eye, and he commended it. 'Really quite like gold,' he said.

'Yes,' said Pullings. 'They do it voluntary – *poojah, poojah*, they say. For days off the island and again when we touched at the Cape, they had a wreath of marigolds around the muzzle. They say their prayers to it, poor fellows, because they think it is like – well, sir, I hardly like to name what they think it is like. But she *is* medium dry, sir, and she *is* roomy – oh, as roomy as a first-rate. I have a vast great spacious cabin to myself. Would you do me the honour of stepping below, sir, and drinking a glass of arrack?'

'I should like it of all things,' said Jack. And stretching himself cautiously on the locker in the vast great spacious cabin, he said, 'How do you come to be here, Pullings, in all your glory?'

'Why, sir, I could not get a ship and they would not confirm me in my rank. "No white lapels for you, Pullings, old cock," they said. "We got too many coves like you, by half." '

'What a damned shame,' cried Jack, who had seen Pullings in action and who knew that the Navy did not and indeed could not possibly have too many coves like him.

'So I tried for a midshipman again, but none of my old captains had a ship themselves; or if they had – and the Honourable Berkely had – no vacancy. I took your letter to Captain Seymour – *Amethyst*, refitting in Hamoaze. Old Cozzens gave me a lift down as far as the Vizes. Captain Seymour received me very polite when I said I was from you, most obliging: nothing starchy or touch-me-not about him, sir. But he scratched his head and damned his wig when he opened the letter and read it. He said he would have blessed the day he could have obliged you, particularly with such advantage to himself, which was the civillest thing I ever heard – turned so neat – but that it was not in his power. He led me to the gun-room and the mids' berth himself to prove he could not take another young gentleman on to his quarter-deck. He was so earnest to be believed, though in course I credited him the moment he opened his mouth, that he desired me to count their chests. Then he gave me a thundering good dinner in his own cabin just him and me – I needed it, sir, for I'd walked the last twenty miles – and after the pudding we went over your action in the *Sophie*: he knew everything, except quite how the wind had veered, and he made me tell just where I had been from the first gun to the last. Then "damn my eyes," says he, "I cannot let one of Captain Aubrey's officers rot on shore without trying to stretch the little interest I have," and he wrote me one letter for Mr Adams at the Admiralty and another for Mr Bowles, a great man at East India House.'

'Mr Bowles married his sister,' observed Jack.

'Yes, sir,' said Pullings. 'But I paid little heed to it just then, because, do you see, Captain Seymour promised that Mr Adams would get me an interview with Old Jarvie himself, and I was in great hopes, for I had always heard, in the service, that he had a kindness for chaps that came in over the bows. So I got back to town again somehow, and there I was, double-shaved and all of a tremble in that old waiting-room for an hour or two. Mr Adams called me in, warns me to speak up loud and clear to his Lordship, and he is going on to say about not mentioning the good word you was so kind as to put in for me, when there's a bloody great din outside, like a boarding-party. Out he goes to see what's o'clock, and comes back with his face as blank as an egg. "The old devil," he said, "he's pressed Lieutenant Salt. Pressed him in the Admiralty itself, and has sent him off to the tender with a file of marines. Eight years' seniority, and he has sent him off with a file of Marines." Did you ever hear of it, sir?'

'Never a word.'

'Well, there was this Mr Salt right desperate for a ship, and he bombarded the First Lord with a letter a day for months and turned up every Wednesday and Friday to ask for an interview. And on the last Friday of all, the day I was there, Old Jarvie winked his eye, said "You want to go to sea? Then to sea you shall go, sir," and had him pressed on the spot.'

'An officer? Pressed for a common sailor?' cried Jack. 'I've never heard of such a thing in my life.'

'Nor nobody else: particularly poor Mr Salt,' said Pullings. 'But that's the way it was, sir. And when I heard that, and when people came in and whispered about it, I felt so timid-like and abashed, that when Mr Adams said perhaps I should try another day, I hurried out into Whitehall and asked the quickest way to East India House of the porter. I fell lucky – Mr Bowles was very kind – and so here I am. It's a good berth: twice the pay, and you are allowed a little venture of your own – I have a chest of China embroidery in the after-hold. But Lord, sir, to be in a man-of-war again!'

'It may not be so long now,' said Jack. 'Pitt's back and Old Jarvie's gone – refused the Channel Fleet – if he weren't a first-rate seaman I'd say the devil go with him – and Dundas is at the Admiralty. Lord Melville. I'm pretty well with him, and if only we can spread a little more canvas and get in before all the plums are snapped up, it will go hard if we don't make a cruise together again.'

Spreading more canvas: that was the difficulty. Ever since his disagreeable experience in latitude 33° N. Captain Spottiswood had been unwilling to set even his topgallant-sails, and the days passed slowly, slowly by. Jack spent much of his time leaning over the taffrail, staring into the *Lord Nelson*'s gentle wake as it stretched away to the south and west, for he did not care to watch the unhurried working of the ship, and the sight of the topgallantmasts struck down on deck filled him with impatience. His most usual companions were the Misses Lamb, good-natured jolly short-legged squat swarthy girls who had gone out to India with the fishing-fleet – they called it that themselves, cheerfully enough – and who were now returning, maidens still, under the protection of their uncle, Major Hill of the Bengal Artillery.

They sat in a line, with Jack between the two girls and a chair for Stephen on the left; and although the *Lord Nelson* was now in the Bay of Biscay, with a fresh breeze in the south-west and the temperature down in the fifties, they kept the deck bravely, cocooned in rugs and shawls, their pink noses peeping out.

'They say the Spanish ladies are amazingly beautiful,' said Miss Lamb. 'Much more so than the French, though not so elegant. Pray, Captain Aubrey, is it so?'

'Why, upon my word,' said Jack, 'I can hardly tell you. I never saw any of 'em.'

'But was you not several months in Spain?' cried Miss Susan.

'Indeed I was, but nearly all the time I was laid up at Dr Maturin's place near Lérida – all arches, painted blue, as they have in those parts; a courtyard inside, and grilles, and orange-trees; but no ladies of Spain that I recall. There was a dear old biddy that fed me pap – would not be denied – and on Sundays she wore a high comb and a mantilla; but she was not what you would call a beauty.'

'Was you very ill, sir?' asked Miss Lamb respectfully.

'I believe I must have been,' said Jack, 'for they shaved my head, clapped on their leeches twice a day, and made me drink warm goat's milk whenever I came to my senses; and by the time it was over I was so weak that I could scarcely sit my horse – we rode no more than fifteen or twenty miles a day for the first week.'

'How fortunate you were travelling with dear Dr Maturin,' said Miss Susan. 'I truly dote upon that man.'

'I have no doubt he pulled me through – quite lost, but for him,' said Jack. 'Always there, ready to bleed or dose me, night and day. Lord, such doses! I dare say I swallowed a moderate-sized apothecary's shop – Stephen,

I was just telling Miss Susan how you tried to poison me with your experimental brews.'

'Do not believe him, Dr Maturin. He has been telling us how you certainly saved his life. We are so grateful; he has taught us to knot laniards and to splice our wool.'

'Aye?' said Stephen. 'I am looking for the captain.' He peered inquisitively under the empty chair. 'I have news that will interest him; it is of interest to us all. The Lascars are suffering not from the buldoo-panee of their own miasmatic plains, whatever Mr Parley may maintain, but from the Spanish influenza! It is whimsical enough to reflect that we, in our haste, should be the cause of our own delay, is it not? For with so few hands we shall no doubt see our topsails handed presently.'

'I am in no hurry. I wish this voyage would go on for ever,' said Miss Lamb, arousing an echo in her sister alone.

'Is it catching?' asked Jack.

'Oh, eminently so, my dear,' said Stephen. 'I dare say it will sweep the ship in the next few days. But I shall dose them; oh, I shall dose them! Young ladies, I desire you will take physic tonight: I have made up a comfortable little prophylactic bottle for you both, and another, of greater strength, for Major Hill. A whale! A whale!'

'Where away?' cried Mr Johnstone, the first officer. He had been in the Greenland fishery when he was young, and his whole being responded to the cry. He had no answer, for Dr Maturin was squatting like a baboon, resting a telescope on the rail and training it with concentrated diligence upon the heaving sea between the ship and the horizon; but directing his gaze along the tube and staring under his two hands cupped Mr Johnstone presently saw the distant spout, followed by the hint of an immense slow roll, gleaming black against the grey.

'Och, she's no good to you at all,' he said, relaxing. 'A finwhale.'

'Could you really see its fins that great way off?' cried Miss Susan. 'How wonderful sailors are! But why is it no good, Mr Johnstone? Not quite wholesome, perhaps, like oysters without an R?'

'There she blows!' cried Mr Johnstone, but in a detached, academic voice, from mere habit. 'Another one. See the spout, Miss Susan. Just a single fountain-jet: that means a finner – your right-whale shows two. Aye, aye, there she goes again. There must be a fair-sized pod. No good to man or beast. It vexes my heart to think of all that prime oil swimming there, no good to man or beast.'

'But *why* is the whale no good?' asked Miss Lamb.

'Why, because she is a finwhale, to be sure.'

'My sister means, what is wrong with being a finwhale? Do you not, Lucy?'

'The finner is too hugeous, ma'am. If you are so rash as to make an attempt upon her – if you creep up in the whale-boat and strike your harpoon home, she will bash the boat like a bowl of neeps as she sounds, maybe, and in any case she will run out your two-hundred-fathom whale-line in less than a minute – you bend on another as quick as you can – she runs it out – another, and still she runs. She tows you under, or she carries all away: you lose your line or your life or both. Which is as who should say, be humble, flee ambition. Canst thou draw up Leviathan with a hook? Confine thyself to the right-whale, thy lawful prey.'

'Oh, I will, Mr Johnstone,' cried Miss Lamb. 'I promise you I shall never attack a finwhale all my life.'

Jack liked to see a whale – amiable creatures – but he could tear himself away from them more easily than either Stephen or the person at the mast-head who was supposed to be looking-out, and for some time now he had been watching the white fleck of sails against the darkening westward sky. A ship, he decided at last: a ship under easy sail on the opposite tack.

A ship she was, the *Bellone*, a Bordeaux privateer,

one of the most beautiful to sail from that port, high and light as a swan, yet stiff; a thirty-four-gun ship-rigged privateer with a clean bottom, a new set of sails and two hundred and sixty men aboard. A fair proportion of those sharp-eyed mariners were at present in the tops or at the crowded mast-heads, and although they could not exactly make the *Lord Nelson* out, they could see enough to make Captain Dumanoir edge cautiously down for a closer look in the failing light.

What he saw was a twenty-six-gun ship, that was certain; probably a man-of-war, but if so then a partially disabled man-of-war, or her topgallantmasts would never have been down on deck in such a breeze. And as Dumanoir and his second captain gazed and pondered in the main crosstrees all notion of the *Lord Nelson*'s being a man-of-war gradually left them. They were old-experienced sailors; they had seen much of the Royal Navy in the last ten years; and there was something about the *Lord Nelson*'s progress that did not square with their experience.

'She's an Indiaman,' said Captain Dumanoir, and although he was only three parts convinced his heart began to thump and his arm to tremble; he hooked it round the topgallant shrouds and repeated, 'An Indiaman.' Short of a Spanish galleon or treasure-ship, a British Indiaman was the richest prize the sea could offer.

A hundred little details confirmed his judgment; yet he might be wrong; he might be leading his precious *Bellone* into an action with one of those stubby English sixth-rates that carried twenty-four-pounder carronades, the genuine smashers, served by a numerous, well-trained, bloody-minded crew; and although Captain Dumanoir had no sort of objection to a dust-up with any vessel roughly his own size, King's ship or not, he was primarily a commerce-destroyer; his function was to provide his owners with a profit, not to cover himself with glory.

He regained his quarterdeck, took one or two turns, glancing up at the western sky. 'Dowse the lights one by one,' he said. 'And in fifteen minutes' time put her about. Courses and foretopsail alone. Matthieu, Jean-Paul, Petit-André, up you go: let them be relieved every glass, Monsieur Vincent.' The *Bellone* was one of the few French ships of the time in which these orders, together with others concerning the preparation of the guns and small-arms, were received without comment and exactly obeyed.

So exactly that even before the lightening of the day the look-out on the *Lord Nelson*'s forecastle felt the loom of a ship to the windward, a ship sailing on a parallel course and not much above a mile away. What he could not see was that the ship was cleared for action – guns run out, shot-racks charged, cartridge filled and waiting, small-arms served out, splinter-netting rigged, yards puddened, boats towing astern – but he did not like her proximity, nor the lack of lights, and when he had stared awhile, wiping his streaming eyes, he hailed the quarterdeck: between his sneezes he gave Mr Pullings to understand that there was a vessel on the larboard beam.

Pullings' mind, lulled by the long even send of the sea, the regular hum of the rigging, the warmth of his pilot-jacket and blackguardly wool hat, exploded into sharp awareness. He was out of his corner by the binnacle, half-way up the weather shrouds, before the sneezing had stopped: three seconds for a long hard stare, and he turned up the watch with the roar he had learnt aboard HMS *Sophie*. The boarding-netting was already rigging out on the long iron cranes by the time he had shaken Captain Spottiswood into full wakefulness – orders confirmed, beat to action, clear the decks, run out the guns, women down into the hold.

He found Jack on deck in his nightshirt. 'She means business,' he said, over the high beating of the eastern drum. The privateer had put up her helm. Her yards were braced round and she was entering a long smooth curve that would cut the *Lord Nelson*'s present course in perhaps a quarter of an hour; her main and fore sails were clewed up, and it was clear that she meant to bear down under topsails alone – could do so with ease, a greyhound after a badger. 'But I have time to put my breeches on.'

Breeches, a pair of pistols. Stephen methodically laying out his instruments by the light of a farthing dip.

'What do you make of her, Jack?' he asked.

'Corvette or a damned big privateer: she means business.'

Up on deck. Much more daylight already, and a scene of less disorder than he had feared, a far better state of things. Captain Spottiswood had put the Indiaman before the wind to gain a few minutes' preparation, the French ship was still half a mile away, still under her topsails, still a little dubious, choosing to probe the *Lord Nelson*'s strength rather than make a dash for it.

Captain Spottiswood might lack decision, but his officers did not, nor the most part of his crew: they were used to the pirates of the South China Sea, to the wicked Malays of the Straits, to the Arabs of the Persian Gulf, and they had the boarding-netting rigged out taut and trim, the arms chest open, and at least half the guns run out.

On the crowded quarterdeck Jack snapped in between two sets of orders, said, 'I am at your disposition, sir.' The drawn, hesitant, elderly face turned towards him. 'Shall I take command of the for'ard division?'

'Do, sir. Do.'

'Come with me,' he said to Major Hill, hovering there at the fringe of the group. They ran along the gangway to the forward eighteen-pounders, two under the forecastle, two bare to the thin rain. Pullings had the waist division; the first officer the twelve-pounders on the quarterdeck; Mr Wand the maindeck eighteen-pounders aft, all encumbered in the stateroom and the cabins; and overhead a tall thin midshipman, looking desperately ill, stood shouting weakly at the bow-gun's crew.

The forward division on the larboard side, guns one,

three, five and seven, were fine modern flintlock pieces; two were already run out – primed, cocked and waiting. Number one's port-lid was jammed, its crew prising with their crows and handspikes in the confined space, thumping it with shot, hauling on the port-tackle, all smelling of brown men in violent emotion. Jack bent low under the beams, straddled the gun: with his hands hard on the carriage he lashed out backwards with all his might. Splinters and flakes of paint dropped from the port: it did not budge – seemed built into the ship. Three times. He slipped off, hobbled round to check the breeching, cried 'Bowse her up' and as the gun's muzzle came hard against the port, 'Stand by, stand by.' He pulled the laniard. A spark, a great sullen crash (damp powder, by God), and the gun leapt back under him. The acrid smoke tore out of the shattered port, and as it thinned Jack saw the sponger already at work, his swab right down the barrel of the gun, while the rest of the crew clapped on to the train-tackle. 'They know their business' he thought with pleasure, leaning out and tearing the wreckage from its hooks. 'Crucify that God-damned gunner!' But this was no time for reflection. Number three was still inboard. Jack and Major Hill tailed on to the side-tackles, and with 'One – two – three' they ran it up, the carriage crashing against the port-sill and the muzzle as far out as it could go. Number five had no more than four Lascars and a midshipman to serve it, an empty shot-rack and only three wads: it must have run itself out on the roll when they cast loose. 'Where are your men?' he asked the boy, taking his dirk and cutting the seizing within the clinch.

'Sick, sir, all sick. Kalim is nearly dead – can't speak.'

'Tell the gunner we must have shot and a cheese of wads. Cut along. Now, sir?' to another midshipman.

'Captain asks what did you fire for, sir,' panted the young man.

'To open the port,' said Jack, smiling into his round-eyed, anxious face. 'Tell him, with my compliments, there

127

is nothing like enough eighteen-pound shot on deck. Cut along now.' The boy shut his mouth on the rest of his message and vanished.

Number seven was in good shape: seven men to its crew, powder-boy standing over to starboard with a cartridge in his hands, gun levelled, tackle-falls neatly faked down; all ship-shape. Its captain, a grizzled European, only replied with a nervous chuckle, keeping his head bent away, feigning to look along the sights. A run seaman, no doubt, a man who had served with him in some commission, who had deserted, and who was afraid of being recognized. Once a quarter-gunner, to judge from the trimness of the gear. 'I hope he can point his piece as well as he . . .'

Jack straightened from his inspection of the flint and pan and glanced right and left. The hammocks were coming up in relays, piling into the netting. Half a dozen very sick men flogged on deck by the serang's mates, were creeping about with shot, and he was standing behind them, obviously in full control; there was still some confusion on the quarterdeck, but the air of frantic haste had gone. This was a breathing-space, and lucky they were to have it. Fore and aft the Indiaman looked like a fighting-ship: thinly manned, decks still encumbered, but a fighting-ship. He looked out over the sea: light enough to see the red of the tricolour five hundred yards away – a severe cold light now the rain had stopped, and a grey, grey sea. Wind steady in the west; high cloud except on the horizon; a long even swell. The *Bellone* still had her larboard tacks aboard: she was hanging off to see what weight of metal the *Lord Nelson* carried. And the *Lord Nelson* was still before the wind, moving heavily – this was one of her many bad points of sailing. If Captain Spottiswood continued to run it was likely that the Frenchman would bear up, and moving two miles for the *Lord Nelson*'s one, cross under her stern and rake her. That was his business: for the moment Jack's world was confined to his guns: there was a comfort in subordination, in small responsibility, no decisions . . .

Seven, five and three were well enough: number one was still too cluttered for a full team to work it fast, and a full team it must have. A last sharp look at the privateer – how beautifully she breasted the swell – and he dived under the forecastle.

Hard, fast, dogged, mechanical work, shifting heavy lumps, bales, casks: he found that what he was whistling under his breath was the adagio from Hummel's piece – Sophia's inept playing of it – Diana's rough splendid dash – a jet of intense feeling for Sophia – loving, protective – a clear image of her on the steps of that house. Some fool, Stephen of all people, had said you could not be both busy and unhappy, sad.

The *Bellone*'s opening gun cut short these reflections. Her starboard bow eight-pounder sent a ball skipping along the *Lord Nelson*'s larboard side; and as though he had needed this to set him going, Captain Spottiswood called out his orders. The yards braced round, the sea-scape turned, and the privateer came into view through the number one gun-port, framed there, bright against the darkness of the low crowded forecastle. The *Lord Nelson* fell off a little, steadied on her new course with the *Bellone* on her larboard quarter, so that now Jack saw no more than her head-sails, four hundred yards away, long musket-shot. And as the Indiaman steadied, so her after guns went off, a six-fold crash, a thin high-pitched cheering, and the word came forward. 'Fire as they bear.'

'This is more like it,' said Jack, plunging out of the forecastle. The long pause before action was always hard to bear, but now in a few seconds everything would vanish but for the living instant – no sadness, no time for fear. Number seven was in good hands, trained right round aft as far as the port would allow, and its captain glaring along the barrel, poised for the roll. The waist guns went off together, and in their eddying smoke – it filled his lungs, a choking exaltation – Jack and Major Hill flung themselves upon the long crows to heave number five, that dull inanimate weight, while the Lascars tailed on to the forward train-tackle to help traverse it to point it at the *Bellone*'s stern, just in view over the dispart-sight. Number seven went off with a poor slow explosion and a great deal of smoke. 'If the powder is all like that,' thought Jack, crouching over number five, his handspike ready to elevate the gun, 'we might as well try boarding right away. But,' he added, 'it is more likely the mumping villain has never drawn it this last week and more.' He waited for the smoke to clear, for the roll of the ship to bring the gun to bear, slowly up and up, and just as he heaved on the laniard he saw the *Bellone* vanish in the white cloud of her own broadside. The gun sprang from under his arched body. He could not see the fall of the shot for the smoke, but from the fine round crash it must have been well pitched up. The privateer's broadside sang and howled overhead – holes in the foretopsail, a bowline hanging loose. The bow-gun overhead went off, and he darted into the forecastle, leaping over the train-tackle as number five was sponged and reloaded. He laid three and one, fired them, and ran back along the line to help run out number five again.

The firing was general now: the *Lord Nelson*'s thirteen larboard guns spoke in ones or twos every half minute or so; the *Bellone*'s seventeen, having fired three steady broadsides in five minutes – a splendid rate even for a man-of-war – had now become irregular, an uninterrupted roll of fire. Her leeward side was veiled in a cloud of smoke that drifted across the intervening sea to join the smoke shot out against the wind by the Indiaman's guns, and through it all there was the stab-stab of orange flame. Only twice could Jack be sure of the flight of his division's shot, once when a flaw in the wind, tearing the curtain aside, showed number seven strike her amidships, just above the main-chains, and again when he saw his own hull her in the bows: her sails were not as pretty as they had been, either, but she had nevertheless closed the distance and she was now on the *Lord Nelson*'s beam, hammering her hard. Would she forge ahead and cross?

There was little time for thought as Jack raced from gun to gun, bearing a hand, running out, swabbing and loading, but it was clear that the *Bellone* had no heavier guns than eight-pounders, that she meant to tear the Indiaman's sails, rigging and spars to pieces rather than to damage her valuable hull and cargo. There was little doubt that she did not relish the eighteen-pound shot that hit her – three or four between wind and water would be very serious, and a single ball might carry away a straining topmast. If they did not hit her hard soon, she would close – abandon her elegant tactics and close. She was an awkward customer, with her formidable gunnery and her repeated attempts at crossing the *Lord Nelson*'s bows; she would be more awkward still at close quarters. 'Deal with that when we come to it,' he thought, tallying on to a rope.

An enormous ringing crash inside his head and filling the outside world. He was down. Blindly struggling away from number five's recoil, he tried to make out whether he was badly wounded or not – impossible to tell at once. He was not. Number seven had exploded, killing three of its servers, blowing its captain's head to pieces – it was his jaw that had gouged the wound across Jack's forearm – and scattering bits of iron in all directions, wounding men as far away as the mainmast – a splinter of iron had grazed his head, knocking him down. The face he was staring at so stupidly was Pullings's, repeating the words, 'You must go below, sir. Below. Let me give you a hand below.'

He came fully to life and cried, 'Secure that gun,' in a voice that he could hear as if from another throat. By the grace of God what was left of the barrel and the carriage had not burst free from the ring-bolts; they made it fast, slid the bodies overboard, and hurried what was left of its gear over to number five.

Three more rounds, three more of those hammer-blow explosions right by his ear, and the bursting gun, the dead men, his own wound, all merged into the one din and the furious activity of battle.

The smoke was thicker, the *Bellone*'s flashes closer, far closer. She was edging down fast. Faster and faster they worked their guns: with the rest of number seven's crew and two men sent up from a dismounted six-pounder on the quarterdeck they plied them without a second's pause. The metal was hot, so hot the guns kicked clear of the deck, flying back with a terrible note on the breeching. Then the *Bellone*'s guns fired a round of grape, followed by a furious discharge of musketry. The smoke swept away and there she was, right upon them, backing her main topsail to check her way and come alongside. Small-arms cracking in her tops to clear the *Lord Nelson*'s decks, men on her yard-arms to lash her spars to theirs, grappling-irons ready in the waist and bows, a dense swarm on her forecastle and in her foreshrouds.

'All hands to repel boarders,' from the quarterdeck, the grinding crash as they touched, the Frenchmen's cheer and here they were cutlasses slashing the boarding-netting, pole-axes, the flash of swords. He snapped one pistol at a determined face coming through the wrecked number seven port, snatched up the great heavy crow, and with an extraordinary feeling of strength and invulnerability – complete certainty – he flung himself at the men in the netting who were trying to come over the bows – the main attack was in the bows. He stood there with one foot on the broken rail, holding the massive crow in the middle, banging, thrusting, beating them down. All around him the shrieking Lascars fought with their pikes, axes, pistols. A rush of Company's men from the waist and the quarterdeck cleared the gangway, where a dozen privateers had come aboard, and carried on to the forecastle, charging with pikes.

The Indiaman's deck was higher by a good spring than the *Bellone*'s; she had a pronounced tumblehome – her sides sloped inwards – which left an awkward space.

But the Frenchmen clung there obstinately, hitting back, striving most desperately, crowding to come aboard. Flung back, yet coming again and again, fresh men by the score and score, until a heave of the sea separated the ships, and a whole group clinging to the forechains fell between them, blasted by Mr Johnstone's blunderbuss fired straight into the mass. The serang ran out on to the yard-arm and cut the lashing, the grappling-irons scraped harmlessly over the rail, and the quarterdeck guns fired three rounds of grape, wounding the French captain, unshipping the *Bellone*'s wheel, and cutting her spanker halliards. She shot up into the wind, and if only the *Lord Nelson* had had enough men both to repel boarders and fight her guns, she could now have raked the *Bellone* at ten yards' range; but not a round could she fire – her head dropped off, and the two ships drifted silently apart.

Jack carried a boy down to the cockpit – both arms slashed to the bone as he flung them up to guard his face – and Stephen said, 'Keep your thumb pressed here till I can come to him. How do we stand?'

'We beat 'em off. Her boats are picking up her men. Two or three hundred she has. We'll be at it again directly. Hurry, Stephen, I cannot wait. We must knot and splice. How many have you here?'

'Thirty or forty,' said Stephen, fastening the tourniquet. 'Boy, you will do very well: lie quiet. Jack, show me your arm, your head.'

'Another time. A couple of lucky shots and we disabled him.'

A lucky shot. How he prayed for it – every time he laid his gun he prayed for it. 'The name of the Father, the Son, and the Holy Ghost.' But in the failing wind the smoke lay thick and heavy all round the *Bellone* – he could see nothing, and he had only two guns firing now. Number one's breeching had gone at the first discharge, wounding two Lascars and a midshipman, and the gun was lying on its side, precariously wedged behind a cask. His crews had thinned – the whole deck had thinned – and the *Lord Nelson*'s fire had slackened to a gun a minute, while the *Bellone* kept up a steady thunder fifty yards to windward. The deck, when he had time to look aft, showed no more than a sparse line of men – no crowded knots at every gun. Some had been wounded, others had run below – the hatches had not been laid – and those that were left were drawn, ashy, weak, their forces drained: they fought without conviction. For a long moment Hill had vanished, but he was back now, laying number three. Jack rammed down the wad, felt behind him for the shot. No shot. That damned powder-boy had run. 'Shot! Shot!' he cried, and there was the boy, waddling from the mainhatch with two heavy balls clasped in his arms – a new boy, absurdly dressed in shore-going rig, new trousers, blue jacket, pigtail in a ribbon. A fat boy. 'Take them from for'ard, you poxed son of a whore,' said Jack into his mute, appalled face, snatching one and thrusting it down the barrel. 'From for'ard, from number one. There's a dozen there. At the double, at the double!' The second wad, rammed hard into the scorching gun. 'Run her up! Run her up!'

Painfully, straining, they forced the great weight up against the roll: one little blue Lascar was vomiting as he heaved. The *Bellone*'s broadside bawled out, all in one; grape and chain, from the shrill scream overhead as they lay to the tackles. He fired, saw Hill snatch the boy from the recoil, and instantly ran forward through the smoke to number three. That damned boy was underfoot. He picked him up, said kindly, 'Stand clear of the guns. You're a good boy – a plucked 'un. Just bring one at a time,' pointing to the forecastle, 'but look alive. Then cartridge. Bear a hand. We must have cartridge.'

The cartridge never came. Jack fired number five, caught a glimpse of topsails towering overhead, saw the *Bellone*'s foreyards glide into the *Lord Nelson*'s shrouds, and heard an enormous cheering, roaring of boarders behind him, *behind* him. The privateer's boats had slipped round unseen in the smoke and there were a hundred Frenchmen coming up the unprotected starboard side.

They filled the *Lord Nelson*'s waist, cutting the quarter-deck off from the forecastle, and the press of men coming in over the bows through the chain-torn netting was so great they could not fight. Faces, chests, arms, so close to him he could not get his long bar free, a little devilish man clinging round his waist. Down, trampled upon, a passing kick. Up and facing them, hitting short-arm blows – a stab. The crowding force, the weight of men. Back, back, step by step, tripping on bodies, back, back. And then a falling void, an impact faintly, faintly heard, as though from another age.

The swinging lantern. He watched it: perhaps for hours. And gradually the world began to fall into place, memory coming back layer by layer, to reach the present. Or nearly so. He could not recall the sequence after the busting of poor Haynes's gun. Haynes, of course: that was his name. A forecastle-man, larboard watch, in the *Resolution*, rated quarter-gunner when they were off the Cape. The rest was darkness: this often happened with a wound. Was he wounded? He was certainly in the cockpit, and that was Stephen moving about among the low, crowded, moaning bodies. 'Stephen,' he said, after a while.

'How then, my dear?' said Stephen. 'How do you find yourself? How are your intellectuals?'

'Pretty well, I thank you. I seem all of a piece.'

'I dare say you are. Limbs and trunk are sound. Coma was all I feared these last few days. You fell down the forehatch. You may take an Almoravian draught, however. The dogs, they did not find half my Almoravian draught.'

'We were taken?'

'Aye, aye, we were taken. We lost thirty-six killed and wounded; and they took us. They plundered us cruelly – stripped to the bone – and for the first few days they kept us under hatches. Here is your draught. However, I extracted a ball from Captain Dumanoir's shoulder and looked after their wounded, and now we are indulged with taking the air on deck. Their second captain, Azéma, is an amiable man, a former King's officer, and he has prevented any gross excess, apart from the plundering.'

'Privateers,' said Jack, trying to shrug. 'But what about those girls? What about the Miss Lambs?'

'They are dressed as men – as boys. I am not sure that they are altogether pleased with the success of their deception.'

'A fair-sized prize-crew?' asked Jack, whose mind had flown to the possibility of retaking the Indiaman.

'Huge,' said Stephen. 'Forty-one. The Company's officers have given their parole; some of the Lascars have taken service for double wages; and the rest are down with this Spanish influenza. They are carrying us into Corunna.'

'Don't they wish they may get us there,' said Jack. 'The chops of the Channel and to westward are alive with cruisers.'

He spoke confidently; he knew that there was truth in what he said; but limping about the quarterdeck on Tuesday, when Stephen allowed him up, he surveyed the ocean with a feeling of despair. A vast great emptiness, with nothing but the trim *Bellone* a little to windward: not a sail, not the smallest lugger on the world's far rim, nor, after hours of unbroken watching, the least reason why any should appear. Emptiness; and somewhere under the leeward horizon, the Spanish port. He remembered coming from the West Indies in the *Alert*, sailing along the busiest sea-route in the whole Atlantic, and they had not seen a living soul until they were in soundings off the Lizard.

In the afternoon Pullings came on deck, pale Pullings, supported by a Miss Lamb on either side. Jack had already seen Pullings (grape-shot in the thigh, a sword-cut on the shoulder and two ribs stove in), just as he had seen Major Hill (down with the influenza) and all the other men under Stephen's hands, but this was the first time he had seen the girls. 'My dear Miss Lamb,' he cried, taking her free hand, 'I hope I see you well. Quite well?' he said earnestly, meaning 'not too much raped?'

'Thank you, sir,' said Miss Lamb, looking conscious and strange – quite another girl, 'my sister and I are perfectly well.'

'Miss Lambs, your most devoted,' said Captain Azéma, coming from the starboard side and bowing. He was a big dark loose-built man, tough, capable, a sailor – a man after Jack's own heart. 'Misses are under my particular protection, sir,' he said. 'I have persuaded them to carry robes, to resume the form divine,' – kissing his fingers. 'They do not risk the least impertinence. Some of my men are villain buggers indeed, impetuous like one says; but quite apart from my protection, not one, *not one*, would want of respect for such heroines.'

'Eh?' said Jack.

'That's right, sir,' cried Pullings, squeezing them. 'Copper-bottomed heroines, trundling shot, running about like mad, powder, match when my flint flew off, wads!! Joan of Arcs.'

'Did they carry powder?' cried Jack. 'Dr Maturin said trousers, or something of that kind, but I – '

'Oh, you horrid two-faced thing!' cried Miss Susan. 'You *saw* her! You shouted out the most dreadful things to Lucy, the most dreadful things I ever heard in my life. You swore at my sister, sir; you know you did. Oh, Captain Aubrey, fie!'

'*Captain* Aubrey?' observed Azéma, adding the head-money for an English officer to his share of the prize – a very handsome sum.

'She's blown the gaff – I'm brought by the lee,' thought Jack. 'They carried powder – What an amazing spirited thing to do.' 'Dear Miss Lambs,' he said most humbly, 'I beg you to forgive me. The last half-hour of the action – a damned warm action too – is a perfect blank to me. I fell on my head; and it is a perfect blank. But to carry powder was the most amazing spirited thing to do: I honour you, my dears. Please forgive me. The smoke – the trousers – what did I say, so that I may unsay it at once?'

'You said,' began Miss Susan, and paused. 'Well, I forget; but it was monstrous . . . '

The sound of a gun made the whole group jerk, an absurd, simultaneous, galvanic leap: they had all been speaking very loud, being still half deafened from the roar of battle, but a gun touched their innermost ears and they all pivoted at once, mechanical toys pointing directly at the *Bellone*.

She had been under double-reefed topsails all this time, to allow the *Lord Nelson* to keep company, but now men were already laying out on the yard to shake out the reefs, and Captain Dumanoir hailed loud and clear, telling his second to make straight for Corunna, 'all sails outside'. He added a good deal that neither Jack nor Pullings could understand, but the general upshot was plain: his look-out had seen a sail to windward; he was not going to take the slightest risk with so valuable a prize; and he meant to beat up to reconnoitre, and as the case fell out, to salute a friend or neutral, to fight an enemy, or, trusting to the *Bellone*'s magnificent sailing qualities, to lead the strange sail astray.

The *Lord Nelson*, trailing a curtain of dark-brown weed, leaking steadily (her pumps had never stopped since the action), and still short of sails, spars and rigging, could only make four knots, even with her topgallantsails set; but the *Bellone*, now a triple pyramid of white, was at her best close-hauled, and in ten minutes they were two miles away from one another. Jack asked permission to go into the top; Captain Azéma not only entreated him to go anywhere he chose, but lent him Stephen's telescope as well.

'Good day,' said the privateersman in the top. Jack had given him a terrible blow with his bar, but he bore no grudge. 'That is one of thy frigates down there.'

'Oh wee?' said Jack, settling his back against the mast. The distant ship sprang close in his objective-glass. Thirty-six guns; no, thirty-eight. Red pennant. *Naiad*? *Minerve*? She had been going large under easy sail when first she sighted the *Bellone*; then studdingsails had appeared – the last were being sheeted home when first Jack had her steadily under view – as she altered course to close the privateer; then she saw the Indiaman and altered course again to know more about her. Upon this the *Bellone* tacked, tacked clumsily, taking an age over what Jack had seen her do in five minutes from 'helm's a-lee' to 'let go and haul'; he heard them laughing, clowning down there on deck. She stood on this tack until she was within a mile of the frigate, steadily beating up against the swell, white water sweeping across her forecastle. A white puff showed at the frigate's bows, and shifting his gaze he saw the red ensign break out at her mizen-peak: he frowned: he would at least have tried the tricolour or, with the big American frigates in those waters, the Stars and Stripes; it might not have worked, but it was worth the attempt. For her part, the *Bellone* was perfectly capable of showing French colours without any distinction, to pass for a national ship and lead the frigate away.

She had done so. She had done just that thing; and the seaman, who had borrowed the glass, licking it with his garlic tongue, chuckled to himself. Jack knew what was passing through the frigate-captain's head; far to leeward a ship, probably a merchantship, possibly a prize, but what sort of prize he could not tell: crossing his bows three-quarters of a mile away there was a French corvette, not very well handled, not very fast, peppering him at random-shot. A simple mind would find no great difficulty about this decision and soon Jack saw the frigate haul her wind. Her studdingsails disappeared, and she turned to pursue the *Bellone*, setting a press of staysails. She would deal with the Frenchman and then come back to see about this hypothetical prize.

'Surely to God you must see she's spilling her wind,' cried Jack within himself. 'Surely to God you've seen that old trick before?' They slipped away and away across the distant sea, the frigate with a fine bold bow-wave at her stern and the *Bellone* keeping just beyond the reach of her chasers; and when they were no more than flecks of white, hull down to the north-north-east, Jack climbed heavily out of the top. The seaman gave him a compassionate yet philosophic nod; this had happened to him before; it was happening to Jack now; it was one of the little miseries of life.

After dark Captain Azéma altered course according to his instructions, and the Indiaman headed into a lonely sea, drawing her slow furrow a hundred miles in the four and twenty hours, never to be seen by the frigate again.

At the far end of that furrow lay Corunna; he had no doubt of Captain Azéma's making his landfall to within a mile or so, for not only was Azéma a thorough-going seaman, but this clear weather continued day after day – perfect weather for observation, for fixing his position. Corunna: Spain. But now that Jack was known for an officer they would never let him ashore. Unless he gave his parole, Azéma would put him in irons, there to lie until the *Bellone* or some chasse-marée carried him to France – his was a valuable carcass.

The next day was a total void: the unbroken round of the sea, the dome of the sky, thin cloud lightening to blue above. And the next was the same, distinguished only by what Jack thought to be the beginnings of the influenza, and a certain skittishness observed in the Misses Lamb, pursued by Azéma's lieutenant and a sixteen-year-old volunteer with flashing eyes.

But Friday's sea was all alive with sails – the ocean

was speckled with the sober drab of a fleet of bankers, coming home with codfish from Newfoundland; they could be smelt a mile downwind. And among the bankers a bean-cod, a double-lateen with a host of odd, haphazard-looking sails, a strange vessel with an archaic prow; and a disagreeable reminder that the coast was near – your bean-cod was no ocean crosser. But though the bean-cod was of absorbing interest to a sailor, the plain cutter far down to leeward wiped it entirely from their attention.

'You see the cutter, sir?' said Pullings.

Jack nodded. The cutter was a rig more favoured by the English than the French; it was used by the Navy and by privateers, by smugglers and by those who pursued smugglers, being fast, nimble and weatherly, lying very close to the wind; it was of no great use to merchants. And this particular little vessel was no merchantman: what merchantman would steer that erratic course among the bankers? She did not belong to the Navy, either, for as soon as she sighted the *Lord Nelson* a gaff-topsail appeared above her mainsail, a modern sail not countenanced in the service. She was a privateer.

This was Captain Azéma's opinion too. He had the guns drawn, reloaded and run out on both sides; he was in no particular hurry, because the cutter had to work straight up into the eye of the wind. Furthermore, as she came nearer, tacking and tacking again, it was clear that she had had a rough time of it not long ago – her mainsail was double-reefed, presumably from some recent damage; there were strangely-patched holes all over it and more in her foresail and ragged jib; her upper works had a chewed appearance; and one of her seven little gun-ports on the starboard side had been hastily repaired. There was not much danger to be feared from her, but still he was going to take no risks: he had new boarding-netting rigged out, a great deal of cartridge filled, and shot brought up; and his acting-bosun, helped by all the Lascars who were capable of work, secured the yards.

The *Lord Nelson* was ready long before the cutter fired a gun and hoisted English colours; but she did not reply at once. Azéma looked at Jack and Pullings. 'I will not ask you to go downstairs,' he said, 'but if you will to hail or to signal, I shall be compelled to shoot you.' He smiled, but he had two pistols in his belt and he meant what he said.

Jack said, 'Just so,' and bowed. Pullings smiled diffidently.

The cutter was lying on the Indiaman's bow, her mainsail shivering; Azéma nodded to the man at the wheel. The *Lord Nelson* turned gently, and Azéma said, 'Fire.' The broadside, the eighteen-pounders alone, parted on the downward roll; beautifully grouped, the shots struck the sea just short of the cutter's larboard bow and beam, ricocheting over her, adding new holes to her sails and knocking away the outer third of her bowsprit. Startled by this reception, the cutter tried to fill and come about, but with so little way on her and with her jib flying in the breeze she would not stay. She fell off, giving the *Lord Nelson* her seven six-pounders as she did so, and wore round on the other tack.

The cutter knew she had come up against a tough'un, a difficult article – half a broadside like this would send her to the bottom; but gathering way she crossed the *Lord Nelson*'s stern, fired again, gybed like a dancer and crossed back to lie upon her starboard bow. At two hundred yards her six-pounders did the Indiaman's thick sides no harm, but they did cut up her rigging, and it was clearly in the cutter's mind to carry on with this manoeuvre.

Azéma was having none of it. The cutter had gone to and fro in spite of his yawing to fire, and now he brought the wind right abeam, swinging the ship through 90°. He ran down the line of guns, speaking to each crew, and sent a deliberate broadside to the space of sea the cutter had filled two seconds earlier – as though by magic, intuition, telepathy, the cutter's master put his helm a-lee the instant

142

of the call to fire, coming about in a flash and heading for the *Lord Nelson*. He did so again two minutes later, less by magic than by a calculation of the time it would take these gunners to have him in their sights again. He was going to board, and he had only one more short tack to bring him up against the *Lord Nelson*'s bows. Jack could see the men there, cutlasses and boarding-axes ready, twenty-five or thirty of them, the master at the tiller, a long sword in his other hand: in a moment now they would start their cheer.

'Fire,' said Azéma again, and as the smoke cleared there was the cutter with her topsail gone, hanging drunkenly over her side, no captain at the tiller, a heap of men struggling or motionless upon her deck. Her way carried her on past the *Lord Nelson*'s bows, out of reach of the next discharge; and now she was racing away, fleeing to gain a hundred yards or so before the *Lord Nelson*'s ponderous turn should bring her starboard broadside to bear.

She survived it, though it was difficult to see how she did so, with so much white water kicked up all round her; and Azéma, who did not feel passionately about either taking or sinking her, sent only a few more shots after her before returning to his course. Ten minutes later she had sent up a new jib and foresail and she was dwindling, smaller and smaller among the distant bankers. Jack felt for his watch; he liked to note the beginning and the end of all engagements – it was gone, of course.

'I think it was temerarious, immoral,' said Azéma. 'Suppose he had killed some of my people! He should be broken on the wheel. I should have sunk him. I am too magnanimous. That is not courage, but hardfooliness.'

'I would agree,' said Jack, 'if it had been the other way around. A sloop that does not strike to a ship of the line is a fool.'

'We see things differently,' said Azéma, still cross over the time lost and the damage to his rigging. 'We have different proportions. But at least' – his good humour

143

returning – 'I hope your countrymen will give us a day of rest tomorrow.'

He had his day of rest, and another morning too; but shortly after he had taken his noon observation – 45° 23' N., 10° 30' W. – and had promised his prisoners Spanish bread and real coffee for breakfast, there was the cry of a sail to windward.

Gradually the white blur resolved itself into a brig; and the brig was clearly giving chase. The hours passed: Captain Azéma was thoughtful and preoccupied during dinner – pecked at his food, and from time to time going up on deck. The *Lord Nelson* was under topgallants, with upper and lower studdingsails, which urged her towards Corunna at five or even six knots as the breeze freshened. He set his royals a little after four, anxiously watching to see how the wounded masts would stand the strain; and for a while it seemed that the brig was falling behind.

'Sir,' said Pullings secretly, coming from those airy heights after a long examination of the brig, 'I am almost sure she is the *Seagull*. My uncle was master of her in ninety-nine, and many's the time I have been aboard.'

'*Seagull*?' said Jack, frowning. 'Did she not change to carronades?'

'That's right, sir. Sixteen twenty-four-pounders, very tight in the bridle-ports: and two long sixes. She can hit hard, if only she gets near enough, but she is amazing slow.'

'Slower than this?'

'Much of a muchness, sir. She's just set her skysails. It may make a difference.'

The difference was small, very small – perhaps a table-cloth or two – but in five hours of steady unchanging weather it was enough to bring the *Seagull* within reach of the *Lord Nelson*'s aftermost starboard eighteen-pounder and of a long eight that Captain Azéma had shifted to fire through the stateroom gallery.

For ten sea miles the brig – and now they were sure she was the *Seagull* – could reply only with her bow six-pounder, which did nothing but make a smoke and encourage her crew; but slowly the *Lord Nelson* neared and then crossed a dark band in the sea, where the wind, backed up by the Spanish Cordillera, combined with the ebbing tide to produce a distinct frontier, a sullen, choppy zone haunted by gulls and other inshore birds.

Within five minutes the *Lord Nelson*'s way fell off perceptibly; the song of her rigging dropped tone by tone; and the *Seagull* ranged up to her starboard quarter. Before the brig crossed the dark water in her turn, she fired the first full broadside of her close-range carronades: it fell short, and so did the next, but a ricocheting twenty-four-pound ball tore through the hammocks and dropped weakly against the mainmast. Captain Azéma looked thoughtfully from the heavy shot to the brig: she still had a quarter of a mile to run before she would lose the full fair breeze. A gain of fifty yards would bring these twenty-four-pounders rattling about his ears, piercing the Indiaman's costly sides and endangering her already damaged masts. His chief feeling was irritation rather than any dread for the outcome: the *Seagull*'s rate of fire and accuracy left much to be desired, whereas he had eight master-gunners aboard; the brig's power of manoeuvring was no greater than his, and he only had to knock away a spar or two to leave her behind and gain the coast. Nevertheless, he was going to need all his concentration.

'She is scarcely commodious, your brig,' he said to Jack. 'We may have serious difficulty with her. I must ask you to go below. Messiers les prisonniers into the hold, if you please – I invite the prisoners to go into the hold.'

There was no denying his authoritative tone. They went below with many a reluctant glance at the evening sea, down hatchway after hatchway to the final grating, which

145

closed over them with a thump and the rattle of a chain. And it was in the crammed bowels of the Indiaman, shut firmly down in the smell of tea, cinnamon and bilgewater that Jack, Pullings, the Company's Europeans and all the passengers witnessed the action. Aural witnesses, of course, no more, since they were below the water-line, with nothing but a swinging lantern and the vague shape of bales to see, but what they heard they heard well. The *Lord Nelson* resonated like a sounding-box to the crash of her eighteen-pounders, transposing the roar an octave lower; and the sea transmitted the *Seagull*'s broadsides – a curious dead thump, like a padded hammer a great way off, a sound devoid of overtones and so distinct that it was sometimes possible to distinguish each of the eight carronades, whose fire would have seemed simultaneous in the open air.

They listened, tried to calculate the direction, worked out the weight of metal – four hundred and thirty-two pounds for the *Lord Nelson*, three hundred and ninety-two for the brig – and the possibility of bringing it into play. 'Azéma is using his big guns alone,' observed Jack. 'Concentrating on her masts, I make no doubt.' Sometimes the *Seagull* hit them, and they cheered, full of speculation as to the place of the strike; once a sudden rush in the well and a renewed activity of the pump made it clear that the *Lord Nelson* had been holed between wind and water, probably in the forepeak; and once a great metallic clang made them think that a gun had been struck; perhaps dismounted.

Towards three o'clock in the morning the candle went out, and they lay in darkness, listening, listening, sometimes regretting their coats, rugs, and pillows and food, and sometimes dozing. The firing went on and on: the *Seagull* had given up her broadsides and was firing gun by gun; the *Lord Nelson* had never done anything else throughout the engagement – a steady, deliberate rhythm hour after hour.

Miss Lamb woke with a scream: 'It was a rat! A monstrous great wet rat! O *how* I regret my trousers!'

Extreme attention slackened as the long night wore on. Once or twice Jack spoke to Major Hill and to Pullings and had no reply. He found that his counting of the shots was mingling with a calculation of the number of sick and wounded under Stephen's hands – with observations made to Sophia – with thoughts of food, of coffee, and the playing of the D minor trio – Diana's rough glissando and the deep sustaining note of the 'cello, as they played three-handed.

A flood of light, the grinding of the chain and grating, and he was conscious that he had been three parts asleep. Not wholly, since he knew that the firing had stopped this last hour and more, but enough to feel shifty and ashamed.

On deck it was raining, a thin drizzle from a high sky – very little wind, and that a land-breeze; Captain Azéma and his people looked deathly pale, tired, but undisturbed – too worn for outward pleasure, but undisturbed. Under her fore and main topsails the *Lord Nelson* was slipping along through the water close-hauled, away from the motionless *Seagull*, far away on her starboard quarter: even at this distance Jack could see that she had suffered badly. Her foreyard was gone, her maintopmast seemed to be tottering, there was a great deal of wreckage on her deck and dangling over her side: four gun-ports beat in: strangely low in the water: pumps hard at work. She had hauled off to refit, to stop her leaks, and the likelihood of her renewing the action – of being able to renew the action – was . . .

Captain Azéma had been bent over a gun, laying it with the very greatest care: he gaged the roll, fired, sending a ball plumb amidships into the repairing party. He waited for the flight of the shot, said 'Carry on, Partre,' and stepped back to his mug of coffee, steaming on the binnacle.

It was perfectly allowable; Jack might have done the

same; but there was something so cold-blooded about it that Jack refused a draught from the mug and turned to look at the *Lord Nelson*'s damage and at the coast, barring the whole eastern horizon now. The damage was heavy but not crippling; Azéma had not made quite the landfall he had expected – that was Cape Prior right ahead – but he would be in Corunna road by noon. Jack ignored the second gun: he tried to make out why it should wound him so, for he had no particular friend aboard the *Seagull*. He could not clarify his mind, but he knew he felt the most furious enmity for Azéma, and it was with more than the ordinary leap of delight, of hope revived when all seemed lost, that he saw the first ship round that Spanish headland, heading north. A homeward-bound line-of-battle ship, HMS *Colossus*, followed by the *Tonnant*, eighty.

The mast-head hailed 'Two ships of the line'. But two more followed: a very powerful squadron, all sails abroad, and holding the weather-gage. There was not the slightest chance of escape. Mute, weary consternation; and in the silence Jack stepped to the pointed eighteen-pounder, laid his hand on the lock and said coldly, 'You must not fire that gun, sir. You must strike your colours to the brig.'

CHAPTER SIX

At five minutes to eight Jack Aubrey walked quickly through the dreary rain over the cobbles of the Admiralty courtyard, pursued by the voice of the hackney coachman. 'Fourpence! Call yourself a gent? The poor bleeding Navy's half-pay shame, that's what I call you.'

He shrugged, and ducking under the overflow from the gutter he hurried into the hall, past the main waiting-room and on to the little office called the Bosun's Chair, for he had a First Lord's appointment, no less. The fire was beginning to draw, sending up a strong writhe of yellow smoke to join the yellow fog outside, and through the yellow shot darts of red, with a pleasant roar and crackle; he stood with his back to the chimneypiece, looking into the rain and mopping his best uniform with a handkerchief. Several figures passed dimly through the Whitehall arch, civilians under umbrellas, officers exposed to the elements: he thought he recognized two or three – certainly that was Brand of the *Implacable* – but the mud deep in the buckles of his shoes occupied him too much for close attention.

He was in a high state of nervous excitement – any sailor waiting to see the First Lord must be in a high state of nervous excitement – yet the surface of his mind was taken up less with his coming interview than with getting the utmost possible service from a single handkerchief and with vague darting reflections upon poverty – an old acquaintance, almost a friend – a more natural state for sea-officers than wealth – wealth very charming – should love to be rich again; but there was the loss of all those little satisfactions of contriving – the triumph of a guinea found in an old waistcoat pocket – the breathless tension over the turn of a card. The hackney-coach had been necessary, however, with the mud ankle-deep, and this damned south-wester: best uniforms did not grow on trees, nor yet silk stockings.

'Captain Aubrey, sir,' said the clerk. 'His lordship will see you now.'

'Captain Aubrey, I am happy to see you,' said Lord Melville. 'How is your father?'

'Thank you, sir, he is very well – delighted with the election, as we all are. But I beg your pardon, my lord. I am out of order. May I offer you my very best congratulations on your peerage?'

'You are very good – very good,' said Lord Melville, and having answered Jack's civil inquiries for Lady Melville and Robert, he went on, 'So you had a lively time of it, coming home?'

'We did indeed, my lord,' cried Jack. 'But I am astonished you should know.'

'Why, it is in the paper – a passenger's letter to her family, describing the Indiaman's capture and recapture. She mentioned you by name – says the handsomest things. Sibbald pointed it out to me.'

That infernal girl, that Lamb, must have sent her letter by the revenue cutter: and there he had been, hurrying up from Plymouth on borrowed money to reach a London filled with bums forewarned, all waiting to arrest him for debt, charmed with the idea of tossing him into the Fleet or the Marshalsea to rot until the war was over and all chance gone. He had known many officers with their careers ruined by a tipstaff – old Baines, Serocold . . . and there he had been, prancing about the town, dressed like the King's birthday for every sneaking attorney to behold. The thought made him feel cold and sick: he said something about 'quite amazed – had posted up from Plymouth with not more than a couple of hours at his father's place – thought he had certainly outrun the news.' Yet it must have made tolerable sense, for Lord Melville only observed in that Scotch voice of his, 'I am sure you used your best endeavours. but I wish you could have come more betimes – weeks, nay, months earlier, before all the plums were gone. I should have liked to do something for you: at the beginning of the war there were commands aplenty. I shall look into this question of promotion that has been urged upon me, but I can hold out no hope of a ship. However, there may be some slight possibility in the Sea-Fencibles or the Impress Service: we are extending both, and they call for active, enterprising men.'

They also called for solvent men, seeing that they were landborne posts: comfort-loving men, devoid of ambition or tired of the sea, willing to look after a kind of fisherman's militia or to attend to the odious work of the press-gang. Clearly it was now or never, all or nothing. Once that hard-faced man the other side of the desk had made a firm offer of a shore appointment there would be no shifting him. 'My lord,' said Jack with all the force and energy he could respectfully express, 'I like a plum, a post-ship, as much as any man alive; but if I might have four pieces of wood that swim, I should be happy, more than happy, to sail them on any service, on any station in the world as a commander or anything else. I have been afloat since I was fourteen, sir, and I have never refused any employment their lordships were good enough to offer me. I believe I may promise you would not regret your decision, sir. All I want is to be at sea again.'

'Heu, heu,' said Lord Melville, in his meditating way, pinning Jack with a grey stare. 'So you make no stipulation of any kind? There was a great deal of clack about your friends wishing you to be made post for the *Cacafuego* affair.'

'None whatsoever, my lord,' said Jack, and shut his mouth. He thought of trying to explain the unfortunate word 'claim' that he had been inspired to use the last time he was in this room: thought better of it, and kept his

151

mouth shut, wearing a look of deferential attention and maintaining it better than he could have done a year ago, although he had a far greater respect for St Vincent than he ever could have for a civilian.

'Weel,' said the First Lord, after a pause, 'I can promise nothing. You can have no conception of the applications, of the interests to be managed, balanced . . . but there might be some remote possibility . . . come and see me next week. In the meantime I will look into this question of promotion, though the post-captain's list is grievously overcharged; and I will turn over the possibilities. Come and see me on Wednesday. Mind me, now, if I do find anything, it will be no plum: that is the one thing I can promise you. But I bind myself in no way at all.'

Jack stood up and made his acknowledgments of his lordship's goodness in seeing him. Lord Melville observed, in an unofficial voice, 'I dare say we shall meet this evening at Lady Keith's: if I can find time, I shall look in.'

'I shall look forward to it extremely, my lord,' said Jack.

'Good day to you,' said Lord Melville, ringing a bell and looking eagerly at his inner door.

'You seem wery cheerful, sir,' said the porter, scanning Jack's face with ancient, red-rimmed eyes. Wery cheerful was an exaggeration; contained satisfaction was more the mark; but at all events it was nothing remotely like the expression of an officer with a flat refusal weighing on his heart.

'Why, Tom, so I am,' said Jack. 'I walked in from Hampstead this morning, as far as Seven Dials. There is nothing like a morning walk to set a man up.'

'Something copper-bottomed, sir?' asked Tom: no tales of morning walks would wash with him. He was old, knowing and familiar; he had known Jack before his first shave, just as he knew almost every other officer on the Navy List below the rank of admiral, and he had a right to a tip if something copper-bottomed turned up while he was on duty.

'Not – not exactly, Tom,' said Jack, looking keenly out through the hall and court to the sodden crowds passing up and down Whitehall – the chops of the Channel, full of shipping; and what cruisers, privateers, chasse-marées, lurking there among them? What unseen rocks? What bums? 'No. But I tell you what it is, Tom: I came out without a cloak and without any money. Just call me a coach and lend me half a guinea, will you?'

Tom had no opinion of sea-officers' powers of discrimination or management on shore; he was not surprised that Jack should have come out lacking the common necessities of life, and from his reading of Jack's expression he was of the opinion that something was on its way – the Fencibles alone would provide a dozen fresh appointments, even if he were not made post. He produced the little coin with a secret, conniving look, and summoned a coach.

Jack plunged into the coach with his hat pulled over his nose and sat huddled low in the corner, peering furtively through the muddy glasses – a curiously deformed, conspicuous figure that excited comment whenever the horse moved at less than a trot. 'An ill-looking parcel of bastards,' he reflected, seeing a bailiff in every full-grown man. 'But my God, what a life. Doing this every day, cooped up with a ledger – what a life.' The cheerless faces went by, hurrying to their dismal work, an endless wet, anxious, cold, grey-yellow stream of people, jostling, pushing past one another like an ugly dream, with here and there a pretty shop-girl or servant to make it more heart-rendingly pathetic.

A convoy of hay-wains came down the Hampstead Road, led by countrymen with long whips. The whips, the drivers' smocks, the horses' tails and manes were trimmed with ribbons, and the men's broad faces shone red, effulgent through the gloom. From Jack's remote and ineffectual schooldays sprang a tag: *O fortunatos nimium, sua si bona norint, agricolas*. 'Come, that is pretty good. How I wish Stephen had been by, to hear it. However, I shall flash it out at him presently.' There would be plenty of opportunity, since they were to travel down the same road that evening to Queenie's rout, and with any luck they would see some agricolas among that pitiable throng.

'Will you tell me about your interview, now?' said Stephen, pushing his report aside and looking into Jack's face with as much attention as the aged porter.

'It was not so bad. Now I have had time to turn it over in my mind, it was not so bad at all. I think they may promote me or give me a ship: one or the other. If they make me post, there is always the possibility of a post-ship in time, and of acting commands; and if they give me a sloop, why, there I am.'

'What are acting commands?'

'When a post-captain is sick, or wants to go ashore for a while – it often happens when they are peers or members of parliament – another post-captain on half-pay is appointed to his ship for the time being. Shall I tell you about it from the beginning?'

'If you please.'

'It started charmingly. The First Lord said he was happy to see me. No First Lord had ever been happy to see me before, or at least he had always managed to contain it – is there any coffee left in that pot, Stephen?'

'There is not. But you may have some beer presently; it is nearly two o'clock.'

'Well, it began charmingly, but then it took the ugliest vile turn imaginable; he made a sad mouth and said it was a pity I had come so late – *he would have liked to do something for me*. Then he made my heart die within me by prating about the Fencibles and the Impress Service and I knew that somehow I must head him off before he made a direct offer.'

'Why?'

'Oh, it would never do to refuse. If you turn down a ship because she don't suit – because she's on the West Indies station, say, and you don't care for the yellow Jack –

154

it is a black mark against you: you may never be employed again. They don't like you to pick and choose. The good of the service must come first, they say: and they are perfectly in the right of it. Then again, I could not tell him I hated both the Fencibles and the press and that in any event I could accept neither without being laid by the heels.'

'So you evaded the proposal?'

'Yes. Dropping my claim to be made post, I told him anything that would float would do for me. I did not drop it in so many words, but he took the point at once, and after some humming and hawing he spoke of *some remote possibility* next week. And he would consider the matter of promotion. I am not to think him in any way committed, but am to call again next week. From a man like Lord Melville I regard that as pretty strong.'

'So do I, my dear,' said Stephen, with as much conviction as he could put into his voice – a good deal of conviction, for he had had dealings with the gentleman in question, who had been in command of the secret funds these many years past. 'So do I. Let us eat, drink and be merry. There are sausages in the scrutoire; there is beer in the green jug. I shall regale myself on toasted cheese.'

The French privateers had taken away his Bréguet watch, as well as most of his clothes, instruments and books, but his stomach was as exact as any timepiece, and as they sat themselves at the little table by the fire, so the church clock told the hour. The crew of the swift-sailing *Bellone* had also taken away the money he had brought from Spain – that had been their first, most anxious care – and since landing at Plymouth he and Jack had been living on the proceeds of one small bill, laboriously negotiated by General Aubrey while their horses waited, and on the hopes of discounting another, drawn on a Barcelona merchant named Mendoza, little known on the London 'change.

At present they were lodging in an idyllic cottage near the Heath with green shutters and a honeysuckle over the door – idyllic in summer, that is to say. They were looking after themselves, living with rigid economy; and there was no greater proof of their friendship than the way their harmony withstood their very grave differences in domestic behaviour. In Jack's opinion Stephen was little better than a slut: his papers, odd bits of dry, garlic'd bread, his razors and small-clothes lay on and about his private table in a miserable squalor; and from the appearance of the grizzled wig that was now acting as a tea-cosy for his milk-saucepan, it was clear that he had breakfasted on marmalade.

Jack took off his coat, covered his waistcoat and breeches with an apron, and carried the dishes into the scullery. 'My plate and saucer will serve again,' said Stephen. 'I have blown upon them. I do wish, Jack,' he cried, 'that you would leave that milk-saucepan alone. It is perfectly clean. What more sanitary, what more wholesome, than scalded milk? Will I dry up?' he called through the open door.

'No, no,' cried Jack, who had seen him do so. 'There is no room – it is nearly done. Just attend to the fire, will you?'

'We might have some music,' said Stephen. 'Your friend's piano is in tolerable tune, and I have found a German flute. What are you doing now?'

'Swabbing out the galley. Give me five minutes, and I am your man.'

'It sounds more like Noah's flood. This peevish attention to cleanliness, Jack, this busy preoccupation with dirt,' said Stephen, shaking his head at the fire, 'has something of the Brahminical superstition about it. It is not very far removed from nastiness, Jack – from cacothymia.'

'I am concerned to hear it,' said Jack. 'Pray, is it catching?' he added, with a private but sweet-natured leer. 'Now, sir,' – appearing in the doorway with the apron rolled under his arm – 'where is your flute? What shall we play?' He sat at the little square piano and ran his fingers up and down, singing,

and don't they wish they may have it? Gibraltar, I mean.'
He went on from one tune to another in an abstracted strumming while Stephen slowly screwed the flute together;
and eventually from this strumming there emerged the
adagio of the Hummel sonata.

'Is it modesty that makes him play like this?' wondered
Stephen, worrying at a crossed thread. 'I could swear
he knows what music is – prizes high music beyond
almost anything. But here he is, playing this as sweetly
as milk, like an anecdote: Jesus, Mary and Joseph. And
the inversion will be worse . . . It is worse – a sentimental
indulgence. He takes pains; he is full of good-will and
industry; and yet he cannot make even his fiddle utter
anything but platitudes, except by mistake. On the piano
it is worse, the notes being true. You would say it was a
girl playing, a sixteen-stone girl. His face is not set in an
expression of sentimentality, however, but of suffering. He
is suffering extremely, I am afraid. This playing is very like
Sophia's. Is he aware of it? Is he consciously imitating her?
I do not know: their styles are much the same in any case
– their absence of style. Perhaps it is diffidence, a feeling
that *they* may not go beyond certain modest limits. They
are much alike. And since Jack, knowing what real music
is, can play like a simpleton, may not Sophia, playing like
a ninny-hammer . . . ? Perhaps I misjudge her. Perhaps it
is a case of the man filled with true poetic feeling who can
only come out with ye flowery meads again – the channels
blocked. Dear me, he is sadly moved. How I hope those
tears will not fall. He is the best of creatures – I love him
dearly – but he is an Englishman, no more – emotional,
lachrymose. Jack, Jack!' he called out. 'You have mistook
the second variation.'

'What? What?' cried passionately. 'Why do you break
in upon me, Stephen?'

'Listen. This is how it goes,' said Stephen, leaning over him and playing.

'No it ain't,' cried Jack. 'I had it right.' He took a turn up and down the room, filling it with his massive form, far larger now with emotion. He looked strangely at Stephen, but after another turn or two he smiled and said, 'Come, let's improvise, as we used to do off Crete. What tune shall we start with?'

'Do you know St Patrick's Day?'

'How does it go?' Stephen played. 'Oh, that? Of course I know it: we call it Bacon and Greens.'

'I must decline to improve on Bacon and Greens. Let us start with Hosier's Ghost, and see where we get to.'

The music wove in and out, one ballad and its variations leading to another, the piano handing it to the flute and back again; and sometimes they sang as well, the forecastle songs they had heard so often at sea.

Come all you brave seamen that ploughs on the main
Give ear to my story I'm true to maintain,
Concerning the Litchfield *that was cast away*
On the Barbary shore by the dawn of the day.

'The light is failing,' observed Stephen, taking his lips from the flute.

'On the Barbary shore by the dawn of the day,' sang Jack again. 'Oh, such a dying fall. So it is but the rain has let up, thank God,' he said, bending to the window. 'The wind has veered into the east – a little north to east. We shall have a dry walk.'

'Where are we going?'

'To Queenie's rout, of course. To Lady Keith's.' Stephen looked doubtfully at his sleeve. 'Your coat will do very well by candlelight,' said Jack. 'And even better when the middle button is sewn on. Just slip it off, will you, and hand along that hussif? I will make all fast while you put on a neckcloth and a pair of stockings

158

– silk stockings, mind. Queenie gave me this hussif when I first went to sea,' he observed, whipping the thread round the shank of the button and biting it off close to the stuff. 'Now let us set your wig to rights – a trifle of flour from the bread-bag as a bow to fashion – now let me brush your coat – splendid – fit for a levee, upon my word and honour.'

'Why are you putting on that blackguardly cloak?'

'By God,' cried Jack, laying his hand on Stephen's bosom. 'I never told you. One of the Miss Lambs wrote to her family – her letter is in the paper – I am mentioned by name – and that fornicating brute of an attorney will have his men out after me. I shall muffle myself up and slouch my hat, and perhaps we may stand ourselves a coach once we get well into the town.'

'Do you have to go? Is it worth running the risk of a sponging-house and the King's Bench for an evening's diversion?'

'Yes. Lord Melville will be there; and I must see Queenie. Even if I did not love her so, I have to keep all my naval interest in play – there will be the admiral and half a dozen other great men. Come. I can explain as we walk. The rout-cake there is famous, too – '

'I hear the squeaking of a pipistrelle! Hark! Stand still. There, there again! So late in the year; it is a prodigy.'

'Does it mean good luck?' asked Jack, cocking his ear for the sound. 'A capital omen, I dare say. But shall we go on now? Gather just a little headway, perhaps?'

They reached Upper Brook Street at the height of the flood – flambeaux, links, a tide of carriages waiting to set down at number three and a counter-current trying to reach number eight, where Mrs Damer was receiving her friends, a dense crowd on the pavements to see the guests and pass remarks upon their clothes, officious unnecessary barefoot boys opening doors or springing up behind, darting and hooting among the horses in a spirit of fun, wonderfully tedious to the anxious or despondent. Jack had meant to fly straight from the coach up the steps, but slow groups of fools, either coming on foot or abandoning their carriages at the corner of Grosvenor Square, clustered like summer bees in the entrance and blocked the way.

He sat there on the edge of his seat, watching for a gap. Arrest for debt was very common – he had always been aware of it – had had several friends carried off to sponging-houses, from which they wrote the most piteous appeals – but it had never happened to him personally and his knowledge of the process and of the law was vague. Sundays were safe, he was sure, and perhaps the King's birthday; he knew that peers could not be seized, that some places such as the Savoy and Whitefriars were sanctuaries, and he hoped that Lord Keith's house might therefore share these qualities: his longing eyes were fixed upon the open door, the lights within.

'Come on, governor,' cried the driver.

'Mind the step, your honour,' said a boy, holding the door.

'Come on, slow-arse,' shouted the coachman behind. 'You ain't going to plant a tree, are you?'

There was no help for it. Jack stepped out on to the pavement and stood by Stephen in the scarcely-moving throng, hitching his cloak even higher round his face.

'It's the Emperor of Morocco,' said a light brightly-painted whore.

'It's the Polish giant from Astley's.'

'Show us your face, sweetheart.'

'Hold your head up, cock.'

Some thought he was a foreigner, French dog of a Turk, others Old Moore, or Mother Shipton in disguise. He shuffled wretchedly towards the lighted doors, and when a hand clapped down on his shoulder he turned with a ferocity that pleased the crowd more than anything they had seen hitherto, except for Miss Rankin treading on her petticoat and coming down full length. 'Aubrey!

160

Jack Aubrey!' cried Dundas, his old shipmate Heneage Dundas. 'I recognized your back at once – should have recognized you anywhere. How do you do? You have a touch of fever, I dare say? Dr Maturin, how do you do? Are you going in here? So am I, ha, ha, ha. How do you get along?' Dundas had recently been made post into the *Franchise*, 36; he loved the world in general, and his cheerful, affectionate flow of talk carried them across the pavement, up the steps and into the hall.

The gathering had a strong naval flavour, but Lady Keith was also a political hostess and the friend of a great many interesting people: Jack left Stephen in conversation with a gentleman who had discovered the adamantine boron and moved through the great drawing-room, through the less crowded gallery and to a little domed room with a buffet in it: Constantia wine, little pies, rout-cakes, more Constantia. Here Lady Keith found him; she was leading a big man in a sky-blue coat with silver buttons and she said, 'Jack, dear, may I introduce Mr Canning? Captain Aubrey, of the Navy.'

Jack liked the look of this man at once, and during the first meaningless civilities this feeling grew: Canning was a broad-shouldered fellow, and although he was not quite so tall as Jack, his way of holding his small round head up and tilted back, with his chin in the air, made him look bigger, more commanding. He wore his own hair – what there was left of it: short tight curls round a shining calvity, though he was in his thirties, no more – and he looked like one of the fatter, more jovial Roman emperors; a humorous, good-natured face, but one that conveyed an impression of great latent strength. 'An ugly customer to have against you,' thought Jack, earnestly recommending 'one of these voluptuous little pies' and a glass of Constantia.

Mr Canning was a Bristol merchant. The news quite astonished Jack. He had never met a merchant before, out of the way of business. A few bankers and money-men, yes; and a poor thin bloodless set of creatures they seemed

– a lower order; but it was impossible to feel superior to Mr Canning. 'I am so particularly happy to be introduced to you, Captain Aubrey,' he said, quickly eating two more little pies, 'because I have known you by reputation for years and because I was reading about you in the paper only yesterday. I wrote you a letter to express my sense of your action with the *Cacafuego* back in '01, and I very nearly posted it: indeed I should have done so, with the least excuse of a nodding acquaintance or a common friend. But it would have been too great a liberty in a complete stranger, alas; and after all, what does my praise amount to? The mere noise of uninformed admiration.'

Jack made the noises of acknowledgment. 'Too kind – an excellent crew – the Spaniard was unlucky in his dispositions.'

'And yet not so wholly uninformed, neither,' went on Canning. 'I fitted out some privateers in the last war, and I took a cruise in one as far as Goree and in another to Bermuda, so I have at least some notion of the sea. No conceivable comparison, of course; but some slight notion of what such an action means.'

'Was you ever in the Service, sir?' asked Jack.

'I? Why, no. I am a Jew,' said Canning, with a look of deep amusement.

'Oh,' said Jack. 'Ah?' He turned, going through the motions of blowing his nose, saw Lord Melville looking at him from the doorway, bowed and called out 'Good evening.'

'And this war I have fitted out seven, with the eighth on the stocks. Now, sir, this brings me to the *Bellone*, of Bordeaux. She snapped up two of my merchantmen the moment war broke out again, and she took the *Nereid*, my heaviest privateer – eighteen twelve-pounders – the cruise before she took you and your Indiama. She is a splendid sailer, sir, is she not?'

'Prodigious, sir, prodigious. Close-hauled, with light airs, she ran away from the *Blanche* as easy as kiss my hand: and spilling her wind by way of a ruse, she still made six knots for *Blanche*'s four, though close-hauled is *Blanche*'s best point of sailing. Very well handled, too: her captain was a former King's officer.'

'Yes. Dumanoir – Dumanoir de Plessy. I have her draught,' said Canning, leaning over the buffet, fairly ablaze with overflowing life and enthusiasm, 'and I am building my eighth on her lines exactly.'

'Are you, by God!' cried Jack. Frigate-sized privateers were not uncommon in France, but they were unknown this side of the Channel.

'But with twenty-four-pounder carronades in place of her long guns, and eighteen-pounder chasers. Do you think she will bear 'em?'

'I should have to look at her draught,' said Jack, considering deeply. 'I believe she would, and to spare: but I should have to look at her draught.'

'But that is a detail,' said Canning, waving his hand. 'The real crux is the command. Everything depends on her commander, of course; and here I should value your advice and guidance beyond anything. I should do a great deal to come by the services of a bold, enterprising captain – a thorough-going seaman, of course. A letter-of-marque is not a King's ship, I admit; but I try to run mine in a way no King's officer would dislike – taut discipline, regularity, cleanliness. But no black lists, no hazing, and very little cat. You are no great believer in the cat, sir, I believe?'

'Not I,' said Jack. 'I find it don't answer the purpose, with fighting-men.'

'Fighting-men: just so. That is another thing I can offer – prime fighting-men, prime seamen. They are mostly smugglers' crews, west-countrymen, born to the sea and up to anything: I have more volunteers than I can find room for; I can pick and choose; and those I choose will follow the right man anywhere, put up with all reasonable discipline and behave like lambs. A right privateer's man is

163

no blackguard when he is led by the right captain. I believe I am right there, sir?'

'I dare say you are, sir,' said Jack slowly.

'And to get the right commander I offer a post-captain's pay and allowances for a seventy-four and I guarantee a thousand a year in prize-money. Not one of my captains has made less, and this new ship will certainly do very much better; she will be more than twice the burden of the others and she will have between two and three hundred men aboard. For when you consider, sir, that a private ship of war spends no time blockading, running messages or carrying troops, but only destroying the enemy's commerce, and when you consider that this frigate can cruise for six months at a time, why, the potentialities are enormous . . . enormous.' Jack nodded: they were, indeed. 'But where can I find my commander?' asked Canning.

'Where did you find your others?'

'They were local men. Excellent, in their way, but they govern smallish crews, relatives, acquaintances, men they have sailed with. This is another problem entirely; it calls for a bigger man, a man on another scale. Might I beg for your advice, Captain Aubrey? Can you think of any man, any former shipmate of yours, perhaps, or . . . ? I should give him a free hand, and I should back him to the hilt.'

'I should have to consider of it,' said Jack.

'Pray do, pray do,' said Canning. No less than a dozen people came up to the buffet at once, and private conversation was at an end. Canning gave Jack his card, pencilling an address upon it, and said in a low tone, 'I shall be here all the week. A word from you, at any time, and I shall be most grateful for a meeting.'

They parted – indeed they were driven apart – and Jack backed until he was brought up by the window. The offer had been as direct as it could be in decency, to a serving officer: he liked Canning, had rarely taken to any man with such immediate sympathy at first sight. He must be most uncommon rich to fit out a six or seven hundred ton letter-of-marque: a huge investment for a private man. Yet Jack's reflection was one of wonder alone, not of doubt – there was not the least question of Canning's honesty in his mind.

'Come, Jack, come, come,' said Lady Keith, tugging his arm. 'Where are your manners? You are behaving like a bear.'

'Dear Queenie,' said he, with a great slow smile, 'forgive me. I am bemused. Your friend Canning wants to make my fortune. He *is* your friend?'

'Yes. His father taught me Hebrew – good evening, Miss Sibyl – such a very wealthy young man, so enterprising. He has a vast admiration for you.'

'That shows a proper candour. Does he speak Hebrew, Queenie?'

'Oh, just enough for his bar mitzvah, you know. He is about as much of a scholar as you are, Jack. He has many friends in the Prince of Wales's set, but don't let that put you off – he is not a flash cove. Come into the gallery.'

'Bar mitzvah,' said Jack, in a grave voice, following her into the crowded gallery; and there, momentarily framed by four men in black coats, he saw the familiar red face of Mrs Williams. She was sitting by the fireplace, looking hot and overdressed, and Cecilia sat next to her: for a moment he could not place them in this context; they belonged to another world and time, another reality. There was no empty place beside them, no vacant chair. As Lady Keith led him up to them she murmured something about Sophia; but her discretion swallowed up her meaning.

'Have you come back to England, Captain Aubrey?' said Mrs Williams, as he made his leg. 'Well, well, upon my word.'

'Where are your other girls?' asked Lady Keith, glancing about.

'I was obliged to leave them at home, your ladyship. Frankie has such a feverish cold, and Sophie has stayed to take care of her.'

'She did not know you would be here,' whispered Cecilia.

'Jack,' said Lady Keith, 'I believe Lord Melville is throwing out a signal. He wants to speak with you.'

'The First Lord?' cried Mrs Williams, half rising in her seat and craning. 'Where? Where? Which is he?'

'The gentleman with the star,' said Lady Keith.

'Just a word, Aubrey,' said Lord Melville, 'and then I must be off. Can you come to see me tomorrow instead of next week? It does not throw you out? Good night to you, then – I am obliged to you, Lady Keith,' he called, kissing his hand and waving it, 'your must humble, devoted . . . '

Jack's face and eyes, as he turned back to the ladies, had a fine glow, a hint of the rising sun. By the law of social metaphysics some of the great man's star had rubbed off on him, as well as a little of young Canning's easy opulence. He felt that he was in command of the situation, of any situation, in spite of the wolves outside the door: his calmness surprised him. What were his feelings beneath this strong bubbling cheerfulness? He could not make it out. So much had happened these last few days – his old cloak still smelt of powder – and indeed was still happening, that he could not make them out. Sometimes you receive a knock in action: it may be your death-wound or just a scratch, a graze – you cannot tell at once. He gave up the attempt and turned his full attention to Mrs Williams, inwardly remarking that the Mrs Williams of Sussex and even of Bath was a different animal from the Mrs Williams in a great London drawing-room; she looked provincial and dowdy; and so, it must be admitted, did Cecilia, with her fussy ornaments and frizzled hair – though indeed she was a good-natured child. Mrs Williams was obscurely aware of this; she looked stupid, uncertain, and almost respectful, though he felt that resentment might not be far away. Having observed how affable Lord Melville was, very much the gentleman, she told Jack that they had read about his escape in the paper: she hoped his return meant that everything was well with him: but how came he to be in India? She had understood he had withdrawn to the Continent in consequence of some . . . to the *Continent*.

'So I did, ma'am. Maturin and I went to France, where that scoundrel Bonaparte very nearly laid us by the heels.'

'But you came home in an Indiaman. I saw it in the papers – in *The Times*.'

'Yes. She touched at Gibraltar.'

'Ah. I see. So now the mystery is cleared up: I thought I should get to the bottom of it at last.'

'How is dear Dr Maturin?' asked Cecilia. 'I hope to see him.'

'Yes, how is the worthy Dr Maturin?' said her mother.

'He is very well, I thank you. He was in the far room some moments ago, talking to the Physician of the Fleet. What a splendid fellow he is: he nursed me through a most devilish fever I caught in the mountains, and dosed me twice a day until we reached Gibraltar. Nothing else would have brought me home.'

'Mountains – Spain,' said Mrs Williams with strong disapproval. 'You will never get *me* there, I can tell you.'

'So you travelled right down through Spain,' said Cecilia. 'I dare say it was prodigiously romantic, with ruins, and monks?'

'There were some ruins and monks, to be sure,' said Jack, smiling at her. 'And hermits too. But the most romantic thing I saw was the Rock, rearing up there at the end of our road like a lion. That, and the orange-tree in Stephen's castle.'

'A castle in Spain!' cried Cecilia, clasping her hands.

'Castle!' cried Mrs Williams. 'Nonsense. Captain Aubrey means some cottage with a whimsical name, my love.'

'No, ma'am. A castle, with towers, battlements, and all that is proper. A marble roof, too. The only whimsical thing about it was the bath, which stood just off a spiral staircase, as bald as an egg: it was marble too, carved out of a single block – amazing. But this orange-tree was in a court with arches all round, a kind of cloister, and it bore oranges, lemons, and tangerines all at the same time! Green fruit, ripe fruit, and flowers, all at the same time and such a scent. There's romance for you! Not many oranges when I was there, but lemons fresh every day. I must have eaten – '

'Am I to understand that Dr Maturin is a man of property?' cried Mrs Williams.

'Certainly you are, ma'am. A thumping great estate up where we crossed the mountains – merino sheep – '

'Merino sheep,' said Mrs Williams, nodding, for she knew the beasts existed – what else could yield merino wool?

' – but his main place is down towards Lérida. By the way, I have not inquired for Mrs Villiers: how rude of me. I hope she is well?'

'Yes, yes – she is here,' – dismissing Diana – 'But I thought he was only a naval surgeon.'

'Did you indeed, ma'am? However, he is a man of considerable estate: a physician, too – they think the world of him in – '

'Then how did he come to be your surgeon?' she asked, in a sudden last burst of suspicion.

'What easier way of seeing the world? Airy, commodious, and *paid for by the King*.' This was utterly conclusive. Mrs Williams relapsed into silence for some moments. She had heard of castles in Spain, but she could not remember whether they were good or bad: they were certainly one or the other. Probably good, seeing that Lord Melville was so affable. Oh yes, very good – certainly very good.

'I hope he will call – I hope you will both call,' she said at last. 'We are staying with my sister Pratt in George Street. Number eleven.'

Jack was most grateful; unhappily official business –

he could not call his time his own – but he was sure Dr Maturin would be delighted; and he begged he might be particularly remembered to Miss Williams and Miss Frances.

'You may have heard, of course, that my Sophie is – ' began Mrs Williams, launched upon the precautionary lie, then regretting it and not knowing how to come off handsomely, ' – that Sophie is, how shall I say – though there is nothing official.'

'There's Di,' whispered Cecilia, poking Jack with her elbow.

She was walking slowly into the gallery between two men, both tall: a dark blue dress, a black velvet band around her throat, splendid white bosom. He had forgotten that her hair was black, *black*, her neck a column and her eyes mere dark smudges in the distance. His feelings needed no analysis: his heart, which had stopped while he searched for the empty place by Mrs Williams, now beat to quarters: a constellation, a galaxy of erotic notions raced through his mind, together with an unmixed pleasure in looking at her. How well-bred she looked! She did not seem pleased, however; she turned her head from the man on her right with a lift of her chin that he knew only too well.

'The gentleman she is walking with is Colonel Colpoys, Admiral Haddock's brother-in-law, from India. Diana is staying with Mrs Colonel Colpoys in Bruton Street. A pokey, inconvenient little house.'

'How beautiful he is,' murmured Cecilia.

'Colonel Colpoys?' cried Mrs Williams.

'No, Mama, the gentleman in the blue coat.'

'Oh, no, my love,' – lowering her voice, speaking behind her hand and staring hard at Canning – 'that gentleman is a jay ee double-u.'

'So he is not beautiful, Mama?'

'Of course not, my dear' – as to an idiot – 'I have just told you he is a' – lowering her voice again – 'jay

169

ee double-u,' pursing her lips and nodding her head with great satisfaction.

'Oh,' said Cecilia, disappointed. 'Well, all I can say,' she muttered to herself, 'is, I wish I had beaux like that following me around. He has been by her all the evening, almost. Men are always following Di around. There is another one.'

The other one, an army officer, was hurrying through the press with a tall thin glass of champagne, bearing it towards her with both hands as though it were a holy object; but before he could urge a fat, staring woman out of his way, Stephen Maturin appeared. Diana's face changed at once – a look of straightforward, almost boyish delight – and as he came up she gave him both hands, crying, 'Oh, Maturin, how very glad I am to see you! Welcome home.'

The soldier, Canning and Jack were watching intently; they saw nothing to give them uneasiness; the delicate pink flush in Diana's face, reaching her ears, was that of spontaneous open uncomplicated pleasure; Maturin's unaltered pallor, his somewhat absent expression, matched her directness. Furthermore, he was looking uncommonly plain – rusty, neglected, undarned.

Jack relaxed in his chair: he had got it wrong, he thought, with a warm and lively pleasure in his mistake: he often got things wrong. He had set up for penetration, and he had got it wrong.

'You are not attending,' said Cecilia. 'You are so busy quizzing the gentleman in blue, that you are not attending. Mama says they mean to go and look at the Magdalene. That is what Dr Maturin is pointing at.'

'Yes? Oh, yes. Certainly. A Guido, I believe?'

'No, sir,' said Mrs Williams, who understood these things better than other people. 'It is an oil painting, a very valuable oil painting, though not quite in the modern taste.'

'Mama, may I run after Dr Maturin and go with them?' asked Cecilia.

'Do, my love, and tell Dr Maturin to come and see me. No, Captain Aubrey, do not get up: you shall tell me about your Spanish journey. There is nothing that interests me more than travel, I declare; and if I had had my health I should have been a great traveller, a second – a second – '

'St Paul?'

'No, no. A second Lady Mary Wortley Montagu. Now tell me about Dr Maturin's establishment.'

Jack could not tell her very much; he had been unwell, delirious at times, and he did not attend to the kind of leases they had in those parts, or the return on capital – Mrs Williams sighed – had not seen the rent-roll, but supposed the estate was 'pretty big' – it took in a good deal of Aragon, as well as Catalonia; it had its drawbacks, however, being sadly infested by porcupines; they were hunted by a pack of pure-bred porcupine-hounds, often by moonlight, the field carrying Cordova-leather umbrellas against the darting of their quills.

'You gentlemen are always so taken up with your sporting, when a little attention to rack-rents and fines and enclosures – I am enclosing Mapes Common – ah, here comes the dear Doctor.'

Stephen's face rarely betrayed much emotion, but her effusive welcome made him stretch his eyes: her first question set him right, however, 'So I hear that you have a marble bath, Dr Maturin? That must be a great comfort to you, in such a climate.'

'Certainly, ma'am. I conceive it to be Visigothic.'

'Not marble?'

'Visigothic marble, my dear madam, from a baptistery destroyed by the Moors.'

'And you have a castle?'

'Oh, it is only a small place. I keep one wing in order, to go up there from time to time.'

'For the porcupine-hunting, no doubt?'

Stephen bowed. 'And for my rents, ma'am. In some

ways Spain is a more direct country than England, and when we say rack-rent in those parts, rack-rent is what we mean – why, we make them pay for the use of the instrument.'

Jack found Diana at the buffet where he had had his conversation with Canning: Canning was no longer with her, but his place had been taken by two more soldiers. She did not give Jack both hands, because one was holding a glass and the other a piece of cake, but her greeting was as gay, cheerful and undisguised as it had been for Stephen: even warmer, perhaps, for she moved away from the group to talk with him – a hundred quick, attentive inquiries – and she said 'How we have missed you at Mapes, Aubrey; how I have missed you! A pack of women mewed up together, bottling gooseberries, God help us. There is that odious Mr Dawkins bearing down. We will go and look at Lady Keith's new picture. Here it is. What do you think of her?'

It was clear that the Magdalene had not yet repented: she was standing on a quay with blue ruins in the background – a blue that swept with varying intensities through her robe to the sea – with gold plates, ewers and basins heaped up on a crimson cloth, and an expression of mild complacency on her face. Her blue dress had blown off – a fresh double-reef topsail breeze – and so had a filmy white garment, exposing handsome limbs and a firm, though opulent bosom. Jack had been a long time at sea, and this drew his attention; however, he shifted his gaze after a moment, surveyed the rest of the picture and sought for something appropriate, perhaps even witty, to say. He longed to produce a subtle and ingenious remark, but he longed in vain – perhaps the day had been too full – and he was obliged to fall back on 'Very fine – such a blue.' Then a small vessel in the lower left-hand corner caught his eye, something in the nature of a pink; she was beating up for the harbour, but it was obvious from the direction of the lady's clothes that the pink would be taken aback the moment she rounded the headland. 'As soon as she catches the land-breeze she will be in trouble,' he said. 'She will never stay, not with those unhandy lateens, and there is no room to wear; so there she is on a lee-shore. Poor fellows. I am afraid there is no hope for them.'

'That is exactly what Maturin told me you would say,' cried Diana, squeezing his arm. 'How well he knows you, Aubrey.'

'Well, a man don't have to be a Nostradamus to tell what a sailor will say, when he sees an infernal tub like that laid by the lee. But Stephen is a very deep old file, to be sure,' he added, his good humour returning. 'And a great cognoscento, I make no doubt. For my part I know nothing about painting at all.'

'Nor do I,' said Diana, staring up at the picture. 'She seems to be making a very good thing of it,' – with a chuckle – 'No lack of admirers. Come, let us see if we can find an ice: I am dying of heat and general distress.'

'Look at the outré way Diana has dragged up her hair,' said Mrs Williams as they passed by towards the great drawing-room. 'It is bound to attract attention. It would do Sophie good, to see her walking about like that, as bold as brass, with poor Captain Aubrey. She has positively taken his arm, I protest.'

'Tell me,' said Diana, 'What are your plans? Are you back for good? Shall we see something of you in Sussex?'

'I am not sure,' said Jack. 'Do you see that man saying good-bye to Lady Keith? But you know him – he was talking to you just now. Canning.'

'Yes?'

'He has offered me the command of a – of a letter-of-marque, a private man of war, a thirty-two gun frigate.'

'Oh, Aubrey, how splendid! A privateer is just the thing for you – Have I said something wrong?'

'No. No, not at all – good evening, sir: that was Admiral Bridges – No, it was just the word privateer. But as

Stephen is always telling me, one must not be the prisoner of words.'

'Of course not. Besides, what does it signify? It is just like taking service with the native princes in India: nobody thinks any the less of you and everybody envies the fortune you make. Oh, how well it would suit you – your own master, no fagging up and down to Whitehall, no admirals to make you do tiresome things and snatch great lumps of your prize-money. A perfect idea for a man like you – for a man of spirit. An independent command! A thirty-two gun frigate!'

'It is a magnificent offer: I am in a maze.'

'And in partnership with Canning! I am sure you would get on famously. My cousin Jersey knows him. The Cannings are absurdly rich, and he is very like a native prince; only he is straightforward and brave, which they are not, on the whole.' Her eager face changed, and looking round Jack saw an elderly man standing by him. 'My dear,' said the elderly man, 'Charlotte sends me to tell you she is thinking of going home presently; we have to drop Charles at the Tower before twelve.'

'I shall come at once,' said Diana.

'No, no, you have plenty of time to finish your ice.'

'Have I, truly? May I introduce Captain Aubrey, of the Navy, Admiral Haddock's neighbour? Colonel Colpoys, who is so sweetly kind as to have me to stay.'

Very small talk for a moment, and the colonel went away to see to his horses.

'When shall I see you again? Will you call at Bruton Street tomorrow morning? I shall be alone. You may take me into the park, and to look at the shops.'

'Diana,' said Jack in a low voice, 'there is a writ out against me. I dare not walk about London.'

'You dare not? You are afraid of being arrested?' Jack nodded. 'Afraid? Upon my word, I never expected to hear that from you. What do you think I introduced you for? It was so you might call.'

'Besides, I am under orders for the Admiralty tomorrow.'

'How unfortunate,' said Diana.

'May I come on Sunday?'

'No, sir, you may not. I do not ask men to come to see me so often . . . No, you must certainly consult your safety: of course you must consult your safety. In any case, I shall no longer be in town.'

'Mr Wells's carriage; Sir John Bridges's carriage; Colonel Colpoys's carriage,' cried a footman.

'Major Lennox,' said Diana, as one of her soldiers went by, 'please be very kind and find me my cloak, will you? I must say good-bye to Lady Keith and my aunt,' she observed to herself, gathering her fan and gloves.

Jack followed the procession of Colonel and Mrs Colpoys, Diana Villiers, the unknown Charles, Lennox and Stephen Maturin, and stood bare-headed, exposed on that brightly-lit pavement while the carriages made their slow way down from the mews: no word, however – not so much as a look. At last the women were handed in and stowed away, the carriage moved off, and Jack walked slowly back into the house with Stephen Maturin.

They went up the broad stairs, making their way against the increasing current of guests who had taken their leave; their conversation was fragmentary and unimportant – a few general remarks – but by the time they had reached the top each knew that their harmony was no longer what it had been these last few months.

'I shall make my farewells,' said Stephen, 'and then I believe I shall walk down to the Physical Society. You will stay a little longer with your friends, I imagine? I do beg you to take a coach from the very door itself and to ride all the way home. Here is the common purse. If you are to see the First Lord in the morning, your mind must be in a condition of easy complaisance, in a placid, rested state. There is milk in the little crock – warmed milk will relax the fibres.'

Jack warmed it, added a dash of rum from his case-bottle, and drank it up; but in spite of his faith in the draught, the fibres remained tense, the placidity of mind a great way off.

Writing a note to tell Stephen that he would be back presently and leaving the candle burning, he walked out on to the Heath. Enough moonlight filtered through the murk to show him his path, pale among the scattered trees; he went fast, and soon he had walked himself into his second wind and a steady rhythm. Into a muck-sweat, too: the cloak became unbearably hot. Steadily on, with the cloak rolled tight under his arm, up hill, down to some ponds, and up again. He almost trod on a courting couple – hard pressed, to lie in such a dismal plash and at such a time – and turned away right-handed, leaving the remote glow of London behind him.

This was the first time in his life he had ever refused a direct challenge. He could hear the whining reasonability of his 'there is a writ out against me' and he blushed in the darkness – pitiful. But how could she have asked him to do such a thing? How could she ask so much? He thought of her with cold hostility. No friend would have done so. She was no fool, no inexperienced girl: she knew what he was risking.

Contempt was very hard to bear. In his place she would have come, bailiffs or no bailiffs; he was sure of that. The Admiralty had sounded a snivelling excuse.

What if he chanced it and appeared at Bruton Street in the morning? If he were to accept the privateer, the appointment in Whitehall would be meaningless. He had been shabbily treated there, more shabbily than any man he could remember, and there was no likelihood, no possibility that tomorrow's meeting would put things right. At the best some unacceptable shore-based post that would salve the First Lord's conscience, that would allow him to say 'We offered him employment, but he did not see fit to accept it.' Conceivably some hulk or storeship; but at

176

all events Lord Melville was not going to make him post and offer him a frigate, the only thing that would do away with the injustice, the only thing that could find him by a sense of proper usage. The recollection of the way he had been treated rose hotter and hotter in his mind: a wretched mean-spirited disingenuous shuffling, and men without a tenth part of his claim being promoted over his head by the dozen. His recommendations ignored, his midshipmen left on the beach.

With Canning as his First Lord, secretary and Board of Admiralty all in one, how different it would be! A well-found ship, a full crew of prime seamen, a free hand, and all the oceans of the world before him – the West Indies for quick returns, the cherished cruising-grounds of the Channel fleet, and if Spain were to come in (which was almost certain), the Mediterranean sea-lanes he knew so well. But even more, far beyond the common range of cruisers and private ships of war, the Mozambique Channel, the approaches to the Isle of France, the Indian Ocean; and eastwards still, the Spice Islands and the Spanish Philippines. South of the Line, right down to the Cape and beyond, there were still French and Dutch Indiamen coming home. And if he were to stretch away on the monsoon, there was Manila under his lee, and the Spanish treasure ships. Even without flying so high, one moderate prize in those latitudes would clear his debts; a second would set him on his feet again; and it would be strange if he could not make two prizes in an almost virgin sea.

The name of Sophia moved insistently up into that part of his mind where words took form. He had repressed it as far as he was able ever since he ran for France. He was not a marriageable man: Sophie was as far out of his reach as an admiral's flag.

She would never have done this to him. In a fit of self-indulgence he imagined that same evening with Sophie – her extraordinary grace of movement, quite different from Diana's quickness, the sweet gentleness with which she would have looked at him – that infinitely touching desire to protect. How would he have stood it in fact, if he had seen Sophie there next to her mother? Would he have turned tail and skulked in the far room until he could make his escape? How would she have behaved?

'Christ,' he said aloud, the new thought striking him with horror, 'what if I had seen them both together?' He dwelt on this possibility for a while, and to get rid of the very unpleasant image of himself, with Sophie's gentle, questioning eyes looking straight at him and wondering, 'Can this scrub be Jack Aubrey?' he turned left and left again, walking fast over the bare Heath until he struck into his first path, where a scattering of birches showed ghastly white in the drizzle. It occurred to him that he should put some order into his thoughts about these two. Yet there was something so very odious, so very grossly indecent, in making any sort of comparison, in weighing up, setting side by side, evaluating. Stephen blamed him for being muddle-headed, wantonly muddle-headed, refusing to follow his ideas to their logical conclusion. 'You have all the English vices, my dear, including muddle-headed sentiment and hypocrisy.' Yet it was nonsense to drag in logic where logic did not apply. To think clearly in such a case was inexpressibly repugnant: logic could apply only to a deliberate seduction or to a marriage of interest.

Taking his bearings, however, was something else again: he had never attempted to do so yet, nor to find out the deep nature of his present feelings. He had a profound distrust for this sort of exercise, but now it was important – it was of the first importance.

'Your money or your life,' said a voice very close at hand.

'What? What? What did you say?'

The man stepped from behind the trees, the rain glinting on his weapon. 'I said, "Your money or your life," ' he said, and coughed.

Instantly the cloak in his face. Jack had him by the

shirt, worrying him, shaking him with terrible vehemence, jerking him high off the ground. The shirt gave way: he stood staggering, his arms out. Jack hit him a great left-handed blow on the ear and kicked his legs from under him as he fell.

He snatched up the cudgel and stood over him, breathing hard and waving his left hand – knuckles split: a damned unhandy blow – it had been like hitting a tree. He was filled with indignation. 'Dog, dog, dog,' he said, watching for a movement. But there was no movement, and after a while Jack's teeth unclenched: he stirred the body with his foot. 'Come, sir. Up you get. Rise and shine.' After a few more orders of this sort, delivered pretty loud, he sat the fellow up and shook him. Head dangling, utterly limp; wet and cold; no breath, no heart-beat, very like a corpse. 'God damn his eyes,' said Jack, 'he's died on me.'

The increasing rain brought his cloak to mind; he found it, put it on, and stood over the body again. Poor wretched little brute – could not be more than seven or eight stone – and as incompetent a footpad as could be imagined – had been within a toucher of adding 'if you please' to his demand – no notion of attack. Was he dead? He was not: one hand scrabbled in vague, disordered motion.

Jack shivered: the heat of walking and of the brief strug-gle had worn off in this waiting pause, and he wrapped his cloak tighter; it was a raw night, with frost a certainty before dawn. More vain, irritated shaking, rough attempts at revival. 'Jesus, what a bore,' he said. At sea there would have been no problem, but here on land it was different – he had a different sense of tidiness ashore – and after a disgusted pause he wrapped the object in his cloak (not from any notion of humanity, but to keep the mud, blood and perhaps worse off his clothes), picked it up and walked off.

Seven stone odd was nothing much for the first hundred yards, nor the second; but the smell of his warmed burden grew unpleasant, and he was pleased to see that he was near the place he had entered the Heath, within sight of his own lit window.

'Stephen will soon set him right,' he thought: it was known that Stephen could raise the dead so long as the tide had not changed – had been seen to do it.

But there was no answer to his hail. The candle was low in its socket, with an unsnuffed mushroom of a wick; the fire was almost out; his note still stood propped against the milk jug. Jack put his footpad down, took the candle and looked at him. A grey, emaciated face: eyes almost closed, showing little crescents of white: stubble: blood over one half of it. A puny little narrow-chested cove, no good to man or beast. 'I had better leave him alone till Stephen comes,' he thought. 'I wonder whether there are any sausages left?'

Hours; the ticking of the clock; the quarter-chimes from the church; steady mending of the fire, staring at the flame; the fibres quite relaxed – a kind of placid happiness at last.

The first light brought Stephen. He paused in the doorway, looking attentively at the sleeping Jack and at the wild eyes of the footpad, lashed into a windsor chair.

'Good morning to you, sir,' he said, with a reserved nod.

'Good morning, sir. Oh sir, if you please – '

'Why, Stephen, there you are,' cried Jack. 'I was quite anxious for you.'

'Aye?' said Stephen, setting a cabbage-leaf parcel on the table and taking an egg from his pocket and a loaf from his bosom. 'I have brought a beef-steak to recruit you for your interview, and what passes for bread in these parts. I strongly urge you to take off your clothes, to sponge yourself all over – the copper will answer admirably – and to lie between sheets for an hour. Rested, shaved, coffee'd, steaked, you will be a different man. I urge the more strongly, because there is a louse crawling up your collar – pediculus vestimenti seeking promotion to p.

180

capitis – and where we *see* one, we may reasonably assume the hidden presence of a score.'

'Pah!' said Jack, flinging off his coat. 'This is what comes of carrying that lousy villain. Damn you, sir.'

'I am most deeply sorry, sir: most heartily ashamed,' said the footpad, hanging his head.

'You might take a look at him, Stephen,' said Jack. 'I gave him a thump on the head. I shall go and light the copper and then turn in. You will give me a call, Stephen?'

'A shrewd thump,' said Stephen, mopping and probing. 'A very shrewd thump, upon my word. Does this hurt?'

'No more than the rest, sir. It is benevolent in you to trouble with me . . . but, oh sir, if I might have the liberty of my hands? I itch unbearably.'

'I dare say you do,' said Stephen, taking the bread-knife to the knot. 'You are strangely infested. What are these marks? They are certainly older than last night.'

'Oh, no more than extravasated blood, sir, under your correction. I tried to take a purse over towards Highgate last week. A person with a wench, which seemed to give me a certain . . . however, he beat me cruelly, and threw me into a pond.'

'It may be that your talents do not altogether fit you for purse-taking: certainly your diet does not.'

'Yet it was my diet, or rather my want of diet, that drove me to the Heath. I have not eaten these five days.'

'Pray, have you had any success?' asked Stephen. He broke the egg into the milk, beat it up with sugar and the remaining drops of rum, and began to feed the footpad with a spoon.

'None, sir. Oh how I thank you: ambrosia. None, sir. A black-pudding snatched from a boy in Flask Lane was my greatest feat. Nectar. None, sir. Yet I am sure if a man threatened me with a cudgel in the dark and desired me to give him my purse, I should do so at once. But not my victims, sir; they either beat me, or they declare they have no purse, or they pay no attention and walk on while I cry "Stand and deliver" beside them, or they take to abusing me – why do I not work? Am I not ashamed? Perhaps I lack the presence, the resolution; perhaps if I could have afforded a pistol . . . Might I take the liberty of begging for a little bread, sir? A very little piece of bread? There is a tiger in my bowels, if not in my appearance.'

'You must masticate deliberately. What do you reply to their suggestions?'

'About work, sir? Why, that I should be very glad to have it, that I should do any work I could find: I am an industrious creature, sir. Might I beg for just another slice? I could have added, that it was work that had been my undoing.'

'Truly?'

'Would it be proper to give an account of myself, sir?'

'A brief account of your undoing would be quite proper.'

'I used to live in Holywell Street, sir; I was a literary man. There were a great many of us, brought up to no trade or calling, but with a smattering of education and money enough to buy pens and a quire of paper, who commenced author and set up in that part of town. It was surprising how many of us were bastards; my own father was said to have been a judge – indeed, he may well have been: someone sent me to school near Slough for a while. A few had some little originality – I believe I had a real turn for verse to begin with – but it was the lower slopes of Helicon, sir, the sort of author that writes *The Universal Directory for Taking Alive Rats* or *The Unhappy Birth, Wicked Life and Miserable End of that Deceitful Apostle, Judas Iscariot* and pamphlets, of course – *Thoughts of the Present Crisis*, by a Nobleman, or *A New Way of Funding the National Debt*. For my part, I took to translating for the book sellers.'

'From what language?'

'Oh, all languages, sir. If it was oriental or classical, there was sure to be a Frenchman there before

182

us; and as for Italian or Spanish, I could generally puzzle it out in the end. High Dutch, too: I was quite a proficient in the High Dutch by the time I had run through Fleischhacker's *Elegant Diversions* and Strumpff's *Nearest Way to Heaven*. I did tolerably well, sir, upon the whole, rarely going hungry or without a lodging, for I was neat, sober, punctual, and as I have said, industrious: I always kept my promised day, the printers could read my hand, and I corrected my proofs as soon as they came. But then a bookseller by the name of – but hush, I must name no names – Mr G sent for me and proposed Boursicot's *South Seas*. I was very happy to accept, for the market was slow, and I had had to live for a month on *The Case of the Druids impartially considered*, a little piece in the *Ladies' Repository*, and the druids did not run to more than bread and milk. We agreed for half a guinea a sheet; I dared not hold out for more, although it was printed very small, with all the notes set in pearl.'

'What might that mean in terms of weekly income?'

'Why, sir, taking the hard places with the smooth, and working twelve hours a day, it might have amounted to as much as five and twenty shillings! I was a cock-a-hoop, for next to the Abbé Prévost, Boursicot is the longest collection of voyages in French I know of, the longest work I had ever engaged in; and I thought I had my living for a great while ahead. My credit was good, so I moved downstairs to the two-pair front, a handsome room, for the sake of the light; I bought some furniture and several books that I should need – some very expensive dictionaries among them.'

'Did you require a dictionary for French, sir?'

'No, sir: I had one. These were Blanckley's *Naval Expositor* and Du Hamel, Aubin, and Saverien, to understand the hard words in the shipwrecks and manoeuvres, and to know what the travellers were about. I find it quite a help in translation to understand the text, sir; I always prefer it. So I worked away in my handsome room, refusing two or three offers from other booksellers and eating in a chop-house twice a week, until the day Mr G sent me his young man to say he had thought better of *my* project of translating Boursicot – that his associates felt the cost of the plate would be too high – and that in the present state of the trade there was no demand for such an article.'

'Did you have a contract?'

'No, sir. It was what the booksellers call a gentleman's agreement.'

'No hope, then?'

'None whatsoever, sir. I tried, of course, and was turned out of doors for my pains. He was angry with me for being ill-used, and he spread tales in the trade of my having grown saucy – the last thing a bookseller can bear in a hack. He even had a harmless little translation of mine abused in the *Literary Review*. I could get no more work. My goods were seized, and my creditors would have had my person too, if I were not so practised at giving them the slip.'

'You are acquainted with bailiffs, arrest for debt, the process of the law?'

'I know few things better, sir. I was born in a debtors' prison, and I have spent years in the Fleet and the Marshalsea. I wrote my *Elements of Agriculture* and my *Plan for the Education of the Young Nobility and Gentry* in the King's Bench.'

'Be so good as to give me a succinct account of the law as it at present stands.'

'Jack,' said Stephen, 'your watch is called.'

'Hey? Hey?' Jack had the sailor's knack of going instantly to sleep, snatching an hour's rest, and starting straight out of it; but this time he had been very far down, very far away, aboard a seventy-four off the Cape, swimming in a milk-warm phosphorescent sea, and for once he sat there on the side of his bed, looking stupid and bringing himself slowly into the present. Lord Melville, Queenie, Canning, Diana.

'What are you going to do with your prize?' asked Stephen.

'Eh? Oh, him. We ought to turn him over to the constable, I suppose.'

'They will hang him.'

'Yes, of course. It is the devil — you cannot have a fellow walking about taking purses; and yet you do not like to see him hang. Perhaps he may be transported.'

'I will give you twelve and sixpence for him.'

'Do you mean to dissect him already?' — Stephen often bought corpses warm from the gallows. 'And do you really possess twelve and sixpence at this moment? No, no, I'll not take your money — you shall have him as a present. I resign him to you. I smell coffee, toast!'

He sat there eating steak, his bright blue eyes protruding with the effort, and with thought and concentration. They were in fact trying to pierce the future, but they happened to be fixed on his captive, who sat mute with dread upon his chair, very secretly scratching and from time to time making little gestures of submission. One of these caught Jack's attention, and he frowned. 'You sir!' he cried in a strong sea-going voice that brought the poor man's heart to his mouth and stopped his searching hand. 'You, sir! You had better eat this and look sharp about it,' cutting an unctuous gobbet — 'I have sold you to the Doctor, so you must obey his orders now, or you will find yourself headed up in a cask and tossed overboard. Do you mind me, hey?'

'Yes, sir.'

'I must be away now, Stephen. We meet this afternoon?'

'My movements are uncertain: I may look into Seething Lane, though it is scarcely worth while until next week.'

The plunge into the Admiralty courtyard; the waiting-room, with half a dozen acquaintances — disconnected gossip, his mind and theirs being elsewhere; the staircase to the First Lord's room, and there, half-way up, a fat officer leaning against the rail, silent weeping, his slab, pale cheeks all wet with tears. A silent marine watched him from the landing, two porters from the hall, aghast.

Lord Melville had been disagreeably affected by his latest interview, that was plain. He had to collect himself and bring immediate business to mind, and for some moments he leafed through the papers on his desk. He said, 'I have just been treated to a display of emotion that has lowered the officer extremely in my opinion. I know that *you* prize fortitude, Captain Aubrey; that *you* are not shaken by disagreeable news.'

'I hope I can bear it, my lord.'

'For I must tell you that I cannot make you post for the *Cacafuego* action. I am bound by my predecessor's decision and I cannot create a precedent. A post-ship is therefore out of the question; and as for sloops, there are only eight-nine in commission, whereas we have four hundred-odd commanders on the list.' He let this sink in, and although there was nothing new about his information – Jack knew the figures by heart, just as he knew that Lord Melville was not being wholly candid, for there were also thirty-four sloops building as well as a dozen for harbour service and in ordinary – its repetition had a deadening effect. 'However,' he went on, 'the former administration also left us a project for an experimental vessel that I am prepared, in certain circumstances, to rate as a sloop rather than a post-ship, although she carries twenty-four thirty-two-pounder carronades. She was designed to carry a particular weapon, a secret weapon that we abandoned after trial, and we are having her completed for general purposes: we have therefore named her the *Polychrest*. Perhaps you would like to see her draught?'

'Very much indeed, my lord.'

'She is an interesting experiment,' he said, opening the portfolio, 'being intended to sail against wind and tide. The projector, Mr Eldon, was a most ingenious man, and he spent a fortune on his plans and models.'

An interesting experiment indeed: he had heard of her. She was known as the *Carpenter's Mistake*, and no one in the service had ever imagined she would be launched. How had she survived St Vincent's reforms? What extraordinary combination of interest had managed to get her off the stocks, let alone on to them? She had head and stern alike, two maintopsailyards, a false bottom, no hold, and sliding keels and rudders. The drawing showed that she was being built in a private yard at Portsmouth – Hickman's, of no savoury reputation.

'It is true that the *Polychrest* was primarily designed as a carrier for this weapon; but she was so far advanced that it would have been an unjustifiable waste to abandon her too; and with the modifications that you see here in green ink, the Board is of the opinion that she will be eminently serviceable in home waters. Her construction does not allow the carrying of stores for a cruise of any duration, but vessels of this size are always required in the Channel, and I have it in contemplation to attach the *Polychrest* to Admiral Harte's squadron in the Downs. For reasons that I shall not enter into, dispatch is called for. Her captain will be required to proceed to Portsmouth immediately, to hasten on her fitting-out, to commission her, and to take her to sea with the utmost expedition. Do you wish to be considered for the appointment, Captain Aubrey?'

The *Polychrest* was a theorizing landsman's vessel, she had been built by a gang of rogues and jobbers; she was to serve under a man he had cuckolded and who would be happy to see him ruined; Cannings's offer would never come again. Lord Melville was no fool, and he was aware of most of these things; he waited for Jack's reply with his head cocked and a considering eye, tapping his fingers on the desk; this was shabby treatment; the *Polychrest* had already been refused; and in spite of his effort with the rating, he would find it hard to justify himself with Lady

Keith – even his own conscience, well seared by years and years of office, gave an uneasy twitch.

'If you please, my lord: I should be most grateful.'

'Very good. Then let us make it so. No – no thanks, I beg,' he said, holding up his hand and looking Jack in the eye. 'This is no plum: I wish it were. But you have a broadside weight of metal greater than many a frigate. Given the opportunity, I am sure you will distinguish yourself, and the Board will be happy to make you post as soon as there is fresh occasion. Now as to officers and followers, I shall be glad to fall in with your wishes as far as possible. Your first lieutenant is already appointed: Mr Parker, recommended by the Duke of Clarence.'

'I should be happy to have my surgeon and Thomas Pullings, my lord, master's mate in the *Sophie*: he passed for lieutenant in '01.'

'You wish him to be made?'

'If you please, my lord.' It was a good deal to ask, and he might have to sacrifice the rest of his patronage; but as he felt the balance of this interview, he could risk it.

'Very well. What else?'

'If I might have two of the midshipmen, my lord?'

'Two? Yes . . . I think so. You mentioned your surgeon. Who was he?'

'Dr Maturin, my lord.'

'Dr Maturin?' said Lord Melville, looking up.

'Yes, my lord: you may have seen him at Lady Keith's. He is my particular friend.'

'Aye,' said Lord Melville, looking down. 'I mind him. Weel, Sir Evan will send you your orders by the messenger today. Or should you rather wait while they are writing out?'

A few hundred yards from the Admiralty, in St James's Park, Dr Maturin and Miss Williams paced the gravel by the ornamental pond. 'It never ceases to amaze me,' said

Stephen, 'when I see these ducks. Coots – any man can swallow coots, those deeply vulgar birds, and even the half-domesticated mallard. But the high-bred pintail, the scaup, the goldeneye! I have crept on my belly in the freezing bog to catch a glimpse of them a furlong off, only to see them lift and away before I had them in my glass; and yet here they are in the heart of a roaring modern city, swimming about as cool as you please, eating bread! Not taken, not pinioned, but straight in from the high northern latitudes! I am *amazed*.'

Sophia looked earnestly at the birds and said that she too found it truly astonishing. 'Poor coots,' she added, 'they always seem so cross. So that is the Admiralty?'

'Yes. And I dare say Jack knows his fate by now. He will be behind one of those tall windows on the left.'

'It is a noble building,' said Sophia. 'Perhaps we might see it a little closer to? To see it in its true proportions. Diana said he was looking quite thin, and not at all well. *Diminished*, was what she said.'

'He has aged, maybe,' said Stephen. 'But he still eats for six; and although I should no longer call him grossly obese, he is far too fat. I wish I could say the same for you, my dear.' Sophia had indeed grown thinner; it suited her in that it took away that last hint of childishness and brought out the hidden strength of her features; but at the same time her removed, mysterious, sleepy look had disappeared, and now she was a young woman wide awake – an adult. 'If you had seen him last night at Lady Keith's, you would not have worried. To be sure, he lost the rest of his ear in the Indiaman – but that was nothing.'

'His ear!' cried Sophia, turning white and coming to a dead halt in the middle of the Parade.

'You are standing in a puddle, my dear. Let me lead you to dry land. Yes, his ear, his right ear, or what there was left of it. But it was nothing. I sewed it on again; and as I say, if you had seen him last night, you would have been easy in your mind.'

'What a good friend you are to him, Dr Maturin. His other friends are so grateful to you.'

'I sew his ears on from time to time, sure.'

'What a providence it is that he has you by: I am afraid he sometimes hazards himself very thoughtlessly.'

'He does, too.'

'Yet I do not think I could have borne to see him. I was very unkind to him when last we met.' Her eyes filled with tears. 'It is dreadful to be unkind: one keeps remembering it.' Stephen looked at her with deep affection: she was a lovely creature, unhappy, with a line across that broad forehead; but he said nothing.

Clocks all over Westminster began to tell the hour, and Sophie cried, 'Oh, we are shockingly late. I promised Mama – she will be so anxious. Come, let us run.'

He gave her his arm and they hurried across the park, Stephen guiding her, for her eyes were dim with tears and every three steps she glanced over her shoulder to look at the windows of the Admiralty.

These windows, for the most part, belonged to the official apartments of the Lords Commissioners; those which sheltered Jack were on the far side of the building, so placed that he could see the courtyard. He was, in fact, in the waiting-room, where he had spent many an anxious, weary hour in the course of his career, and where he had now been waiting since his interview long enough to count a hundred and twenty-three men and two women walk in or out of the archway. A good many other officers shared the room with him, the company changing as the day wore on; but none of them were waiting, as he was waiting, with their appointment and their orders crackling in their bosoms – his was as strange a case of waiting as the porters had ever seen, and it excited their curiosity.

His was an absurd position. In one pocket he had this beautiful document requesting and requiring him to repair on board His Majesty's sloop *Polychrest*, and in the other a flaccid purse with a clipped groat in it and no more, all the rest having gone in customary presents. The *Polychrest* meant safety, or so he believed, and the Portsmouth mail left at eleven o'clock that night; but he would have to get from Whitehall to Lombard Street without being taken; he would have to traverse London, a conspicuous uniformed figure. In any case he must communicate with Stephen, who expected him at the cottage. Yet he dared not leave the Admiralty: if he were taken at this stage he would hang himself out of mere fury, and he had already had a most unpleasant fright when he was crossing the hall from the Secretary's office and a porter told him that 'a little cove in black and a scrub wig had been asking for him by name.'

'Send him about his business, will you? Is Tom here?'

'Oh, no, sir. Tom's not on duty till Sunday night. a shifty little cove in black, sir.'

For the last forty minutes he had seen this slight black vaguely legal figure crossing and recrossing the passage into Whitehall, peering into coaches as they stopped and even mounting on the step: once he had seen him talking with two burly great fellows, Irish chairmen or bailiff's men dressed as chairmen – a common disguise for bums.

Jack was not in good odour with the porters that day; he had not produced a shower of gold, not as who should say a shower; but they had a smell of the truth and they naturally took his part against the civil power. When one came in with fresh coals he quietly observed, 'Your little chap with the cauliflower ear is still hanging about outside the arch, sir.'

'Cauliflower ear' – had he heard that before how happy he would have been! He darted to the window, and after some minutes of peering he said, 'Be a good fellow and desire him to step into the hall. I will see him at once.'

Mr Scriven, the literary man, came across the court-yard; he was looking old and tired; his ear was hideously swollen. 'Sir,' he said in a voice that quavered with anxiety, 'Dr Maturin bids me tell you that all was well in Seething Lane, and he hopes you will join him at the Grapes, by the

Savoy, if you are not bespoke. I am to fetch a coach into the court. I have been trying to do my errand, sir . . . I hope . . . '

'Excellent. Capital. Make it so, Mr – . Bring it into the yard and I am with you.'

At the mention of the Savoy, that blessed haven, the porter's suspicions were confirmed; a benevolent grin spread across his face and he hurried out with Mr Scriven to find a coach, bring it in through the arch (an irregular proceeding) and manoeuvre it so close to the steps that Jack could step in unseen.

'Perhaps it would be wise to sit on the floor, on this cloak, sir,' said Mr Scriven. 'It has been baked,' he added, sensing a certain reluctance. 'And Dr Maturin was good enough to shave me all over, to parboil me in the copper, and to new-clothe me from head to foot.'

'I am sorry I gave your ear such a knock,' said Jack from the depths of the straw. 'Does it hurt a great deal?'

'You are very good, sir. I do not feel it now. Dr Maturin was so kind as to dress it with an ointment from the oriental apothecary's at the corner of Bruton Street, and it is almost insensible. Now, sir, you can sit up, if you choose: we are in the duchy.'

'What duchy?'

'The duchy of Lancaster, sir. From Cecil Street to the other side of Exeter Change it is part of the duchy, neither London nor Westminster, and the law is different – writs not the same as London writs: why, even the chapel is a royal peculiar.'

'Peculiar, is she?' said Jack with real satisfaction. 'A damned agreeable peculiarity, too. I wish there were more of 'em. What is your name, sir?'

'Scriven, sir, at your service. Adam Scriven.'

'You are an honest fellow, Mr Scriven. Here we are: this is the Grapes. Can you pay the man? Capital.'

'Stephen,' he cried, 'how happy I am to see you. We have a chance yet – we breathe! We hope! I have a ship, and if only I can get to Portsmouth, and if she floats, we shall make our fortunes. Here are my orders: there are yours. Ha, ha, ha. What luck did you have? I hope you did not hear bad news. You look pretty hipped.'

'No, no,' said Stephen, smiling in spite of himself. 'I have negotiated the bill on Mendoza. At only twelve and a half per cent discount, which surprised me; but then the bill was backed. Here are eight-five guineas,' sliding a leather bag across the table.

'Thank you, thank you, Stephen,' cried Jack, shaking him by the hand. 'What a charming sound – they ring out like freedom, ha, ha. I am as hungry as a man can well be, without perishing of mere want – nothing since breakfast.' He began to halloo for the woman of the house, who told him he might have a nice pair of ducks or a nice piece of cold sturgeon with cucumber, fresh that morning in Billingsgate.

'Let us start with the sturgeon, and if you put the ducks down to the fire this very minute, they will be ready by the time we have done. What are you drinking, Stephen?'

'Gin and water, cold.'

'What a God-forsaken melancholy tope. Let us call for champagne: it is not every day we get a ship, and such a ship. I will tell you all about it.' He gave Stephen a detailed account of his interview, drawing the *Polychrest*'s curious shape in watered gin. 'She is a vile job, of course, and how she survived Old Jarvie's reforms I cannot conceive. When I looked at her sheer-plan, and when I thought of Canning's frigate, building under his eye according to the draught of the *Bellone* – why, it made me feel very strange, for a moment. But I have scarcely had time to tell you of the handsome offer he made me. Forgive me for a moment while I write him a note to say I regret extremely that official business makes it impossible, and so on: turn it in the most obliging way I can manage, very civil and friendly, and get it into the penny post tonight;

for really, it was the handsomest, most flattering offer. I took to Canning amazingly; I hope to see him again. You would like him, Stephen. Full of life, intelligent, gets the point at once, interested in everything – civil, too, delicate and modest; perfectly gentlemanlike; you would swear he was an Englishman. You must meet.'

'That is a recommendation, to be sure; but I am already acquainted with Mr Canning.'

'You know him?'

'We met at Bruton Street today.' In a flash Jack understood why the sound of Bruton Street had run so unpleasantly just now. 'I called on Diana Villiers after walking with Sophie in the park.'

A look of intense pain came over Jack's face. 'How was Sophie?' he asked, looking down.

'She was not looking well. Thinner, unhappy. But she has grown up: I think her more beautiful now than when we knew her in Sussex.'

Jack leant over the back of his chair, saying nothing. A clatter of plates and dishes, a busy waving of table-cloth and napkins, and the sturgeon and the champagne came in. They ate, with a few generalities about sturgeon – a fish-royal – the first time Jack had eaten it – a rather insipid, disappointing fish – and then he said, 'How was Diana?'

'Her spirits appeared sometimes elated and sometimes oppressed; but she was in splendid looks; and she too was full of life.' He might have added, 'And of wanton unkindness.'

Jack said, 'I had no notion you would call at Bruton Street.' Stephen made no reply other than a bend of his head. 'Were there many other people?'

'Three soldiers, an Indian judge, and Mr Canning.'

'Yes. She told me she knew him. Here come the ducks. They look famous, do they not?' he cried with a show of spirit. 'Pray carve them, Stephen. You do it so cleverly. Shall we send some down to Scriven? What do you make of him, by the bye?'

'He is a man, like another. I feel a certain sympathy for him.'

'Do you mean to keep him?'

'I might, too. Will I help you to some stuffing?'

'As much as ever you like. When shall we eat sage and onions again? When he has eaten his duck, do you think Scriven could cut along and take our places on the mail, while we are packing at Hampstead? He might still get insides.'

'It would be safer for you to go post, Jack. The papers have an account of Lady Keith's reception, and your name is in the *Chronicle*, if not the rest: your creditors must have taken notice of it. Their agents in Portsmouth are perfectly capable of meeting the coach. Mr Scriven is thoroughly acquainted with their ingenious devilish malignity: he tells me they are as watchful and eager as thief-takers. You must drive straight to the yard in a post-chaise and go aboard. I will attend to your dunnage and send it down by the waggon.'

'Ain't you coming, Stephen?' cried Jack, pushing his plate away and staring across the table, perfectly aghast.

'I had not thought of going to sea at present,' said Stephen. 'Lord Keith offered me the flagship as physician, but I begged to be excused. I have many things that call for my attention here; and it is a long while since I was in Ireland – '

'But I had taken it absolutely for granted that we were to sail together, Stephen,' cried Jack. 'And I was so happy to bring you these orders. What shall I . . . ' He checked himself, and then in a much lower tone he said, 'But of course, I had not the least right to make such an assumption. I do beg your pardon; and I will explain to the Admiralty at once – entirely my fault. A flagship, after all, by God! It is not more than you deserve. I am afraid I have been very presumptuous.'

'No, no, no, my dear,' cried Stephen. 'It is nothing to do with the flagship. I do not give a fig for a flagship. Put that clear out of your mind. I should far prefer a sloop or a frigate. No. It is that I had not quite made up my mind to a cruise just now. However, let us leave things as they stand for the moment. Indeed, I should not like to have the name of a take-it-and-drop it, shilly-shallying, missish "son of a bitch" at the Navy Board,' he said with a smile. 'Never be so put about, joy: it was only the abruptness that disturbed me – I am more deliberate in my motions than you sanguine, briny creatures. I am engaged until the end of the week, but then, unless I write, I will join you with my sea-chest on Monday. Come, drink up your wine – admirable stuff for a little small shebeen – and we will have another bottle. And before we put you aboard your chaise, I will tell you what I know about the English law of debt.'

CHAPTER SEVEN

My dear Sir,

This is to tell you that I have reached Portsmouth
a day earlier than I had proposed; to solicit the indulgence of not reporting aboard until this evening; and
to beg for the pleasure of your company at dinner.

I am, my dear Sir,

Your affectionate humble servant,

Stephen Maturin

He folded the paper, wrote 'Captain Aubrey, RN, HM
Sloop Polychrest', sealed it and rang the bell. 'Do you
know where the *Polychrest* lies?' he asked.

'Oh, yes, sir,' replied the man with a knowing smile.
'She's getting her guns in at the Ordnance; and a rare old
time of it she had, last tide.'

'Then be so good as to have this note taken to her
directly. And these other letters are to be put into the
post.'

He turned back to the table, and opening his diary he
wrote, 'I sign myself his affectionate humble servant; and
affection it is that brings me here, no doubt. Even a frigid,
self-sufficing man needs something of this interchange if
he is not to die in his unmechanical part: natural philoso-
phy, music, dead men's conversation, is not enough. I like
to think, indeed I do think, that JA has as real an affection
for me as is consonant with his unreflecting, jovial nature,
and I know mine for him – I know how moved I was by
his distress; but how long will this affection withstand
the attrition of mute daily conflict? His kindness for me
will not prevent him from pursuing Diana. And what he
does not wish to see, he will not see: I do not imply a

conscious hypocrisy, but the *quod volunt credere* applies with particular force to him. As for her, I am at a loss – this kindness and then the turning away as though from an enemy. It is as though in playing with JA she had become herself entangled. (Yet would she ever part with her ambition? Surely not. And he is even less marriageable than I; less a lawful prize. Can this be a vicious inclination? JA, though no Adonis by my measure, is well-looking, which I am not.) It is as though his ludicrous account of my wealth, passing through Mrs Williams and gathering force by the conviction in that block-head's tone, had turned me from an ally, a friend, even an accomplice, into an opponent. It is as though – oh, a thousand wild possibilities. I am lost, and I am disturbed. Yet I think I may be cured; this is a fever of the blood, and laudanum will cool it, distance will cool it, business and action will do the same. What I dread is the contrary heating effect of jealousy: I had never felt jealousy before this, and although all knowledge of the world, all experience, literature, history, common observation told me of its strength, I had no sense of its true nature at all. *Gnosce teipsum* – my dreams appal me. This morning, when I was walking beside the coach as it laboured up Ports Down Hill and I came to the top, with all Portsmouth harbour suddenly spread below me, and Gosport, Spithead and perhaps half the Channel fleet glittering there – a powerful squadron moving out past Haslar in line ahead, all studdingsails abroad – I felt a longing for the sea. It has a great cleanliness. There are moments when everything on land seems to me tortuous, dark, and squalid; though to be sure, squalor is not lacking aboard a man-of-war.

'I am not sure how far JA practised upon Mrs Williams's avid credulity: pretty far, to judge by her obsequious reception of me. It has had this curious result, that JA's stock has risen with her in almost the same proportion as mine. She would have no objection to him if his estate were clear. Nor, I swear, would Sophie. Yet I do believe that

that good child is so firm in the principles she has been taught, that she would wither away an old maid, rather than disobey her mother – marry without her consent. No Gretna Green. She is a dear good child; and she is one of those rare creatures in whom principle does not do away with humour. This is no time for roaring mirth, to be sure, but I remember very well to have noted, again and again at Mapes, that she is quietly and privately *jolly*. A great rarity in women (Diana included, apart from an appreciation of wit and now and then a flash of it), who are often as solemn as owls, though given to noisy laughter. How deeply sorry, how more than sorry I should be if she were to take the habit of unhappiness: it is coming on her fast. The structure of her face is changing.' He stood looking out of the window. It was a clear, frosty morning, and the blackguardly town looked as well as it could. Officers passed in and out of the Port Admiral's house, over against the inn; the pavements were full of uniforms, blue coats and red, church-going officers' wives in pretty mantuas, with here and there a fur pelisse; scrubbed children with Sunday faces.

'A gentleman to see you, sir,' said the waiter. 'A lieutenant.'

'A lieutenant?' said Stephen; and after a pause, 'Desire him to walk up.'

A thundering on the stairs, as though someone had released a bull; the door burst inwards, trembling, and Pullings appeared, lighting up the room with his happiness and his new blue coat. 'I'm made, sir,' he cried, seizing Stephen's hand. 'Made at last! My commission came down with the mail. Oh, wish me joy!'

'Why, so I do,' said Stephen, wincing in that iron grip, 'if more joy you can contain – if more felicity will not make your cup overflow. Have you been drinking, Lieutenant Pullings? Pray sit in a chair like a rational being, and do not spring about the room.'

'Oh say it again, sir,' said the lieutenant, sitting and

gazing at Stephen with pure love beaming from his face. 'Not a drop.'

'Then it is with present happiness you are drunk. Well. Long, long may it last.'

'Ha, ha, ha! That is exactly what Parker said. "Long may it last," says he; but envious, like, you know – the grey old toad. Howsomever, I dare say even I might grow a trifle sour, or rancid, like, five and thirty years without a ship of my own, and this cruel fitting-out. And he is a good, righteous man, I am sure; though he was proper pixy-led before the captain came.'

'Lieutenant, will you drink a glass of wine, a glass of sherry-wine?'

'You've said it again, sir,' cried Pullings, with another burst of effulgence. ('You would swear that light actually emanated from that face,' observed Stephen privately.) 'I take it very kind. Just a drop, if you please. I am not going to get drunk until tomorrow night – my feast. Would it be proper for me to propose a sentiment? Then here's to Captain Aubrey – my dear love to him, and may he have all his heart desires. Bottoms up. Without him I should never have got my step. Which reminds me of my errand, sir. Captain Aubrey's compliments to Dr Maturin, congratulates him upon his safe arrival, and will be very happy to dine with him at the George this day at three o'clock; has not yet shipped paper, pens, or ink, and begs to be excused the informality of his reply.'

'It would give me great pleasure if you would keep us company.'

'Thankee, sir, thankee. But in just half an hour I am taking the long-boat out off of the Wight. The *Lord Mornington* Indiaman passed Start Point on Thursday, and I hope to press half a dozen prime seamen out of her about dawn.'

'Will the cruising frigates and the Plymouth tenders have left you anything to take?'

'Love you, sir, I made two voyages in her. There are

hidey-holes under her half-deck you would never dream of, without you helped to stow men into 'em. I'll have half a dozen men out of her, or you may say, "black's the white of your eye, Tom Pullings." Lieutenant Tom Pullings,' he added, secretly.

'We are short-handed, so?'

'Why it's pretty bad, of course. We are thirty-two men short of our complement, but 'tis not so short as poor. The receiving-ship sent us eighteen Lord Mayor's men and twenty-odd from the Huntingdonshire and Rutland quotas, chaps taken off the parish and out of the gaols – never seen the sea in their life. It's seamen we're short of. Still, we do have a few prime hands, and two old Sophies among 'em – old Allen, fo'c'sleman, and John Lakey, maintop. Do you remember him? You sewed him up very near, the first time you ever sailed with us and we had a brush with an Algerine. He swears you saved his – his privates, sir, and is most uncommon grateful: would feel proper old fashioned without 'em, he says. Oh, Captain Aubrey will lick 'em into shape, I'm certain sure. And there's Mr Parker seems pretty taut; and Babbington and me will have the hide off of any bastard as don't attend to his duty – the Captain need not fear for that.'

'What of the other officers?'

'Why, sir, I have not rightly had time to come to know 'em, not with all this day-of-judgment hell and shindy of fitting-out – purser in the Victualling Yard, gunner at the Ordnance, master in the hold, or where the hold would be if there was a hold, which there ain't.'

'She is constructed on new principles, I find?'

'Well, sir, I hope she's constructed to swim, that's all. I would not say it to any but a shipmate, sir, but I never seen anything like her, Pearl River, Hugli or Guinea coast. You can't tell whether she's coming or going. Not but what she's a gallows deal more handsome than the common run,' he added, as though taking himself up for disloyalty. 'Mr Parker seen to that – gold-leaf, bright-work galore, special patent blacking for the bends and yards, blocks stropped with red leather. Was you ever at a fitting-out, sir?'

'Not I.'

'It's a right old Bedlam,' said Pullings, shaking his head and laughing. 'Dockyard mateys underfoot, stores all over the deck, new drafts milling about like lost souls, nobody knowing who anyone is or where to go – a right old Bedlam, and the Port Admiral sending down every five minutes to know why you're not ready for sea – is everybody observing the Sabbath aboard the *Polychrest*, ha, ha, ha!' In the gaiety of his heart Tom Pullings sang

'We'll give you a bit of our mind, old hound:
Port Admiral, you be damned.

'I haven't had my clothes off since we commissioned her,' he observed. 'Captain Aubrey turns up at crack of dawn – posted all the way – reads himself in to me and Parker and the Marines and half a dozen loobies which was all we had then, and up goes his pennant. And before his last words are rightly out – fail not as you will answer the contrary at your peril – "Mr Pullings, that topsail-sheet block needs a dog-bitch thimble, if you please," in his own voice exactly. But Lord, you should have heard him carrying on at the riggers when he found they had been giving us twice-laid stuff; they had to call the Master-Attendant to soothe his horrid passion. Then "Lose not a minute," says he, driving us all though fit to drop, merry as a grig and laughing when half the people run to the stern thinking it is the bows, and t'other way about. Why, sir, he'll be glad of his dinner, I'm sure: he's not had above a bit of bread and cold beef in his hand since I been aboard, And now I must take my leave. He would give his eye-teeth for a boat-load of thorough-paced seamen.'

Stephen returned to his window, watched the lithe young form of Thomas Pullings weave through the traffic, cross to the far side and hurry away with that easy, loose-limbed rolling gait of his kind towards the Point and his long night's wait in an open boat far out in the Channel. 'Devotion is a fine thing, a moving thing to see,' he reflected. 'But who is going to pay for that amiable young man's zeal? What blows, oaths, moral violence, brutalities?'

The scene had changed: church-going was over, and the respectable part of the town had vanished behind doors, into an odour of mutton; now groups of sailors straggled up and down, walking wide, like countrymen in London, and among them small greasy tradesmen, routs, hucksters, and the thick local girls and women called brutes. A confused bellowing, something between merriment and a riot turning ugly, and the *Impregnable*'s liberty-men, in shore-going rig and a prize divided in their pockets, came staggering by with a troop of whores, a fiddler walking backwards in front of them and small boys skirmishing on every side, like sheepdogs. Some of the whores were old, some had torn dresses with yellow flesh beneath, all had dyed and frizzled hair, and all looked pinched with cold.

The warmth and happiness of young Pullings' joy receded. 'All ports I have seen are much the same,' he reflected. 'All the places where sailors congregate: I do not believe that this reflects their nature, however, but rather the nature of the land.' He sank into a train of thought – man's nature how defined? Where the constant factors of identity? What allows the statement 'I am I' from which he was aroused by the sight of Jack, walking along with the fine easy freedom of Sunday – no bowed head, no anxious looks over his shoulder. There were many other people in the street, but two, some fifty yards behind Jack and keeping pace with him, caught Stephen's eye: burly fellows, of no obvious trade or calling, and there was something odd about them, some intentness, some want of casual staring about, that made him look harder, withdrawing from the window and fixing them until they came abreast of the George.

'Jack,' he said, 'there are two men following you. Come over here and look out discreetly. There they are, standing on the Port Admiral's steps.'

'Yes,' said Jack. 'I know the one with the broken nose. He tried to come aboard the other day – no go, however; I smoked him at once. I dare say he is putting the other on to my line, the pragmatical bastard. Oh, be damned to them,' he said, hurrying to the fire. 'Stephen, what do you say to a drink? I spent the whole morning in the foretop, starved with cold.'

'A little brandy will answer the case, I think; a glass of right Nantes. Indeed, you look quite destroyed. Drink this up, and we will go straight to the dining-room. I have ordered a halibut with anchovy sauce, mutton, and a venison pasty – simple island fare.'

The worn lines eased out of Jack Aubrey's face, a rosy glow replaced the unhealthy grey; he seemed to fill his uniform again. 'How much better a man feels when he is mixed with halibut and leg of mutton and roebuck,' he said, toying with a piece of Stilton cheese. 'You are a much better host than I am, Stephen,' he observed. 'All the things I stood most in need of but hardly name. I remember a wretched dinner I invited you to in Mahon, the first we ever ate together, and they got it all wrong, being ignorant of Spanish, my sort of Spanish.'

'It was a very good meal, a very welcome meal,' said Stephen. 'I remember it perfectly. Shall we take our tea upstairs? I wish to hear about the *Polychrest*.' The big room was an almost unbroken spread of blue, with here and there a Royal Marine, and conversation was little more private than signals on the open sea.

'We shall make a go of her, once we get used to her ways, I make no doubt,' said Jack. 'She may be a little odd to look at, to the prejudiced eye; but she floats, and that is the essential, do you see? She floats; and as a floating battery – why, I have rarely seen the like! We only have to get her there, and then we have four and twenty thirty-two pounders to bring into play. Carronades, you may say; but thirty-two pounder carronades! We can take on any French sloop afloat, for these are your genuine smashers – we could tackle a thirty-six-gun frigate, if only we could get close enough.'

'By this same argument of proximation you could also set about a three-decker, a first-rate, at six inches; or two, indeed, if you could wedge yourself between them and fire both sides. But believe me, my dear, it is a fallacious argument, God forbid. How far do these carronades of yours fling their vast prodigious missiles?'

'Why, you must engage within pistol shot if you want to hit what you point them at; but at yard-arm to yard-arm, oh, how they smash through the oak!'

'And what is your enemy doing with his long guns, while you labour to approach him? But I am not to teach you your own trade, however.'

'Approach him . . . ' said Jack. 'There's the rub. I must have hands to work the ship. We are thirty-two men short of our complement – no hope of another draft – and I dare say you will reject some of the cripples and Abraham-men the receiving-ship has sent us: sad thievish little creatures. Men I must have, and the glass is running out . . . tell me, did you bring Scriven with you?'

'I did. I thought he might be found some small employment.'

'He is an eminent hand at writing, is he not? Pamphlets and such? I have tried dashing off a poster – even three or four volunteers would be worth their weight in gold – but I have had no time, and anyhow it don't seem to answer. Look.' He brought some papers out of his pocket.

'Well,' said Stephen, reading. 'No: perhaps it don't.' He rang the bell and bade the man ask Mr Scriven to walk up. 'Mr Scriven,' he said, 'be so good as to look at these – you see the problem – and to draft a sheet to the purpose. There is paper and ink on the table over there.'

Scriven withdrew to the window, reading, noting and

grunting to himself; and Jack, as he sat there, warm and comfortable by the fire, felt a delicious total relaxation creep over his person; it espoused the leather chair, sinking into its curves, no tension anywhere at all. He lost the thread of Stephen's remarks, answering oh and ah at the pauses, or smiling and moving his head with ambiguous appreciation. Sometimes his legs would give a violent twitch, jerking him out of this state of bliss; but each time he sank back, happier than before.

'I said "You do move with the utmost caution, I am sure?" ' said Stephen, now touching him on the knee.

'Oh, certainly,' said Jack, at once grasping the subject. 'I have never set foot on shore except for Sunday, and every boat that comes alongside is examined. In any case, I am moving out to Spithead on tomorrow's tide, which will prevent surprises. I have refused all Dockyard invitations, even the Commissioner himself. The only one I shall accept is Pullings' feast, where there is no risk of any kind – a little place in Gosport by the landing-stage, quite out of the way. I cannot disappoint him: he is bringing his people and his sweetheart up from the country.'

'Sir,' said Mr Scriven, 'may I show you my attempt?'

£5,000 a man! (or more)
WEALTH   EASE   DISTINCTION
YOUR LAST CHANCE OF A FORTUNE!

HMS *Polychrest* will shortly sail to scour the seas of ALL KING GEORGE'S enemies. She is desined to SAIL AGAINST WIND AND TIDE and she will Take, Sink and Destroy the Tyrant's helpless man-of-war, without Mercy, sweeping the Ocean of his Trade. There is no time to be lost! Once the *Polychrest* has gone by there will be no more PRIZES, no more fat French and cowardly Dutch merchantmen, loaded with Treasure, Jewels, Silks, Satins and Costly Delicacies for the immoral and luxurious Usurper's Court.

This Amazing New Vessel, built on Scientific Principles, is commanded by the renowned

CAPTAIN AUBREY!

whose brig *Sophie*, with a 28lb broadside, captured £100,000's worth of enemy shipping last war. 28lb, and the *Polychrest* fires 384lb from either side! So what will she do, in this proportion? More than TWELVE TIMES as much! The Enemy must soon be Bankrupt – the End is Nigh. Come and join the Fun before it is too late, and then set up your Carriage!

Captain Aubrey has been prevailed upon to accept a few more Hands. Only exceptionally wide-awake, intelligent men will be entertained, capable of lifting a Winchester bushel of Gold; but PERHAPS YOU ARE THE LUCKY MAN! Hurry, there is no time to be lost. Hurry to the Rendezvous at the – YOU MAY BE THE LUCKY MAN WHO IS ACCEPTED!
No troublesome formalities. The best of provisions at 16 oz to the pound, 4lb of tobacco a month. Free beer, wine and grog! Dancing and fiddling aboard. A health-giving, wealth-giving cruise. Be healthy and wealthy and wise, and bless the day you came aboard the Polychrest*!*

GOD SAVE THE KING

'The figures I have ventured to put are merely for the form,' he said, looking into their faces as they read.

'It is coming it a trifle high,' said Jack, writing sums that could be attempted to be believed. 'But I like it. I am obliged to you, Mr Scriven. Will you take it round to the Courier office and explain to them how it is to be printed?

You understand these things admirably. They may strike off a hundred posters and two hundred as handbills, to be given out where the country waggons and coaches come in. Here is a couple of guineas. Stephen, we must get under way. There will still be light enough to check the new patent slides, and you have two drafts to sort out: pray do not reject anything that can haul a rope.'

'You will like to meet the other officers,' he said, as they stood waiting for their boat. 'They may look a little rough, just at first. They have been led a devil of a dance with it, with this fitting-out, especially Parker. The man who was the first to be offered *Polychrest* dilly-dallied – could not be found, could not make up his mind – and Pullings, bless him, did not come until I was here. So it was all on Parker's shoulders.'

He stepped into the boat and sat there silent, thinking about his first lieutenant. Mr Parker was a man in his middle fifties, grey, precise, strict, a great one for spit and polish and details of uniform – this had earned him Prince William's good word – and brave, active, conscientious; but he tired easily, he did not seem very intelligent, and he was somewhat deaf. Far worse, he had no sense of the men – his black-list was as long as his arm, but the real seamen took little notice of him – and Jack suspected that he had no sense of the sea either. Jack also suspected, more than suspected, that Parker's was the little discipline, the hazing discipline; that under Parker uncontrolled the *Polychrest* would be a flash ship, all paint outside and no order within, the cat in daily use and the crew sullen, unwilling and brutal – an unhappy ship, and an inefficient fighting-machine.

It would not be easy to deal with him. There must be no discord on the quarterdeck; Parker must be seen to be in charge of the day-to-day running of the *Polychrest*, with no easy-going captain to undermine his authority. Not that Jack was in the least easy-going; he was a taut officer and he liked a taut ship, but he had served in one hell afloat, he had seen others, and he wanted no part of it.

'There she lies,' he observed, nodding towards the *Polychrest*, a certain defensive note in his voice.

'That is she?' said Stephen. A three-masted vessel – he hesitated to call her a ship, however – very trim, rather high in the water: shining black sides with a brilliant lemon streak broken by twelve portlids, also black; and above the lemon a line of blue, topped with white; gold scroll-work running into the blue from either extremity. 'She does not look so mighty strange to me, except that she seems to have both ends sharp, and no beak-head, in the sense of that dip, that anfractuosity, to which we are accustomed; but after all, the same remarks apply to the curragh in which Saint Brendan made his voyage. I do not understand what all the coil is about.'

'His curragh stayed well? She sailed against wind and tide?'

'Certainly. Did he not reach the Islands of the Blessed?'

By Friday Jack's spirits were higher than they had been since he took his first command down the long harbour of Port Mahon and out to sea. Not only had Pullings brought back seven cross but able seamen from the *Lord Mornington*, but Scriven's poster had induced five youths from Salisbury to come aboard 'to ask for details'. And better was in store: Jack and Stephen were on deck, waiting to go to Pullings' feast, waiting in the grey fog until the unhandy crew, badgered by Mr Parker and harassed by the bosun, should succeed in getting the launch into the water, when a wherry came alongside, suddenly appearing through the murk. There were two men in it, dressed in short blue jackets with brass buttons down one side, white trousers, and tarpaulin hats; this with their long pigtails, gold earrings and black silk neck-cloths, made them look more like man-of-war's men than was quite right, and

Jack stared down at them hard from the rail. To his astonishment he found himself looking straight into the face of Barret Bonden, his former coxswain, and another old Sophie, a man whose name escaped him.

'They may come aboard,' he said. 'Bonden, come a-board. I am very happy to see you,' he went on, as Bonden stood beaming at him on the quarterdeck. 'How do you come along, eh? Pretty spry, I trust? Have you brought me a message?' This was the only rational explanation for the presence of a seaman, bobbing about on the crowded waters of Spithead as though the hottest press in years were a matter of unconcern: but there was no ship's name to the ribbon flying from the hat in Bonden's hand, and there was something about his delighted bearing that kindled hope.

'No, your honour,' said Bonden. 'Which our Joe,' – jerking his thumb at his companion (Joseph Plaice, Bonden's cousin, of course: sheet-anchor man, starboard watch, elderly, deeply stupid, but reliable when sober, and a wonderful hand at a variant of the Matthew Walker knot, sober or speechless) – 'said you was afloat again, so we come round from Priddy's Hard to enter volunteerly, if so be you can find room, sir.' This was as near an approach to open mirth as decency would allow.

'I shall stretch a point for you, Bonden,' said Jack. 'Plaice, you will have to earn your *place* by learning the boys your Matthew Walker.' This flight was beyond Joseph Plaice, but he looked pleased and touched his knuckle to his forehead. 'Mr Parker, enter these men, if you please, and rate them Plaice fo'csle'man, Bonden my cox'n.'

Five minutes later he and Stephen were in the launch, Bonden steering, as he had steered for Jack in many a bloody cutting-out expedition on the Spanish coast. How did he come to be at liberty at such a time, and how had he managed to traverse the great man-hungry port without being pressed? It would be useless to ask him; he would only answer with a pack of lies. So as they neared the dim harbour entrance Jack said, 'How is your nephew?' meaning George Lucock, a most promising youth whom he had rated midshipman in the *Sophie*.

'Our George, sir?' said Bonden, in a low voice. 'He was in the *York*.' The *York* had foundered in the North Sea with the loss of all hands. 'He was only a foremast jack: pressed out of a Domingoman.'

'He would have made his way,' said Jack, shaking his head. He could see that young man, bright with joy at his promotion, shining in the Mediterranean sun, and the flash of polished brass as he took the noon altitude with his sextant, that mark of the quarterdeck. And he remembered that the *York* had come from Hickman's yard – that there were tales of her having put to sea with timbers in such a state that no lanterns were needed in the hold, because of the glow of rotten wood. At all events she was in no condition to meet a full gale, a North Sea widow-maker.

These thoughts occupied him as they wove through the shipping, ducking under cables that stretched away to the great shadowy forms of three-deckers, crossing the paths of the countless boats plying to and fro, sometimes with outbursts of rage or wit from the licensed watermen – once the cry of 'What ho, the Carpenter's Mistake' floated from behind a buoy, followed by a burst of maniac laughter; and they brought his spirits low.

Stephen remained perfectly mute in some dark study of his own, and it was not until they were coming in to the landing-stage that the sight of Pullings waiting for him lighted some cheerfulness in Jack's mind. The young man was standing there with his parents and an astonishingly pretty girl, a sweet little pink creature in lace mittens with immense blue eyes and an expression of grave alarm. 'I should like to take her home and keep her as a pet,' thought Jack, looking down at her with great benevolence.

The elder Mr Pullings was a farmer in a small way on the skirts of the New Forest, and he had brought a couple of sucking-pigs, a great deal of the King's game, and a pie that was obliged to be accommodated with a table of its own, while the inn provided the turtle soup, the wine and the fish. The other guests were junior lieutenants and master's mates, and to begin with the feast was stiffer and more funereal than might have been wished; Mr Pullings was too shy to see or hear, and once he had delivered his piece about their sense of Captain Aubrey's kindness to their Tom in a burring undertone whose drift Jack seized only half-way through, he set himself to his bottle with a dreadful silent perseverance. However, the young men were all sharp-set, for this was well past their dinner-hour, and presently the huge amounts of food they ate engendered talk. After a while there was a steady hum, the sound of laughter, general merriment, and Jack could relax and give his attention to Mrs Pullings's low, confidential account of her anxiety when Tom ran away to sea 'with no change of linen, nothing to shift into – not even so much as his good woollen stockings'.

'Truffles!' cried Stephen, deep in the monumental pie, Mrs Pullings's particular dish, her masterpiece (young hen pheasants, boned, stuffed tight with truffles, in a jelly of their own life's blood, Madeira and calves' foot). 'Truffles! My dear madam, where did you find these princely truffles?' – holding one up on his fork.

'The stuffing, sir? We call 'em yearth-grobbets; and Pullings has a little old spayed sow turns 'em up by the score along the edge of the forest.'

Truffles, morells, blewits, jew's ears (perfectly wholesome if not indulged in to excess; and even then, only a few cases of convulsions, a certain rigidity of the neck over in two or three days – nonsense to complain) occupied Stephen and Mrs Pullings until the cloth disappeared, the ladies retired, and the port began to go round. By now rank had evened out: at least one young man was as grand, royal and spreading as an admiral, and in the vinous, candle-lit haze Jack's nagging anxiety about what the *Polychrest* would do in a capful of wind with all that tophamper, about her ballast, trim, construction, crew and stores dropped away, leaving him the cheerful lieutenant he had been not so very long ago.

They had drunk the King, the First Lord ('O bless him, God bless him,' cried Pullings), Lord Nelson with three times three, wives and sweethearts, Miss Chubb (the pink child) and other young ladies; they had carried the elder Mr Pullings to his bed, and they were singing

> *We'll rant and we'll roar like true British sailors,*
> *We'll range and we'll roam over all the salt seas,*
> *Until we strike soundings in the Channel of old*
>   *England:*
> *From Ushant to Scilly 'tis thirty-five leagues.*
>
> *We hove our ship to when the wind was south-west,*
>   *boys,*
> *We hove our ship to for to strike soundings clear,*
> *Then we filled our main-topsail and bore right away,*
>   *boys,*
> *And right up the Channel our course we did steer.*
>
> *We'll rant and we'll roar . . .*

The din was so great that Stephen alone noticed the door open just enough for Scriven's questing head: he placed a warning hand on Jack's elbow, but the rest were roaring still when it swung wide and the bailiffs rushed in.

'Pullings, pin that whore with the staff,' cried Stephen, tossing his chair under their legs and clasping Broken-nose round the middle.

Jack darted to the window, flung up the sash, jumped on to the sill and stood there poised while behind him the bailiffs struggled in the confusion, reaching out their staffs with ludicrous earnestness, trying to touch him, taking no notice of the clogging arms round their waists, knees and chests. They were powerful, determined fellows; the reward was high, and the mêlée surged towards the open window – one touch amounted to a lawful arrest.

A leap and he was away: but the head tipstaff was fly – he had posted a gang outside, and they were looking up eagerly, calling out 'jump for it, sir – we'll break your fall – it's only one storey.' Holding on to the window he craned out, looking down the lane towards the shore – he could see the gleam of water – towards the place where by rights the Polychrests should be drinking Pullings' beer, sent to them together with the second sucking-pig; and surely Bonden could be relied upon? He filled his lungs and hailed 'Polychrest' in a tone that echoed back from Portsmouth and stopped the mild gossip in the launch stone dead. 'Polychrest!'

'Sir?' came back Bonden's voice out of the dripping gloom.

'Double up to the inn, d'ye hear me? Up the lane. Bring your stretchers.'

'Aye-aye, sir.'

In a moment the launch was empty. Stretchers, the boat's long wooden footrests, meant a row. The captain was no doubt pressing some hands, and they, pressed men themselves, did not mean to miss a second of the fun.

The pounding of feet at the end of the lane, coming nearer: behind, the sway and crash of chairs, oaths, a doubtful battle. 'Here, here! Right under the window,' cried Jack, and there they were, a little wet mob, gasping, gaping up. 'Make a ring, now. Stand from under!' He jumped, picked himself up and cried, 'Down to the boat. Bear a hand, bear a hand!'

For the first moment the gang in the street hung back, but as the head tipstaff and his men came racing out of the inn shouting 'In the name of the law! Way there, in the name of the law!' they closed, and the narrow lane was filled with the sound of hard dry blows, grunts, the crash of wood upon wood. The sailors, with Jack in the middle, pushed fast in the direction of the sea.

'In the name of the law!' cried the tipstaff again, making a most desperate attempt to break through.

' – the law,' cried the seamen, and Bonden, grappling with the bailiff, wrenched the staff from him. He flung it right down the lane, fairly into the water, and said, 'You've lost your commission now, mate. I can hit you now, mate, so you watch out, I say. You watch out, cully, or you'll come home by Weeping Cross.'

The bailiff uttered a low growl, pulled out his hanger and hurled himself at Jack. 'Artful, eh?' said Bonden, and brought his stretcher down on his head. He fell in the mud, to be trampled upon by Pullings and his friends, pouring out of the inn. At this the gang broke and fled, calling out that they should fetch their friends, the watch, the military, and leaving two of their number stretched upon the ground.

'Mr Pullings, press those men, if you please,' cried Jack from the boat. 'And that fellow in the mud. Two more? Capital. All aboard? Where's the Doctor? Pass the word for the Doctor. Ah, there you are. Shove off. Altogether, now, give way. Give way cheerly. What a prime hand he will make, to be sure,' he added in an aside, 'once he's used to our ways – a proper bulldog of a man.'

At two bells that morning watch the *Polychrest* was slipping quietly through the cold grey sea, the cold grey air, for at midnight the wind had come a little east of south, and in order not to lose a minute (a ship could be windbound for weeks on end in the Channel at this season) Jack had given orders to unmoor, although the tide was making. A gentle breeze it was, not enough to dispel the fog or raise more than a ripple on the long oily swell, and the *Polychrest* could have carried a great spread of canvas; however, she was under little more than her topsails, and she ghosted along, with little more than a whisper of water the length of her side.

The tall dark form of her captain, much larger in his foul-weather clothes, stood over on the windward side of the quarterdeck. At the sound of the log being heaved, the cry of 'Turn' and 'stop' and the thump of its coming aboard again, he turned. 'Mr Babbington, what do you have?' he called.

'Two knots and a three fathom, if you please, sir.'

Jack nodded. Somewhere out there in the darkness on the larboard bow there would be Selsey Bill, and presently he might have to tack: for the moment he had plenty of room – the persistent howling under the lee came from the horns of the inshore fishing-boats, and they were a good mile away. To seaward there was the thump of a gun every few minutes – a man-of-war bound for Portsmouth, no doubt, on the opposite tack – and the *Polychrest*'s bow carronade answered regularly with quarter charges.

'At least there will be four men who know how to handle one by morning,' he reflected.

In a way it was unfortunate that this first acquaintance with his ship should come at a time when there was no horizon, when sea and air could not be told apart; but he was not sorry for it, upon the whole – it gained him some hours at least, it sent Gosport, its squalors and its possible complications far astern, and in any case he had been on fire to know how she handled in the open sea ever since he had set eyes on the *Polychrest*. She had the strangest motion, a kind of nervous lift and shudder like a horse about to shy, as she rose to the swell, a kind of twist in her roll that he had never known before.

Mr Goodridge, the master, could be seen in the glow of the binnacle, standing by the quartermaster at the con. He was a reserved, elderly man of great experience, once the master of a ship of the line, but broken for fighting with the chaplain and only recently put on the list again; and he was as intent upon the *Polychrest*'s behaviour as his captain.

'What do you make of her, Mr Goodridge?' asked Jack, walking over to the wheel.

'Why, sir, for ardent griping, I have never seen the like.'

Jack took the wheel, and indeed, even at the rate of sailing, there was a steady, powerful thrust against him: the *Polychrest* wanted to get her head right up into the eye of the wind. He let her have her way, and then, just before the sails began to shiver the griping stopped; the helm went dead under his hand, and her odd corkscrew motion changed its rhythm entirely. He could not make it out, but stood there puzzling as he gently eased the *Polychrest* back on to her course. It was as though she had two centres of rotation, two pivots: if not three . . . obviously jib, foresail and a reef in the mizen topsail would keep her off, but that was not the trouble – that would not account for this sluggish helm, this sudden lack of response.

'Three inches in the well, sir,' said the carpenter's mate, making his routine report.

'Three inches in the well, if you please, sir,' said the master.

'Ay,' said Jack. It was negligible: she had not had anything of a trial yet, no working in a heavy sea; but at least it proved that those strange sliding keels and the nameless peculiarity of her quickwork did not mean that the water poured straight in: a comfortable reflection, for he had misgivings. 'No doubt we shall find what trim suits her best,' he observed to the master and went back to the rail, half consciously trying to recreate his quarterdeck pacing in the little *Sophie*, while his mind, worn fine by Pullings' feast, by the prolonged turmoil of unmooring with a foul hawse and by the anxiety of getting under way in a crowded road, turned to the problem of the forces acting upon the vessel.

The new-lit galley stove sent a whiff of smoke eddying aft, together with the smell of burgoo, and at the same time he heard the head-pumps beginning to work. Up and down, up and down, with his hands behind his back and his chin tucked into his griego against the biting air: up and down. The figure of the *Polychrest* was as clear in his mind as if she had been a model held up to a lamp, and he studied her reaction to the creeping influence of the tide, and the lateral thrust of the wind, the eddies deep under her strangely placed rudders . . .

The after-guard were sprinkling the quarterdeck with their buckets, carefully avoiding his walk, and after them came the sand-men. The bosun was on deck: Malloch, a short, bull-like young fellow; had been bosun's mate in the crack *Ixion*. Jack heard his shout and the thwack of his cane as he started a man on the fo'c'sle. And all the time there was the measured thump of the carronade, the now distant gun of the man-of-war, the horns away to port, the steady chant of the man heaving the lead in the chains – 'by the mark nine . . . ho yo ho yo . . . and a quarter nine.'

The rake of the masts was a great consideration, of course. Jack was an intuitive rather than a scientific sailor, and in his mental image of the *Polychrest* her backstays tautened until the angle of her masts looked right and some inner voice said 'Belay there'. The holystones began their steady grinding: the decks could do with it, after the shambles of a hurried fitting-out. These were such familiar sounds and smells, these innumerable difficulties were so very much part of the world he had known from childhood, that he felt as though he had been returned to his own element. It was not that he did not like the land – capital place; such games, such fun – but the difficulties there, the complications, were so vague and imprecise, reaching one behind another, no end to them: nothing a man could get hold of. Here, although life was complex enough in all conscience, he could at least attempt to cope with anything that turned up. Life at sea had the great advantage that . . . something was amiss. He tried to place it, glancing sharply fore and aft in the greyness of approaching day. The fishing-boats that had been sailing on a parallel course were now astern: their melancholy wailing sounded almost

218

from the *Polychrest*'s wake. The Bill must be no great way ahead. It was time to go about. A damned foolish moment to choose, with the people busy, and he would have preferred to wait until the watch below was on deck; but she might have made even more leeway than he had allowed for, and only a fool would run any risk for the sake of neatness.

'We will put her about, Mr Goodridge,' he said.

The bosun started his call. Brooms, buckets, swabs, squeegees, holystones, prayer-books, brass rags flew into sheltered places as his mates roared down the hatches 'All hands, all hands 'bout ship' and then vanished below to drive the sleepers up – those few so worn with toil, seasickness and desolation, that they were unconscious in spite of the carronade and the echoing thunder of the holystones. The score or so of right seamen had been at their stations ten minutes – Pullings and the bosun on the fo'c'sle, the gunner and his mates at the maintack, the carpenter at the foresheet, the Marines at the mainsheet, the maintopmen and the after-guard on the quarterdeck, at the braces – before the last desperate half-clothed bewildered landsman was hunted up, shoved and beaten and cobbed into his place.

'Bear up,' said Jack to the timoneer, waiting for this Bartholomew Fair performance to come to an end – a bosun's mate was now belabouring the former tipstaff with his persuader, to help him understand the difference between a stay and a bowline. And when he felt a little more way on the sloop, saw something like order on deck, and judged the moment ripe, he called, 'Ready about.'

'Ready about, sir,' came the answer.

'Luff up handsomely, now,' he said quietly to the man at the wheel, and then loud and clear, 'Helm's a-lee. Fore topsheet, fore topbowline, stays'l sheet, let go.' The full-bellied curves of the headsails sagged and collapsed; the *Polychrest* moved in a long smooth curve up towards the direction of the wind.

'Off tacks and sheets.'

Everything was ready for the decisive order that would bring the yards flying round; everything was as calm and unhurried as the sloop's slow curve through this grey, heaving, formless world; there was time and to spare. And that was just as well, he thought, seeing the way they were shifting the sheets over the stays – something between cat's cradle and puss-in-the-corner.

Her curve was slower now; and now the swell was coming more and more on to her starboard bow, heaving against her course. Slowly up and up: within two points of the wind, a point and a half, and the words 'Mainsail haul' had been long formed in his mouth when he realized that the deep steady sound to port and astern, the sound that was coming so clear and loud through the intent, waiting silence, was that of the breakers on Selsey Bill. She had made twice and three times the leeway he and the master had reckoned for. At the same moment he felt an essential change in her motion, a dead sullenness: she was going to miss stays. She was not going to travel up into the eye of the wind and carry on beyond it, so that the sails, braced round, would fill on the larboard side and bear her out to sea.

A ship that would not stay must wear – she must fall off from the wind, right round the way she came and much farther still, pivoting about her stern in a great leeward sweep until she had the wind aft, turning, turning until she could bring it astern and then at last on her other side, turning still until she was heading in the direction she desired – a long, long turn: and in this case, with this tide, swell and wind, the *Polychrest* would need a mile to accomplish it, a mile of leeway before she could brace up sharp and head out into the Channel.

She was losing her headway; her sails were flapping dismally in the silence; with every thrust of the sea she was nearer the unseen shore. The alternatives flew through his mind: he could let her fall off, set the driver and try

220

again; he could wear and risk it, coming to an anchor if he had cut it too fine – an ignominious, horribly time-wasting process, or he could box-haul her. But dared he box-haul her with this crew? While these possibilities ran past his inner scrutineer a remote corner of his mind called out shrilly against the injustice of missing stays – unknown in such conditions, monstrous, a malignancy designed to make him late on his station, to allow Harte to call him unofficerlike, no seaman, a dawdling Sybarite, a slow-arse. That was the danger: there was no peril in this sea, nothing but a consciousness of having misjudged things, and the likelihood of an ugly, unanswerable rebuke from a man he despised.

These thoughts had their being between the time he heard the splash of the lead and the cry 'By the deep eight'. As the next cry came, 'A half less eight' he said to himself, 'I shall box-haul her.' And aloud, 'Haul up main and mizen tops'ls. Fore tops'l sheet hard a-weather. Foretops'l sharp aback: clap on to that brace. Look alive on the foc's'le there. Lee bowlines, lee bowlines.'

As if she had run into a gentle cushion, the *Polychrest*'s headway stopped – he felt her underfoot – and she began to move backwards, the headsails and her lee-helm paying her round as she went. 'Square main and mizen yards. Jump to those braces, now.'

She might not like turning up into the wind, but with her strange sharp stern she was very good at going back-wards. He had never known such a sternway.

'And a half eight,' from the chains.

Round she went: the squared main and mizen yards lay parallel with the wind, the topsails shaking. Farther, farther; and now the wind was abaft her beam, and by rights her sternway should have stopped; but it did not; she was still travelling with remarkable speed in the wrong direction. He filled the topsails, gave her weather helm, and still she slid backwards in this insane contradiction of all known principles. For a moment all the certainties of his world quivered – he caught a dumbfounded, appalled glance from the master – and then with a sigh from the masts and stays, the strangest straining groan, the *Polychrest*'s motion passed through a barely perceptible immobility to headway. She brought the wind right aft, then on to her larboard quarter; and hauling out the mizen and trimming all sharp, he set the course, dismissed the watch below, and walked into his cabin, relief flooding into him. The bases of the universe were firm again, the *Polychrest* was heading straight out into the offing with the wind one point free; the crew had not done very badly, no time worth mentioning had been lost; and with any luck his steward would have brewed a decent pot of coffee. He sat on a locker, wedging himself against the bulkhead as she rolled: over his head there was the hurrying of feet as ropes were coiled down and made trim, and then came the long-interrupted sounds of cleaning – a bear, a great padded, shot-laden block of stone, started growling on the deck eighteen inches from his ears: he blinked once or twice, smiled, and smiling went fast asleep.

He was still asleep when the hands were piped to dinner, sleeping still when the gun-room sat down to its gammon and spinach, and for the first time Stephen saw all the *Polychrest*'s officers together – all except for Pullings, who had the watch, and who was walking the quarterdeck with his hands behind his back, pacing in as close an imitation of Captain Aubrey as his form could manage, and remembering, every now and then, to look stern, devilish, as like a right tartar as possible, in spite of his bubbling happiness. At the head of the table sat Mr Parker, an acquaintance of some days' standing, a tall, spare, disapproving man, rather good-looking, apart from the expression on his face; then the lieutenant of Marines in his scarlet coat, a black-haired Scotsman from the Hebrides whose face was so marked by the smallpox that it was difficult to make out what habitual expression it might wear; he had a very well-bred turn, however; and Macdonald was his name. Mr Jones the purser, his neighbour, was also a black man, but there the likeness stopped; the purser was a drooping little flaccid man with pendulous cheeks either side of a fleshy red mouth; his face was the colour of cheese, and this uniform pallor swept up his high forehead to a baldness that reached from ear to ear. His straight hair grew only in a fringe round this pool, hanging some way down his neck, and in whiskers; yet a strong beard showed blue on his waxy cheeks, a very powerful growth. His appearance was that of a small shopkeeper; but there was little time to judge of his conversation, for at the sight of his plate he started from the table with a watery belch, rushed staggering to the quarter-gallery, and was seen no more. Then there was the master, still yawning from his morning watch. He was a slight, elderly, grizzled man with bright blue eyes, and he said little as he set to his table at the beginning of the meal: Stephen was habitually silent; the others were feeling their way with their new messmates, and their knowledge that the surgeon was the captain's particular friend acted as a further check.

However, as Stephen's appetite waned, so his desire for information increased, and laying down his knife and fork he said to the master, 'Pray, sir, what is the function of the curious sloping metal-lined cylindrical place immediately in front of my store-room? What is its name?'

'Why, Doctor,' said Mr Goodridge, 'what to call it I do not rightly know, other than an abomination; but the ship-wrights spoke of it as the combustion-chamber, so I take it it was where the secret weapon was stowed. It used to lead out on deck where the fo'c'sle is now.'

'What kind of a secret weapon?' asked Macdonald.

'Something in the nature of a rocket, I believe.'

'Yes,' said the first lieutenant, 'a kind of enormous rocket without a stick. It was the ship that was to be the stick, and those levered chutes for shot were intended to bring her by the head or by the stern for elevation: the weapon was calculated to destroy a first-rate at the distance of a mile, but it had to be amidships, to counteract the roll, and that was the reason for the system of lateral keels and rudders.'

'If the rocket was the calibre of the chamber, then the recoil must have been prodigious,' said Macdonald.

'Prodigious,' said Mr Parker. 'That was why the sharp stern was imagined, to prevent the sudden thrust destroying her bottom – the whole ship recoiled, whereas a square stern, by resisting, would be crushed. Even so, they had to put a mass of timber where the stern-post should be, to take the first impact.' A very exalted personage had been present at the experimental firing that had cost the inventor his life, and he had told Mr Parker that the ship had darted back her whole length, at the same time being pressed down in the water as far as her wing-transoms. The exalted personage had been against it from the start; Mr Congreve, who went down with the party, had said it would never answer; and it had not answered – these innovations never did. Mr Parker was against any break with tradition; it would never answer in the Navy; he did not care for these flint-locks for the guns, for example; although indeed they took a fine polish, and looked well enough, for an inspection.

'How did the poor gentleman come to be killed?' asked the master.

'It seems that he would light the fuse himself, and as it hung fire, he put his head into the chamber to see what was amiss, when it exploded.'

'Well, I am sorry for him,' said Mr Goodridge. 'But if it had to be, it might have been as well if he had sent the ship to the bottom at the same time. A cranker, more unseaworthy craft I never saw, and I have seen a mort in my time. She made more leeway than a common raft between St Helen's and the Bill, for all the sharp floor and sliding keels, and she gripes like a man-trap. Then she

224

goes and misses stays in a mill-pond. There is no pleasing her. She reminds me of Mrs Goodridge – whatever you do is wrong. If the captain had not box-hauled her in a flash, why, I don't know where we might have come to. A most seamanlike manoeuvre, I must say; though I should not have ventured it myself, not with such a ragamuffin crew. And indeed she had more sternway upon her than I should have thought possible. As you say, sir, she was built to recoil, and I thought she was going to go on recoiling until we were brought up all standing on the coast of France. A crinkum-crankum piece of work, in my opinion, and 'tis the Lord's blessing we have a right seaman in command; but what even he will do, or what the Archangel Gabriel would do, if it comes on to blow, I do not know, I am sure. The Channel is not so broad as all that; and in point of searoom, what this here craft requires, is the great Southern Ocean, at its widest part.'

The master's words were prompted by the *Polychrest*'s increasing roll; it sent the bread-barge careering over the table, and a midshipman into Jack's cabin, with the news that the wind was shifting into the east, a little mouse-like child, stiff in his best uniform, with his dirk at his side – he had slept with it.

'Thank you, Mr – ' said Jack. 'I do not believe I remember your name.'

'Parslow, sir, if you please.'

Of course. The Commissioner's protégé, a naval widow's son. 'What have you been doing to your face, Mr Parslow?' he asked, looking at the red, gaping, lint-flecked wound that ran across that smooth oval cheek from ear to chin.

'I was shaving, sir,' said Mr Parslow with a pride he could not conceal. 'Shaving, sir, and a huge great wave came.'

'Show it to the doctor, and tell him, with my compliments, that I should be glad if he would drink tea with me. Why are you in your number one rig?'

225

'They said – it was thought I ought to show an example to the men, sir, this being my first day at sea.'

'Very proper. But I should put on some foul-weather clothes now. Tell me, did they send you for the key of the keelson?'

'Yes, sir; and I looked for it everywhere. Bonden told me he thought the gunner's daughter might have it, but when I asked Mr Rolfe, he said he was sorry, he was not a married man.'

'Well, well. You have foul-weather clothes?'

'Why, sir, there are a great many things in my chest, my *sea*-chest, that the shopman told Mama I should be equipped with. And I have my father's sou-wester.'

'Mr Babbington will show you what to put on. Tell him with my compliments, that he will show you what to put on,' he added, remembering that gentleman's inhuman barbarity. 'Do not wipe your nose upon your sleeve, Mr Parslow. It ain't genteel.'

'No, sir. Beg pardon, sir.'

'Cut along then,' said Jack irritably. 'Am I a God-damned wet nurse?' he asked his pea-jacket.

On deck he was greeted by a squall of rain mixed with sleet and spray. The wind had increased to a fine fresh breeze, sweeping the fog away and replacing it by a low sky – bands of weeping cloud against a steely grey, black on the eastern horizon; a nasty short choppy sea was getting up against the tide, and although the *Polychrest* was holding her course well enough, she was shipping a good deal of water, and her very moderate spread of canvas laid her over as though she had topgallants abroad. So she was as crank as he had feared; and a wet ship into the bargain. There were two men at the wheel, and from the way they were cramped on to the spokes it was clear they were having to fight hard to keep her from flying up into the wind.

He studied the log-board, made a rough calculation of the position, adding a triple leeway, and decided to wear in half an hour, when both watches would be on deck. He had plenty of room, and there was no point in harassing the few good men he had aboard, particularly as the sky looked changeable, menacing, damned unpleasant – they might have a dirty night of it. And he would get the topgallantmasts down on deck before long. 'Mr Parker,' he said, 'we will take another reef in the foretopsail, if you please.'

The bosun's call, the rush of hands, the volley of orders through Parker's speaking-trumpet – 'Halliards let fly – clap on to that brace – Mr Malloch, touch up those hands at the brace.' The yards came round, the wind spilled from the sail and the *Polychrest* righted herself, at the same time making such a cruel gripe that the man at the con had to fling himself at the wheel to prevent her being taken aback. 'Lay out – look alive, there – you, sir, you on the yardarm, are you asleep? Are you going to pass the – weather earing? Damn your eyes, are you going to stow that bunt? Mr Rossall, take that man's name. Lay in.'

Through the clamour Jack watched the men aloft. The man on the yardarm was young Haines, from the *Lord Mornington*; he knew his trade; might make a good captain of the foretop. He saw his foot slip as he scrambled in towards the mast – those horses wanted mousing.

'Send the last man off the yard aft,' called the first lieutenant, red in the face from shouting. 'Start him, Mr Malloch.'

This same old foolery – the last man off was the first man on, the man who went right out on to the yardarm. It was a hard service – it had to be a hard service – but there was no need to make it harder, discouraging the willing hands. The people were going to have plenty to do: it was a pity for them to waste their strength beating one another. And yet again it was easy to seek a cheap popularity by checking an officer in public – easy, and disastrous in the long run.

'Sail ho!' hailed the look-out.

'Where away?'

'Right astern, sir.'

She came up out of a dark smudge of half-frozen rain, a frigate hull-up already, on the same tack as the *Polychrest* and overhauling her very fast. French or English? He was no great way from Cherbourg. 'Make the private signal,' said Jack. 'Mr Parker, your glass, if you please.'

He fixed the frigate in the grey round of the objective, swaying to counterbalance the sloop's roll, pitch and shudder, and as the *Polychrest*'s windward gun went off behind him he saw the blue-white-blue break out aboard her, curving far out to leeward, and the momentary whiff from her answering gun. 'Make our number,' he said, relaxing. He gave orders for the mousing of the horses, desired Mr Parker to see what he could make of the frigate, sent Haines forward, and settled to watch in peace.

'Three of them, sir,' said Mr Parker. 'And I think the first is *Amethyst*.'

Three there were, in line ahead. '*Amethyst* she is, sir,' said the signal midshipman, huddling his book under the shelter of his bosom. They were directly in his wake, steering the same course. But the *Polychrest*'s leeway was such that in a very short while he saw them not head-on, but from an angle, an angle that increased with alarming speed, so that in five minutes he was watching them over the weather quarter. They had already struck their topgallantmasts, but they were still carrying their topsails atrip – their full, expert crews could reef them in a moment. The first was indeed the *Amethyst*; the second he could not make out – perhaps the *Minerve*; the third was the *Franchise*, with his old friend Heneage Dundas aboard, a post captain, in command of a beautiful French-built thirty-six-gun frigate; Dundas, five years junior to him as a lieutenant, thirteen months as master and commander; Jack had cobbed him repeatedly in the midshipmen's berth of Old Ironsides: and would do so again. There he was, standing up on the slide of a quarter-deck carronade, as pleased as Punch, waving his hat. Jack raised his own, and the wind took his bright yellow hair, tearing it from the ribbon behind, and streamed it away north-westward. As if in reply a hoist ran up to the *Franchise*'s mizen-peak.

'Alphabetic, sir,' said the midshipman, spelling it out. 'P S – oh yes, Psalms. Psalms cxlvii, 10.'

'Acknowledge,' said Jack who was no Biblical scholar.

Two guns from the *Amethyst*, and the frigates tacked in succession, moving like so many models on a sheet of glass: round they went, each exactly in the same piece of water, keeping their stations as though they were linked together. It was a beautifully executed manoeuvre, above all with such a head-sea and such a wind, the result of years of training – a crew that pulled together, officers that knew their ship.

He shook his head, staring after the frigates as they vanished into the gloom. Eight bells struck. 'Mr Parker,' he said, 'we will get the topgallantmasts down on deck, and then we will wear.' By the time the masts were struck there would be no satirical friends to watch from a distance.

'I beg your pardon, sir?' asked Parker, with an anxious poke of his head.

Jack repeated his order and retired to the taffrail to let his first lieutenant carry on.

Glancing at the *Polychrest*'s wake to judge her leeway he noticed a little dark bird, fluttering weakly just over the water with its legs dangling; it vanished under the larboard quarter, and as he moved across to make sure of it, he tripped over something soft, about knee-height, something very like a limpet – the child Parslow, under his sou-wester.

'Why, Mr Parslow,' he said, picking him up, 'you are properly rigged now, I see. You will be glad of it. Run below to the doctor and tell him, if he chooses to see a stormy petrel, he has but to come on deck.'

It was not a stormy petrel, but a much rarer cousin with yellow feet – so rare that Stephen could not identify him until he pittered across a wave so close that those yellow feet showed clear.

'If rarity and the force of the storm are in direct proportion,' he reflected, watching it attentively, 'then we are in for a most prodigious hurricane. I shall not mention it, however.'

A frightful crash forward: the foretopgallantmast brought itself down on deck more briskly than in the smartest frigate, half stunning Mr Parker and plunging Jack into manoeuvres more suitable for a petrel than a mariner. Throughout the night the wind backed until it was blowing hard from the north; there it stayed, north-east, north, or north-west, never allowing more than close-reefed topsails, if that, for nine days on end, nine days of rain, snow, steep wicked seas, and a perpetual fighting for their lives; nine days in which Jack rarely left the deck and young Parslow never once took off his clothes; nine days of wearing, lying to, scudding under bare poles, and never a sight of the sun – no notion of their position within fifty miles and more. And when at last a strong south-wester allowed them to make up their enormous leeway, their noonday observation showed that they were where they had started from.

Early in the blow a lee-lurch, laying the *Polychrest* on her beam-ends, had shot the dazed first lieutenant down the main hatchway, damaging his shoulder, and he had spent the rest of the time in his cot, with the water washing about it often enough, and in great pain. Jack was sorry for the pain, in an abstract way, though it seemed fair that one so fond of inflicting agony should feel a touch of it, but he was heartily glad of Parker's absence – the man was incompetent, incompetent for such a situation as this. He was conscientious, he did his duty as he understood it; but he was no seaman.

The master, Pullings, Rossall, the senior master's mate,

the bosun and the gunner were seamen; so were a dozen of the hands. Babbington and Allen, another oldster, were shaping well; and as for the rest of the people, they at least knew what they were to haul upon at the word of command. This long week's blow, when they were close on foundering twice a day and when everybody knew it, had crammed a deal of training into a short time – short when measured by the calendar rather than by mortal dread. Training in manoeuvres of every kind, but particularly in the use of the pumps: they had not stopped for an hour since the second day of the blow.

Now as they sailed up the Channel, passing Selsey Bill with a light air on the quarter and topgallantsails set, with the galley fires lighted at last and a hot dinner in their bellies, he felt that they might not be disgraced when the *Polychrest* reached her station; and she would reach it now, he was sure, even if she had to tide it all the way – no unlikely event, with this wind dying on him. She would not be disgraced: he was short-handed, of course, and there were seventeen men in the sick-bay – two hernias, five bad falls with broken bones, and the rest the usual wounds from falling spars or blocks or ropes crossing a hand or leg. One landsman, an unemployed glover from Shepton Mallet, had been lost overboard, and a thief from the Winchester assizes had gone raving, staring, barking mad off Ushant: yet on the other hand, sea-sickness had vanished, and even the quota-men from the inland gaols could walk about the deck without much danger to themselves or others. The crew were a poor-looking set, upon the whole, but when he had had time to exercise them at the guns, it was not impossible that he might make a passable man-of-war out of the *Polychrest*. He knew her tolerably well now: he and the master (he had a great esteem for Mr Goodridge) had worked out a sail-plan that made the most of what qualities she possessed, and when he could alter her trim to bring her by the head and rake her masts she might do better; but he could not love her. She was a mean-spirited vessel, radically vicious, cross-grained, laboursome, cruel in her unreliability; and he could not love her. She had disappointed him so often when even a log canoe would have risen to the occasion that his strong natural affection for his command had dwindled quite away. He had sailed in some rough old tubs, ponderous things with no perceptible virtue to the outsider, but he had always been able to find excuses for them – they had always been the finest ships in the history of the Navy for some particular quality – and this had never happened to him before. The feeling was so strange, the disloyalty so uncomfortable, that it was some time before he would acknowledge it; and when he did – he was pacing the quarterdeck after his solitary dinner at the time – it gave him such uneasiness of mind that he turned to the midshipman of the watch, who was clinging motionless to a stanchion, and said, 'Mr Parslow, you will find the Doctor in the sick-bay . . . '

'Find him yourself,' said Parslow.

Was it possible that these words had been uttered? Jack paused in his stride. From the rigid blankness of the quartermaster, the man at the wheel, and the gunner's mates busy with the aftermost port carronade, and from the mute writhing of the midshipmen on the gangway, it was clear that they had.

'I tell you what it is, Goldilocks,' went on Parslow, closing one eye, 'don't you try to come it high over me, for I've a spirit that won't brook it. Find him yourself.'

'Pass the word for the bosun's mate,' said Jack. 'Quartermaster, Mr Parslow's hammock, if you please.' The bosun's mate came running aft, his starter in his hand. 'Seize the young gentleman to the gun in my cabin.'

The young gentleman had released his hold on the stanchion; he was now lying on the deck, protesting that he should not be beaten, that he should dirk any man who presumed to lay a hand upon him – he was an officer. The bosun's mate picked him up by the small of the back:

the sentry opened and closed the cabin door. A startled cry and then some treble oaths that made the grinning quarterdeck stretch its eyes, the whole punctuated by the measured thump of a rope's end; and then Mr Parslow, sobbing bitterly, was led out by the hand. 'Lash him into his hammock, Rogers,' said Jack. 'Mr Pullings, Mr Pullings, the grog for the midshipmen's berth is stopped until further orders.'

That evening in his cabin he said to Stephen, 'Do you know what those blackguards in the midshipmen's berth did to young Parslow?'

'Whether or no, you are going to tell me,' observed Stephen, helping himself to rum.

'They made him beastly drunk and then sent him on deck. Almost the first day they might have turned in for their watch below, the first time they are not up to their knees in water, they can think of nothing better to do than to make a youngster drunk. They shall not do it again, however. I have stopped their grog.'

'It would be as well if you were to stop the whole ship's grog. A most pernicious custom, a very gross abuse of animal appetite, a monstrous aberration – half a pint of rum, forsooth! I should not have a quarter of the men under my care, was it not for your vile rum. They are brought down with their limbs, ribs, collar-bones shattered, having fallen from the rigging drunk – diligent, stout, attentive men who would never fall when sober. Come, let us pour it secretly away.'

'And have a mutiny on our hands? Thank you very kindly. No: I should rather have them three sheets in the wind now and again, but willing to do their duty the rest of the time. Mutiny. It makes your blood run cold to think of it. Men you have worked with right through the commission and liked, growing cold and secret; no jokes, no singing out, no good will; the ship falling into two camps, with the undecided men puzzled and wretched in between. And then the shot-rolling by night.'

'Shot-rolling?'

'They roll shot along the deck in the night-watches, to let you know their mind, and maybe to catch an officer's legs.'

'As for mutinies in general,' said Stephen, 'I am all in favour of 'em. You take men from their homes or their chosen occupations, you confine them in insalubrious conditions upon a wholly inadequate diet, you subject them to the tyranny of bosun's mates, you expose them to unimagined perils; what is more, you defraud them of their meagre food, pay and allowances – everything but this sacred rum of yours. Had I been at Spithead, I should certainly have joined the mutineers. Indeed, I am astonished at their moderation.'

'Pray, Stephen, do not speak like this, nattering about the service; it makes me so very low. I know things are not perfect, but I cannot reform the world *and* run a man-of-war. In any case, be candid, and think of the *Sophie* – think of any happy ship.'

'There are such things, sure; but they depend upon the whim, the digestion and the virtue of one or two men, and that is iniquitous. I am opposed to authority, that egg of misery and oppression; I am opposed to it largely for what it does to those who exercise it.'

'Well,' said Jack, 'it has done me no good. This afternoon I was savaged by a midshipman, and now I am harassed by my own surgeon. Come, Stephen, drink up, and let us have some music.' But instead of tuning his fiddle he reached beyond it, saying, 'Here is something that will interest you. Have you ever heard of robber-bolts?'

'I have not.'

'This is one.' He held out a short solid copper cylinder with a great nut on the end of it. 'As you know, bolts are to hold the hull together, going right through her timbers; and the best are copper, against the corrosion. They are expensive – I believe two pounds of copper, a short piece

234

of bolt, will pay a shipwright's wages for a day. But if you are a damned villain, you cut off the middle, drive each end home and pocket the money for the length of copper in between. Nobody is any the wiser until the frame opens; and that may not happen until the ship is on the other side of the world. And even then she may founder, leaving no witnesses.'

'When did you know this?'

'I suspected it from the start. I knew she would be a damned job, coming from Hickman's; and then the fellows at the yard were so fulsome, so free with their hampers. But I was certain only the other day. Now that she has worked a little, it is easier to be certain. I pulled this one out with my fingers.'

'Could you not have made representations in the proper quarters?'

'Yes. I could have asked for a survey and waited for a month or six weeks: and then where should I have been? It is a dockyard matter, and you hear very rum tales of ships being passed whatever their state, and small clerks setting up their carriages. No. I preferred to take her out; and indeed, she has withstood quite a blow. I shall have her hove down if ever I can – if ever I can find the right moment, or if she will not float without it.'

They remained silent for a while, and all the time the steady throb of the pumps sounded through the cabin, and, almost keeping time, the barking of the lunatic.

'I must give that man some more of my laudanum,' said Stephen, half to himself.

Jack's mind was still on bolts, timbers, and the other powers that held his ship together. 'What do you say to Parker's shoulder?' he asked. 'He will not be fit for duty for a great while, I dare say? Should lay up ashore, no doubt, and take the waters?'

'Not at all,' said Stephen. 'He is coming along admirably – Dr Ramis's thin water gruel has answered admirably, and the low diet. Properly slung, he may come on deck tomorrow.'

'Oh,' said Jack. 'No sick ticket? No long leave? You do not feel that the waters might help his deafness, too?' He looked wistfully into Stephen's face, but without much hope: in what he conceived to be his duty as a medical man, Stephen Maturin would not budge for man, God or beast. In such matters he was beyond the reach of reason or even of friendship. They never discussed the officers with whom Stephen messed, but Jack's desire to be shot of his first lieutenant, his opinion of Mr Parker, was clear enough to anyone who knew him well: yet Stephen merely looked dogged, reached for the fiddle and ran up and down the scale. 'Where did you get this?' he asked.

'I picked it up in a pawnshop near the Sally-Port. It cost twelve and six.'

'You were not cheated, my dear. I like its tone extremely – warm, mellow. You are a great judge of a fiddle, to be sure. Come, come, there is not a moment to lose; I make my rounds at seven bells. One, two, three,' he cried, tapping his foot, and the cabin was filled with the opening movement of Boccherini's Corelli sonata, a glorious texture of sound, the violin sending up brilliant jets through the 'cello's involutions, and they soared up and away from the grind of pumps, the tireless barking, the problems of command, up, the one answering the other, joining, separating, twining, rising into their native air.

A keen, pale, wintry morning in the Downs: the hands at breakfast, Jack walking up and down.

'The admiral is making our number, sir,' said the signal midshipman.

'Very well,' said Jack. 'Man the gig.' He had been expecting this since before dawn, when he reported his presence; the gig was already alongside and his best coat was lying spread out on his cot. He reappeared, wearing it, and went over the side to the twittering of the bosun's pipes.

The sea was as calm as a sea can well be; the tide was at the full, and the whole grey surface under the frozen sky had the air of waiting – not a ripple, scarcely a hint of living swell. Behind him, beyond the dwindling *Polychrest*, lay the town of Deal, and away beyond it, the North Foreland. Ahead of him, the massive bulk of the *Cumberland*, 74, with the blue ensign at the mizen; then two cables' lengths away, the *Melpomène*, a lovely frigate, then two sloops and a cutter; and beyond them again, between the squadron and the Goodwin sands, the whole of the West Indies, Turkey, Guinea and India trade, a hundred and forty sail of merchantmen lying there in the road, a wood of masts, waiting for a wind and a convoy, every yard and spar distinct in this cold air – almost no colour, only line, but that line unbelievably sharp and clear.

However, Jack had been gazing at this scene ever since the pale disc of the sun had made it visible, and during the pull to the flagship his mind was taken up with other things: his expression was grave and contained as he went up the side, saluted the quarterdeck, greeted the *Cumberland*'s captain, and was shown into the great cabin.

Admiral Harte was eating kippers and drinking tea, his secretary and a mass of papers on the other side of the table. He had aged shockingly since Jack had last seen him; his shallow eyes seemed to have moved even closer together and his look of falsity to have grown even more pronounced.

'So here you are at last,' he cried – with a smile, however, and reaching up an unctuous hand. 'You must have come dawdling up the Channel; I expected you three tides ago, upon my honour.' Admiral Harte's honour and Jack's dawdling were much on a par, and Jack only bowed. The remark was not intended to be answered, in any case – a mere automatic unpleasantness – and Harte went on, with an awkward assumption of familiarity and good fellowship. 'Sit down. What have you been doing with yourself? You look ten years older. The girls at the back of Portsmouth Point, I dare say. Do you want a cup of tea?'

Money was Harte's nearest approach to joy, his ruling passion: in the Mediterranean, where they had served together, Jack had been remarkably successful in the article of prizes; he had been given cruise after cruise, and he had put more than ten thousand pounds into his admiral's pocket. Captain Harte, as commandant of Port Mahon, hd come in for no share of this, of course, and his dislike for Jack had remained unaffected; but now the case was altered; now he stood to gain by Jack's exertions, and he meant to conciliate his good will.

Jack was rowed back again, still over this silent water, but with something less of gravity in his look. He could not understand Harte's drift; it made him uneasy, and the lukewarm tea was disagreeable in his stomach; but he had met with no open hostility, and his immediate future was clear – the *Polychrest* was not to go with this convoy, but was to spend some time in the Downs, seeing to the manning of the squadron and the harassing of the invasion flotilla over the way.

Aboard the *Polychrest* his officers stood waiting for him; the hammocks were up, as neat as art could make them, the decks were clean, the ropes flemished, the Marines geometrically exact as they presented arms and all the officers saluted; yet something was out of tune. The odd flush on Parker's face, the lowering obstinacy on Stephen's, the concern on Pullings', Goodridge's and Macdonald's, gave him a notion of what was afoot; and this notion was confirmed five minutes later, when the first lieutenant came into his cabin and said, 'I am very much concerned to have to report a serious breach of discipline, sir.'

A little after breakfast, while Jack was aboard the admiral, Stephen had come on deck: the first thing he had seen there was a man running aft with a bosun's mate beating him from behind – not an uncommon sight in a man-of-war. But this man had a heavy iron marline-spike between his teeth, held tight with spunyarn, and as he screamed, blood ran from either side of his mouth. He came to a dead halt at the break of the quarterdeck, and Stephen, taking a lancet from his waistcoat pocket, stepped up to him, cut the spunyarn, took the spike and threw it into the sea.

'I remonstrated with him – I told him that the punishment was inflicted upon my orders – and he attacked me with an extreme ferocity.'

'Physically?'

'No, sir. Verbally. He cast out reflections upon my courage and my fitness to command. I should have taken decided measures, but I knew that you were shortly to return, and I understood he was your friend. I hinted that he should withdraw to his cabin: he did not see fit to comply, but stayed pacing the quarterdeck, on the starboard side, although it was represented to him that with the captain out of the ship, this was *my* prerogative.'

'My friendship for Dr Maturin is neither here nor there, Mr Parker: I am surprised that you should have mentioned it. You must understand that he is an Irish gentleman of great eminence in his profession, that he knows very little, almost nothing, of the service, and that he is extremely impatient of being practised upon – being made game of. He does not always know when we are earnest and when we are not. I dare say there has been some misunderstanding in this case. I remember him to have flown out very savagely at the master of the *Sophie* over what he conceived to be a misplaced joke about a trysailmast.'

'A master is not a lieutenant.'

'Now, sir, do you instruct me upon rank? Do you pretend to tell me something that is clear to a newly-joined midshipman?' Jack did not raise his voice, but he was pale with anger, not only at Parker's stupid impertinence but

239

even more at the whole situation, and at what must come. 'Let me tell you, sir, that your methods of discipline do not please me, I had wished to avoid this: I had supposed that when I observed to you that your punishment of Isaac Barrow was perfectly illegal, that you would have taken the hint. And there were other occasions. Let us understand one another. I am not a preachee-flogee captain: I will have a taut ship, by flogging if need be, but I will have no unnecessary brutality. What is the name of the man you gagged?'

'I am sorry to say I do not recall his name for the moment, sir. A landsman, sir – a waister in the larboard watch.'

'It is usual in the service for an efficient first lieutenant to know the names of the men. You will oblige me by finding it directly.'

'William Edwards, sir,' said Parker, some moments later.

'William Edwards. Just so. A scavenger from Rutland: took the bounty. Had never seen the sea or a ship or an officer in his life – no notion of discipline. He answered, I suppose?'

'Yes, sir. Said, "I came as fast as I could, and who are you, any gait?" on being rebuked for slackness.'

'Why was he being started?'

'He left his post without leave, to go to the head.'

'There must be some discrimination, Mr Parker. When he has been aboard long enough to know his duty, to know the officers and for the officers to know him – and I repeat that it is an officer's duty to know his men – then he may be gagged for answering. If indeed he should do so, a most unlikely event in a ship even half well run. And the same applies to most of the crew; it is useless and detrimental to the good of the service to beat them until they know what is required of them. You, an experienced officer, clearly misunderstood Edwards: you thought he intended gross disrespect. It is exceedingly possible that Dr Maturin, with no experience whatsoever, misunderstood you. Be so good as to show me your defaulters list. This will not do, Mr Parker. Glave, Brown, Stindall, Burnet, all newly-joined landsmen: and so it runs, a list long enough for a first-rate, an ill-conducted first-rate. We shall deal with this later. Pass the word for Dr Maturin.'

This was a Jack Aubrey he had never seen before, larger than life, hard, cold, and strong with a hundred years of tradition behind him, utterly convinced that he was right. 'Good morning, Dr Maturin,' he said. 'There has been a misunderstanding between you and Mr Parker. You were not aware that gagging is a customary punishment in the Navy. No doubt you looked upon it as a piece of rough horseplay.'

'I looked upon it as a piece of extreme brutality. Edwards's teeth are in a state of advanced decay – he has been under my hands – and this iron bar had crushed two molars. I removed the bar at once, and . . .'

'You removed it on medical grounds. You were not aware that it was a customary punishment, awarded by an officer – you knew nothing of the reason for the punishment?'

'No, sir.'

'You did wrong, sir: you acted inconsiderately. And in your agitation, in the heat of the moment, you spoke hastily to Mr Parker. You must express your sense of regret that this misunderstanding should have arisen.'

'Mr Parker,' said Stephen, 'I regret that there has been this misunderstanding. I regret the remarks that passed between us; and if you wish I will repeat my apology on the quarterdeck, before those who heard them.'

Parker reddened, looked stiff and awkward; his right hand, the usual instrument for acknowledging such declarations, was immobilized in his sling. He bowed and said something about 'being entirely satisfied – more than enough – for his part he too regretted any disobliging expression that might have escaped him.'

241

There was a pause. 'I will not detain you, gentlemen,' said Jack coldly. 'Mr Parker, let the starboard watch be exercised at the great guns and the larboard at reefing topsails. Mr Pullings will take the small-arms men. What is that infernal row. Hallows,' – to the Marine sentry outside the door – 'what is that din?'

'Beg pardon, your Honour,' said the soldier, 'it's the captain's steward and the gun-room steward fighting over the use of the coffee-pot.'

'God damn their eyes,' cried Jack. 'I'll tan their hides – I'll give them a bloody shirt – I'll stop their capers. Old seamen, too: rot them. Mr Parker, let us establish a little order in this sloop.'

'Jack, Jack,' said Stephen, when the lamp was lit, 'I fear I am a sad embarrassment to you. I think I shall pack my chest and go ashore.'

'No, soul, never say that,' said Jack wearily. 'This explanation with Parker had to come: I had hoped to avoid it, but he did not catch my drift; and really I am just as glad to have had it out.'

'Still and all, I think I will go ashore.'

'And desert your patients?'

'Sea-surgeons are ten a penny.'

'And your friends?'

'Why, upon my word, Jack, I think you would be better without me. I am not suited for a sea-life. You know far better than I, that discord among the officers is of no use to your ship; and I do not care to be a witness of this kind of brutality, or any party to it.'

'Ours is a hard service, I admit. But you will find as much brutality by land.'

'I am not a party to it by land.'

'Yet you did not so much mind the flogging in the *Sophie*?'

'No. The world in general, and even more your briny

world, accepts flogging. It is this perpetual arbitrary harassing, bullying, hitting, brow-beating, starting – these capricious torments, spreadeagling, gagging – this general atmosphere of oppression. I should have told you earlier. But it is a delicate subject, between you and me.'

'I know. It is the devil . . . At the beginning of a commission a raw, ugly crew (and we have some precious hard bargains, you know) – has to be driven hard, and startled into prompt obedience; but this had gone too far. Parker and the bosun are not bad fellows – I did not give them a strong enough lead at the beginning – I was remiss. It will not be the same in the future.'

'You must forgive me, my dear. Those men are dropsical with authority, permanently deranged, I must go.'

'I say you shall not,' said Jack, with a smile.

'I say I shall.'

'Do you know, my dear Stephen, that you may not come and go as you please?' said Jack, leaning back in his chair and gazing at Stephen with placid triumph. 'Do not you know that you are under martial law? That if you was to stir without my leave, I should be obliged to put an R against your name, have you taken up, brought back in irons and most severely punished? What do you say to a flogging through the feet, ha? You have no notion of the powers of a captain of a man-of-war. *He* is dropsical with authority, if you like.'

'Must I not go ashore?'

'No, of course you must not, and that's the end to it. You must make your bed and lie on it.' He paused, with a feeling that this was not quite the epigram that he had wished. 'Now let me tell you of my interview with that scrub Harte . . . '

'If, then, as I understand you, we are to spend some time in this place, you will have no objection to granting me some days' leave of absence. Apart from all other considerations, I must get my dement and my compound

243

fracture of the femur ashore: the hospital at Dover is at an inconsiderable distance – a most eligible port.'

'Certainly,' cried Jack, 'if you give me your word not to run, so that I have all the trouble of careering over the country after you with a posse – a posse navitatum. Certainly. Any time you like to name.'

'And when I am there,' said Stephen deliberately, 'I shall ride over to Mapes.'

CHAPTER EIGHT

'A gentleman to see Miss Williams,' said the maid.

'Who is it, Peggy?' cried Cecilia.

'I believe it is Dr Maturin, Miss.'

'I will come at once,' said Sophia, throwing her needle-work into a corner and casting a distracted glance at the mirror.

'It must be for me,' said Cecilia. 'Dr Maturin is my young man.'

'Oh, Cissy, what stuff,' said Sophia, hurrying down-stairs.

'You have one, no *two* already,' whispered Cecilia, catching her in the corridor. 'You can't have three. Oh, it's so unfair,' she hissed, as the door closed and Sophia walked into the morning-room with a great air of composure.

'How happy I am to see you,' they said, both together, looking so pleased that a casual observer would have sworn they were lovers, or at least that there was a particular attachment between them.

'Mama will be so disappointed to have missed you,' said Sophia. 'She has taken Frankie up to town, to have her teeth filed, poor pet.'

'I hope Mrs Williams is well, and Miss Cecilia? How is Mrs Villiers?'

'Diana is not here, but the others are very well, I thank you. How are you, and how is Captain Aubrey?'

'Blooming, blooming, thank you, my dear. That is to say, I am blooming: poor Jack is a little under the weather, what with his new command, and a crew of left-handed hedgecreepers from half the gaols in the kingdom.'

'Oh,' cried Sophie, clasping her hands, 'I am sure he works too hard. Do beg him not to work too hard, Dr

Maturin. He will listen to you – I sometimes think you are the only person he will listen to. But surely the men must love him? I remember how the dear sailors at Melbury ran to do whatever he said, so cheerfully; and he was so good to them – never gruff or commanding, as some people are with their servants.'

'I dare say they will come to love him presently, when they appreciate his virtues,' said Stephen. 'But for the moment we are all at sixes and sevens. However, we have four old Sophies aboard – his coxswain volunteered – and they are a great comfort.'

'I can quite see they would follow him anywhere in the world,' said Sophia. 'Dear things, with their pigtails and buckled shoes. But tell me, is the *Polychrest* really so very – ? Admiral Haddock says she can never swim, but he loves to make our flesh creep, which is very ill-natured in him. He says she has two main topsail yards, in such a sneering, contemptuous way. I have no patience with him. Not that he means it unkindly, of course; but surely it is very wrong to speak lightly of such important things, and to say she will certainly go to the bottom? It is not true, is it, Dr Maturin? And surely two main topsail yards are better than one?'

'I am no sailor, as you know, my dear, but I should have thought so. She is an odd, pragmatical vessel, however, and she has this way of going backwards when they mean her to go forwards. Other ships find it entertaining, but it does not seem to please our officers or seamen. As for her not floating, you may set your mind at rest. We had a nine days' blow that took us far out into the chops of the Channel, with an ugly, pounding sea that partially submerged us, shaking away spars, booms, ropes; and she survived that. I do not suppose Jack was off the deck more than three hours at a time – I remember seeing him lashed to the bitts, up to his middle in the water, bidding the helmsman ease her as the seas came in; and on catching sight of me said, "She'll live yet." So you may be quite easy.'

'Oh dear, oh dear,' said Sophia in a low voice. 'At least, I do hope he eats well, to keep up his strength.'

'No,' said Stephen, with great satisfaction, 'that he does not. I am glad to say he does not eat at all well. I used to tell him over and over again, when he had Louis Durand as his cook, that he was digging his grave with his teeth: he ate far, far too much three times a day. Now he has no cook; now he makes do with our common fare; and he is much the better for it – has lost two stone at least. He is very poor now, as you know, and cannot afford to poison himself; to ruin his constitution: it is true that he cannot afford to poison any guests either, which grieves him. He no longer keeps a table. But you, my dear, how are you? It seems to me that you are more in need of attention than our honest tar.' He had been watching her all this time, and although that unbelievable complexion was as lovely as ever, it was lovely in a lower tone, once the pinkness of surprise had faded; there was tiredness, sorrow, a want of light in her eyes; and something of the straight spring had gone. 'Let me see your tongue, my dear,' he said taking her wrist. 'I love the smell of this house,' he said, as he counted automatically. 'Orris-root, I believe? There was orris-root everywhere in my childhood home – smelt it as soon as you opened the door. Yes, yes. Just as I thought. You are not eating enough. What do you weigh?'

'Eight stone and five pounds,' said Sophia, hanging her head.

'You are fine-boned, sure; but for an upstanding young woman like you it is not nearly enough. You must take porter with your dinner. I shall tell your mother. A pint of good stout will do all that is required: or almost all.'

'A gentleman to see Miss Williams,' said the maid. 'Mr Bowles,' she added, with a knowing look.

'I am not at home, Peggy,' said Sophie. 'Beg Miss Cecilia to see him in the drawing-room. Now I have told a lie,' she said, catching her lip behind her teeth. 'How dreadful. Dr

Maturin, would you mind coming for a walk in the park, and then it will be true?'

'With all the pleasure in life, lamb,' said Stephen.

She took his arm and led him quickly through the shrubbery. When they came to the wicket into the park she said, 'I am so wretchedly unhappy, you know.' Stephen pressed her arm, but said nothing. 'It is that Mr Bowles. They want me to marry him.'

'Is he disagreeable to you?'

'He is perfectly hateful to me. Oh, I don't mean he is rude or unkind or in the least disrespectful – no, no, he is the worthiest, most respectable young man. But he is such a bore, and he has moist hands. He sits and gasps – he thinks he ought to gasp, I believe – he sits with me for hours and hours, and sometimes I feel that if he gasps at me just once more, I shall run my scissors into him.' She was speaking very quick, and now indignation had given her colour again. 'I always try to keep Cissy in the room, but she slips away – Mama calls her – and he tries to get hold of my hand. We edge slowly round and round the table – it is really too ridiculous. Mama – nobody could mean to be kinder than my dear Mama, I am sure – makes me see him – she will be so vexed when she hears I was not at home to him today – and I have to teach Sunday school, with those odious little tracts. I don't mind the children, much – poor little things, with their Sundays spoilt, after all that long church – but visiting the cottagers makes me perfectly wretched and ashamed – teaching women twice my age, with families, who know a hundred times more about life than I do, how to be economical and clean, and not to buy the best cuts of meat for their husbands, because it is *luxurious*, and God meant them to be poor. And they are so polite and I know they must think me so conceited and stupid. I can sew a little, and I can make a chocolate mousse, but I could no more run a cottage with a husband and little children in it on ten shillings a week than I could sail a first rate. Who do

248

they think they are?' she cried. 'Just because they can read and write.'

'I have often wondered,' said Stephen. 'The gentleman is a parson, I take it?'

'Yes. His father is the bishop. And I will not marry him, no, not if I have to lead apes in Hell. There is one man in the world I will ever marry, if he would have me – and I had him and I threw him away.'

The tears that had been brimming now rolled down her cheeks, and silently Stephen passed her a clean pocket-handkerchief.

They walked in silence: dead leaves, frosted, withered grass, gaunt trees; they passed the same palings twice, a third time.

'Might you not let him know?' asked Stephen. '*He* cannot move in the matter. You know very well what the world thinks of a man who offers marriage to an heiress when he has no money, no prospects, and a load of debts. You know very well what your mother would say to such a proposal: and he is delicate in the point of honour.'

'I did write to him: I said all I could in modesty; and indeed it was the most forward, dreadful thing. It was not modest at all.'

'It came too late . . .'

'*Too late*. Oh, how often I have said that to myself, and with such grief. If he had come to Bath just once again, I know we should have come to an understanding.'

'A secret engagement?'

'No. I should never have consented to that: but an understanding – not to bind him, you understand, but just to say that I should always wait. Anyhow, that is what I agreed in myself; but he never came again. Yet I did say it, and I feel myself bound in honour, whatever happens, unless he should marry elsewhere. I should wait and wait, even if it means giving up babies – and I should love to have babies. Oh, I am not a romantic girl: I am nearly thirty, and I know what I am talking about.'

'But surely now you could make him understand your mind?'

'He did not come in London. I cannot pursue him, and perhaps distress and embarrass him. He may have formed other attachments – I mean no blame: these things are quite different with men, I know.'

'There was that wretched story of an engagement to marry a Mr Allen.'

'I know.' A long pause. 'That is what makes me so cross and ill-natured,' said Sophia at last, 'when I think that if I had not been such an odious ninny, so jealous, I might now be . . . But they need not think I shall ever marry Mr Bowles, for I shall not.'

'Would you marry without your mother's consent?'

'Oh, no. Never. That would be terribly wrong. Besides, quite apart from its being wicked – and I should never do it – if I were to run away, I should not have a penny; and I should love to be a help to my husband, not a burden. But marrying where you are told, because it is *suitable*, and *unexceptionable*, is quite different. Quite different. Quick – this way. There is Admiral Haddock, behind the laurels. He has not seen us – we will go round by the lake: no one ever comes there. Do you know he is going to sea again, by the way?' she asked in another tone.

'In command?' cried Stephen, astonished.

'No. To do something at Plymouth – the Fencibles or the Impress Service – I did not attend. But he is going by sea. An old friend is to give him a lift in the *Généreux*.'

'That is the ship Jack brought into Mahon when Lord Nelson's squadron took her.'

'Yes, I know: he was second of the *Foudroyant* then. And the admiral is so excited, turning over all his old uniform-cases and taking in his laced coats. He has asked Cissy and me for the summer, for he has an official residence down there. Cissy is wild to go. This is where I come to sit when I cannot bear it any longer in the house,' she said, pointing to a little green-mouldy Grecian temple, leprous and scaling. 'And this is where Diana and I had our quarrel.'

'I never heard you had quarrelled.'

'I should have thought we could have been heard all over the county, at least. It was my fault; I was horrid that day. I had had Mr Bowles to endure all the afternoon, and I felt as though I had been flayed: so I went for a ride as far as Gatacre, and then came back here. But she should not have taunted me with London, and how she could see him whenever she liked, and that he had not gone down to Portsmouth the next day at all. It was unkind, even if I had deserved it. So I told her she was an ill-natured woman, and she called me something worse, and suddenly there we were, calling names and shouting at one another like a couple of fishwives – oh, it is so humiliating to remember. Then she said something so cruel about letters and how she could marry him any moment she chose, but she had no notion of a half-pay captain nor any other woman's leavings that I quite lost my temper, and swore I should thrash her with my riding-crop if she spoke to me like that. I should have, too: but then Mama came, and she was terribly frightened and tried to make us kiss and be friends. But I would not; nor the next day, either. And in the end Diana went away, to Mr Lowndes, that cousin in Dover.'

'Sophie,' said Stephen, 'you have confided so much in me, and so trustingly . . . '

'I cannot tell you what a relief it has been, and what a comfort to me.'

' . . . that it would be monstrous not to be equally candid with you. I am very much attached to Diana.'

'Oh,' cried Sophia. 'Oh, how I hope I have not hurt you. I thought it was Jack – oh, what have I said?'

'Never be distressed, honey. I know her faults as well as any man.'

'Of course, she is very beautiful,' said Sophia, glancing at him timidly.

251

'Yes. Tell me, is Diana wholly in love with Jack?'

'I may be wrong,' she said, after a pause, 'I know very little about these things, or anything else; but I do not believe Diana knows what love is at all.'

'This gentleman asks whether Mrs Villiers is at home,' said the Teapot's butler, bringing in a salver with a card upon it.

'Show him into the parlour,' said Diana. She hurried into her bedroom, changed her dress, combed her hair up, looked searchingly into her face in the glass, and went down.

'Good day to you now, Villiers,' said Stephen. 'No man on earth could call you a fast woman. I have read the paper twice through – invasion flotilla, loyal addresses, price of Government stock and list of bankrupts. Here is a bottle of scent.'

'Oh thank you, thank you, Stephen,' she cried, kissing him. 'It is the real Marcillac! Where on earth did you find it?'

'In a Deal smuggler's cottage.'

'What a good, forgiving creature you are, Maturin. Smell – it is like the Moghul's harem. I thought I should never see you again. I am sorry I was so disagreeable in London. How did you find me out? Where are you? What have you been doing? You look very well. I dote upon your blue coat.'

'I come from Mapes. They told me you were here.'

'Did they tell you of my battle with Sophie?'

'I understood there had been a disagreement.'

'She angered me with her mooning about the lake and her tragic airs – if she had wanted him, why did she not have him when she could? I do loathe and despise want of decision – shilly-shallying. And anyhow, she has a perfectly suitable admirer, an evangelical clergyman full of good works: good connections too, and plenty of money. I

252

dare say he will be a bishop. But upon my word, Maturin, I never knew she had such spirit! She set about me like a tiger, all ablaze; and I had only quizzed her a little about Jack Aubrey. Such a set-to! There we were roaring away by the little stone bridge, with her mare hitched to the post, starting and wincing – oh, I don't know how long – a good fifteen rounds. How you would have laughed. We took ourselves so seriously; and such energy! I was hoarse for a week after. But she was worse than me – as loud as a hog in a gate; and her words tumbling over one another, in a most horrid passion. But I tell you what, Maturin, if you really want to frighten a woman, offer to slash her across the face with your riding whip, and look as if you meant it. I was quite glad when my aunt Williams came up, screeching and hallooing loud enough to drown the both of us. And for her part she was just as glad to send me packing, because she was afraid for the parson; not that I would ever have laid a finger on him, the greasy oaf. So here I am again, a sort of keeper or upper-servant to the Teapot. Will you drink some of his honour's sherry? You are looking quite glum, Maturin. Don't be mumchance, there's a good fellow. I have not said an unkind thing since you appeared: it is your duty to be gay and amusing. Though harking back, I was just as pleased to come away too, with my face intact: it is my fortune, you know. You have not paid it a single compliment, though I was liberal enough to you. Reassure me, Maturin – I shall be thirty soon, and I dare not trust my looking-glass.'

'It is a good face,' said Stephen, looking at it steadily. She held her head up in the hard cold light of the winter sun and now for the first time he saw the middle-aged woman: India had not been kind to her complexion: it was good, but nothing to Sophia's; that faintest of lines by her eyes would reach out; the hint of drawn strength would grow more pronounced – haggard; in a few years other people would see that Sophie had slashed it deep. He hid his discovery behind all the command and dissimulation that he was master of and went on, 'An astonishing face. A damned good figurehead, as we say in the Navy. And it has launched one ship, at least.'

'A good damned figurehead,' she said bitterly.

'Now for the harrow,' he reflected.

'And after all,' she said, pouring out the wine, 'why do you pursue me like this? I give you no encouragement. I never have. I told you plainly at Bruton Street that I liked you as a friend but had no use for you as a lover. Why do you persecute me? What do you want of me? If you think to gain your point by wearing me out, you have reckoned short; and even if you were to succeed, you would only regret it. You do not know who I am at all; everything proves it.'

'I must go,' he said, getting up.

She was pacing nervously up and down the room. 'Go, then,' she cried, 'and tell your lord and master I never want to see him again, either. He is a coward.'

Mr Lowndes walked into the parlour. He was a tall, stout, cheerful gentleman of about sixty, wearing a flowered silk dressing-gown, breeches unbuckled at the knees, and a tea-cosy in lieu of a wig, or nightcap: he raised the cosy and bowed.

'Dr Maturin – Mr Lowndes,' said Diana, with a quick beseeching look at Stephen – deprecation combined with concern, vexation, and the remains of anger.

'I am very happy to see you, sir, most honoured: I do not believe I have had the pleasure,' said Mr Lowndes, gazing at Stephen with extreme intensity. 'I see from your coat that you are not a mad-doctor, sir. Unless, indeed, this is an innocent deception?'

'Not at all, sir. I am a naval surgeon.'

'Very good – you are *upon* the sea but not *in* it: you are not an advocate for cold baths. The sea, the sea! Where should we be without it? Frizzled to a mere toast, sir; parched, desiccated by the simoom, the dread simoom. Dr Maturin would like a cup of tea, my dear, against

254

the desiccation. I can offer you a superlative cup of tea, sir.'

'Dr Maturin is drinking sherry, Cousin Edward.'

'He would do better to drink a cup of tea,' said Mr Lowndes, with a look of keen disappointment. 'However, I do not presume to dictate to my guests,' he added, hanging down his head.

'I shall be very happy to take a cup of tea, sir, as soon as I have drunk up my wine,' said Stephen.

'Yes, yes!' cried Mr Lowndes, brightening at once. 'And you shall have the pot to take with you on your voyages. Molly, Sue, Diana, pray make it in the little round pot Queen Anne gave my grandmama; it makes the best tea in the house. And while it is making, sir, I will tell you a little poem; you are a literary man, I know,' he said, dancing a few paces and bowing right and left.

The butler brought in the tray, looked sharply from Mr Lowndes to Diana: she shook her head slightly, eased her cousin into a wing-chair, tidied him, tied a napkin round his neck, and, as the spirit-lamp brought the kettle to the boil, measured out the tea and brewed it.

'Now for my poem,' said Mr Lowndes. 'Attend! Attend! *Arma virumque cano*, etc. There, ain't it capital?'

'Admirable, sir. Thank you very much.'

'Ha, ha, ha!' cried Mr Lowndes, cramming his mouth with cake, red with sudden pleasure. 'I knew you were a man of exquisite sensibilities. Take the bun!' He flung a little round cake at Stephen's head, and added, 'I have a turn for verse. Sometimes my fancy runs to Sapphics, sometimes to catalectic Glyconics and Pherecrateans – the Priapic metre, my dear sir. Are you a Grecian? Should you like to hear some of my Priapean odes?'

'In Greek, sir?'

'No, sir, in English.'

'Perhaps at another time, sir, when we are alone – when no ladies are present, it would give me great pleasure.'

'You have noticed that young woman, have you? You are

255

a sharp one. But then you are a young man, sir. I too was a young man. As a physical gentleman, sir, do you really think incest so very undesirable?'

'Cousin Edward, it is time for your bath,' said Diana; but he grew confused and unhappy – he was sure it would not do to let that fellow alone with a valuable teapot, but he was too polite to say so; his oblique references to it as 'the dread simoom' were not understood, and it took her five minutes of coaxing to get him out of the room.

'What news from Mapes, shipmate?' asked Jack.

'What? I cannot hear a word with all this screeching and bawling overhead.'

'You are as bad as Parker,' said Jack, and poking his head out of the cabin he called, ''Vast heaving the after carronades. Mr Pullings, let these hands reef tops'ls. I said "What news from Mapes?" '

'A miscellaneous bag. I saw Sophie alone: she and Diana have parted brass-rags. Diana is looking after her cousin in Dover. I called on her. She asked us both to dinner on Friday, to eat a dish of Dover soles. I accepted for myself, but said I could not answer for you: you might not find it possible to go ashore.'

'She asked me?' cried Jack. 'Are you sure? What is it, Babbington?'

'I beg your pardon, sir, but the flagship is signalling all captains.'

'Very well. Let me know the moment *Melpomène*'s barge touches the water. Stephen, chuck me my breeches, will you?' He was in working clothes – canvas trousers, a guernsey frock and a frieze jacket – and as he stripped the criss-cross of wounds showed plain: bullets, splinters, cutlasses, a boarding-axe; and the last, a raking thrust from a pike, still showed red about the edges. 'Half an inch to the left – if that pike had gone in half an inch to the left, you would have been a dead man,' observed Stephen.

'My God,' said Jack, 'there are times when I wish –
however, I must not whine.' From under his clean white
shirt he asked, 'How was Sophie?'

'Low in her spirits. She is subjected to the attentions of
a moneyed parson.' No reply. No emergence of the head.
He went on, 'I also saw to everything at Melbury: all is
well there, though the lawyer's men have been hanging
about. Preserved Killick asks may he join the ship? I took
it upon myself to say that he should come and ask you
himself. You will be happy to have the skilled attendance
of Preserved Killick. I reduced my femur at the hospital –
the leg may be saved – and wished my dement on to them,
with a slime-draught to make him easy. I also bought your
thread, music-paper, and strings: these I found at a shop
in Folkstone.'

'Thank you, Stephen. I am very much obliged to you.
You must have had a damned long ride of it. Indeed,
you look dog-tired, quite done up. Just tie my hair for
me, like a good fellow, and then you shall turn in. I
must get you an assistant, a surgeon's mate: you work
too hard.'

'You have some grey hairs,' said Stephen, tying the
yellow queue.

'Do you wonder?' said Jack. He buckled on his sword,
sat down on the locker, and said, 'I had almost forgot.
I had a pleasant surprise today. Canning came aboard!
You remember Canning, that admirable chap I liked
so much in town, and who offered me his privateer?
He has a couple of merchantmen in the road and he
came round from the Nore to see them off. I have asked
him to dinner tomorrow; and that reminds me . . . ' It
reminded him of the fact that he had no money, and
that he should like to borrow some. He had drawn three
lunar months' pay on joining his ship, but his expenses
in Portsmouth – customary presents, vails, a bare minimum of equipment – had swallowed twenty-five guineas
and more in a week, quite apart from Stephen's loan.

It had not allowed him to lay in stores, and that was another thing that was wrong with the running of the *Polychrest* – he hardly knew his officers except on duty. He had invited Parker and he had dined once with the gun-room during their long calm, tiding up the Channel, but he had barely exchanged half a dozen words with Macdonald or Allen, for example, outside the line of duty; yet they were men upon whom the ship, and his own life and reputation, might depend. Parker and Macdonald had private means and they had entertained him well: he had scarcely entertained them at all. He was not keeping up the dignity of a captain: a captain's dignity depended in some degree upon the state of his store-room – a captain must not look a scrub – and as his silly, talkative, consequential temporary steward kept telling him so officiously, his was empty apart from a hundredweight of orange marmalade, a present from Mrs Babbington. 'Where shall I stow the wine, sir? – What shall I do about the live-stock? – When are the sheep coming? – What does your Honour wish me to do about the hen-coops?' Furthermore, he would soon have to invite the admiral and the other captains of the squadron; and tomorrow there would be Canning. Ordinarily he would have turned at once to Stephen, for although Stephen was an abstemious man, indifferent to money beyond the bare necessities of life, and strangely ill-informed, even unperceptive, about discipline, the finer points of ceremonial, the complexity of the service and the importance of entertaining, he would always give way at once when it was represented to him that tradition called for an outlay. He would produce money from the odd drawers and pots where it lay, disregarded, as though Jack were doing him a particular favour by borrowing it: in other hands he would have been the 'easiest touch' afloat. These reflections darted through Jack's mind as he sat there, stroking the worn lion's head on the pommel of his sword; but something in the atmosphere, some chill or reserve or inward scruple of his own, prevented him from completing his sentence before the *Melpomène*'s barge was reported to be in the water.

This was not a Sunday afternoon, with ship-visiting and liberty boats plying to and fro in the squadron; it was an ordinary working day, with all hands creeping up and down the rigging or exercising at the great guns; nothing but a Dover bumboat and a Deal hoveller came anywhere near the *Polychrest*; and yet long before Jack's return it was known throughout the ship that she was on the wing. Where bound, no one could tell, though many tried (to the westward, to Botany Bay, the Mediterranean to carry presents to the Dey of Algiers and redeem Christian slaves). But the rumour was so strong that Mr Parker cleared her hawse, heaved short, and, with a hideous memory of unmooring at Spithead, sent the crew to their stations for this manoeuvre again and again, until even the dullest could find the capstan and his place on the bar. He received Jack back aboard with a look of discreet but earnest inquiry, and Jack, who had seen his preparations, said, 'No, no, Mr Parker, you may veer away astern; it is not for today. Desire Mr Babbington to come into the cabin, if you please.'

'Mr Babbington,' he said, 'you are in a very repellent state of filth.'

'Yes, sir,' said Babbington, who had spent the first dog-watch in the maintop with two buckets of flush from the galley, showing a framework-knitter, two thatchers (brothers: much given to poaching), and a monoglot Finn how to grease the masts, sheets and running-rigging generally, and who was liberally plastered with condemned butter and skimmings from the coppers in which salt pork had been boiled. 'Beg pardon, sir.'

'Be so good as to scrub yourself from clew to earring, to shave – you may borrow Mr Parslow's razor, I dare say – to put on your best uniform and report back here. My compliments to Mr Parker and you are to take the blue cutter to Dover with Bonden and six reliable men who deserve liberty until the evening gun. The same to Dr Maturin, and I should be glad to see him.'

'Aye, aye, sir. Oh thank you, sir.'

He turned to his desk:

> Polychrest
> in the Downs
>
> Captain Aubrey presents his best compliments to Mrs Villiers and much regrets that duty prevents him from accepting her very kind invitation to dine on Friday. However, he hopes to have the honour, and the pleasure, of waiting on her when he returns.

'Stephen,' he said, looking up, 'I am writing to decline Diana's invitation – we are ordered to sea tomorrow night. Should you wish to add a word or send a message? Babbington is making our excuses.'

'Let Babbington bear mine by word of mouth, if you please. I am so glad you are not going ashore. It would have been the extreme of folly, with the *Polychrest* known to be on the station.'

Babbington came in, shining with cleanliness, in a frilled shirt and fine white breeches.

'You remember Mrs Villiers?' said Jack.

'Oh *yes*, sir. Besides, I drove her to the ball.'

'She is in Dover, at the house where you called for her – New Place. Be so good as to give her this note; and I believe Dr Maturin has a message.'

'Compliments: regrets,' said Stephen.

'Now turn out your pockets,' said Jack.

Babbington's face fell. A little heap of objects appeared, some partially eaten, and a surprising number of coins – silver, a gold piece. Jack returned fourpence, observing that that would set him up handsomely in cheesecakes,

260

recommended him to bring back all his men as he should answer the contrary at his peril, and desired him to 'top his boom'.

'It is the only way of keeping him even passably chaste,' he said to Stephen. 'There are a great many loose women in Dover, I am afraid.'

'I beg your pardon, sir,' said Mr Parker, 'but a man by the name of Killick asks permission to come aboard.'

'Certainly, Mr Parker,' cried Jack. 'He is my steward. There you are, Killick,' he said, coming on deck. 'I am happy to see you. What have you got there?'

'Hampers, sir,' said Killick, pleased to see his captain, but unable to restrain a wondering eye from running up and down the *Polychrest*. 'One from Admiral Haddock. T'other from the ladies up at Mapes, or rather, from Miss Sophie, to speak correct: pig, cheeses, butter, cream, poultry and such, from Mapes; game from next door. Admiral's clearing off his land, sir. There's a prime bold roebuck there, sir, hung this sennight past, and any number of hares and such.'

'Mr Malloch, a whip – no, a double whip to the main-yard. Easy with those hampers, now. What's the third bundle?'

'Another roebuck, sir.'

'Where from?'

'Which it fouled the wheels of the tax-cart I come in and hurt its leg, sir,' said Killick, looking at the flagship in the distance with a kind of mild wonder. 'Just half a mile after the turning to Provender bridge. No, I lie – maybe a furlong closer to Newton Priors. So I put it out of its misery, sir.'

'Ah,' said Jack. 'The Mapes hamper is directed to Dr Maturin, I see.'

'It's all one, sir,' said Killick. 'Miss told me to say the pig weighs twenty-seven and a half pound the quarter, and I am to set the hams to the tub the very minute I come aboard – the souse she put aside in thicky jar, knowing

261

you liked 'un. The white puddings is for the Doctor's breakfast.'

'Very good, Killick, very good indeed,' said Jack. 'Stow 'em away. Handsomely with that buck – don't you bruise him on any account.'

'To think a man's heart could break over a soused hog's face,' he reflected, feigning to turn over the admiral's game; partridge, pheasant, woodcock, snipe, mallard, wigeon, teal, hares. 'You brought the rest of the wine Killick?'

'Which the bottles broke, sir: all but half a dozen of the Burgundy.'

Jack cocked his eye, sighed, but said nothing. Six bottles would do pretty well, with what was left of his corruption from the yard. 'Mr Parker, Mr Macdonald, I hope you will give me the pleasure of dining in the cabin tomorrow? I am expecting a guest.'

They bowed, smiled, and said they should be very happy; they did indeed feel a real pleasure, for Jack had declined the gunroom's last invitation, and this had created an uneasiness in their minds – an unpleasant beginning to a commission.

Stephen said the same in effect, when he could be brought to understand. 'Yes, yes, certainly, of course – much obliged. I did not grasp your meaning.'

'Yet it was plain enough, in all conscience,' said Jack, 'and adapted to the meanest understanding. I said. "Will you have dinner with me tomorrow? Canning is coming, and I have asked Parker, Macdonald and Pullings." '

'My mind dwells with real concern, and yet with what I might term an *inquisitive*, slightly vulgar concern, upon the state of Mother Williams's heart when she finds her dairy, poultry-yard, pig-house, larder, stripped bare. Will it burst? Will it stop beating altogether? Dry to a total desiccation – no great step? What the effect upon her visceral humours? How will Sophie reply? Will she attempt concealment, prevarication? She lies with as much skill as

Preserved Killick – a desperate stare, and her face the most perfect damask rose. My mind, I say, wanders in this region, lost. I have no acquaintance with English family life, with English *female* family life: it is to me a region quite unknown.'

It was not a region in which Jack chose to dwell: with a start of intense pain he jerked his mind away. 'Lord, I love that Sophie so,' he cried within. He took a quick turn on deck, going right forward to pat the gammoning of the bowsprit – a private consolation from his very earliest days at sea. When he came back he said, 'A most damnable unpleasant thought has just struck me. I know I must not give Canning swine's flesh, he being a Jew; but can he eat a buck? Is a buck unclean? And hare would not answer, either, for I dare say they are rated with the coney and her kind.'

'I have no idea. You have no Bible, I suppose?'

'Indeed I have a Bible. I used it to check Heneage's signal – The Lord taketh no pleasure in the strength of an horse, do you remember? What did he mean by that, do you suppose? It was not so very witty, or original; for after all, everyone knows the Lord taketh no pleasure in the strength of an horse. He had crossed his tiller-ropes, I dare say. However, I have also been reading it, these last few days.'

'Ah?'

'Yes. I may preach a sermon to the ship's company next Sunday.'

'You? Preach a sermon?'

'Certainly. Captains often do, when no chaplain is carried. I always made do with the Articles of War in the *Sophie*, but now I think I shall give them a clear, well-reasoned – come, what's the matter? What is so very entertaining about my preaching a sermon? Damn your eyes, Stephen.' Stephen was doubled in his chair, rocking to and fro, uttering harsh spasmodic squeaks: tears ran down his face. 'What a spectacle you are, to be sure. Now

I come to think of it, I do not believe I have ever heard you laugh before. It is a damned illiberal row, I can tell you – it don't suit you at all. Squeak, squeak. Very well: you shall laugh your bellyful.' He turned away with something about 'pragmatical apes – simpering, tittering' and affected to look into the Bible without the least concern; but there are not many who can find themselves the object of open, whole-hearted, sincere, prostrating laughter without being put out of countenance, and Jack was not one of these few. However, Stephen's mirth died away in time – a few last crowing whoops and it was over. He got to his feet, and dabbing his face with a handkerchief he took Jack by the hand. 'I am so sorry,' he said. 'I beg your pardon. I would not have vexed you for the world. But there is something so essentially *ludicrous*, so fundamentally comic . . . that is to say, I had so droll an association of ideas – pray do not take it personally at all. Of course you shall preach to the men; I am persuaded it will have a most striking effect.'

'Well,' said Jack, with a suspicious glance, 'I am glad it afforded you so much innocent merriment at all events. Though what you find . . . '

'What is your text, pray?'

'Are you making game of me, Stephen?'

'Never, upon my word: would scorn it.'

'Well, it is the one about I say come and he cometh; for I am a centurion. I want them to understand it is God's will, and it must be so – there must be discipline – 'tis in the Book – and any infernal bastard that disobeys is therefore a blasphemer too, and will certainly be damned. That it is no good kicking against the pricks: which is in the Book too, as I shall point out.'

'You feel that it will make it easier for them to bear their station, when they learn that it is providential?'

'Yes, yes, that's it. It is all here, you know' – tapping the Bible. 'There are an amazing number of useful things in it,' said Jack, with a candid gaze out of the scuttle. 'I had no idea. And, by the way, it seems that roebuck is not unclean, which is a comfort, and a very great one, I can tell you. I was quite anxious about this dinner.'

The next day brought countless duties – the raking of the *Polychrest*'s masts, the restowing of what part of her ballast they could come at, the mending of a chain-pump – but this anxiety remained, to come into full flower in the last quarter of an hour before the arrival of his guests. He stood fussing in his day-cabin, twitching the cloth, teasing the stove until its colour was cherry-pink, worrying Killick and his attendant boys, wondering whether after all the table should not have been athwart-ships, and contemplating a last-minute alteration. Could it really seat six in even moderate comfort? The *Polychrest* was a larger vessel than the *Sophie*, his last command, but because of the singularity of her construction the cabin had no stern-gallery, no fine curving sweep of windows to give an impression of light, air and indeed a certain magnificence to even a little room; the actual space was greater and the head-room was such that he could stand with no more than a slight stoop, but this space had no generosity of breadth – it drew out in length, narrowing almost to a point aft, and all that it had in the way of day was a skylight and a couple of small scuttles. Leading forward from this shield-shaped apartment was a short passage, with his sleeping-cabin on one side and his quarter-gallery on the other: it was not a true gallery, a projection, in the *Polychrest* at all, of course, nor was it strictly on her quarter, but it served the purpose of a privy as well as if it had been both. In addition to the necessary pot it contained a thirty-two pounder carronade and a small hanging lantern, in case the bull's eye in the port-lid should not be enough to show the unwary guest the consequences of a false step. Jack looked in to see whether it was burning bright and stepped out into the passage just as the sentry opened the door to admit the midshipman of the watch with the message that 'the gentleman was alongside, if you please, sir.'

As soon as Jack saw Canning come aboard he knew

265

his party would be a success. He was dressed in a plain buff coat, with no attempt at a seafaring appearance, but he came up the side like a good 'un, moving his bulk with a strong, easy agility, judging the roll just so. His cheerful face appeared in the gangway, looking sharply from left to right; then the rest of him, and he stood there, quite filling the space, with his hat off and his bald crown gleaming in the rain.

The first lieutenant received him, led him the three paces to Jack, who shook him very warmly by the hand, performed the necessary introductions, and guided the assembled body into the cabin, for he had little temptation to linger in the icy drizzle and none at all to show the *Polychrest* in her present state, to an eye so keen and knowing as his guest's.

Dinner began quietly enough with a dish of codlings caught over the side that morning and with little in the way of conversation apart from banalities – the weather, of course, inquiries after common acquaintance – 'How was Lady Keith? When last seen? What news of Mrs Villiers? Did Dover suit her? Captain Dundas, was he well, and happy in his new command? Had Mr Canning heard any good music lately? Oh yes! Such a *Figaro* at the Opera, he had gone three times.' Parker, Macdonald and Pullings were mere dead weights, bound by the convention that equated their captain, at his own table, with royalty, and forbade anything but answers to proposals set up by him. However, Stephen had no notion of this convention – he gave them an account of nitrous oxide, the laughing gas, exhilaration in a bottle, philosophic merriment; and it did not apply to Canning at all. Jack worked hard with an easy flow of tiny talk; and presently the dead weight began to move. Canning did not refer to the *Polychrest* (Jack noticed this with a pang, but with gratitude as well) apart from saying that she must be a very interesting ship, with prodigious capabilities, and that he had never seen such paintwork – such elegance and taste – the completest thing

– one would have supposed a royal yacht – but he spoke of the service in general with obvious knowledge and deep appreciation. Few sailors can hear sincere, informed praise of the Navy without pleasure, and the reserved atmosphere in the cabin relaxed, warmed, grew positively gay.

The codlings were succeeded by partridges, which Jack carved by the simple process of putting one on each man's plate; the corrupt claret began to go about, the gaiety increased, the conversation became general, and the watch on deck heard the sound of laughter coming from the cabin in a steady flow.

After the partridges came no less than four removes of game, culminating in a saddle of venison borne in by Killick and the gun-room steward on a scrubbed scuttle-hatch with a runnel gouged out for the gravy. 'The burgundy, Killick,' murmured Jack, standing up to carve. They watched him earnestly as he laboured, their talk dying away; and they bent with equal attention to their plates.

'Upon my word, gentlemen,' said Canning, laying down his knife and fork, 'you do yourselves pretty well in the Navy – such a feast! The Mansion House is nothing to it. Captain Aubrey, sir, this is the best venison I have ever tasted in my life: it is a *solemn* dish. And such burgundy! A Musigny, I believe?'

'Chambolles-Musigny, sir, of '85. I am afraid it is a little past its prime: I have just these few bottles left – happily my steward does not care for burgundy. Mr Pullings, a trifle of the brown end?'

It was indeed a most capital buck, tender, juicy, full of savour; Jack set to his own mound with an easy mind at last: more or less everybody was talking – Pullings and Parker explaining Bonaparte's intentions to Canning – the new French gunboats, the ship-rigged prams of the invasion flotilla – and Stephen and Macdonald leaning far over their plates to hear one another, or rather to be heard, in an argument that was still mild enough, but that threatened to grow a little warm.

'Ossian,' said Jack, at a moment when both their mouths were full, 'was he not the gentleman that was quite exploded by Dr Johnson?'

'Not at all, sir,' cried Macdonald, swallowing faster than Stephen. 'Dr Johnson was a respectable man in some ways, no doubt, though in no degree related to the Johnstones of Ballintubber; but for some reason he had conceived a narrow prejudice against Scotland. He had no notion of the sublime, and therefore no appreciation of Ossian.'

'I have never read Ossian myself,' said Jack, 'being no great hand with poetry. But I remember Lady Keith to have said that Dr Johnson raised some mighty cogent objections.'

'Produce your manuscripts,' said Stephen.

'Do you expect a Highland gentleman to produce his manuscripts upon compulsion?' said Macdonald to Stephen, and to Jack, 'Dr Johnson, sir, was capable of very inaccurate statements. He affected to see no trees in his tour of the kingdom: now I have travelled the very same road many times, and I know several trees within a hundred yards of it – ten, or even more. I do not regard him as any authority upon any subject. I appeal to your candour, sir – what do you say to a man who defines the mainsheet as the largest sail in a ship, or to belay as to splice, or a bight as the circumference of a rope? And that in a buke that professes to be a dictionary of the English language? Hoot, toot.'

'Did he indeed say that?' cried Jack. 'I shall never think the same of him again. I have no doubt your Ossian was a very honest fellow.'

'He did, sir, upon my honour,' cried Macdonald, laying his right hand flat upon the table. 'And falsum in uno, falsum in omnibus, I say.'

'Why, yes,' said Jack, who was as well acquainted with old omnibus as any man there present. 'Falsum in omnibus. What do you say to omnibus, Stephen?'

'I concede the victory,' said Stephen smiling. 'Omnibus routs me.'

'A glass of wine with you, Doctor,' said Macdonald.

'Allow me to help you to a little of the underside,' said Jack. 'Killick, the Doctor's plate.'

'More dead men, Joe?' asked the sentry at the door, peering into the basket.

'God love us, how they do stow it away, to be sure,' said Joe, with a chuckle. 'The big cove, the civilian – it's a pleasure to see him eat. And there's figgy-dowdy to come, and woodcocks on toast, and then the punch.'

'You ain't forgotten me, Joe?' said the sentry.

'The bottle with the yellow wax. They'll be singing any minute now.'

The sentry put the bottle to his lips, raised it up and up, wiped his mouth with the back of his hand, and observed, 'Rum stuff they drink in the cabin: like blackstrap, only thinner. How's my gent?'

'You'll carry him to his cot, mate: he's coming along royal, sheets aflowing. Which the same goes for buff waistcoat. A bosun's chair for him.'

'Now, sir,' said Jack to Canning, 'we have a Navy dish that I thought might amuse you. We call it figgy-dowdy. You do not have to eat it, unless you choose – this is Liberty Hall. For my part, I find it settles a meal; but perhaps it is an acquired taste.'

Canning eyed the pale, amorphous, gleaming, slightly translucent mass and asked how it was made; he did not think he had ever seen anything quite like it.

'We take ship's biscuit, put it in a stout canvas bag – ' said Jack.

'Pound it with a marlin-spike for half an hour – ' said Pullings.

'Add bits of pork fat, plums, figs, rum, currants,' said Parker.

'Send it to the galley, and serve it up with bosun's grog,' said Macdonald.

Canning said he would be delighted – a new experience – he had never had the honour of dining aboard a man-of-war – happy to acquire any naval taste. 'And really,' he said, 'it is excellent, quite excellent. And so this is bosun's grog. I believe I must beg for another glass. Capital, capital. I was telling you, sir,' he said, leaning confidentially over towards Jack, 'I was telling you some ten or twenty courses back, that I had heard a wonderful *Figaro* at the Opera. You must run up if you possibly can; there is a new woman, La Colonna, who sings Susanna with a grace and a purity I have never heard in my life – a revelation. She drops true on the middle of her note, and it swells, swells . . . Ottoboni is the Contessa, and their duet would bring tears to your eyes. I forget the words, but you know it, of course.' He hummed, his bass making the glasses tremble.

Jack beat the time with his spoon and struck in with 'Sotto i pini . . . '

They sang it through, then through again; the others gazed at them with a mild, bemused, contemplative satisfaction; at this stage it seemed natural that their captain should personate a Spanish lady's maid, and even, somewhat later, three blind mice.

Before the mice, however, there was an event that confirmed them in their affectionate regard for Mr Canning: the port went round, and, the loyal toast being proposed, Canning leapt to his feet, struck his head against a beam and collapsed into his chair as though pole-axed. They had always known it might happen to some land-soldier or civilian, had never actually seen it, and, since he had done himself no lasting injury, they were enchanted. They comforted him, standing round his chair, dressing the lump with rum, assuring him that it was quite all right – it would soon pass – they often banged their heads – no harm in it – no bones broken. Jack called for the punch, telling the steward in a rapid undertone that a bosun's chair was to be rigged, and administered a tot with a medical air, observing, 'We are privileged to drink the King seated in the Navy, sir; we may do so without the least disrespect. Few people know it however – quite recent – it must seem very strange.'

'Yes. Yes.' said Canning, staring heavily straight at Pullings. 'Yes. I remember now.' Then, as the punch spread new life throughout his vitals he smiled round the table and said, 'What a green hand I must look to all you gentlemen.'

It passed, as they had told him it would, and a little while later he joined them in these mice, the Bay of Biscay-o, Drops of Brandy, the Female Lieutenant, and the catch about the lily-white boys, in which he excelled them all, roaring out.

> *Three, three the rivals*
> *Two, two the lily-white boys, clothed all in green-o,*
> *But one is one and all alone*
> *And evermore shall be so*

ending with a power and a depth that none of them could reach: Boanerges.

'There is a symbolism there that escapes me,' said Stephen, his right-hand neighbour, when the confused cheering had died away.

'Does it not refer to – ' began Canning; but the others had returned to their mice, all singing in voices calculated to reach the foretop in an Atlantic gale, all except Parker, that is to say, who could not tell one tune from another and who merely opened and closed his mouth with an expression of polite good-fellowship, in a state of exquisite boredom; and Canning broke off to join them.

He was still with the mice as he was steered into the bosun's chair and lowered gently into his boat, still with them as he was rowed over the sea towards the great dark assembly of ships under the Goodwin sands; and Jack, leaning over the rail, heard his voice growing fainter and fainter – *see* how they run, *see* how they run – until at last it turned back to Three, three the rivals, dying quite away.

'That was as successful a dinner-party as I remember, afloat,' said Stephen at his side. 'I thank you for my part in it.'

'Do you really think so?' said Jack. 'I was so glad you enjoyed it. I particularly wished to do Canning well: apart from anything else, he is a very rich man, and one does not like the ship to look scrape-farthing. I was sorry to call a halt so soon, however; but I must have a little light for manoeuvring. Mr Goodridge, Mr Goodridge, how is your tide?'

'She'll be making for another glass, sir.'

'Your fender-men are ready?'

'Ready, all ready, sir.'

The wind was fair, but at slack water they were to unmoor and pass through the squadron and the convoy: Jack had a mortal dread that the *Polychrest* might foul one of the men-of-war or half the straggling convoy, and he had armed a party with long poles to shove her off.

'Then let us step into your cabin.' When they were below he said, 'You have the charts spread out, I see. I believe you are a Channel pilot, Master?'

'Yes, sir.'

'Just as well: I know the West Indian waters and the Mediterranean better than these. Now I want you to lay the sloop half a mile off Gris Nez at three in the morning, the steeple bearing north fifty-seven east and the tower on the cliff south sixty-three east.'

Towards four bells in the middle watch Jack came on deck: the *Polychrest* was lying to under foretopsail and mizen, bowing the swell with her odd nervous lift and jerk. The night was still sharp and clear, bright moonlight, and eastwards a pale host of stars – Altair rising over the dark mass of Cap Gris Nez under the starboard quarter.

And the wind was still this same nipping breeze out of the north-west. But far over on the larboard bow trouble was brewing: no stars above Castor and Pollux, and the moon was sinking towards a black bar right across the horizon. With a falling glass this might mean a blow from the same quarter – an uncomfortable position, with the shore so close under his lee. 'I wish it were over,' he said, beginning his ritual pace. His orders required him to be off the headland at three in the morning, to fire a blue light, and to receive a passenger from a boat that should answer his hail with the word *Bourbon*: he was then to proceed with all possible dispatch to Dover. If no boat appeared or if he were driven off his station by stress of weather, then he was to repeat the operation on the three succeeding nights, remaining out of sight by day.

This was Pullings' watch, but the master was also on deck, standing over by the break of the quarterdeck, keeping an eye on his landmarks, while the quiet business of the ship went on. From time to time Pullings trimmed the sails to keep them exactly balanced; the carpenter's mate reported the depth of water in the well – eighteen inches, which was more than was right; the master-at-arms made his rounds; the glass turned, the bell rang, the sentinels called 'All's well' from their various posts, the look-outs and the helm were relieved. The watch took a turn at the pumps; and all the while the breeze hummed through the rigging, the sum of the notes rising and falling through a full tone as the ship rolled, her masts straining their shrouds and braces now this side, now that.

'Look out afore, there,' called Pullings.

'Aye-aye, thir,' came the distant voice. Bolton, one of the men pressed from the Indiaman, a glowering, surly, murderous brute with no front teeth – yellow fangs each side of a lisping gap; but a good seaman.

Jack held his watch to the moonlight: still a long time to go, and now the dark bar in the north-west had swallowed up Capella. He was thinking of sending a couple of men to the mast-head when the look-out hailed. 'Upon deck, thir. Boat on the thtarboard quarter.'

He reached up into the shrouds and swung himself to the rail, searching the dark sea. Nothing. 'Where away?' he called.

'Right on the quarter. Maybe half a point off now. Pulling like hell, three of a thide.'

He caught sight of her as she crossed the path of the moon. About a mile away: very long, very low, very narrow, more like a line on the water: travelling fast towards the land. This was not his boat – wrong shape, wrong time, wrong direction.

'What do you make of her, Mr Goodridge?' he asked.

'Why, sir, she's one of those Deal shells – death-or-money boats, they call 'em, or guinea-boats as some say; and by the look of her, she's got a main heavy cargo aboard. They must have seen a revenue cutter or a cruiser early on, for now they've got to pull against the ebb, and it runs cruel hard off the point. Do you mean to snap her up, sir? It's now or never with the race off the headland. What a bit of luck.'

He had not seen one before, but he knew them by reputation, of course: they were more like racing-craft for a quiet river than anything built to face a sea – every notion of safety sacrificed to speed; but the profit on smuggling gold was so great that the Deal men would take them clean across the Channel. They could run away from anything, pulling into the eye of the wind, and although the men were sometimes drowned, they were very rarely caught. Unless, as it might fall out, they chanced to be right under the lee of a pursuer, hampered by a swift tide, and tired out by their long pull. Or if they ran straight into a waiting man-of-war.

Gold packed very small: there might be five or six hundred pounds for him in that frail shell, as well as seven prime hands, the best seamen on the coast – lawful prize, for their protections would be of no sort of use to them whatsoever now. He had the weather-gage. He had but to fill his foretopsail, pay round, set everything she could carry, and bear down. To run from him she would have to pull dead against the tide, and they would not be able to keep that up for long. Twenty minutes: perhaps half an hour. Yes, but then he would have to beat back again to his station; and he knew the *Polychrest*'s powers in that direction, alas.

'There's the best part of an hour to go before three, sir,' said the master at his side. Jack held up his watch again; the master-at-arms held his lantern to light it; the listening quarterdeck fell unnaturally silent. They were all seamen aft, but by now even the framework-knitter in the waist knew what was afoot.

'I only make it seven minutes past, sir,' said the master. No. It would not do. 'Mind your helm.' snapped Jack as the *Polychrest* yawed a full point to starboard. 'Mr Pullings, check the blue lights,' he said, and resumed his pacing. For the first five minutes it was hard to bear: every time he reached the taffrail there was that boat, drawing in nearer and nearer to the land, but still in extreme danger. After his twentieth turn she had crossed the invisible line into safety: the sloop could no longer cut her off – he could no longer change his mind.

Five bells: he checked their position, bringing the bearing-compass on to the steeple and the tower. The dirty weather in the north-west was skirting the Great Bear now. Six bells, and the blue light soared up, burst, and drifted away to leeward, lighting all their upturned faces with an unnatural emphasis – open mouths, mindless wonder.

'Mr Pullings, be so good as to send a reliable man into the top with a night-glass,' said Jack. And five minutes later, 'Maintop, there. What do you see? Any boat pulling from under the land?'

A pause. 'Nothing, sir. I got the line of surf in my glass, and nothing ain't pulled off yet.'

Seven bells. Three well-lit ships passed out at sea,

running down the Channel – neutrals, of course. Eight bells, and the changing watch found the *Polychrest* still there. 'Take her out into the offing, Mr Parker,' said Jack. 'Sink the land entirely, making as little southing as ever you can. We must be here again tomorrow night.'

But the *Polychrest* spent tomorrow night on the other side of the Channel, lying to under Dungeness, shipping such seas that Jack thought he should have to run for the shelter of the Isle of Wight, and report back to the admiral with his tail between his legs, his mission unaccomplished; but the wind chopped round westwards at dawn, and the sloop, pumping hard, began to creep back under close-reefed topsails across the angry water – a sea so short and steep that she proceeded by sickening and often unpredictable jerks, and in the gun-room no amount of fiddles or ingenuity on the parts of the diners would keep their food on the table.

The purser's place was empty, as it usually was as soon as the first reef was taken in; and Pullings was dozing as he sat.

'You do not suffer from the sea-sickness, sir?' said Stephen to Macdonald.

'Why, no, sir. But then I come from the Western Isles, and we are in boats as soon as we are breeched.'

'The Western Isles . . . The Western Isles. There was a Lord of the Isles – of your family, I presume, sir?' – Macdonald bowed. 'And that always seemed to me the most romantic title that ever was. We, indeed, have our White Knight, and the Knight of the Glen, the O'Connor Don, the McCarthy Mor, O'Sionnach the Fox, and so on; but the Lord of the Isles . . . it gives a feeling of indeterminate magnificence. That reminds me: I had the strangest impression today – an impression of time recovered. Two of your men, both by the name of Macrea, I believe, were speaking privately, furbishing their equipment with one piece of pipeclay between them as I stood near them – nothing of any consequence, you understand, just small disagreement about the pipeclay, the first desiring the second to kiss his arse and the second wishing the soul of the first to the Devil and a good deal more to the same effect. And I understood directly, without the least thought or conscious effort of will!'

'You have the Gaelic, sir?' cried Macdonald.

'No, sir,' said Stephen, 'and that is what is so curious. I no longer speak it; I thought I no longer understood it. And yet there at once, with no volition on my part, there was complete understanding. I had no idea the Erse and the Irish were so close; I had imagined the dialects had moved far apart. Pray, is there a mutual understanding between your Hebrideans and the Highlanders on the one, and let us say the native Ulstermen on the other?'

'Why, yes, sir; there is. They converse tolerably well, on general subjects, on boats, fishing, and bawdy. There are some different words, to be sure, and great differences of intonation, but with perseverance and repetition they can make themselves understood very well – a tolerably free communication. There are some Irishmen among the pressed hands, and I have heard them and my marines speaking together.'

'If I had heard them, they would be on the defaulters' list,' said Parker, who had come below, dripping like a Newfoundland dog.

'Why is this?' asked Stephen.

'Irish is forbidden in the Navy,' said Parker. 'It is prejudicial to discipline; a secret language is calculated to foment mutiny.'

'Another roll like that, and we shall have no masts,' said Pullings, as the remaining crockery, the glasses and the inhabitants of the gun-room all shot over to the lee. 'We'll lose the mizen first, Doctor,' – picking Stephen tenderly out of the wreckage – 'and so we'll be a brig; then we'll lose the foremast, so we'll be a right little old sloop; then we'll lose the main, and we'll be a raft, which is what we ought to have begun as.'

277

By some miracle of dexterity Macdonald had seized, and preserved, the decanter; holding it up he said, 'If you can find a whole glass, Doctor, I should be happy to drink a wee doodly of wine with you, and to lead your mind back to the subject of Ossian. From the obliging way in which you spoke of my ancestor, it is clear that you have a fine delicate notion of the sublime; and sublimity, sir, is the greatest internal evidence of Ossian's authenticity. Allow me to recite you a short description of the dawn.'

Once again the blue light shone down on the deck of the *Polychrest* and the uplifted faces of the watch; but this time it drifted off to the north-east, for the wind had come right round, bringing a thin rain and the promise of more, and this time it was almost instantly answered by musketry on the shore – red points of flame and a remote pop-pop-pop.

'Boat pulling off, sir,' called the man in the top. And two minutes later, 'On deck, on deck there! Another boat, sir. Firing on the first one.'

'All hands to make sail,' cried Jack, and the *Polychrest* woke to urgent life. 'Fo'c'sle, there; cast loose two and four. Mr Rolfe, fire on the second boat as I run inshore. Fire the moment they bear – full elevation. Mr Parker, tops'ls and courses.' They were half a mile off, well out of range of his carronades, but if only he could get under way he would soon shorten it. Oh, for just one long gun, a chaser . . .

The supplementary orders came thick and fast, a continuous, repetitive, exasperated clamour. 'Lay aloft, jump to it, trice up, lay out, lay out – will you lay out there on the maintops'lyard? Let fall, God damn your – eyes, let fall, mizen tops'l. Sheet home. Hoist with a will, now, hoist away.'

Christ, it was agony: it might have been an undermanned merchantman, a dung-scow in pandemonium:

he clasped his hands behind his back and stepped to the rail to prevent himself running forward to sort out the confused bellowing on the fo'c'sle. The boats were coming straight for him, the second firing two or three muskets and a spatter of pistols.

At last the bosun piped belay and the *Polychrest* began to surge forward, lying over to the wind. Keeping his eye on the advancing boats he said, 'Mr Goodridge, lay her in to give the gunner a clear shot. Mr Macdonald, your marksmen into the top – fire at the second boat.'

Now the sloop was really moving, opening the angle between the two boats: but at the same time the first boat began to turn towards her, shielding its pursuer from his fire. 'The boat ahoy,' he roared. 'Steer clear of my stern – pull a-starboard.'

Whether they heard, whether they understood or no, a gap appeared between the boats. The forward carronades went off – a deep crash and a long tongue of flame. He did not see the fall of the shot, but it had no effect on the following boat, which kept up its excited fire. Again, and this time he caught it, a split-second plume in the grey, well short, but in the right direction. The first musket cracked out overhead, followed by three or four together. A carronade again, and this time the ball was pitched well up to the second boat, for the *Polychrest* had moved two or three hundred yards: it must have ricocheted over their heads, for it damped their ardour. They came on still, but at the next shot the pursuing boat spun round, fired a last wanton musket and pulled fast out of range.

'Heave her to, Mr Goodridge,' said Jack. 'Back the mizen tops'l. The boat, ahoy! What boat?' There was a gabbling out there on the water, fifty yards away. 'What boat?' he hailed again, leaning far over the rail, the rain driving in on his face.

'Bourbon,' came a faint cry, followed by a strong shout, 'Bourbon' again.

'Pull under my lee,' said Jack. The way was off the

Polychrest, and she lay there pitching and groaning. The boat touched alongside, hooked to the mainchains, and in the glow of the battle-lanterns he saw a body crumpled in the stern-sheets.

'Le monsieur est touché,' said the man with the boat-hook.

'Is he badly hurt – mauvaisement blessay?'

'Sais pas, commandant. Il parle plus: je crois bien que c'est un macchabée à présent. Y à du sang partout. Vous voulez pas me faire passer une élingue, commandant?'

'Eh? Parlez – pass the word for the Doctor.'

It was not until they had got his patient into Jack's cabin that Stephen saw his face. Jean Anquetil, a nervous, timid-brave, procrastinating, unlucky young man: and he was bleeding to death. The bullet had nicked his aorta, and there was nothing, nothing he could do: the blood was pumping out in great throbs.

'It will be over in a few minutes,' he said, turning to Jack.

'And so, sir, he died within minutes of being brought aboard,' said Jack.

Admiral Harte grunted. He said, 'That is everything he had on him?'

'Yes, sir. Greatcoat, boots, clothes and papers: they are very bloody, I am afraid.'

'Well, that is a matter for the Admiralty. But what about this death-or-money boat?'

So that was the reason for his ill-humour. 'I sighted the boat when I was on my station, sir; there were fifty-three minutes to go before the rendezvous, and if I had borne down I must necessarily have been late – I could never have beaten back in time. You know what the *Polychrest* is on a bowline, sir.'

'And you know the tag about workmen and their tools, Captain Aubrey. Anyhow, there is such a thing as being too scrupulous by half. The fellow was never at the rendezvous at all: these foreigners never are. And in any case, half an hour or so . . . and it positively could not have been more, even with a crew of old women. Are you aware, sir, that *Amethyst*'s boats picked up that Deal bugger as he was running into Ambleteuse with eleven hundred guineas aboard? It makes me mad to think of it . . . made a cock of the whole thing.' He drummed his fingers on the table. The *Amethyst* was cruising under Admiralty orders, Jack reflected; the flag-officer had no share in her prize-money; Harte had lost about a hundred and fifty pounds; he was not pleased. 'However,' went on the admiral, 'it is no use crying over spilt milk. As soon as the wind gets out of the south, I am taking the convoy down. You will wait here for the Guinea-men to join, and the ships in the list Spalding will give you: you are to escort them as far as the Rock of Lisbon, and I have no doubt on your way back you will make good this little mess. Spalding will give you your orders: you will find no cast-iron rigid rendezvous.'

By morning the wind had shifted into the west-north-west, and the blue peter broke out at a hundred foretopmastheads: boats by the score hurried merchant captains, mates, passengers and their relatives from Sandwich, Walmer, Deal and even Dover, and many a cruel extortionate bargain was struck when the flagship's signals, reinforced by insistent guns, made it clear that time was short, that this time was the true departure. Towards eleven o'clock the whole body, apart from those that had fallen foul of one another, was under way in three straggling divisions, or rather heaps. Orderly or disorderly, however, they made a splendid sight, white sails stretching over four or five miles of grey sea, and the high, torn sky sometimes as grey as the one or as white as the other. An impressive illustration of the enormous importance of trade to the island, too; one that might have served the *Polychrest*'s midshipmen as a lesson in political economy and on the powers of the

average seaman at evading the press – there were some
thousands of them there, sailing unscathed from the very
heart of the Impress Service.

But they, in common with the rest of the ship's
company, were witnessing punishment. The grating was
rigged, the bosun's mates stood by, the master-at-arms
brought up his delinquents, a long tally charged with
drunkenness – gin had been coming aboard from the
bum-boats, as it always did – contempt, neglect of duty,
smoking tobacco outside the galley, playing dice, theft.
On these occasions Jack always felt gloomy, displeased
with everybody aboard, innocent and guilty alike: he
looked tall, cold, withdrawn, and, to those under his
power, his nearly absolute power, horribly savage, a
right hard horse. This was early in the commission
and he had to establish an unquestioning discipline;
he had to support his officers' authority. At the same
time he had to steer fine between self-defeating harshness
and (although indeed some of these charges were trivial
enough, in spite of his words with Parker) fatal softness;
and he had to do so without really knowing three quarters
of his men. It was a difficult task, and his face grew more
and more lowering. He imposed extra duties, cut grog for
three days, a week, a fortnight, awarded four men six
lashes apiece, one nine, and the thief a dozen. It was not
much, as flogging went; but in the old *Sophie* they had
sometimes gone two months and more without bringing
the cat out of its red baize bag: it was not much, but even
so it made quite a ceremony, with the relevant Articles of
War read out, the drum-roll, and the gravity of a hundred
men assembled.

The swabbers cleaned up the mess, and Stephen went
below to patch or anoint the men who had been flogged
– those, that is to say, who reported to him. The seamen
put on their shirts again and went about their business,
trusting to dinner and grog to set them right: the landsmen
who had not been beaten navy-fashion before were much

more affected – quite knocked up; and the thieves' cat had made an ugly mess of thief Carlow's back, the bosun's mate being first cousin to the man he robbed.

He came on deck again shortly before the men were piped to dinner, and seeing the first lieutenant walking up and down looking pleased with himself, he said to him, 'Mr Parker, will you indulge me in the use of a small boat in let us say an hour? I could wish to walk upon the Goodwin sands at low tide. The sea is calm; the day propitious.'

'Certainly, Doctor,' said the first lieutenant, always good-humoured after a flogging. 'You shall have the blue cutter. But will you not miss your dinner?'

'I shall take some bread, and a piece of meat.'

So he paced this strange, absolute and silent landscape of firm damp sand with rivulets running to its edges and the lapping sea, eating bread with one hand and cold beef with the other. He was so low to the sea that Deal and its coast were out of sight; he was surrounded by an unbroken disc of quiet grey sea, and even the boat, which lay off an inlet at the far rim of the sand, seemed a great way off, or rather upon another plane. Sand stretched before him, gently undulating, with here and there the black half-buried carcasses of wrecks, some massive, others ribbed skeletons, in a kind of order whose sense escaped him, but which he might seize, he thought, if only his mind would make a certain shift, as simple as starting the alphabet at X – simple, if only he could catch the first clue. A different air, a different light, a sense of overwhelming permanence and therefore a different time; it was not at all unlike a certain laudanum-state. Wave ripples on the sand: the traces of annelids, solens, clams: a distant flight of dunlins, close-packed, flying fast, all wheeling together and changing colour as they wheeled.

His domain grew larger with the ebbing of the tide; fresh sandpits appeared, stretching far, far away to the north under the cold even light; islands joined one another, gleaming water disappeared, and only on the far rim of his world was there the least noise – the lap of small waves, and the remote scream of gulls.

It grew smaller, insensibly diminishing grain by grain; everywhere there was a secret drawing-in, apparent only in the widening channels between the sandbanks, where the water was now running frankly from the sea.

The boat's crew had been contentedly fishing for dabs all this time, and they had filled two moderate baskets with their catch.

'There's the Doctor,' said Nehemiah Lee, 'a-waving of his arms. Is he talking to hisself, or does he mean to hail us?'

'He's a-talking to hisself,' said John Lakes, an old Sophie. 'He often does. He's a very learned cove.'

'He'll get cut off, if he don't mind out,' said Arthur Simmons, an elderly, cross-grained forecastleman. 'He looks fair mazed, to me. Little better than a foreigner.'

'You can stow that, Art Simmons,' said Plaice. 'Or I'll stop your gob.'

'You and who to help you?' asked Simmons, moving his face close to his shipmate's.

'Ain't you got no respect for learning?' said Plaice. 'Four books at once I seen him read. Nay, with these very eyes, here in my head,' – pointing to them – 'I seen him whip a man's skull off, rouse out his brains, set 'em to rights, stow 'em back again, clap on a silver plate, and sew up his scalp, which it was drooling over one ear, obscuring his dial, with a flat-seam needle and a pegging-awl, as neat as the sail-maker of a King's yacht.'

'And when did you bury the poor bugger?' asked Simmons, with an offensive knowingness.

'Which he's walking the deck of a seventy-four at this very moment, you fat slob,' cried Plaice. 'Mr Day, gunner of the *Elephant*, by name, better than new, and promoted. So you can stuff that up your arse, Art Simmons. Learning? Why, I seen him sew on a man's arm when it was hanging by a thread, passing remarks in Greek.'

284

'And my parts,' said Lakey, looking modestly at the gunwale.

'I remember the way he set about old Parker when he gagged that poor bugger in the larboard watch,' said Abraham Bates. 'Those was learned words: even I couldn't understand above the half of 'em.'

'Well,' said Simmons, vexed by their devotion, that deeply irritating quality, 'he's lost his boots now, for all his learning.'

This was true. Stephen retracted his footsteps towards the stump of a mast protruding from the sand where he had left his boots and stockings, and to his concern he found that these prints emerged fresh and clear directly from the sea. No boots: only spreading water, and one stocking afloat in a little scum a hundred yards away. He reflected for a while upon the phenomenon of the tide, gradually bringing his mind to the surface, and then he deliberately took off his wig, his coat, his neckcloth and his waistcoat.

'Oh dear, oh dear,' cried Plaice. 'He's a-taking off his coat. We should never have let him off alone on those – – sands. Mr Babbington said "Do not let him go a-wandering on them – – sands, Plaice, or I'll have the hide off your – back". Ahoy! The Doctor ahoy, sir! Come on, mates, stretch out, now. Ahoy, there!'

Stephen took off his shirt, his drawers, his catskin comforter, and walked straight into the sea, clenching his mouth and looking fixedly at what he took to be the stump of mast under the pellucid surface. They were valuable boots, soled with lead, and he was attached to them. In the back of his mind he heard the roaring desperate hails, but he paid no attention: arrived at a given depth, he seized his nose with one hand, and plunged.

A boathook caught his ankle, an oar struck the nape of his neck, partly stunning him and driving his face deep into the sand at the bottom: his foot emerged, and he was seized and hauled into the boat, still grasping his boots.

They were furious. 'Did he not know he might catch cold? – Why did he not answer their hail? It was no good his telling them he had not heard; they knew better; *he* had not got flannel ears – Why had he not waited for them? – What was a boat for? – Was this a proper time to go a-swimming? – Did he think this was midsummer? Or Lammas? – He was to see how cold he was, blue and trembling like a fucking jelly. – Would a new-joined ship's boy have done such a wicked thing? No, sir, he would not. – What would the skipper, what would Mr Pullings and Mr Babbington say, when they heard of his capers? – As God loved them, they had never seen anything so foolish: He might strike them blind, else. – Where had he left his intellectuals? Aboard the sloop?' They dried him with handkerchiefs, dressed him by force, and rowed him quickly back to the *Polychrest*. He was to go below directly, turn in between blankets – no sheets, mind – with a pint of grog and have a good sweat. He was to go up the side now, like a Christian, and nobody would notice. Plaice and Lakey were perhaps the strongest men in the ship, with arms like gorillas; they thrust him aboard and hurried him to his cabin without so much as by your leave, and left him there in the charge of his servant, with recommendations for his present care.

'Is all well, Doctor?' asked Pullings looking in with an anxious face.

'Why, yes, I thank you, Mr Pullings. Why do you ask?'

'Well, sir, seeing your wig was shipped arsy-versy and your comforter all ends up, I thought may be you had had a misfortune, like.'

'Oh, no: not at all, I am obliged to you. I recovered them none the worse – I flatter myself there is not such a pair in the kingdom. The very best Cordova ass's leather. *They* will not suffer from a thoughtless hour's immersion. Pray, what was all the ceremony as I came into the ship?'

'It was for the Captain. He was only a little way behind you – came aboard not five minutes ago.'

'Ah? I was not aware he had been out of the ship.'

Jack was obviously in high spirits. 'I trust I do not disturb you,' he said. 'I said to Killick, "Do not disturb him on any account, if he is busy." But I thought that with such a damned unpleasant night outside, and the stove drawing so well in, that we might have some music. But first take a sup of this madeira and tell me what you think of it. Canning sent me a whole anker – so good-natured of him. I find it wonderfully grateful to the palate. Eh?'

Stephen had identified the smell that hung about Jack's person and that wafted towards him as he passed the wine. It was the French scent he had bought in Deal. He put down his glass composedly and said, 'You must excuse me this evening, I am not quite well, and I believe I shall turn in.'

'My dear fellow, I am so sorry,' cried Jack, with a look of concern. 'I do hope you have not caught a chill. Was there any truth in that nonsense they were telling me, about your swimming off the sands? You must certainly turn in at once. Should you not take physic? Allow me to mix you a strong . . .'

Shut firmly in his cabin, Stephen wrote. 'It is unspeakably childish to be upset by a whiff of scent; but I am upset, and I shall certainly exceed my allowance, to the extent of five hundred drops.' He poured himself out a wineglassful of laudanum, closed one eye, and drank it off. 'Smell is of all senses by far the most evocative: perhaps because we have no vocabulary for it – nothing but a few poverty-stricken approximations to describe the whole vast complexity of odour – and therefore the scent, unnamed and unnamable, remains pure of association; it cannot be called upon again and again, and blunted, by the use of a word; and so it strikes afresh every time, bringing with it all the circumstances of its first perception. This is particularly true when a considerable period of time has elapsed. The whiff, the gust, of which I speak brought me the Diana of the St Vincent ball, vividly alive, exactly as I knew her then, with none of the vulgarity or loss of looks I see today. As for that loss, that very trifling loss, I applaud it and wish it may continue. She will always have that quality of being more intensely alive, that spirit, dash and courage, that almost ludicrous, infinitely touching unstudied unconscious grace. But if, as she says, her face is her fortune, then she is no longer Croesus; her wealth is diminishing; it will continue to diminish, by her standard, and even before her fatal thirtieth year it may reach a level at which I am no longer an object of contempt. That, at all events, is my only hope; and hope I must. The vulgarity is new, and it is painful beyond my power of words to express: there was the appearance of it before, even at that very ball, but *then* it was either factious or the outcome of the received notions of her kind – the reflected vulgarity of others; *now* it is not. The result of her hatred for Sophia, perhaps? Or is that too simple? If it grows, will it destroy her grace? Shall I one day find her making postures, moving with artful negligence? That would destroy me. Vulgarity: how far am I answerable for it? In a relationship of this kind each makes the other, to some extent. No man could give her more opportunity for exercising all her worst side than I. But there is far, far more to mutual destruction than that. I am reminded of the purser, though the link is tenuous enough. Before we reached the Downs he came to me in great secrecy and asked me for an antaphrodisiac.

'*Purser Jones:* I am a married man, Doctor.

'*SM:* Yes.

'*Jones:* But Mrs J is a very religious woman, is a very virtuous woman; and she don't like it.

'*SM:* I am concerned to hear it.

'*Jones:* Her mind is not given that way, sir. It is not

that she is not fond and loving, and dutiful, and handsome – everything a man could wish. But there you are: I am a very full-blooded man, Doctor. I am only thirty-five, though you might not think it, bald and pot-bellied and cetera and cetera. Sometimes I toss and turn all night, and burn, as the Epistle says; but it is to no purpose, and sometimes I am afraid I will do her a mischief, it is so . . . That is why I went to sea, sir; though I am not suited for a naval life, as you know all too well.

'*SM:* This is very bad, Mr Jones. Do you represent to Mrs Jones that . . .

'*Jones:* Oh, I do, sir. And she cries and vows she will be a better wife to me – hers is not an ungrateful mind, she says – and so, for a day or two, she turns to me. But it is all duty, sir, all duty. And in a little while it is the same again. A man cannot still be asking; and what you ask for is not given free – it is never the same – no more like than chalk and cheese. A man cannot make a whore of his own wife.

'He was pale and sweating, pitiably earnest; said he was always glad to sail away, although he hated the sea; that she was coming round to Deal to meet him; that as there were drugs that promoted venereal desire, so he hoped there might be some that took it away and that I should prescribe it for him, so that they could be sweethearts. He swore "he should rather be cut" than go on like this, and he repeated that "a man could not make a whore of his own wife." '

Some days later the diary continued: 'Since Wednesday JA has been his own master; and I believe he is abusing his position. As I understand it, the convoy was complete yesterday, if not before: the masters came aboard for their instructions, the wind was fair and the tide served; but the sailing was put off. He takes insensate risks, going ashore, and any observation of mine has the appearance of bad faith. This morning the devil suggestd to me that

289

I should have him laid by the heels; I could so with no difficulty at all. He presented the suggestion with a wealth of good reasons, mostly of an altruistic nature, and mentioned both honour and duty; I wonder he did not add patriotism. To some extent JA is aware of my feelings, and when he brought her renewed invitation to dinner he spoke of "happening to run into her again", and expatiated on the coincidence in a way that made me feel a surge of affection for him in spite of my animal jealousy. He is the most inept liar and the most penetrable, with his deep, involved, long-winded policy, that I have ever met. The dinner was agreeable; I find that given warning I can support more than I had supposed. We spoke companionably of former times, ate very well, and played – the cousin is one of the most accomplished flautists I have heard. I know little of DV, but it appears to me that her sense of hospitality (she is wonderfully generous) overcame all her more turbid feelings; I also think she has a kind of affection for the both of us; although in that case, how she can ask so much of JA passes my understanding. She showed at her best; it was a delightful evening; but how I long for tomorrow and a fair wind. If it comes round into the south – if he is windbound for a week or ten days, he is lost: he must be taken.'

CHAPTER NINE

The *Polychrest* left her convoy in 38° 30′ N., 11° W., with the wind at south-west and the Rock of Lisbon bearing S87E., 47 leagues. She fired a gun, exchanged signals with the merchantmen, and wore laboriously round until the wind was on her larboard quarter and her head was pointing north.

The signals were polite, but brief; they wished one another a prosperous voyage and so parted company, with none of those long, often inaccurate hoists that some grateful convoys would keep flying until they were hidden by the convexity of the earthly sphere. And although the previous day had been fine and calm, with an easy swell and warm variable airs from the west and south, the merchant captains had not invited the King's officers to dinner: it was not a grateful convoy, and in fact it had nothing to be grateful for. The *Polychrest* had delayed their departure, so that they had missed their tide and the best part of a favourable breeze, and had held them back in their sailing all the way, not only by her slowness, but by her inveterate sagging to leeward, so that they were all perpetually having to bear up for her, they being a weatherly set of ships. She had fallen aboard the *Trade's Increase* by night, when they were lying-to off the Lizard, and had carried away her bowsprit; and when they met with a strong south-wester in the Bay of Biscay she rolled her mizenmast out. Her maintopmast had gone with it and they had been obliged to stand by while she set up a jury-rig. Nothing had appeared to threaten their security, not so much as a lugger on the horizon, and the *Polychrest* had had no occasion to protect them or to show what teeth she might possess. They turned from her with loathing, and pursued their voyage at their own far brisker pace, setting topgallants and royals at last.

But the *Polychrest* had little time for attending to the convoy as it disappeared, for this was Thursday, and the people were to be mustered. Scarcely had she steadied on her new course before five bells in the forenoon watch struck and the drum began to beat: the crew came hurrying aft and stood in a cluster abaft the mainmast on the larboard side. They had all been aboard some time now, and they had been mustered again and again; but some were still so stupid that they had to be shoved into place by their mates. However, by this time they were all decently dressed in the purser's blue shirts and white trousers; none showed the ghastly pallor of gaol or sea-sickness any more, and indeed the enforced cleanliness, the sea-air and the recent sun had given most the appearance of health. The food might have done something, too, for it was at least as good as that which many of them had been eating, and more plentiful.

The first part of the alphabet happened to contain most of the *Polychrest*'s seamen. There were some awkward brutes among them, such as that gap-toothed Bolton, but most were the right strong-faced long-armed bow-legged pigtailed sort; they called out 'Here, sir' to their names, touching their foreheads and walking cheerfully past their captain to the starboard gangway. They gave that part of the ship something of the air of the *Sophie*, an efficient, happy ship, if ever there was one, where even the waisters could hand, reef and steer . . . how fortunate he had been in his lieutenant. But Lord, how few the seamen were! After the letter G there were hardly more than two among all the names that were called. Poor meagre little creatures for the most part little stouter than the boys. And either surly or apprehensive or both: not a smile as they answered their names and crossed over. There had been too much flogging, too much starting: but what else could you do in an emergency? Oldfield, Parsons, Pond, Quayle . . . sad little objects; the last much given to informing; had been turned out of his mess twice already. And they were not the bottom of the barrel.

Eighty-seven men and boys, no more, for he was still thirty-three short of his complement. Perhaps thirty of them knew their duty, and some were learning; indeed, most had learnt a little, and there were no longer the scenes of total incompetence that had made a nightmare of the earliest days. He knew all these faces now; some had improved almost out of recognition; some had deteriorated – too much unfamiliar misery; dull minds unused to learning yet forced to learn a difficult trade in a driving hurry. Three categories: a top quarter of good sound able hands; then the vague middle half that might go up or might go down, according to the atmosphere of the ship and how they were handled; and then the bottom quarter, with some hard cases among them, brutal, or stupid, or even downright wicked. As the last names were called his heart sank farther: Wright, Wilson and Young were the very bottom. Men like them were to be found aboard most men-of-war in a time of hot press, and an established ship's company could wear a certain number without much harm. But the *Polychrest*'s was not an established ship's company; and in any case the proportion was far too high.

The clerk closed the book, the first lieutenant reported the muster complete, and Jack gave them a last look before sending them to their tasks: a thoughtful look, for these were the men he might have to lead on to the deck of a French man-of-war tomorrow. How many would follow him?

'Well, well,' he thought, 'one thing at a time,' and he turned with relief to the problem in hand, to the new-rigging of the *Polychrest*. It would be complicated enough in all conscience, with her strange hull and the calculation of the forces acting upon it, but in comparison with the task of making a crew of man-of-war's men out of the rag, tag, and bobtail from G to Y it was as simple and direct as kiss my hand. And here he was seconded by good officers: Mr Gray, the carpenter, knew his trade thoroughly; the bosun, though still too free with his cane, was active, willing and competent where rigging was concerned; and the master had a fine sense of a ship's nature. In theory, Admiralty regulations forbade Jack to shift so much as his backstays, but Biscay had shifted them for him, and a good deal more besides; he had a free hand, fine calm weather, a long day before him, and he meant to make the most of it.

For form's sake he invited Parker to join their deliberations, but the first lieutenant was more concerned with his paintwork and gold-leaf than with getting the ship to move faster through the water. He did not seem to understand what they were driving at, and presently they forgot his presence, though they listened politely to his plea for a larger crow-foot to extend a double awning – 'In the *Andromeda*, Prince William always used to say that his awning gave the quarterdeck the air of a ballroom.' As he spoke of the dimensions of the heroic euphroe that suspended this awning and the number of cloths that went into the awning itself, Jack looked at him curiously. Here was a man who had fought at the battle of the Saintes and in Howe's great action, and yet still he thought his yard-blacking more important than sailing half a point closer to the wind. 'I used to tell him it was no use racing one mast against the other in reefing topsails until the people at least knew how to lay aloft: I was wasting my breath. Very well, gentlemen,' he said aloud, 'let us make it so. There is not a moment to lose. We could not ask for better weather, but who can tell how long it will last?'

The *Polychrest*, fresh from the yard, was reasonably well supplied with bosun's and carpenter's stores; but in any event, Jack's intention was rather to cut down than to add. She had always been crank and overmasted, so that she lay down in a capful of wind; and her foremast had always been stepped too far aft, because of her original purpose in life, which made her gripe even with her mizen furled – made her do a great many other unpleasant things too. In spite of his fervent longing, he could do nothing about the stepping without official consent and the help of a dockyard, but he could do something to improve the mast by raking it forward and by a new system of stays, jibs and staysails; and he could make her less crank by stubbing her topmasts, striking topgallants, and setting up bentincks, triangular courses that would not press her down in the water so much and that would relieve her top-hamper.

This was work he understood and loved; for once he was not in a tearing hurry, and he paced about the deck, seeing his plan take form, going from one group to the next as they prepared the spars, rigging and canvas. The carpenter and his mates were in the waist, their saws and adzes piling up heaps of chips and sawdust between the holy guns – guns that lay still today for the first time since he had hoisted his pennant; the sailmaker and his two parties spread over the forecastle and the greater part of the quarterdeck, canvas in every direction; and the bosun piled his coils of rope and his blocks in due order, checking them on his list, sweating up and down to his store-room, with no time to knock the hands about or even to curse them, except as a mechanical, unmeaning afterthought.

They worked steadily, and better than he had expected: his three pressed tailors squatted there cross-legged, very much at home, plying needle and palm with the desperate speed they had learnt in the sweat-shop, and an out-of-work nailmaker from Birmingham showed an extraordinary skill in turning out iron rings from the armourer's forge: 'Crinkum-cankum, round she goes', a twist of his tongs, a knowing triple rap with his hammer, and the glowing ring hissed into a bucket.

Eight bells in the afternoon watch, and the sun pouring down on the busy deck. 'Shall I pipe the hands to supper, sir?' asked Pullings.

'No, Mr Pullings,' said Jack. 'We shall sway up the maintopmast first. Proper flats we should look, was a Frenchman to heave in sight,' he observed, looking up and down the confusion. The foremast was clothed already, with a fine potential spread of canvas but little drawing, for want of stays; the jury-mizen still wore its little odd lateen, to give steerage-way; but the massive topmast was athwart the gangways, and this, together with the rest of the spars littering the deck, and all the other activities, made it almost impossible to move about – quite impossible to work the ship briskly. There was no room, although the boats were towing astern and everything that could be moved below had disappeared. She was making an easy three knots in the quartering breeze, but any emergency would find her helpless. 'Mr Malloch, there. Is your hawser to the capstan?'

'All along, sir.'

'Hands to the capstan, then. Are you ready at the word, there for'ard?'

'Ready, aye ready, sir.'

'Silence, fore and aft. Heave. Heave handsomely.' The capstan turned, the hawser tightened. It led from the capstan through a block on deck to another block on the mainmast head, thence to the head of the topmast, down to the square fid-hole in its heel, and so back to the topmast head, where it was made fast; bands of spun-yarn held it to the mast at intervals, and as it tightened so it began to raise the head. The topmast, a great iron-hooped column of wood some forty feet long, lay across the waist, its ends protruding far out on either side; as its head rose, so Jack called orders to the party on the other side to ease its heel in over the rail, timing each heave to the roll. 'Pawl, there. Stand to your bars. Heave. Heave and rally. Pawl.' The mast tilted up, nearer and nearer to the vertical. Now it was all inboard, no longer sloping but perfectly upright, swaying with the roll, an enormous, dangerous pendulum in spite of the controlling guys. Its head pointed at the trestle-trees, at the block high on the mainmast: the men in the top guided it through them, and still it rose with the turning of the capstan, to pause with its heel a few feet above the deck while they put on the cap. Up again, and they cut the spun-yarn as it reached the block: another pause, and they set the square over the mainmast head, banging it down with a maul, a thump-thump-thump that echoed through the silent, attentive ship.

'They must be getting the cap over,' said Stephen's patient in the sick-bay, a young topman. 'Oh, sir, I wish I was there. He'll splice the mainbrace for sure – it was night on eight bells when you come below.'

'You will be there presently,' said Stephen. 'but none of your mainbrace, none of your nasty grog, my friend, until you learn to avoid the ladies of Portsmouth Point, and the fireships of the Sally-Port. No ardent spirits at all for you. Not a drop, until you are cured. And even then, you would be far better with mild unctuous cocoa, or burgoo.'

'Which she told me she was a virgin,' said the sailor, in a low, resentful tone.

The mast rose up and up, the thrust coming from nearer and nearer to the fid-hole as the spun-yarn bands were cut in succession. They had cast off the hawser in favour of the top-rope; they had got the topmast shrouds over, the stays and the backstays; and now the top-tackle was swaying it up with a smooth, steady motion interrupted only by the roll of the ship. A hitch at this point – the top-rope parting, a block-spindle breaking – might be fatal. The last cautious six inches, and the fid-hole appeared above the trestle-trees. The captain of the top waved his hand: Jack cried 'Pawl, there.' The captain of the top banged home the long iron fid, cried 'Launch ho', and it was done. The topmast could no longer plunge like a gigantic arrow down through the deck, down through the ship's bottom, and send them all to their long account. They eased the top-rope and the mast settled on its fid with a gentle groan, firmly supported below, fore, aft, and on either side.

Jack let out a sigh, and when Pullings reported 'Main-topmast swayed up, sir,' he smiled. 'Very good, Mr Pullings,' he said. 'Let the laniards be well greased and bowsed taut, and then pipe to supper. The people have worked well, and I believe we may splice the mainbrace.'

'How pleasant it is to see the sun,' he called over the taffrail, later in the afternoon.

'Eh?' said Stephen, looking up from a tube thrust deep into the water.

'I said how pleasant it was to see the sun,' said Jack, smiling down at him there in the barge – smiling, too, with general benevolence. He was warm through and through after months of English drizzle; the mild wind caressed him through his open shirt and old canvas trousers; behind him the work was going steadily along, but now it was a matter for expert hands, the bosun, his mates, the quartermasters and forecastlemen; the mere hauling on ropes was over, and the mass of the crew forward were making cheerful noises – with this day's rational work, with no cleaning and no harassing, the feeling aboard had changed. The charming weather and the extra allowance of rum had also helped, no doubt.

'Yes,' said Stephen. 'It is. At a depth of two feet, Fahrenheit's thermometer shows no less than sixty-eight degrees. A southern current, I presume. There is a shark following up, a shark of the blue species, a carcharias. He revels in the warmth.'

'Where is he? Do you see him? Mr Parslow there, fetch me a couple of muskets.'

'He is under the dark belly of the ship. But no doubt he will come out presently. I give him gobbets of decayed flesh from time to time.'

From the sky forward there was a guttural shriek – a man falling from the yard, grabbing at air, almost motionless for a flash of time, head back, strained madly

298

up; then falling, faster, faster, faster. He hit a backstay. It bounced him clear of the side and he splashed into the sea by the mizen-chains.

'Man overboard!' shouted a dozen hands, flinging things into the water and running about.

'Mr Goodridge, bring her to the wind, if you please,' said Jack, kicking off his shoes and diving from the rail. 'How fresh – perfect!' he thought as the bubbles rushed thundering past his ears and the good taste of clean sea filled his nose. He curved upwards, looking at the rippled silver underside of the surface, rose strongly out of the water, snorting and shaking his yellow head, saw the man floundering fifty yards away. Jack was a powerful rather than a graceful swimmer, and he surged through the water with his head and shoulders out, like a questing dog, fixing the point in case the man should sink. He reached him – starting eyes, inhuman face belching water, stretching up, the terror of the deep (like most sailors he could not swim) – circled him, seized him by the root of his pigtail and said, 'Easy, easy, now, Bolton. Hold up.' Bolton writhed and grasped with convulsive strength. Jack kicked him free and bawled right into his ear, 'Clasp your hands, you fool. Clasp your hands, I say. There's a shark just by, and if you splash he'll have you.'

The word *shark* went home even to that terrified, half-drunk, water-logged mind. Bolton clasped his hands as though the force of his grip might keep him safe: he went perfectly rigid: Jack kept him afloat, and there they lay, rising and falling on the swell until the boat picked them up.

Bolton sat confused, obscurely ashamed and stupid in the bottom of the boat, gushing water; to cover his confusion he assumed a lumpish catalepsy, and had to be handed up the side. 'Carry him below,' said Jack. 'You had better have a look at him, Doctor, if you would be so kind.'

'He has a contusion on his chest,' said Stephen, coming

back to where Jack stood dripping on the quarterdeck, drying as he leaned on the rail and enjoyed the progress of the work on the running rigging. 'But no ribs are broken. May I congratulate you upon saving him? The boat would never have come up in time. Such promptitude of mind – such decision! I honour it.'

'It was pretty good, was it not?' said Jack. 'This is capital, upon my word,' – nodding to the mainmast – 'and at this rate we shall have the bentincks bent tomorrow. Did you smoke that? I said, the bentincks *bent*. Ha, ha, ha!'

Was he making light of it out of coxcombery, fanfaronade? From embarrassment? No, Stephen decided. It was as genuine as his mirth at his ignoble tiny pun, or adumbration of a pun, the utmost limit of naval wit.

'Was you not afraid,' he asked, 'when you reflected upon the shark – his notorious voracity?'

'Him? Oh, sharks are mostly gammon, you know: all cry and no wool. Unless there's blood about, they prefer galley leavings any day. On the West Indies station I once went in after a jolly and dived plump on to the back of a huge great brute: he never turned a hair.'

'Tell me, is this a matter of frequent occurrence with you? Does it in no way mark an epocha in your life, at all?'

'Epocha? Why, no; I can't say it does. Bolton here must make the twenty-second since I first went to sea: or maybe the twenty-third. The Humane chaps sent me a gold medal once. Very civil in them, too; with a most obliging letter. I pawned it in Gibraltar.'

'You never told me this.'

'You never asked. But there is nothing to it, you know, once you get used to their grappling. You feel good, and worthy – deserve well of the republic, and so on, for a while, which is agreeable, I don't deny; but there is really nothing to it – it don't signify. I should go in for a dog, let alone an able seaman: why, if it were warm, I dare say I should go in for a surgeon, ha, ha, ha! Mr Parker,

300

I think we may rig the sheets tonight and get the stump of the mizzen out first thing tomorrow. Then you will be able to priddy the deck and make all shipshape.'

'It is all ahoo at present, sir, indeed,' said the first lieutenant. 'But I must beg your pardon, sir, for not receiving you aboard in a proper fashion just now. May I offer my congratulations?'

'Why thank you, Mr Parker: an able seaman is a valuable prize. Bolton is one of our best upper-yardsmen.'

'He was drunk, sir. I have him in my list.'

'Perhaps we may overlook it this once, Mr Parker. Now the sheers can go with one foot here and the other by the scuttle, with a guy to the third hoop of the mainmast.'

In the evening, when it was too dark to work but too delightful to go below, Stephen observed, 'If you make it your study to depreciate rescues of this nature, will you not find that they are not valued? That you get no gratitude?'

'Now you come to mention it, I suppose it is so,' said Jack. 'It depends: some take it very kind. Bonden, for example. I pulled him out of the Mediterranean, as I dare say you remember, and no one could be more sensible of it. But most think it no great matter, I find. I can't say I should myself, unless it was a particular friend, who knew it was me, and who went in saying "Why, damn me, I shall pull Jack Aubrey out." No. Upon the whole,' he said, reflecting and looking wise, 'it seems to me, that in the article of pulling people out of the sea, virtue is its own reward.'

They lapsed into silence, their minds following different paths as the wake stretched out behind and the stars rose in procession over Portugal.

'I am determined at last,' cried Stephen, striking his hand upon his knee, 'I am at last determined – determined, I say – that I shall learn to swim.'

'I believe,' said Jack, 'that by the setting of the water tomorrow, we shall have our bentincks drawing.'

* * *

'The bentincks draw, the bentincks draw, the bentincks draw fu' weel,' said Mr Macdonald.

'Is the Captain pleased?' asked Stephen.

'He is delighted. There is no great wind to try them, but she seems much improved. Have you not remarked her motion is far more easy? We may have the pleasure of the purser's company once more. I tell you, Doctor, if that man belches of set purpose just once again, or picks his teeth at table, I shall destroy him.'

'That is why you are cleaning your pistols, I presume. But I am glad to hear what you tell me, about these sails. Perhaps now we shall hear less of selvagees and booms – the inner jib, the outer jib – nay, to crown all, the jibs of jibs, God forbid. Your mariner is an honest fellow, none better; but he is sadly given to jargon. Those are elegant, elegant pistols. May I handle them?'

'Pretty, are they not?' said Macdonald, passing the case. 'Joe Manton made them for me. Do these things interest you?'

'It is long since I had a pistol in my hand,' said Stephen. 'Or a small-sword. But when I was younger I delighted in them – I still do. They have a beauty of their own. Then again, they have a real utility. In Ireland, you know, we go out more often than the English do. I believe it is the same with you?'

Macdonald thought it was, though there was a great difference between the Highlands and the rest of the kingdom; what did Dr Maturin mean by 'often'? Stephen said he meant twenty or thirty times in a twelvemonth; in his first year at the university he had known men who exceeded this. 'At that time I attached a perhaps undue importance to staying alive, and I became moderately proficient with both the pistol and the small-sword. I have a childish longing to be at it again. Ha, ha – carte, tierce, tierce, sagoon, a hit!'

'Should you like to try a pass or two with me on deck?'

'Would that be quite regular? I have a horror of the least appearance of eccentricity.'

'Oh, yes, yes! It is perfectly usual. In the *Boreas* I used to give the midshipmen lessons as soon as I had finished exercising the Marines; and one or two of the lieutenants were quite good. Come, let us take the pistols too.'

On the quarterdeck they foined and lunged, stamping, crying 'Ha!' and the clash and hiss of steel upon steel seduced the midshipmen of the watch from their duty until they were banished to the heights, leaving their happier friends to watch the venomous wicked dart and flash entranced.

'Stop, stop! Hold – belay, avast,' cried Stephen, stepping back at last. 'I have no breath – I gasp – I melt.'

'Well,' said Macdonald, 'I have been a dead man these ten minutes past. I have only been fighting speeritually.'

'Sure, we were both corpses from very early in the battle.'

'Bless us all,' said Jack, 'I had no notion you were such a man of blood, dear Doctor.'

'You must be uncommon deadly when you are in practice,' said Macdonald. 'A horrid quick murdering lunge. I should not care to go out with you, sir. You may call me pudding, and I will bear it meekly. Do you choose to try the pistols?'

Jack, watching from his side of the quarterdeck, was wholly amazed: he had no idea that Stephen could hold a sword, nor yet load a pistol, still less knock the pips out of a playing-card at twenty paces: yet he had known him intimately. He was pleased that his friend was doing so well; he was pleased at the respectful silence; but he was a little sad that he could not join in, that he stood necessarily aloof – the captain could not compete – and he was obscurely uneasy. There was something disagreeable, and somehow reptilian, about the cold, contained way Stephen took up his stance, raised his pistol, looked along the barrel with his pale eyes, and shot the head off

303

the king of hearts. Jack's certainties wavered; he turned to look at his new bentincks, smoothly filled, drawing to perfection. Finisterre would be under their lee by now, some sixty leagues away; and presently, about midnight, he would alter course eastward – eastward, for Ortegal and the Bay.

Just before eight bells in the first watch Pullings came on deck, pushing a yawning, bleary-eyed Parslow before him.

'You are a good relief, Mr Pullings,' said the master. 'I shall be right glad to turn in.' He caught the yawn from the midshipman, gaped enormously and went on, 'Well, here you have her. Courses, main and fore tops'ls, forestays'l and jib. Course nor-nor-east, to be altered due east at two bells. Captain to be called if you sight any sail. Oh, my dear cot, how she calls. A good night to you, then. That child could do with a bucket of water over him,' he added, moving towards the hatchway.

Deep in his sleep Jack was aware of the changing watch – sixty men hurrying about in a ship a hundred and thirty feet long can hardly do so in silence – but it did not stir him more than one point from the deepest level of unconsciousness; it did not bring him half so near the surface as the change of course, which followed one hour later. He swam up, between sleeping and waking, knowing that his body was no longer lying in the same relationship to the north. And that the *Polychrest* was going large: the quick nervous rise and fall had given way to a long, easy glide. No roaring or calling out on deck. Pullings had put her before the wind with a few quiet remarks: all wool and no cry: how fortunate he was to have that good young fellow. But there was something not quite right. The sails had been trimmed, yet feet were pattering about at a great rate: through the open skylight he caught quick excited words, and he was fully awake, quite prepared for the opening of his door and the dim form of a midshipman beside his cot.

'Mr Pullings' duty, sir, and he believes there is a sail on the larboard bow.'

'Thank you, Mr Parslow. I shall be with him directly.'

He reached the glow of the binnacle as Pullings came sliding down a backstay from the top, thump on to the quarterdeck. 'I think I picked 'un out, sir,' he said, offering his telescope. 'Three points on the larboard bow, maybe a couple of mile away.'

It was a darkish night: an open sky, but hazy at the edges, the great stars little more than golden points and the small ones lost; the new moon had set long ago. When his eyes grew accustomed to the darkness he could make out the horizon well enough, a lighter bar against the black sky, with Saturn just dipping now. The wind had veered a trifle northerly; it had strengthened, and white water flecked the rise of every swell. Several times he thought he had the topsails of a ship in his glass, but every time they dissolved, never to reappear.

'You must have good eyes,' he said.

'She fired a gun, sir, and I caught the flash; but I did not like to call you till I had made certain sure. There she is, sir, just under the sprits'l yard. Tops'ls: maybe mizen t'garns'l. Close-hauled, I take it.'

'By God, I am getting old,' thought Jack, lowering the glass. Then he saw her, a ghostly flash that did not dissolve – vanished, but reappeared in the same place. A whiteness that the glass showed as a pale bar – topsails braced up sharp so that they overlapped. And a hint of white above: the mizen topgallant. She was on the starboard tack, close hauled on the fresh north-westerly breeze, probably heading west-south-west or a little south of it. If she had fired a gun, just one gun, it meant that she had consorts – that she was tacking and that they were to do the same. He searched the darkness eastward, and this time he saw one, perhaps two, of those dim but lasting wafts. On this course their

305

paths would intersect. But for how long would the remote unknown hold on to his present tack? No great while, for Cape Ortegal lay under his lee, an iron-bound coast with cruel reefs.

'Let us haul our wind, Mr Pullings,' he said. And to the helmsman, 'Luff up and touch her.'

The *Polychrest* came up and up; the stars turned, sweeping an arc in the sky, and he stood, listening intently for the first flutter of canvas that would mean she was as close to the wind as she would lie. The breeze blew on his left cheek-bone now; a dash of spray came over the rail to wet his face, and forward the leech of the foretopsail began to shake.

Jack took the wheel, eased her a trifle. 'Sharp that bow-line, there,' he called. 'Mr Pullings, I believe we can come up a trifle more. See to the braces and the bowlines.'

Pullings ran forward over the pale deck: a dark group on the forecastle heaved, 'One, two, three, belay,' and as he came aft so ropes tightened, yards creaked round an extra few inches. Now she was trimmed as sharp as she could be, and gradually Jack heaved on the spokes against the strong living pressure, bringing her head closer, closer to the wind. The pole-star vanished behind the maintopsail. Closer, still closer: and that was her limit. He had not believed she could do so well. She was lying not far from five points off the wind, as opposed to her old six and a half, and even if she made her usual extravagant leeway she could still eat the wind out of the stranger, so long as she had a very careful hand at the wheel and paid great attention to her trim: and he had the feeling she was sagging less, too. 'Thus, very well thus,' he said to the helmsman, looking into his face by the binnacle light. 'Ah, it is Haines, I see. Well, Haines, you will have to oblige me with a double trick at the wheel: this calls for a right seaman. Dyce, do you mind me, now? Not a hair's breadth off.'

'Aye, aye, sir. Dyce it is.'

'Carry on, Mr Pullings. Check all breechings and shot-racks. You may shake out a reef in the maintopsail if the breeze slackens. Call me if you find any change.'

He went below, pulled on his shirt and breeches and lay down on his cot, leafing through Steel's Navy List: but he could not rest, and presently he was on the quarterdeck again, pacing the lee side with his hands behind his back, a glance over the dark sea at every turn.

Two ships, perhaps three, tacking by signal: they might be anything – British frigates, French ships of the line, neutrals. But they might also be enemy merchantmen, slipping out by the dark of the moon: a hint of incautious light as the second rose on the swell made merchantmen more probable; and then again, it was unlikely that men-of-war should straggle over such an expanse of sea. He would get a better idea as the sky lightened; and in any case, whether they tacked or not, he would have the weather-gage at dawn – he would be up-wind of them.

He watched the side, he watched the wake: leeway she was making, of course; but it was distinctly less. Each heave of the log showed a steady three knots and a half: slow, but he wanted nothing more – at this point he would have reduced sail if she had been moving faster, for fear of finding himself too far away by morning.

Far over the sea on the *Polychrest*'s quarter a flash lit up the sky, and more than a heartbeat later he heard the boom: they were tacking again. Now he and the unknown were sailing on parallel courses, and the *Polychrest* had the weather-gage at its most perfect: she was directly in the eye of the wind from the leading ship of the three – the third was a certainty now, and had been so this last half hour.

Eight bells. It would be light before very long. 'Mr Pullings, keep the watch on deck. In main and mizen topsails. Mr Parker, good morning to you. Let the galley fires be lit at once, if you please: the hands will go to breakfast as soon as possible – a substantial breakfast, Mr

Parker. Rouse up the idlers. And then you may begin to clear the ship for action: we will beat to quarters at two bells. Where are the relief midshipmen? Quartermaster, go cut down their hammocks this instant. Pass the word for the gunner. Now, sir,' – to the appalled Rossall and Babbington – 'what do you mean by this vile conduct? Not appearing on deck in time for your watch? Nightcaps, dirty faces, by God! You are unwashed idle lubbers, both of you. Ah, Mr Rolfe, there you are: how much powder have you filled?'

The preparations went smoothly ahead, and each watch breakfasted in turn. 'Now you'll see summat, mates,' said William Screech, an old Sophie, as he rammed down his meal – cheese and portable soup. 'Now you'll see old Goldilocks cut one of his capers over them forringers.'

'It's time we see summat,' said a landsman. 'Where are all these golden dollars we were promised? It has been more kicks than ha'pence, so far.'

'They are a-lying just to leeward, mate,' said Screech. 'All you got to do, is to mind your duty and serve your gun brisk, and bob's your uncle Dick.'

'I wish I was at home with my old loom,' said a weaver, 'golden dollars or no golden dollars.'

Now the galley fires were dowsed in stench and hissing: the fearnought screens appeared at the hatchways: Jack's cabin vanished, Killick hurrying his belongings to the depths and the carpenters taking away the bulkheads: the gun-room poultry went clucking below in their coops: and all this while Jack stared out over the sea. The eastern sky was showing a hint of light by the time the bosun came to report a difficulty in his pudding – did the Captain wish it to be above the new clench or below? This question took no great consideration, but when Jack had given his answer and could look over the side again, the stranger was there as clear as he could desire: on the dull silver of the sea her hull showed black as it rose, something under a mile away on the starboard quarter. And behind her, far to leeward, the two others. They were no great sailers, that was clear, for although they had a fine spread of canvas abroad they were finding it hard to come up with her: she had hauled up her courses to let them close the distance, and now they were perhaps three parts of a mile from her. One seemed to be jury-rigged. Tucking his glass into his bosom, he climbed to the maintop. At the first glance he took, once he had settled firmly and had brought the leading ship into focus, he pursed his mouth and uttered a silent whistle. A thirty-two, no, a thirty-four gun frigate, no less. At the second he smiled, and without taking his eye from the telescope he called, 'Mr Pullings, pray come into the top. Here, take my glass. What do you make of her?'

'A thirty-two, no, a thirty-four gun frigate, sir. French, by the cut of her jib. No. No! By God, sir, she's the *Bellone*.'

The *Bellone* she was, in her old accustomed cruising-ground. She had undertaken to escort two Bordeaux mer-chantmen as far as twenty degrees west and forty-five north, and she had brought them successfully across the Bay of Biscay, not without trouble, for they were slow brutes, and one had lost her fore and main topmasts: she had stood by them, but she had no sharper sense of her obligations than any other privateer and now she was keenly interested in this odd triangular thing bob-bing about to windward. Her contract had no stipulations against her making prizes during her trip, and for the last quarter of an hour, or ever since she had sighted the *Polychrest*, the *Bellone* had been hauled a point closer to the wind to close her, and the *Bellone*'s captain had been doing exactly what Jack was at now, staring hard through his glass from the top.

The *Bellone*. She could outrun any square-rigged ship afloat, on a wind; but for the next ten or twenty minutes Jack had the initiative. He had the weather-gage, and he could decide whether to bring her to action or not. But this would not last long: he must think fast – make up his mind before she could shoot ahead. She had thirty-four guns to his four and twenty: but they were eight and six pounders – she threw a broadside of a hundred and twenty-six pounds, and with his three hundred and eighty-four he could blow her out of the water, given the right conditions. Only eight-pounders: but they were long brass eight-pounders, beautiful guns and very well served – she could start hitting him at a mile and more, whereas his short, inaccurate carronades, with their scratch crews, needed to be within pistol-shot for any certainty of execution. At fifty yards, or even at a hundred, he could give her such a dose! Near, but not too near. There was no question of boarding her, not with her two or three hundred keen privateersmen, not with this crew. Nor must he be boarded, Lord above.

'Mr Pullings,' he said, 'desire Mr Macdonald to get his men's red jackets off. Fling sailcloth over the guns in the waist. Drabble it about all ahoo, but so that it can be whipped off in a flash. Two or three empty casks on the fo'c'sle. Make her look like a slut.'

How neatly the roles were reversed! This time the *Bellone* had not been preparing herself for a couple of hours; *her* decks would not be clear fore and aft; and she would still be in a state of doubt – it was *she* who would be taken by surprise.

Taken: the word rang like a trumpet. He hurried down to the quarterdeck, his mind made up. 'Mr Parker, what are you about?'

'These mats are to protect my gold-leaf, sir,' said the first lieutenant.

'Do not square them, Mr Parker: they are very well so.' Indeed, they looked charmingly mercantile. 'All hands aft, if you please.'

They stood before him in the grey light, some few delighted, some amazed, many despondent, anxious, apt to stare over the water at that dark shape.

'Shipmates,' he said, loud and clear, smiling at them,

'that fellow down there is only a privateer. I know him well. He has a long row of gun-ports, but there are only six- and eight-pounders behind 'em, and ours are twenty-fours, though he don't know it. Presently I shall edge down on him – he may pepper us a while with his little guns, but it don't signify – and then, when we are so close we cannot miss, why, we shall give him such a broadside! A broadside with every gun low at his mizen. Not a shot, now, till the drum beats, and then ply 'em like heroes. Thump it into her! Five minutes' brisk and she strikes. Now go to your quarters, and remember, not a shot till the drum beats, and then every ball low at his mizen. Ply 'em quick, and waste not a shot.' Turning, he saw Stephen watching him from the companion hatchway. 'Good morning, good morning!' he cried, smiling with great affection. 'Here's our old friend the *Bellone* just to leeward.'

'Ay. So Pullings tell me. Do you mean to fight with her?'

'I mean to sink, take, burn or destroy her,' said Jack, a smile flashing across his face.

'I dare say you do. Please to remember the watch they took from me. A Bréguet repeater, number 365, with a centre seconds hand. And three pairs of drawers, I should know them anywhere. I must go below.'

The day was dawning fast; the east was golden – a clear sky with white clouds streaked across; the merchantmen were crowding sail to come up with the privateer.

'Mr Parker, lay the hatches, if you please. Mr Macdonald, your best marksmen into the tops at the last minute: they are to sweep the quarterdeck, nothing but the quarterdeck.'

This was his simple plan: he would edge down, never allowing her to forereach him, keeping rigorously to windward, puzzling her as long as he possibly could, and so batter her at close quarters, keeping her there by taking the wind out of her sails. Anything more complex he dared not attempt, not with this ship, not with these men – no quick

311

manoeuvres, no crossing under her stern – just as he dared not hide his men below, these raw hands who had never seen an angry gun.

'Ease her half a point, Mr Goodridge.'

Their courses were converging. How near would the *Bellone* let him come? Every hundred yards meant a minute less of enduring her long-range fire. Nearer, nearer . . .

If he could dismast her, shoot away her wheel – and it was just abaft the mizen in the *Bellone* . . . Now he could see the white of the faces on her quarterdeck. And yet still they sailed, on and on, drawing together, closer, closer. When would she fire? 'Another quarter, Mr Goodridge. Mr Rossall, you have the Papenburg . . . ?'

A puff of smoke from the *Bellone*'s bows, and a shot came skipping along the *Polychrest*'s side. The British colours appeared aboard the Frenchman. 'She's English!' cried a voice in the waist, with such relief, poor fellow. A hail, just audible in a lull of wind: 'Shorten sail and heave to, you infernal buggers.' Jack smiled. 'Slowly, Mr Rossall,' he said. 'Blunder around a little. Half up, down and up again.' The Papenburg flag wavered up to the mizenpeak and appeared at last, streaming out towards the privateer.

'That will puzzle him,' said Jack. The moment's doubt brought the two ships yet closer. Then another shot, one that hit the *Polychrest* square amidships: an ultimatum.

'Up foretopsheet,' cried Jack. He could afford to let the *Bellone* range up a little, and the confusion might gain another half minute.

But now the *Bellone* had had enough: the white ensign came down, the tricolour ran up: the frigate's side vanished in a long cloud and a hundredweight of iron hurtled across the five hundred yards of sea. Three balls struck the *Polychrest*'s hull; the rest screamed overhead. 'Clap on to that sheet there, for'ard,' he cried: and as the sail filled, 'Very well, Mr Goodridge, lay me alongside her at pistol-shot. Our colours, Mr Rossall. Mr Pullings, off canvas, casks over the side.'

An odd gun or two from the *Bellone*, and for a hideous moment Jack thought she was going to tack, cross his stern, and try a luffing-match to gain the wind, hitting him from a distance all the time. 'God send her broadside,' he muttered; and it came, a great rolling crash, but ragged – by no means in the *Bellone*'s finest style. Now the privateer was committed to a quick finish, out of hand. All that remained was to wait while the master took the *Polychrest* down into action, foiling every attempt at forereaching, keeping her just so in relation to the wind and the *Bellone* – to last out those minutes while the gap was narrowed.

'Mr Macdonald, Marines away aloft,' he said. 'Drummer, are you ready?'

Across the water the guns were being run out and aimed again; as the last thrust out its muzzle he roared 'Lie down. Flat down on deck.' This was a mixed broadside, mostly grape: it tore through the lower rigging and across the deck. Blocks rattled down, ropes parted, and there was Macdonald at his side, staggering, a hand clapped to his arm. A wretched little man was running about, trying to get down the forehatch: several others on their hands and knees, looking wild, watching to see if he would succeed. The bosun tripped him up, seized him and flung him back to his gun. The smoke cleared, and now Jack could see the dead-eyes in the *Bellone*'s shrouds. 'Stand to your guns,' he cried. 'Stand by. Wait for the drum. All at the mizen, now.'

The officers and the captains of the guns were traversing the carronades, training them at the *Bellone*, glaring along the barrels. The little drummer's huge eyes were fixed on Jack's face. Closer, even closer . . . He judged the roll, felt the ship reach the long slow peak, and the instant she began to go down he nodded and cried 'Fire!' The drum-roll was drowned by the universal blast of all the starboard guns, stunning the wind, so that the smoke lay thick, impenetrable. He fanned it with his hand, leaning out over the rail. It cleared, sweeping leeward, and he saw the murderous effect – a great gaping hole in the *Bellone*'s side, her mizenchains destroyed, the mast wounded, three gun-ports beaten in, bodies on her quarterdeck.

A furious, savage cheer from the *Polychrest*. 'Another, another,' he cried. 'Another and she strikes!'

But her colours were flying still, her wheel was unhurt, and on her quarterdeck Captain Dumanoir waved his hat to Jack, shouting orders to his men. To his horror Jack saw that the *Polychrest*'s cursed leeway was carrying her fast aboard the privateer. The Frenchmen, all but the gun-crews, were massing in the bows, some two hundred of them.

'Luff up, Goodridge . . .' and his words were annihilated by the double broadside, the *Bellone*'s and the *Polychrest*'s, almost yardarm to yardarm.

'All hands to repel boarders – pikes, pikes, pikes!' he shouted, drawing his sword and racing to the forecastle, the likely point of impact, vaulting a dismounted gun, a couple of bodies, and reaching it before the smoke cleared away. He stood there with twenty or thirty men around him, waiting for the grinding thump of the two ships coming together. Through the cloud there was an enormous shouting – orders in French – cheering – and now far astern a rending, tearing crash. Clear air, brilliant light, and there was the *Bellone* sheering off, falling off from the wind, turning; and the gap between them was twenty yards already. Her mizen had gone by the board, and she could not keep to the wind. The fallen mast lay over her starboard quarter, hanging by the shrouds, acting as a huge rudder, swinging her head away.

'To your guns,' he shouted. The *Bellone*'s stern was turning towards them – a raking broadside now would destroy her.

'She's struck, she's struck!' cried a fool. And now the

lack of training told – now the disorganized gun-crews ran about – match-tubs upset, shot, cartridge, swabs, rammers everywhere. Some men cheering, others capering like half-wits – guns in, guns out – Bedlam. 'Pullings, Babbington, Parker, get those guns firing – jump to it, God damn you all. Up with the helm, Goodridge – keep her bearing.' He knocked down a little silly weaver, skipping there for joy, banged two men's heads together, compelled them to their guns, heaved one carronade in, ran another out, fired it into the *Bellone*'s open stern, and ran back to the quarter-deck, crying 'Bear up, Goodridge, bear up, I say.'

And now the vile *Polychrest* would not answer her helm. Hardly a sheet of her headsails remained after that last broadside, and all her old griping was back. The helm was hard over, but she would not pay off; and the precious seconds were flying.

Malloch and his mates were busy with the sheets, knotting like fury: here and there a carronade spoke out – one twenty-four-pound ball hit the *Bellone* plumb on the stern-post. But the privateer had squared her yards; she was right before the wind, and they were separating at a hundred yards a minute. Before the headsheets were hauled aft, so that the *Polychrest* could pay off and pursue the *Bellone*, there was quarter of a mile of open water between them; and now the *Bellone* was replying with her stern-chaser.

'Mr Parker, get two guns into the bows,' said Jack. The *Polychrest* was gathering way: the *Bellone*, hampered by her trailing mast, yawed strangely. The distance narrowed. 'Mr Parslow, fetch me a glass.' His own lay shattered by the fife-rail.

'A glass? What glass, sir?' The little pale dazed face peered up, anxious, worried.

'Any glass – a telescope, boy,' he said kindly. 'In the gun-room. Look sharp.'

He glanced up and down his ship. The bentincks holed like sieves, two staysails hanging limp, foretopsail in rags, half a dozen shrouds parted: jibs and mizen drawing well, however. Something like order on deck. Two guns dismounted, but one being crowed up and re-breached. The rest run out, ready, their crews complete, the men looking eager and determined. A great heap of hammocks in the waist, blasted out of their netting by the *Bellone*'s last broadside. The wounded carried below, skirting the heap.

'The glass, sir.'

'Thank you, Mr Parslow. Tell Mr Rolfe the bow carronades are to fire the moment they can be run out.'

Aboard the *Bellone* they were hacking at the starboard mizen-shrouds with axes. The last pair parted, the floating mast tore clear, and the frigate surged forward, drawing clear away, going, going from them. But as he watched, her maintopmast lurched, lurched again, and with a heavy pitch of the sea it fell bodily over the side.

A cheer went up from the *Polychrest*. They were gaining on her – they were gaining! The bow carronade went off: the shot fell short, but almost hit the *Bellone* on the ricochet. Another cheer. 'You'll cheer the other side of your faces when she hauls her wind and rakes us,' he thought. The two ships were some five hundred yards apart, both directly before the wind, with the *Polychrest* on the *Bellone*'s larboard quarter: the privateer had but to put her helm a-lee to show them her broadside and rake them from stem to stern. She could not come right up into the wind with no sails aft, but she could bring it on to her beam, and less than that would be enough.

Yet she did not do so. The topmast was cut away, but still the *Bellone* ran before the wind. And focusing his glass upon her stern he saw why – she had no helm to put a-lee. That last lucky shot had unseated her rudder. She could not steer. She could only run before the wind.

They were coming down to the merchantmen now, broad low ships still on the larboard tack. Did they mean to give any trouble? To stand by their friend? They had five gun-ports of a side, and the *Bellone* would pass within a cable's length of them. 'Mr Parker, run out the larboard guns.' No: they did not. They were slowly edging away, heading north: one was a lame duck – juryrigged fore and main topmasts. The *Polychrest*'s bow gun sent a fountain of water over the *Bellone*'s stern. They were gaining. Should he snap up the merchantmen and then go on after the privateer? Content himself with the merchants? At this moment they could not escape: but in five minutes he would be to leeward of them, and slow though they might be, it would be a task to bring them to. In half an hour it would be impossible.

The carronade was firing two shots for the *Bellone*'s one; but that one came from a long eight, a more accurate gun by far. A little before they came abreast of the merchant ships it sent a ball low over the *Polychrest*'s deck, killing a seaman near the wheel, flinging his body on to Parslow as he stood there, waiting for orders. Jack pulled the body off, disentangled the blood-stained child, said 'Are you all right, Parslow?' and in reply to Parker's 'The merchantmen have struck, sir,' he cried, 'Yes, yes. See if it is possible to lace on a bonnet.' A minute gain in speed would allow him to draw up on the *Bellone*, yaw and hammer her with his broadside again. They swept close by the merchantmen, who let fly their sheets in submission. Even in this heat of battle, with the guns answering one another as fast as they could be loaded, powder-smoke swirling between them, bodies on deck, blood running fresh in the scuppers, there were eyes that glanced wistfully at their prizes – fair-sized ships: ten, twenty, even thirty thousand guineas, perhaps. They knew very well that the moment the *Polychrest* had run a mile to leeward, all that money would get under way, spread every possible stitch of canvas, haul to the wind, and fly: kiss my hand to a fortune.

South-east they ran, the merchant ships dwindling fast astern. They ran firing steadily, first the one gaining a little as damaged rigging was repaired, then the other;

neither dared risk the pause to bend new sails; neither dared risk sending up a new topmast or topgallants in this steep pitching sea; and as they stood they were exactly matched. The least damage to either would be decisive, the least respite fatal; and so they ran, and the glass turned and the bell rang right through the forenoon watch, hour after hour, in a state of extreme tension – hardly a word on deck, apart from orders – never much more or less than a quarter of a mile away from one another. Both tried setting studdingsails: both had them blown away. Both started their water over the side, lightening themselves by several tons – every trick, device, contrivance known to seamen for an even greater urgency of thrust. At one point Jack thought the *Bellone* was throwing her stores overboard, but it was only her dead. Forty splashes he counted: the slaughter in that close-packed ship must have been appalling. And still they fired.

By noon, when they raised the high land of Spain among the clouds on the southern horizon, the *Polychrest*'s bows were pockmarked with shot-holes, her foremast and foretopsailyard had been gashed again and again, and she was making water fast. The *Bellone*'s stern was shattered to an extraordinary degree and her great mainsail was a collection of holes; but she was steering again. This she did by a cable veered out of the stern-port, which allowed her to turn a couple of points from the wind – not much, but more than she could do by steering with her sheets. She altered course deliberately on sighting Cape Peñas, and it cost her dear: the drag of the cable lost her a hundred yards – a great distance in that desperate race – and Rolfe, the *Polychrest*'s master-gunner, red-eyed, black with powder, but in his element, sent a ball smashing into her stern-chaser, and from dead silence the *Polychrest* burst into wild cheering. Now the *Bellone* ran mute, apart from musket-fire. But still she ran, and it was Gijon that she was running for. Gijon, a Spanish port and therefore closed to British ships, though open to the French.

Yet there were still some miles to go, and any shot that touched her mainyard or her sheets would cripple her. Now her guns were going overboard to win back that hundred yards. Jack shook his head – it would do her little good, with the wind right aft and only headsails left.

'On deck, there,' hailed the look-out. 'A sail on the starboard bow.'

She was a Spanish frigate, rounding Cape Peñ˜as and bearing up for Gijon: she should have been sighted long ago, if every eye had not been fixed upon the flying privateer. 'Damn her,' said Jack, with the fleeting thought that it was strange to see such perfection of canvas, pyramids of white, after all this time staring at tattered rags: and how fast she moved!

An explosion forward – not the right crash of the carronade. Shouts, a high dog-like howling of agony. The over-heated gun had burst, killing the gunner stone dead and wounding three more – one man jerking clear of the deck as he screamed, leaping so that twice he escaped from his mates' arms, carrying him below. They slid the gunner over the side, cleared the wreckage, worked furiously to shift the other carronade into its place, but it was a slow job – ring-bolts and all had gone; and all the while the *Bellone*'s muskets played on them in the bows.

Now they ran silently, with eager, inveterate malice; the coast drew nearer – the savage cliffs and the white water on the reefs were in view; and without a pause the animal screaming came up from the cockpit far below.

A gun from the Spanish frigate, a hoist of signals. 'Damn her,' said Jack again. The *Bellone* was veering out her cable again to turn to port, to turn for the entrance to Gijon – Dumanoir must haul up a good two points, or he would be on the rocks.

'No you don't, God damn you,' cried Jack. 'Stand to your guns, there. Train 'em sharp for'ard. Three degrees' elevation. Fire as they bear on her main mast. Mr Goodridge, bring her up.'

319

The *Polychrest* swerved violently to larboard, bringing her side slanting to the privateer. Her guns went off in succession, three, six and three. Great gaps appeared in the *Bellone*'s mainsail, the yard tilted, held only by the preventerlift; but still she ran.

'The Spaniard is firing, sir,' said Parker. And indeed a shot whipped across the *Polychrest*'s stem. The frigate had altered course to run between them: she was very close.

'Damn him,' said Jack, and taking the wheel he put the ship before the wind, straight for the privateer. He might have time for one more broadside more before the Spaniard crossed his hawse – one chance to cripple the *Bellone* before she cleared the reef and reached the open channel for the port.

'Stand to your guns,' he said in the silence. 'Steady, steady now. Three degrees. For her mainmast. Make sure of every ball.'

He glanced over his shoulder, saw the Spaniard – a magnificent spread of sail – heard her hail loud and clear, clenched his mouth, and spun the wheel. If the Spaniard caught his broadside, that was his affair.

Round, round she came, the helm hard over. The guns went off in one great rolling deliberate thunder. The *Bellone*'s mainmast came slowly down, down, right over her side, all her canvas with it. The next moment she was in the surf. He saw the copper of her hull: she drove farther on to the reef in two great heaves and there lay on her side, the waves making a clean breach over her.

'And so, sir, I drove her on to the rock before Gijon. I wished to send in the boats to burn her at low tide, but the Spaniards represented to me that she was in territorial waters, and that they should oppose any such measure. They added, however, that she was hopelessly bilged, her back broken.'

Admiral Harte stared at him with sincere dislike. 'So

as I understand it,' he said, 'you left these valuable merchantmen when you could have tossed a biscuit on to their deck, to chase a blackguardly privateer, which you did not take either.'

'I destroyed her, sir.'

'Oh, I dare say. We have all heard of these ships driven on the rocks and bilged and so on and so forth, and then next month they reappear as good as new. It is easy enough to say "I drove her on the rocks". Anyone can say that, but no one has yet got any head-money or gun-money out of it – not a brass farthing. No, no, it is all the fault of this damn-fool sail-plan of yours: if you could have spread your topgallants you would have had plenty of time to pick up the merchants and then have really knocked hell out of the bugger you claim to have destroyed. These bentincks, in anything but a gale wind – I have no notion of them.'

'I could never have worked to windward of the convoy without them, sir; and I do assure you that with the *Polychrest* a greater spread of canvas would only have pressed her down.'

'So we are to understand that the less sail you spread the faster you go?' said Harte, with a look at his secretary, who tittered. 'No, no: an admiral is generally reckoned to know more about these things than a commander – let us hear no more of this fancy rig. Your sloop is peculiar enough, without making her look like a poxed cocked hat, the laughing-stock of the fleet, creeping about at five knots because you don't choose to set more sail. Anyhow, what have you to say about this Dutch galliot?'

'I must confess she ran clean away from me, sir.'

'And who picked her up the next day, with her gold-dust and elephant's teeth? *Amethyst*, of course. *Amethyst* again, and you were not even in sight. I don't touch a – that is to say, you don't share. Seymour is the lucky man: ten thousand guineas at the lowest mark. I am deeply disappointed in you, Captain Aubrey. I give you what amounts to a cruise in a brand-new sloop, and what do you do with it? You come back empty-handed – you bring her in looking like I don't know what, pumping night and day, half her spars and cordage gone, five men dead and seven wounded, with a tale about driving a little privateer on to some more or less imaginary rocks and clamouring for a refit. Don't tell me about bolts and twice-laid stuff,' he said, holding up his hand. 'I've heard it all before. And I've heard about your carrying on ashore, before I came in. Let me remind you that a captain is not allowed to sleep out of his ship without permission.'

'Indeed, sir?' asked Jack, leaning forward. 'May I beg you to be more particular? Am I reproached with sleeping out of my ship?'

'I never said you *slept* out of it, did I?' said Harte.

'Then may I ask what I am to understand by your remark?'

'Never mind,' said Harte, fiddling with his paper-knife: and then in an unconquerable jet of waspishness, 'but I will tell you this – your topsails are a disgrace to the service. Why can't you furl them in a body?'

The malignance was too obvious to bite. Crack frigates with a full, expert crew might furl their sails in a body rather than in the bunt, but only in harbour or for a Spithead review. 'Well,' said Harte, aware of this, 'I am disappointed in you, as I say. You will go on the Baltic convoys, and the rest of the time I dare say the sloop will be employed up and down the Channel. That's more your mark. The Baltic convoy should be complete in a few days' time. And that reminds me: I have had a very extraordinary communication from the Admiralty. Your surgeon, a fellow by the name of Maturin, is to be given this sealed envelope; he is to have leave of absence, and they have sent down an assistant to take his place while he is away and to help him when he sees fit to return to his duty. I wish he may not give himself airs – a sealed envelope, forsooth.'

CHAPTER TEN

The post-chaise drove briskly forward over the Sussex downs, with Stephen Maturin and Diana Villiers sitting in it with the glasses down, very companionably eating bread and butter.

'So now you have seen your dew-pond,' she said comfortably. 'How did you like it?'

'It came up to my highest expectations,' said Stephen. 'And I had looked forward to it extremely.'

'And I look forward to Brighton extremely, too: I hope I may be as pleased as you are. Oh, I cannot fail to be delighted, can I, Maturin? A whole week's holiday from the Teapot! And even if it rains all the time, there is the Pavilion – how I long to see the Pavilion.'

'Was not candour the soul of friendship, I should say, "Why Villiers, I am sure it will delight you," affecting not to know that you were there last week.'

'Who told you?' she asked, her bread and butter poised.

'Babbington was there with his parents.'

'Well, I never said I had not been – it was just a flying visit – I did not see the Pavilion. That is what I meant. Do not be disagreeable, Maturin: we have been so pleasant all the way. Did he mention it in public?'

'He did. Jack was much concerned. He thinks Brighton a very dissolute town, full of male and female rakes – a great deal of temptation. He does not like the Prince of Wales, either. There is an ill-looking smear of butter on your chin.'

'Poor Jack,' said Diana, wiping it off. 'Do you remember – oh how long ago it seems – I told you he was little more than a huge boy? I was pretty severe about it: I preferred something more mature, a fully-grown man. But how I miss all that fun and laughter! What has happened to his gaiety? He is growing quite a bore. Preaching and moralizing. Maturin, could you not tell him to be less prosy? He would listen to you.'

'I could not. Men are perhaps less free with such recommendations than you imagine. In any case I am very sorry to say we are no longer on such terms that I could venture anything of the kind – if indeed we ever were. Certainly not since last Sunday's dinner. We still play a little music together now and then, but it is damnably out of tune.'

'It was not a very successful dinner: though I took such care with the pudding. Did he say anything?'

'In my direction? No. But he made some illiberal flings at Jews in general.'

'That was why he was so glum, then. I *see*.'

'Of course you see. You are not a fool, Villiers. The preference was very marked.'

'Oh no, no, Stephen. It was only common civility. Canning was the stranger, and you two were old friends of the house; he had to sit beside me, and be attended to. Oh, what is that bird?'

'It is a wheatear. We have seen between two and three hundred since we set out, and I have told your their name twice, nay, three times.'

The postillion reined in, twisted about and asked whether the gentleman would like to see another dew-pond? There was one not a furlong off.

'I cannot make it out,' said Stephen, climbing back into the chaise. 'The dew, per se, is inconsiderable; and yet they are full. They are always full, as the frog bears witness. *She* does not spawn in your uncertain, fugitive ponds; *her* tadpoles do not reach maturity in your mere temporary puddle; and yet here they are – ' holding out a perfect frog the size of his little finger nail – 'by the hundred, after three weeks of drought.'

'He is entrancing,' said Diana. 'Pray put him out, on

the grass. Do you think I may ask what this delightful smell is, without being abused?'

'Thyme,' said Stephen absently. 'Mother of thyme, crushed by our carriage-wheels.'

'So Aubrey is bound for the Baltic,' said Diana, after a while. 'He will not have this charming weather. I hate the cold.'

'The Baltic and northwards: just so,' said Stephen, recollecting himself. 'Lord, I wish I were going with him. The eider-duck, the phalarope, the narwhal! Ever since I was breeched I have pined to see a narwhal.'

'What will happen to your patients when you are gone?'

'Oh, they have sent me a cheerful brisk noisy good-natured foolish young man with scrofulous ears – a vicious habit of body – to be my assistant. Those who are not dead will survive him.'

'And where are you going now? Lord, Stephen, how prying and inquisitive I am. Just like my aunt Williams. I trust I have not been indiscreet.'

'Oh,' cried Stephen, suddenly filled with a strong temptation to tell her that he was going to be landed on the Spanish coast at the dark of the moon – the classical temptation of the secret agent in his loneliness, but one that he had never felt before. 'Oh, 'tis only a dismal piece of law-business. I shall go to town first, then to Plymouth, and so perhaps to Ireland for a while.'

'To town? But Brighton is quite out of your way – I had imagined you had to go to Portsmouth, when you offered me a lift. Why have you come so far out of your way?'

'The dew-ponds, the wheatears, the pleasure of driving over grass.'

'What a dogged brute you are, Maturin, upon my honour,' said Diana. 'I shall lay out for no more compliments.'

'No, but in all sadness,' said Stephen, 'I like sitting in a chaise with you; above all when you are like this. I could wish this road might go on for ever.'

There was a pause; the chaise was filled with waiting;

but he did not go on, and after a moment she said with a forced laugh, 'Well done, Maturin. You are quite a courtier. But I am afraid I can see its end already. There is the sea, and this must be the beginning of the Devil's Punchbowl. And will you really drive me up to the door in style? I thought I should have to arrive in a pair of pattens – I brought them in that little basket with the flap. I am so grateful; and you shall certainly have your narwhal. Pray, where are they to be had? At the poulterer's, I suppose.'

'You are too good, my dear. Would you be prepared to reveal the address at which you are to be set down?'

'Lady Jersey's, in the Parade.'

'Lady Jersey's?' She was the Prince of Wales's mistress: and Canning was a member of that set.

'She is a Villiers cousin by marriage, you know,' said Diana quickly. 'And there is nothing in those vulgar newspaper reports. They like one another: that is all. Why, Mrs Fitzherbert is devoted to her.'

'Ay? Sure, I know nothing of these things. Will I tell you about poor Macdonald's arm, now?'

'Oh, *do*,' cried Diana. 'I have been longing to ask, ever since we left Dover.'

They parted at Lady Jersey's door, having said nothing more, amidst the flurry of servants and baggage: tension, artificial smiles.

'A gentlemen to see Miss Williams,' said Admiral Haddock's butler.

'Who is it, Rowley?' asked Sophia.

'The gentleman did not mention his name, ma'am. A sea-officer, ma'am. He asked for my master, and then for Miss Williams, so I showed him into the library.'

'Is he a tall, very good-looking midshipman?' asked Cecilia. 'Are you sure he did not ask for me?'

'Is he a commander?' asked Sophia, dropping her roses.

'The gentleman is in a cloak, ma'am: I could not see his

326

rank. He might be a commander, though – not a midshipman, oh no, dear me. He come in a four-horse shay.'

From the library window Stephen saw Sophia running across the lawn, holding up her skirt and trailing rose-petals. She took the steps up to the terrace three at a time: 'A deer might have taken them with such sweet grace,' he observed. He saw her stop dead and close her eyes for a second when she understood that the gentleman in the library was Dr Maturin; but she opened the door with hardly a pause and cried, 'What a delightful surprise! How kind to come to see us. Are you in Plymouth? I thought you were ordered for the Baltic.'

'The *Polychrest* is in the Baltic,' he said, kissing her heartily. 'I am on leave of absence.' He turned her to the light and observed, 'You are looking well – very well – quite a remarkable pink.'

'Dear, dear Dr Maturin,' she said, 'you really must not salute young ladies like that. Not in England. Of course I am pink – scarlet, I dare say. You kissed me!'

'Did I, my dear? Well, no great harm. Do you take your porter?'

'Most religiously, in a silver tankard: I almost like it, now. What may I offer you? The admiral always takes his grog about this time. Are you in Plymouth for long? I do hope you will stay.'

'If you could give me a cup of coffee, you would do me a most essential service. I lay at Exeter, and they gave me the vilest brew . . . No, I am on the wing – I sail with this tide – but I did not like to pass without paying my respects. I have been travelling since Friday, and to sit with my friends for half an hour is a charming respite.

'Since Friday? Then perhaps you have not heard the splendid news?'

'Never a word, at all.'

'The Patriotic Fund have voted Captain Aubrey a sword of a hundred guineas, and the merchants a piece of plate, for destroying the *Bellone*. Is it not splendid news?

327

Though no more than he deserves, I am sure – indeed, not nearly enough. Will he be promoted, do you think?'

'For a letter of marque, a privateer? No. And he does not look for it. Promotion is the very devil these days. There are not enough ships to go round. Old Jarvie did not build them, but he did make men post. So we have herds of unemployed captains; shoals of unpromoted commanders.'

'But none so deserving as Captain Aubrey,' said Sophia, dismissing the rest of the Navy List. 'You have not told me how he is.'

'Nor have you asked after your cousin Diana.'

'How shocking of me; I beg your pardon. I hope she is quite well.'

'Very well. In charming spirits. We drove from Dover to Brighton together some days ago: she is to spend a week with Lady Jersey.'

It was clear that Sophia had never heard of Lady Jersey. She said, 'I am so glad. No one can be better company than Diana when she is in – ' she quickly changed 'a good temper' to a weak 'in charming spirits.'

'As for Jack, I am sorry to say I cannot congratulate *him* upon charming spirits; nor indeed upon any spirits at all. He is unhappy. His ship is a very miserable vessel; his admiral is a scrub; he has a great many worries ashore and afloat. And I tell you bluntly, my dear, he is jealous of me and I of him. I love him as much as I have loved any man, but often these last months I have wondered whether we can stay in the same ship without fighting. I am no longer what small comfort I was to him, but a present irritation and a constraint – our friendship is constrained. And the tension, cooped up in a little small ship day after day, is very great – covert words, the risk of misunderstanding, watching the things we say or even sing. It is well enough when we are far out in the ocean. But with Channel service, in and out of the Downs – no, it cannot last.'

'Does he know of your feelings for Diana? Surely not. Surely, to his best friend, he would never . . . He loves you dearly.'

'Oh, as to that – yes, I believe he does, in his own way; and I believe if he had never been led into this by a series of unhappy misunderstandings, he would never have "crossed my hawse", as he would put it. As for his knowing the nature of my feelings, I like to think he does not. Certainly not with any sharp clarity, in the forefront of his mind. Jack is not quick in such matters; he is not in any way an analytical thinker, except aboard a ship in action: but light creeps in, from time to time.'

They were interrupted by the appearance of the coffee, and for some time they sat without speaking, each deep in thought.

'You know, my dear,' said Stephen, stirring his cup, 'where women are concerned, a man is very helpless against direct attack. I do not mean in the nature of a challenge, which of course he is bound in honour to take up, but in the nature of a plain statement of affection.'

'I could not, could not possibly write to him again.'

'No. But if for example the *Polychrest* were to put in here, which is very likely in the course of the summer, you could perfectly well ask, or the Admiral could ask him to give you and your sister a lift to the Downs – nothing more usual – nothing more conducive to an understanding.'

'Oh, I could never do so. Dear Dr Maturin, do but think how immodest, how pushing – and the risk of a refusal. I should die.'

'Had you seen his tears over your kindness, your hampers, you would not speak of refusal. He was all a-swim.'

'Yes, you told me in your dear letter. But no, really, it is quite impossible – unthinkable. A man might do so, but for a woman it is quite impossible.'

'There is much to be said for directness.'

'Oh, yes, yes! There is. Everything would be so much simpler if one only said what one thought, or felt. Tell me,' she said shyly, after a pause, 'may I say something to you, perhaps quite improper and wrong?'

'I should take it very friendly in you, my dear.'

'Then if you were perfectly direct with Diana, and proposed marriage to her, might not we all be perfectly happy? Depend upon it, that is what she expects.'

'I? Make her an offer? My dearest Sophie, you know what kind of a match I am. A little ugly small man, with no name and no fortune. And you know her pride and ambition and connections.'

'You think too little of yourself, indeed you do. Far, far too little. You are much too humble. In your own way you are quite as good looking as Captain Aubrey – everybody says so. Besides, you have your castle.'

'Honey-love, a castle in Spain is not a castle in Kent. Mine is mostly ruin – the sheep shelter in the part with a roof. And the great part of my land is mere mountain; even in peace-time it hardly brings me in two or three hundred English pounds a year.'

'But that is *plenty* to live on. If she loves you just a little, and I cannot see how any woman could not, she would be delighted with an offer.'

'Your sweet partiality blinds you, my dear. And as for love – love, that amiable, unmeaning word – however you may define it, I do not believe she knows what it is, as you told me once yourself. Affection, kindness, friendship, good nature sometimes, yes: beyond that, nothing. No. I must wait. It may come, perhaps; and in any case, I am content to be a pis aller. I too know how to wait. I dare not risk a direct refusal – perhaps a contemptuous refusal.'

'What is a pis aller?'

'What one accepts when one can do no better. It is my only hope.'

'You are too humble. Oh, you are. I am sure you are mistaken. Believe me, Stephen: I am a woman, after all.'

'Besides, I am a Catholic, you know. A Papist.'

'What does that matter, above all to her? Anyhow,

330

the Howards are Catholics – Mrs Fitzherbert is a Catholic.'

'Mrs Fitzherbert? How odd you should mention her. My dear, I must go. I thank you for your loving care of me. I may write again? There was no unkindness because of my letters?'

'None. I do not mention them.'

'Not for a month or so, however: and perhaps I may pass by Mapes. How is your Mama, your sisters? May I ask after Mr Bowles?'

'They are very well, thank you. As for him,' she said, with a flash of her eye, the calm grey growing fierce, 'I sent him about his business. He became impertinent – "Can it be that your affections are engaged elsewhere?" says he. "Yes, sir, they are," I replied. "Without your mother's consent?" he cried, and I desired him to leave the room at once. It was the boldest thing done this age.'

'Sophie, your very humble servant,' said Stephen, standing up. 'Pray make my compliments to the Admiral.'

'Too humble, oh far too humble,' said Sophie, offering her cheek.

Tides, tides, the Cove of Cork, the embarkation waiting on the moon, a tall swift-pacing mule in the bare torrid mountains quivering in the sun, palmetto-scrub, Señor don Esteban Maturin y Domanova kisses the feet of the very reverend Lord Abbot of Montserrat and begs the honour of an audience. The endless white road winding, the inhuman landscape of Aragon, cruel sun and weariness, dust, weariness to the heart, and doubt. What was independence but a word? What did any form of government matter? Freedom: to do what? Disgust, so strong that he leant against the saddle, hardly able to bring himself to mount. A shower on the Maladetta, and everywhere the scent of thyme: eagles wheeling under thunder-clouds, rising, rising. 'My mind is too confused for anything but direct action,' he said. 'The flight disguised as an advance.'

The lonely beach, lanterns flashing from the offing, an infinity of sea. Ireland again, with such memories at every turn. 'If I could throw off some of this burden of memory,' said Stephen to his second glass of laudanum, 'I should be more nearly sane. Here's to you, Villiers, my dear.' The Holyhead mail and two hundred and seventy miles of rattling jerking, falling asleep, waking in another country: rain, rain, rain: Welsh voices in the night. London, and his report, trying to disentangle the strands of altruism, silliness, mere enthusiasm, self-seeking, love of violence, personal resentment; trying too to give the impossible plain answer to the question 'Is Spain going to join France against us, and if so, when?' And there he was in Deal once more, sitting alone in the snug of the Rose and Crown, watching the shipping in the Downs and drinking a pot of tea: he had an odd detachment from all this familiar scene – the uniforms that passed outside his bow-window were intimately well known, but it was as though they belonged to another world, a world at one or two removes, and as though their inhabitants, walking, laughing, talking out there on the other side of the pane were mute, devoid both of colour and real substance.

Yet the good tea (an unrivalled cholagogue), the muffin, the comfort of his chair, the ease and relaxation after these weeks and months of jading hurry and incessant motion – tension, danger and suspicion too – insensibly eased him back into this frame, re-attached him to this life of which he had been an integral part. He had been much caressed at the Admiralty; a very civil, acute, intelligent old gentleman called in from the Foreign Office had said the most obliging things; and Lord Melville had repeatedly mentioned their sense of obligation, their desire to acknowledge it by some suitable expression of their esteem – any appointment, any request that Dr Maturin might choose to make would receive the most earnest and sympathetic consideration. He was recalling the scene and sipping his tea with little sounds of inward complacency when he saw Heneage Dundas stop on the pavement outside, shade his eyes, and peer in through the window, evidently looking for a friend. His nose came into contact with the glass, and its tip flattened into a pale disc. 'Not unlike the foot of a gasteropod,' observed Stephen, and when he had considered its loss of superficial circulation for a while he attracted Dundas's attention, beckoning him in and offering him a cup of tea and a piece of muffin.

'I have not seen you these months past,' said Dundas in a very friendly tone. 'I asked for you several times, whenever *Polychrest* was in, and they told me you was on leave. How brown you are! Where have you been?'

'In Ireland – tedious family business.'

'In Ireland? You astonish me. Every time I have been in Ireland it has rained. If you had not told me, I should have sworn you had been in the Med, ha, ha, ha. Well, I asked for you several times: I had something particular to say. Excellent muffin, eh? If there is one thing I like better than another with my tea, it is a well-turned piece of muffin.' After this promising beginning, Dundas fell strangely mute: it was clear that he wanted to say something of importance, but did not know how to get it out handsomely – or, indeed, at all. Did he want to borrow money? Was some disease preying on his mind?

'You have a particular kindness for Jack Aubrey, Dr Maturin, I believe?'

'I have a great liking for him, sure.'

'So have I. So have I. We were shipmates even before we were rated midshipmen – served in half a dozen commissions together. But he don't listen to me, you know; he don't attend. I was junior to him all along, and that counts, of course; besides, there are some things you cannot tell a man. What I wanted to say to you was, do you think you might just hint to him that he is – I will not say ruining his career, but sailing very close to the wind? He does not

333

clear his convoys – there have been complaints – he puts into the Downs when the weather is not so very terrible – and people have a tolerable good notion why, and it won't answer, not in Whitehall.'

'Lingering in port is a practice not unknown to the Navy.'

'I know what you mean. But it is a practice confined to admirals with a couple of fleet actions and a peerage behind them, not to commanders. It won't do, Maturin. I do beg you will tell him so.'

'I will do what I can. God knows what will come of it. I thank you for this mark of confidence, Dundas.'

'The *Polychrest* is trying to weather the South Foreland now; I saw her from the *Goliath*, missing stays and having to wear again. She has been over the way, looking at the French gunboats in Etaples. She should manage it when the sea-breeze sets in; but God help us, what leeway that ship does make. She has no right to be afloat.'

'I shall take a boat and meet her,' said Stephen. 'I am quite impatient to see my shipmates again.'

They received him kindly, very kindly; but they were busy, anxious and overwrought. Both watches were on deck to moor the *Polychrest*, and as he watched them at their work it was clear to Stephen that the feeling in the ship had not improved at all. Oh very far from it. He knew enough about the sea to tell the difference between a willing crew and a dogged, sullen set of men who had to be driven. Jack was in his cabin, writing his report, and Parker had the deck: was the man deranged? An incessant barking flow of orders, threats, insults, diversified with kicks and blows: more vehement than when Stephen had left the ship, and surely now there was a note of hysteria? Not far behind him in vociferation there was Macdonald's replacement, a stout pink and white young man with thick pale lips; his authority extended only to his soldiers, but he made up for this by his activity, bounding about with his cane like a jack-in-a-box.

When he went below this impression was confirmed. His assistant, Mr Thompson, was not perhaps very wise nor very skilful – his attempt at a Cheseldon's lithotomy had an ominous smell of gangrene – but he did not seem at all brutal or even unkind; yet as they went round their patients there was not a smile – proper answers, but no sort of interchange, no friendliness whatsoever, except from one old Sophie, a Pole by the name of Jackruckie, whose hernia was troubling him again. And even his strange jargon (he spoke very little English) was uneasy, conscious, and inhibited. In the next cot lay a man with a bandaged head. Gummata, the sequelae of an old depressed fracture, malingering? In an eager attempt to justify his diagnosis, Thompson darted a pointing finger at the man's head, and instantly the crooked protective arm shot up.

By the time he had finished his rounds and settled in his cabin, the *Polychrest* was moored. Jack had gone off to make his report, and something nearer to peace had come down on the ship. There was only the steady grind of the pumps and the now almost voiceless bark of the first lieutenant getting the courses, the *square* courses, and topsails furled in a body, smooth enough for a royal review.

He walked into the gun-room, which was empty but for the Marine officer. He was reclining upon two chairs with his feet on the table; and craning up his neck he cried, 'Why, you must be the sawbones back again. I'm glad to see you. My name is Smithers. Forgive me if I do not get up; I am quite fagged out with mooring the ship.'

'I noticed that you were very active.'

'Pretty brisk, pretty brisk. I like my men to know who's who and what's what and to move smart – *they'll* smart else, you catch my meaning, ha, ha. They tell me you are quite a hand with a cello. We must have a bout some night. I play the German flute.'

'I dare say you are a remarkable performer.'

'Pretty brisk, pretty brisk. I don't like to boast, but I fancy I was the best player at Eton in my time. If I

chose to do it professionally, I should make twice what
they give me for fighting His Majesty's wars for him – not
that the pewter matters to *me*, of course. It's precious slow
in this ship, don't you find? Nobody to talk to; nothing
but ha'penny whist and convoy-duty and looking out for
the French prams. What do you say to a hand of cards?'

'Is the captain returned, do you know?'

'No. He won't be back for hours and hours. You have
plenty of time. Come let us have a hand of piquet.'

'I play very little.'

'You need not be afraid of him. He'll be pulling down
to Dover against the tide – he's got a luscious piece there
– won't be back for hours and hours. A luscious piece, by
God: I could wear it. I'd have a mind to cut him out, if he
weren't my captain: it's a wonder what a red coat will do,
believe you me. I dare say I could, too; she invited all the
officers last week, and she looked at me . . . '

'You cannot be speaking of Mrs Villiers, sir?'

'A pretty young widow – yes, that's right. Do you
know her?'

'Yes, sir: and I should be sorry to hear her spoken
of with disrespect.'

'Oh, well, if she's a friend of yours,' cried Smithers,
with a knowing leer, 'that's different. I have said nothing.
Mum's the word. Now what about our game?'

'Do you play well?'

'I was born with a pack of cards in my hand.'

'I must warn you I never play for small stakes: it
bores me.'

'Oh, I'm not afraid of you. I've played at White's –
I played at Almack's with my friend Lord Craven till
daylight put the candles out! What do you think of that?'

The other officers came down one by one and watched
them play; watched them in silence until the end of
the sixth partie, when Stephen laid down a point of
eight followed by a quart major, and Pullings, who had
been sitting behind him, straining his stomach to the

groaning-point to make him win, burst out with 'Ha, ha, you picked a wrong 'un when you tackled the Doctor.'

'Do be quiet, can't you, when gentlemen are playing cards. And smoking that vile stinking pipe in the gun-room – it is turning the place into one of your low pot-houses. How can a man concentrate his mind with all this noise? Now you have made me lose my score. What do you make it, Doctor?'

'With repique and capot, that is a hundred and thirty; and since I believe you are two short of your hundred, I must add your score to mine.'

'You will take my note of hand, I suppose?'

'We agreed to play for cash, you remember.'

'Then I shall have to fetch it. It will leave me short. But you will have to give me my revenge.'

'Captain's coming aboard, gentlemen,' said a quartermaster. Then reappearing a moment later, 'Port side, gents.' They relaxed: he was returning with no ceremony.

'I must leave you,' said Stephen. 'Thank you for the game.'

'But you can't go away just when you have won all that money,' cried Smithers.

'On the contrary,' said Stephen. 'It is the very best moment to leave.'

'Well, it ain't very sporting. That's all I say. It ain't very sporting.'

'You think not? Then when you have laid down the gold you may cut double or quits. Sans revanche, eh?'

Smithers came back with two rouleaux of guineas and part of a third. 'It's not the money,' he said. 'It's the principle of the thing.'

'Aces high,' said Stephen, looking impatiently at his watch. 'Please to cut.'

A low heart: knave of diamonds. 'Now you will have to take my note for the rest,' said Smithers.

'Jack,' said Stephen, 'may I come in?'

'Come in, come in, my dear fellow, come in,' cried Jack, springing forward and guiding him to a chair. 'I have scarcely seen you – how very pleasant this is! I cannot tell you how dreary the ship has been without you. How brown you are!'

In spite of an animal revulsion at the catch of the scent that hung about Jack's coat – never was there a more unlucky present – Stephen felt a warmth in his heart. His face displayed no more than a severe questioning, professional look, however, and he said, 'Jack, what have you been doing to yourself? You are thin, grey – costive, no doubt. You have lost another couple of stone: the skin under your eyes is a disagreeable yellow. Has the bullet-wound been giving trouble? Come, take off your shirt. I was never happy that I had extracted all the lead; my probe still seemed to grate on something.'

'No, no. It has quite healed over again. I am very well. It is only that I don't sleep. Toss, turn, can't get off, then ill dreams and I wake up some time in the middle watch – never get off again, and I am stupid all the rest of the day. And damned ill-tempered, Stephen; I sway away on all top-ropes for a nothing, and then I am sorry afterwards. Is it my liver, do you think? Not yesterday, but the day before I had a damned unpleasant surprise: I was shaving, and thinking of something else; and Killick had hung the glass aft the scuttle instead of its usual place. So just for a moment I caught sight of my face as though it was a stranger looking in. When I understood it was me, I said, "Where did I get that damned forbidding ship's corporal's face?" and determined not to look like that again – it reminded me of that unhappy fellow Pigot, of the *Hermione*. And this morning there it was again, glaring back at me out of the glass. That is another reason why I am so glad to see you: you will give me one of your treble-shotted slime-draughts to get me to sleep. It's the devil, you know, not sleeping: no wonder a man looks

338

like a ship's corporal. And these dreams – do you dream, Stephen?'

'No, sir.'

'I thought not. You have a head-piece . . . however, I had one some nights ago, about your narwhal; and Sophie was mixed up with it in some way. It sounds nonsense, but it was so full of unhappiness that I woke blubbering like a child. Here it is, by the way.' He reached behind him and passed the long tapering spiral of ivory.

Stephen's eyes gleamed as he took it and turned it slowly round and round in his hands. 'Oh thank you, thank you, Jack,' he cried. 'It is perfect – the very apotheosis of a tooth.'

'There were some longer ones, well over a fathom, but they had lost their tips, and I thought you would like to *get the point, ha, ha, ha.*' It was a flash of his old idiot self, and he wheezed and chuckled for some time, his blue eyes as clear and delighted as they had been long ago: wild glee over an infinitesimal grain of merriment.

'It is a most prodigious phenomenon,' said Stephen, cherishing it. 'How much do I owe you, Jack?' He put his hand in his pocket and pulled out a handkerchief, which he laid on the table, then a handful of gold, then another, and scrabbled for the odd coins, observing that it was foolish to carry it loose: far better made a bundle of.

'Good God,' cried Jack, staring. 'What on earth have you been at? Have you taken a treasure-ship? I have never seen so much money all at once in my life.'

'I have been stripping a jackeen that annoyed me: the young nagin, the coxcomb in the red coat. The *lobster*, as you would say.'

'Smithers. But this is gaming, Stephen, not mere play.'

'Yes. He seemed concerned at his loss: a lardish sweat. But he has all the appearance of wealth – all its petulant arrogance, certainly.'

'He has private means, I know; but you must have left him very short – this is more than a year's pay.'

'So much the better. I intended he should smart.'

'Stephen, I must ask you not to do it again. He is an under-bred puppy, I grant you, and I wonder the jollies ever took him, they being so particular; but the ship is in a bad enough way as it is, without getting a name for gaming. Will you not let him have it back?'

'I will not. But since you wish it, I shall not play with him again. Now how much do I owe you, my dear?'

'Oh, nothing, nothing. Do me the pleasure of accepting it as a present. Pray do. It was very little, and the prize paid for it.'

'You took a prize, so?'

'Yes. Just one. No chance of any more – the *Polychrest* can be recognized the moment she is hull up on the horizon, now that she is known. I am sorry you were not aboard, though it did not amount to much: I sold my share to Parker for seventy-five pounds, being short at the time, and he did not make a great deal out of it. She was a little Dutch shalloop, creeping along the back of the Dogger, laden with deals; and we crept just that trifle less almighty slow. A contemptible prize – we should have let her go in the *Sophie* – but I thought I ought to blood the hands at last. Not that it did much good. The ship is in a bad way; and Harte rides me hard.'

'Pray show me your honorary sword and the merchants' piece of plate. I called upon Sophie, and she told me about them.'

'Sophie?' cried Jack, as though he had been kicked. 'Oh. Oh, yes – yes, of course. You called upon her.' As an attempt at diverting his mind to happier thoughts, this was not a success. After a moment he said, 'I am sorry, they are not here. I ran short again. For the time being, they are in Dover.'

'Dover,' said Stephen, and thought for a while, running the narwhal's horn through his fingers. 'Dover. Listen, Jack, you take insane risks, going ashore so often, particularly in Dover.'

340

'Why particularly in Dover?'

'Because your often presence there is notorious. If it is notorious to your friends, how much more so to your enemies? It is known in Whitehall; it must be known to your creditors in Mincing Lane. Do not look angerly now, Jack, but let me tell you three things: I must do so, as a friend. First, you will certainly be arrested for debt if you continue to go ashore. Second, it is said in the service that you cling to this station; and what harm that may do you professionally, you know better than I. No, let me finish. Third, have you considered how you expose Diana Villiers by your very open attentions, in circumstances of such known danger?'

'Has Diana Villiers put herself under your protection? Has she commissioned you to say this to me?'

'No, sir.'

'Then I do not see what right you have to speak to me in this way.'

'Sure, Jack, my dear, I have the right of a friend, have I not? I will not say duty, for that smells of cant.'

'A friend who wants a clear field, maybe. I may not be very clever, no God-damned Macchiavelli, but I believe I know a ruse de guerre when I see one. For a long time I did not know what to think about you and Diana Villiers – first one thing and then another – for you are a devilish sly fox, and break back upon your line. But now I see the reason for this standing off and on, this "not at home", and all this damned unkind treatment, and all this cracking-up of clever, amusing Stephen Maturin, who understands people and never preaches, whereas I am a heavy-handed fool that understands nothing. It is time we had a clear explanation about Diana Villiers, so that we may know where we stand.'

'I desire no explanations. They are never of any use, particularly in matters of this kind, where what one might term *sexuality* is concerned – reason flies out of the window; all candour with it. In any case, even where this passion is not concerned, language is so imperfect, that . . . '

'Any bastard can cowardly evade the issue by a flood of words.'

'You have said enough, sir,' said Stephen, standing up. 'Too much by far: you must withdraw.'

'I shall not withdraw,' cried Jack, very pale. 'And I will add, that when a man comes back from leave as brown as a Gibraltar Jew, and says he had delicate weather in Ireland, he lies. I will stand by that, and I am perfectly willing to give you any satisfaction you may choose to ask for.'

'It is odd enough,' said Stephen, in a low voice, 'that our acquaintance should have begun with a challenge, and that it should end with one.'

'Dundas,' he said, in the small room of the Rose and Crown, 'how good of you to come so soon. I am sorry to say I must ask you to be my second. I tried to follow your excellent suggestion, but I mishandled it – I did not succeed. I should have seen he was in a state of unhappy passion, but I persisted untimely, and he called me a coward and a liar.'

Dundas's face changed to one of horror. 'Oh, that is very bad,' he cried. 'Oh, Lord.' A long, unhappy pause. 'No question of an apology, I suppose?'

'None whatsoever. One word he did withdraw,' – Captain Aubrey presents his compliments to Dr Maturin, and begs to say that an expression escaped him yesterday evening, a common expression to do with birth, that might have been taken to have a personal bearing. None was intended, and Captain Aubrey withdraws that word, at the same time regretting that, in the hurry of the moment, he made use of it. The other remarks he stands by – 'but the gratuitous lie remains. It is not easy of digestion.'

'Of course not. What a sad, sad business. We shall

have to fit it in between voyages. I feel horribly responsible. Maturin, have you been out before? I should never forgive myself if anything were to happen to you. Jack is an old hand.'

'I can look after myself.'

'Well,' said Dundas, looking at him dubiously, 'I shall go and see him at once. Oh, what a damned unlucky thing. It may take some time, unless we can arrange it tonight. That is the wretched thing about the Navy: soldiers can always settle out of hand, but with us I have known an affair hang fire three months and more.'

It could not be arranged that night, for on the evening tide the *Polychrest* was ordered to sea. She bore away to the south-west with a couple of store-ships, carrying with her more than her usual load of unhappiness.

The news of their disagreement spread throughout the ship; the extent and the deadly nature of it were quite unknown, but so close an intimacy could not come to a sudden end without being noticed, and Stephen watched the reactions of his shipmates with a certain interest. He knew that in many ships the captain played the part of a monarch and the officers that of a court – that there was eager competition for Caesar's favour; but he had never thought of himself as the favourite; he had never known how much the respect paid to him was a reflection of the great man's power. Parker, who revered authority far more than he disliked his captain, drew away from Stephen; so did the featureless Jones; and Smithers did not attempt to conceal his animosity. Pullings behaved with marked kindness in the gun-room; but Pullings owed everything to Jack, and on the quarterdeck he seemed a little shy of Stephen's company. Not that he was often put to this trial, however, for convention required that the principals in a duel, like bride and bridegroom, should see nothing of one another before they reached the altar. Most of the old Sophies shared Pullings' distress; they looked at him with anxious constraint, never with unkindness; but it was clear to Stephen that quite apart from any question of interest, their prime loyalty lay with Jack, and he embarrassed them as little as he could.

He spent the chief of his time with his patients – the lithotomy called for radical measures: a fascinating case and one that called for hours of close surveillance – reading in his cabin, and playing chess with the master, who surprised him by showing particular consideration and friendliness. Mr Goodridge had sailed as a midshipman and master's mate with Cook; he was a good mathematician, an excellent navigator, and he would have reached commissioned rank if it had not been for his unfortunate battle with the chaplain of the *Bellerophon*.

'No, Doctor,' said he, leaning back from the board, 'you may struggle and wruggle as you please, but I have him pinned. It is mate in three.'

'It is muchwhat like,' said Stephen. 'Must I resign?'

'I think you must. Though I like a man that fights, to be sure. Doctor,' he said, 'have you reflected upon the phoenix?'

'Not, perhaps, as often as I should have done. As I remember, she makes her nest in Arabia Felix, using cinnamon for the purpose; and with cinnamon at six and eight-pence, surely this is a thoughtless thing to do?'

'You are pleased to be facetious, Doctor. But the phoenix, now, is worth your serious consideration. Not the bird of the tales, of course, which cannot be attempted to be believed in by a philosophical gentleman like you, but what I might call the bird behind the bird. I should not care to have it known in the ship, but in my opinion, the phoenix is Halley's comet.'

'Halley's comet, Mr Goodridge?' cried Stephen.

'Halley's comet, Doctor; and others,' said the master, pleased with the effect of his words. 'And when I say opinion, I might say fact, for to a candid mind the thing is proved beyond the slightest doubt. A little calculation makes it plain. The best authors give 500, 1416, and

7006 years as the proper intervals between phoenixes; and Tacitus tells us that one appeared under Sesostris, another under Amasis, another in the reign of the third Ptolemy, and another in the twentieth year of Tiberius; and we know of many more. Now let us take the periods of Halley's, Biela's, Lexel's, and Encke's comets and plot them against our phoenixes, just allowing for lunar years and errors of computation in the ancients, and the thing is done! I could show you calculations, with respect to their orbits, that would amaze you; the astronomers are sadly out, because they do not take account of the phoenix in their equations. They do not see that for the ancients the pretended phoenix was a poetical way of saying a blazing heavenly phenomenon – that the phoenix was an emblem; and they are too proud and sullen and dogged and wanting in candour to believe it when told. The chaplain of the *Bellerophon*, who set up for an astronomer, would not be convinced. I stretched him out on deck with a heaving-mallet.'

'I am quite convinced, Mr Goodridge.'

'It ruined my career,' – with a fiery look into the past – 'It ruined my career; but I should do it again, the contumelious dog, the . . . however, I must not swear; and he was a clergyman. Since then I have not told many people, but in time I mean to publish – *The Phoenix Impartially Considered, A Modest Proposal*, by an Officer of Rank in the Royal Navy – and that will flutter some dovecotes I could mention; that will bring them up with a round turn. My phoenixes, Doctor, tell me we may expect a comet in 1805; I will not give the month, because of a doubt in Ussher as to the exact length of the reign of Nabonidus.'

'I shall look forward to it with confident expectation,' said Stephen; and he reflected, 'I wish they could foretell an end to this waiting.'

'How strangely I dread the event,' he said, sitting down by his patient and counting his respirations, 'and yet how hard I find it to wait.'

In the far corner of the sick-bay the low murmur of conversation began again; the men were used to his presence, and to his absences – more than once a messmate had brought in the forbidden grog, walking right past the Doctor without being noticed – and he did not disturb them. At present two Highlanders were talking slowly to an Irishman, slowly and repetitively in Gaelic, as he lay there on his stomach to ease his flayed back.

'I follow them best when I do not attend at all,' observed Stephen. 'When I do not strain, or try to isolate any word. It is the child in long clothes that understands, myself in Cahirciveen. They are of the opinion that we shall anchor in the Downs before eight bells. I hope they are right; I hope I find Dundas.'

They were right, and before the way was off the *Polychrest* he heard the sentry hail a boat and the answering cry of '*Franchise*' that meant her captain was coming aboard. The bosun's pipe, the proper respect shown to a post captain, the stumping of feet overhead, and then 'Captain Dundas's compliments, and might he have a word with Dr Maturin, when at leisure?'

Discretion was of first importance in these matters, and Heneage Dundas, knowing how public a spoken word might be in a crowded sloop, had written his message on a piece of paper. 'Will half past six on Saturday suit? In the dunes. I will come for you.' He handed the paper, with a grave, meaning look. Stephen glanced at it, nodded, and said, 'Perfect. I am obliged to you. Will you give me a lift ashore? I should spend tomorrow in Deal, should I not? Perhaps you would be so very kind as to mention it to Captain Aubrey.'

'I have: we may go now, if you wish.'

'I will be with you in two minutes.' There were some papers that must not be seen, a few manuscripts and letters that he prized; but these were almost ready, and his necessary bag was at hand. In two minutes he followed Dundas up the companion-ladder and they rowed away over the calm sea to Deal. Speaking in such a way as to be clear to Stephen alone, Dundas gave him to understand that Jack's second, a Colonel Rankin, could not get down until tomorrow night – Friday; that he had seen Rankin earlier in the week, and that they had decided on an excellent spot near the castle often used for this purpose and convenient in every way. 'You are provided, I suppose?' he asked, just before the boat touched.

'I think so,' said Stephen. 'If not, I will call on you.'

'Goodbye, then,' said Dundas, shaking his hand. 'I must go back to my ship. If I do not see you before, then at the time we agreed.'

Stephen settled in at the Rose and Crown, called for a horse, and rode slowly towards Dover, reflecting upon the nature of dunes; upon the extraordinary loneliness surrounding each man; and on the inadequacy of language – a thought that he would have developed to Jack if he had been given time. 'And yet for all its inadequacy, how marvellously well it allows them to deal with material things,' he said, looking at the ships in the roadstead, the unbelievable complexity of named ropes, blocks, sails that would carry the crowd of isolated individuals to the Bosphorus, the West Indies, Sumatra, or the South Sea whaling grounds. And as he looked, his eyes running along the odd cocked-hat form of the *Polychrest* he saw her captain's gig pull away from the side, set its lugsail, and head for Dover.

'Knowing them both, as I do,' he observed, 'I should be surprised if there were much liking between them. It is a perverse relationship. That, indeed, may be the source of its violence.'

Reaching Dover, he went directly to the hospital and examined his patients: his lunatic was motionless, crouched in a ball, sunk even below tears; but Macdonald's stump was healing well. The flaps were as neat as a parcel, and he noted with pleasure that the hair on them continued to grow in its former direction.

'You will soon be quite well,' he said, pointing this out to the Marine. 'I congratulate you upon an excellent healthy constitution. In a few weeks' time you will rival Nelson, spring one-handed from ship to ship – happier than the Admiral in that you have your sword-arm still.'

'How you relieve my mind,' said Macdonald. 'I had been mortally afraid of gangrene. I owe you a great deal, Doctor: believe me, I am sensible of it.' Stephen protested that any butcher, any butcher's boy, could have done as much – a simple operation – a real pleasure to cut into such healthy flesh – and their conversation drifted away to the likelihood of a French invasion, of a breach with Spain, and to the odd rumours of St Vincent impeaching Lord Melville for malversation, before it returned to Nelson.

'He is a hero of yours, I believe?' said Macdonald.

'Oh, I hardly know anything of the gentleman,' said Stephen. 'I have never even seen him. But from what I understand, he seems quite an active, zealous, enterprising officer. He is much loved in the service, surely? Captain Aubrey thinks the world of him.'

'Maybe,' said Macdonald. 'But he is no hero of mine. Caracciolo sticks in my gullet. And then there is his example.'

'Could there be a better example, for a sea-officer?'

'I have been thinking, as I lie here in bed,' said Macdonald. 'I have been thinking of justification.' Stephen's heart sank: he knew the reputation of the Scots for theological discussion, and he dreaded an outpouring of Calvinistical views, flavoured, perhaps, with some doctrines peculiar to the Royal Marines. 'Men, particularly Lowlanders, are never content with taking their sins upon their own heads, or with making their own law; a young fellow will play the blackguard, not because he is satisfied that his other parts will outweigh the fact, but because Tom Jones was paid for lying with a woman – and since Tom Jones was a hero, it is quite in order for him to do the same. It might have been better for the Navy if

Nelson had been put to a stable bucket when he was a wee bairn. If the justification that a fellow in a play or a tale can provide, is enough to confirm a blackguard, think what a live hero can do! Whoremongering – lingering in port – hanging officers who surrender on terms. A pretty example!' Stephen looked at him attentively for signs of fever; they were certainly there, but to no dangerous degree at present. Macdonald stared out of the window, and whatever he may have seen there, apart from the blank wall, prompted him to say, 'I hate women. They are entirely destructive. They drain a man, sap him, take away all his good: and none the better for it themselves.' After a pause, 'Nasty, nasty queans.'

Stephen said, 'I have a service to beg of you, Mr Macdonald.'

'Name it, sir, I beg: nothing could give me greater pleasure.'

'The loan of your pistols, if you please.'

'For any purpose but to shoot a Marine officer, they are yours and welcome. In my canteen there, under the window, if you would be so good.'

'Thank you, I will bring them back, or cause them to be brought, as soon as they have served their purpose.'

The evening, as he rode back, was as sweet as an early autumn evening could be, still, intensely humid, a royal blue sea on the right hand, pure dunes on the left, and a benign warmth rising from the ground. The mild horse, a good-natured creature, had a comfortable walk; it knew its way, but it seemed to be in no hurry to reach its stable – indeed, it paused from time to time to take leaves from a shrub that he could not identify; and Stephen sank into an agreeable languor, almost separated from his body: a pair of eyes, no more, floating above the white road, looking from left to right. 'There are days – good evening to you, sir' – a parson went by, walking with his cat, the smoke from his pipe keeping him company as he walked – 'there are days,' he reflected, 'when one sees as though one had been blind the rest of one's life. Such clarity – perfection in everything, not merely in the extraordinary. One lives in the very present moment; lives intently. There is no urge to be doing: being is the highest good. However,' he said, guiding the horse left-handed into the dunes, 'doing of some kind there must be.' He slid from the saddle and said to the horse, 'Now how can I be sure of your company, my dear?' The horse gazed at him with glistening, intelligent eyes, and brought its ears to bear. 'Yes, yes, you are an honest fellow, no doubt. But you may not like the bangs; and I may be longer than you choose to wait. Come, let me hobble you with this small convenient strap. How little I know about dunes,' he said, pacing out his distance and placing a folded handkerchief at the proper height on a sandy slope. 'A most curious study – a flora and a fauna entirely of its own, no doubt.' He spread his coat to preserve the pistols from the sand and loaded them carefully. 'What one is *bound* to do, one usually does with little acknowledged feeling; a vague desperation, no more,' he said, taking up his stance. Yet as he did so his face assumed a cold, dangerous aspect and his body moved with the easy precision of a machine. The sand spat up from the edge of the handkerchief; the smoke lay hardly stirring; the horse was little affected by the noise, but it watched idly for the first dozen shots or so.

'I have never known such consistently accurate weapons,' he said aloud. 'I wonder, can I still do Dillon's old trick?' He took a coin from his pocket, tossed it high, and shot it fair and square on the top of its rise, between climbing and falling. 'Charming instruments indeed: I must cover them from the dew.' The sun had set; the light had so far diminished that the red tongue of flame lit up the misty hollow at each discharge; the handkerchief was long ago reduced to its component threads. 'Lord, I shall sleep tonight. Oh, what a prodigious dew.'

In Dover, sheltered by the western heights, the darkness fell earlier. Jack Aubrey, having done what little business he had to do, and having called in vain at New Place – 'Mr Lowndes was indisposed: Mrs Villiers was not at home' – sat drinking beer in an ale-house near the Castle. It was a sad, dirty, squalid little booth – a knocking-shop for the soldiers upstairs – but it had two ways out, and with Bonden and Lakey in the front room he felt reasonably safe from surprise. He was as low as he had ever been in his life, a dull, savage lowness; and the stupidity that came from the two pots he had drunk did nothing to raise it. Anger and indignation were his only refuge, and although they were foreign to his nature, he was steadily angry and indignant.

An ensign and his flimsy little wench came in, hesitated on seeing Jack, and settled in the far corner, slapping and pushing each other for want of words. The woman of the house brought candles and asked whether he should like anything more; he looked out of the window at the gathering twilight and said no – what did he owe her, and for the men in the tap?

'One and ninepence,' said the woman; and while he felt in his pockets she stared him full in the face with an open, ignorant, suspicious, avid curiosity, her eyes screwed close and her upper lip drawn back over her three yellow teeth. She did not like the cloak he wore over his uniform; she did not like the sobriety of his men, nor the way they kept themselves to themselves; again, gentlemen as were gentlemen called for wine, not beer; he had made no response to Betty's advances nor to her own modest proposal of accommodation; she wanted no pouffes in her house, and she should rather have his room than his company.

He looked into the tap, told Bonden to wait for him at the boat, and walked out by the back way, straight into a company of whores and soldiers. Two of the whores were fighting there in the alley, tearing one another's hair and clothes, but the rest were cheerful enough, and two of the women called to him, coming alongside to whisper their talents, their prices, and their clean bill of health.

He walked up to New Place. The demure look that accompanied the 'not at home' had convinced him that he should see Diana's light. A faint glow between the drawn curtains up there: he checked it twice, walking up and down the road, and then fetched a long cast round the houses to reach a lane that led behind New Place. The palings of the wilderness were no great obstacle, but the walled inner garden needed his cloak over the broken glass on top and then a most determined run and leap. Down in the garden the noise of the sea was suddenly cut off – a total, listening silence and the falling dew as he stood there amongst the crown imperials. Gradually the silence listened less; there were sounds inside the house – talking from various windows, somebody locking doors, closing the lower shutters. Then a quick heavy thudding on the path, the deep wuff-wuff of dog Fred, the mastiff, who was free of the garden and the yard by night, and who slept in the summerhouse. But dog Fred was a mute creature; he knew Captain Aubrey – thrust his wet nose into his hand – and said no more. He was not altogether easy in his mind, however, and when at last Jack gained the mossy path he followed him to the house, grumbling, pushing the back of his knees. Jack took off his coat, folded it on the ground, and then his sword: Fred at once lay on the coat, guarding both it and the sword.

For months and months past a builder had been replacing the roof-tiles of New Place; his improvised crane, with its pulley, projecting from the parapet and its rope hung there still, hooked to a bucket. Jack quickly made the ends fast, tried it, took the strain, and swung himself up. Up, hand over hand, past the library, where Mr Lowndes was writing at his desk, past a window giving on to the stairs, up to the parapet. From this point it was only a few steps to Diana's window, but half-way up, before ever he reached the parapet, he had recognized Canning's great

352

delighted laugh, a crowing noise that rose from a deep bass, a particular laugh, that could not be mistaken. For all that he went the whole way, until he was there, sitting on the parapet with a sharp-angled view of all of the room that mattered. For three deep breaths he might have burst through: it was extraordinarily vivid, the lit room, the faces, their expressions picked out by the candlelight, their intense life and their unconsciousness of a third person. Then shame, unhappiness, extreme weariness put out the rest, extinguished it utterly. No rage, no fire: all gone, and nothing to take their place. He moved some paces off to hear and see no more, and after a while he reached out to the end of the crane for the rope; automatically he frapped the two strands, took a sailor's grip on it, swung himself out into the darkness, and went down, down and down, pursued by that intensely amused laughter.

Stephen spent Friday morning writing, coding and decoding; he had rarely worked so fast or so well, and he had the agreeable feeling that he had produced a clear statement of a complex situation. From a moral scruple he had refrained from his habitual dose, and he had spent the greater part of the night in a state of lucid consideration. When he had tied up all the ends, sealed his papers in a double cover and addressed the outer to Captain Dundas, he turned to his diary. 'This is perhaps the final detachment; and this is perhaps the only way to live – free, surprisingly light and well, no diminution of interest but no commitment: a liberty I have hardly ever known. Life in its purest form – admirable in every way, only for the fact that it is not living, as I have ever understood the word. How it changes the nature of time! The minutes and the hours stretch out; there is leisure to see the movement of the present. I shall walk out beyond Walmer Castle, by way of the sand-dunes: there is a wilderness of time in that arenaceous world.'

Jack also took a spell at his writing-table, but in the forenoon he was called away to the flagship.

'I have worn you down a trifle, my spark,' thought Admiral Harte, looking at him with satisfaction. 'Captain Aubrey, I have orders for you. You are to look into Chaulieu. *Thetis* and *Andromeda* chased a corvette into the harbour. She is believed to be the *Fanciulla*. There are also said to be a number of gunboats and prams preparing to move up the coast. You are to take all possible measures, consistent with the safety of your ship, to disable the one and to destroy the others. And the utmost despatch is essential, do you hear me?'

'Yes, sir. But form's sake, I must represent to you that the *Polychrest* needs to be docked, that I am still twenty-three men short of my complement, that she is making eighteen inches of water an hour in a dead calm, and that her leeway renders inshore navigation extremely hazardous.'

'Stuff, Captain Aubrey: my carpenters say you can perfectly well stay out another month. As for her leeway, we all make leeway: the French make leeway, but they are not shy of running in and out of Chaulieu.' In case the hint should not have been clear enough, he repeated his last remark, dwelling on the word *shy*.

'Oh, certainly, sir,' said Jack with real indifference. 'I spoke, as I say, purely for form's sake.'

'I dare say you want your orders in writing?'

'No, thank you, sir; I believe I shall remember them quite easily.'

Returning to the ship he wondered whether Harte understood the nature of the service he required of the *Polychrest* – how very like a death-warrant these orders might be: he was not much of a seaman. On the other hand, he had vessels at his command more suitable by far for the intricate passage of the Ras du Point and the inner roads – the *Aetna* and the *Tartarus* would do the job admirably. Ignorance and malice in fairly even parts,

354

he decided. Then again, Harte might have relied upon his contesting the order, insisting upon a survey, and so dishing himself: if so, he had chosen the moment well, as far as the *Polychrest* was concerned. 'But what does it signify?' he said, running up the side with a look of cheerful confidence. He gave the necessary orders, and a few minutes later the blue peter broke out at the foretopmasthead, with a gun to call attention to it. Stephen heard the gun, saw the signal, and hurried back to Deal.

There were several other Polychrests ashore – Mr Goodridge, Pullings to see his sweetheart, Babbington with his doting parents, half a dozen liberty-men. He joined them on the shingle, where they were bargaining for a hoveller, and in ten minutes he was back in the pharmaceutical-bilgewater-damp-book smell of his own cabin. He had hardly closed his door before a hundred minute ties began to fasten insensibly on him, drawing him back into the role of a responsible naval surgeon, committed to complex daily life with a hundred other men.

For once the *Polychrest* cast prettily to larboard and bore away on the height of the tide. A gentle breeze abaft the beam carried her shaving round the South Foreland, and by the time the hands were piped to supper they were in sight of Dover. Stephen came on deck by way of the fore-hatch from the sick-bay, and walked into the bows. As he stepped on to the forecastle the talk stopped dead, and he noticed an odd, sullen, shifty glance from old Plaice and Lakey. He had grown used to reserve from Bonden these last few days, for Bonden was the captain's coxswain, and he supposed Plaice had caught it by family affection; but it surprised him from Lakey, a noisy man with an open, cheerful heart. Presently he went below again, and he was busy with Mr Thompson when he heard 'All hands 'bout ship' as the *Polychrest* stood out into the offing. It was generally known that they were bound down-Channel to look into a French port: some said Wimereux, others Boulogne, and some pushed as far as Dieppe; but when

355

the gun-room sat down to supper the news went about that Chaulieu was their goal.

Stephen had never heard of the place. Smithers (who had recovered his spirits) knew it well: 'My friend, the Marquis of Dorset, was always there in his yacht, during the peace; and he was for ever begging me to run across with him – "'Tis absolutely no more than a day and a night in my cutter," he would say. "You should come, George – we can't do without you and your flute." '

Mr Goodridge, who looked thoughtful and withdrawn, added nothing to the conversation. After a discussion of yachts, their astonishing luxury and sailing qualities, it returned to Mr Smithers's triumphs, his yacht-owning friends, and their touching devotion to him; to the fatigues of the London season, and the difficulty of keeping débutantes at a decent distance. Once again Stephen noticed that all this pleased Parker; that although Parker was a man of respectable family and, in his way, a 'hard horse', he encouraged Smithers, listening attentively, and as it were taking something of it to himself. It surprised Stephen, but it did not raise his spirits; and leaning across the table he said privately to the master, 'I should be obliged, Mr Goodridge, if you would tell me something about this port.'

'Come with me, then, Doctor,' said the master. 'I have the charts spread out in my cabin. It will be easier to explain with these shoals laid down before us.'

'These, I take it, are sandbanks,' said Stephen.

'Just so. And the little figures show the depth at high water and at low: the red is where they are above the surface.'

'A perilous maze. I did not know that so much sand could congregate in one place.'

'Why, it is the set of the tides, do you see – they run precious fast round Point Noir and the Prelleys – and these old rivers. In ancient times they must have been much bigger, to have carried down all that silt.'

'Have you a larger map, to give me a general view?'

'Just behind you, sir, under Bishop Ussher.'

This was more like the maps he was used to: it showed the Channel coast of France, running almost north and south below Etaples until a little beyond the mouth of the Risle, where it tended away westwards for three or four miles to form a shallow bay, or rather a rounded corner, ending on the west with the Ile Saint-Jacques, a little pear-shaped island five hundred yards from the shore, which then resumed its southerly direction and ran off the page in the direction of Abbeville. In the inner angle of this rounded corner, the point where the coast began to run westward, there was a rectangle marked Square Tower, then nothing, not even a hamlet, for a mile westward, until a headland thrust out into the sea for two hundred yards: a star on top of it, and the name Fort de la Convention. Its shape was like that of the island, but in this case the pear had not quite succeeded in dropping off the mainland. These two pears, St Jacques and Convention, were something less than two miles apart, and between them, at the mouth of a modest stream called the Divonne, lay Chaulieu. It had been a considerable port in mediaeval times, but it had silted up; and the notorious banks in the bay had still further discouraged its trade. Yet it had its advantages: the island sheltered it from western gales and the banks from the north; the fierce tides kept its inner and outer roads clear, and for the last few years the French government had been cleaning the harbour, carrying an ambitious breakwater out to protect it from the north-east, and deepening the channels. The work had gone on right through the Peace of Amiens, for Chaulieu revived would be a valuable port for Bonaparte's invasion-flotilla as it crept up the coast from every port or even fishing-village capable of building a lugger right down to Biarritz – crept up to its assembly-points, Etaples, Boulogne, Wimereux and the rest. There were already over two thousand of these prams, cannonières and transports, and Chaulieu had built a dozen.

'This is where their slips are,' said Goodridge, pointing to the mouth of the little river. 'And this is where they are doing most of their dredging and stone-work, just inside the harbour jetty. It makes the harbour almost useless for the moment, but they don't care for that. They can lie snug in the inner road, under Convention; or in the outer, for that matter, under St Jacques, unless it comes on to blow from the north-east. And now I come to think of it, I believe I have a print. Yes: here we are.' He held out an odd-shaped volume with long strips of the coast seen from the offing, half a dozen to a page. A dull low coast, with nothing but these curious chalky rises each side of the mean village: both much of a height, and both, as he saw looking closely, crowned by the unmistakable hand of the industrious, ubiquitous Vauban.

'Vauban,' observed Stephen, 'is like aniseed in a cake: a little is excellent; but how soon one sickens – these inevitable pepper-pots, from Alsace to the Roussillon.' He turned back to the chart. Now it was clear to him that the inner road, starting just outside the harbour and running up north-east past the Fort de la Convention on its headland, was protected by two long sandbanks, half a mile off the shore, labelled West Anvil and East Anvil; and that the outer road, parallel to the first, but on the seaward side of the Anvils, was sheltered on the east by the island and on the north by Old Paul Hill's bank. These two good anchorages sloped diagonally across the page, from low left to high right, and they were separated by the Anvils: but whereas the inner road was not much above half a mile wide and two long, the outer was a fine stretch of water, certainly twice that size. 'How curious that these banks should have English names,' he said. 'Pray, is this usual?'

'Oh, yes: anything by sea, we feel we own, just as we call Setubal St Ubes, and Coruña The Groyne, and so on: this one here we call the Galloper, after ours, it being much the same shape. And the Anvils we call anvils because with a north-wester and a making tide, the hollow seas bang away on them rap-rap, first the one and the other, like you was in a smithy. I ran in here once in a cutter, by the Goulet' – pointing to the narrow passage between the island and the main – 'in '88 or '89, with a stiff north-wester, into the inner road, and the spoondrift came in off the bank so thick you could hardly breathe.'

'There is an odd symmetry in the arrangement of these banks, and in these promontories: perhaps there may be a connection. What a maze of channels! How shall you come in? Not by the Goulet, I presume, since it is so close to the fort on the island – I should not have called it a promontory: it is an island, though from the print it looks much the same, being seen head-on.'

'It depends on the wind, of course; but with anything north, I should hope to follow the channel between the Galloper and Morgan's Knock to the outer road, run past St Jacques, and then either go between the Anvils or round the tail of the West Anvil to come to the harbour-mouth; then out again on the ebb, with God's blessing, by the Ras du Point – here, beyond the East Anvil – and so get into the offing before Convention knocks our masts away. They mount forty-two pounders: a mighty heavy gun. We must start to come in on the first half of the flood, do you see, to get off if we touch and to do our business at high water. Then away with the ebb, so as not to be heaved in by the making tide when they have chawed us up a little, and we have not quite the control we could wish. And chaw us up they will, playing their heavy pieces on us, unless we can take them by surprise: capital practice those French gunners make, to be sure. How glad I am I left the *Modest Proposal* with Mrs G., fair-copied and ready for the press.'

'So the tide is all-important,' observed Stephen, after a pause.

'Yes. Wind and tide, and surprise if we can manage

it. The tides we can work. I reckon to bring her there, with the island bearing due south and the square tower south-east a half east, with the flood, not of tomorrow night, but of the night after – Sunday, as ever is. And we must pray for a gentle west or north-west breeze to take us in: and out again, maybe.'

CHAPTER ELEVEN

Stephen sat by his patient in the gently rocking sick-bay. He had almost certainly pulled him through the crisis – the faint thready pulse had strengthened this last hour, temperature had dropped, breathing was almost normal – but this triumph occupied only a remote corner of his mind: the rest was filled with dread. As a listener, a half unconscious listener, he had heard too much good of himself – 'The Doctor is all right – the Doctor will not see us abused – the Doctor is for liberty – he has instruction; he has the French – he is an Irish person, too.' The murmur of conversation at the far end had dropped to an expectant silence; the men were looking eagerly towards him, nudging one another; and a tall Irishman, visiting a sick shipmate, stood up, his face turned towards the Doctor. At his first movement Stephen slipped out of the sick-bay: on the quarterdeck he saw Parker, talking with the Marine lieutenant, both gazing at a line-of-battle ship, a three-decker standing south-west with all her canvas abroad, studdingsails port and starboard, tearing down the Channel with a white bow-wave streaming along her side. Two midshipmen, off duty, sat making a complex object out of rope in the gangway. 'Mr Parslow,' said Stephen, 'pray be so good as to ask the Captain if he is at leisure.'

'I'll go when I've finished this,' said Parslow coolly, without getting up.

Babbington dropped his fid, kicked Parslow vehemently down the ladder and said, 'I'll go, sir.' A later moment he came running back. 'Captain has Chips with him just now, sir, but will be very happy in five minutes.'

Very happy was a conventional phrase, and it was

obvious that Captain Aubrey had had an unpleasant conversation with his carpenter: there was a lump of rotten wood with a drawn bolt in it on his desk and a shattered, bludgeoned look on his face. He stood up, awkward, doubtful, embarrassed, his head bent under the beam.

'I am sorry to have to ask for this interview, sir,' said Stephen. 'But it is probable there will be a mutiny tomorrow night, when the ship is in with the French coast. The intention is to carry her into Saint-Valéry.'

Jack nodded. This confirmed his reading of the situation – the Sophies' downcast, wretched looks, the men's demeanour, the twenty-four-pound shot that had left their racks to trundle about the deck in the middle watch. His ship was falling to pieces under his feet, his crew were falling away from their duty and their allegiance. 'Can you tell me who are the ringleaders?'

'I cannot. No, sir: you may call me many things, but not an informer. I have said enough, more than enough.'

No. Many surgeons, with a foot in each world, were more than half in sympathy with mutineers: there had been that man at the Nore, and the unfortunate Davidson they hanged for it at Bombay. And even Killick, his own servant, even Bonden – and they must have known something of what was brewing – would not inform on their shipmates, although they were very close to him.

'Thank you for having come to see me,' he said stiffly.

When the door had closed behind Stephen he sat down with his head in his hands and let himself go to total unhappiness – to something near despair – so many things together, and now this cold evil look: he reproached himself most bitterly for not having seized this chance for an apology. 'If only I could have got it out; but he spoke so quick, and he was so very cold. Though indeed, I should have looked the same if any man had given me the lie; it is not to be borne. What in God's name possessed me? So trivial, so beside the point – as gross as a schoolboy calling names – unmanly. However, he shall make a hole

362

in me whenever he chooses. And then again, what should I have the air of, suddenly growing abject now that I know he is such a deadly old file?' Yet throughout this period of indulgence some other part of his brain was dealing with the immediate problem, and almost without a transition he said, 'By God, I wish I had Macdonald.' This had nothing to do with a desire for comfort or council – he knew that Macdonald disapproved of him – but for efficiency. Macdonald was an officerlike man; this puppy Smithers was not. Still, he might not be wholly inept.

He rang his bell, and said, 'Pass the word for Mr Smithers.'

'Sit down, Mr Smithers. Tell me over the names of your Marines, if you please. Very good: and there is your sergeant, of course. Now listen to what I say. Think of each of these men separately, with great attention, and tell me whether or no each is to be relied upon.'

'Why, of course they are, sir,' cried Smithers.

'No, no. Think, man, think,' said Jack, trying to force some responsibility from that pink smirk. 'Think, and reply when you have really thought. This is of the very first consequence.'

His look was exceedingly penetrating and savage; it had effect. Smithers lost countenance and began to swear. He did evidently put his mind into painful motion; his lips could be seen moving, telling over the muster; and after some time he came up with the answer, 'Perfectly reliable, sir. Except for a man called – well, he has the same name as me; but no sort of connection, of course – a Papist from Ireland.'

'You will answer for that? You are dead certain of what you say? I say dead certain?'

'Yes, sir,' said Smithers, staring, terribly upset.

'Thank you, Mr Smithers. You are to mention this conversation to no one. That is a direct, absolute order. And you are to display no uneasiness. Pray desire Mr Goodridge to come here at once.'

'Mr Goodridge,' he said, standing at his chart-table, 'be so good as to give me our position.'

'Exact, sir, or within a league or two?' asked the master, with his head on one side and his left eye closed.

'Exact.'

'I must bring the log-board, sir.' Jack nodded. The master returned, took up scale and compasses, and pricked the chart. 'There, sir.'

'I see. We are under courses and topsails?'

'Yes, sir. We agreed to run down easy for Sunday's tide, if you remember, so as not to hang about in the offing, we being so recognizable.'

'I believe, I believe,' said Jack, studying the chart and the board, 'I believe that we may catch this evening's tide. What do you say, Master?'

'If the wind holds, sir, so we may, by cracking on regardless. I should not care to answer for the wind, though. The glass is rising.'

'Not mine,' said Jack, looking at his barometer. 'I should like to see Mr Parker, if you please: and in the meantime it would be as well to get the stuns'ls, royals and skylines into the tops.

'Mr Parker, we have a mutiny on our hands. I intend to take the *Polychrest* into action at the earliest possible moment, by way of dealing with the situation. We shall crowd sail to reach Chaulieu tonight. But before making sail I shall speak to the men. Let the gunner load the two aftermost guns with grape. The officers are to assemble on the quarterdeck at six bells – in ten minutes – with their side-arms. The Marines will fall in with their muskets on the fo'c'sle. No hurry or concern will be shown before that time. When all hands are called the guns will be traversed for'ard, with an oldster standing by each one. When I have spoken to the hands and we make sail, no man is to be struck or started until further orders.'

'May I offer an observation, sir?'

'Thank you, Mr Parker, no. Those are my orders.'

'Very good, sir.'

He had no confidence in Parker's judgment. If he had asked the advice of any man aboard it would have been Goodridge. But this was his responsibility as captain of the ship and his alone. In any case, he felt that he knew more about mutinous hands than anyone on the quarterdeck of the *Polychrest*: as a disrated midshipman he had served before the mast in a discontented ship on the Cape station – he knew it from the other side. He had a great affection for the foremast jack, and if he did not know for certain what would go with the lower deck, at least he was quite sure what would not.

He looked at his watch, put on his best coat, and walked on to the quarterdeck. Six bells in the forenoon watch. His officers were gathering round him, silent, very grave.

'All hands aft, if you please, Mr Parker,' he said.

The shrill pipes, the roaring down hatchways, the stampede, the red coats trooping forward through the throng. Silence, but for the tapping of the reef-points overhead.

'Men,' said Jack, 'I know damned well what's going on. I know damned well what's going on; and I won't have it. What simple fellows you are, to listen to a parcel of makee-clever sea-lawyers and politicians, glib, quick-talking coves. Some of you have put your necks into the noose. I say your necks into the noose. You see the *Ville de Paris* over there?' Every head turned to the line-of-battle ship on the horizon. 'I have only to signal her, or half a dozen other cruisers, and run you up to the yardarm with the Rogue's March playing. Damned fools, to listen to such talk. But I am not going to signal to the *Ville de Paris* nor to any other king's ship. Why not? Because the *Polychrest* is going into action this very night, that's why. I am not going to have it said in the fleet that any Polychrest is afraid of hard knocks.'

'That's right,' said a voice – Joe Plaice, well out in front, his mouth wide open.

'It's not you, sir,' said another, unseen. 'It's him, old Parker, the hard-horse bugger'.

'I'm going to take the *Polychrest* in tonight,' Jack went on, in a growing roar of conviction, 'and I'm going to hammer the Frenchmen in Chaulieu, in their own port, d'ye hear me? If there's any man here afraid of hard knocks, he'd better stay behind. Is there any man here, afraid of hard knocks?'

A kind of universal growl, not ill-natured: some laughter; further cries of 'that hard-horse bugger'.

'Silence fore and aft. Well, I'm glad there ain't. There are some awkward hands among us still – look at that wicked ugly slab-line – and some men that talk too much, but I never thought there was a faint heart aboard. They may say the *Polychrest* ain't very quick in stays; they may say she don't furl her tops'ls all that pretty; but if they say she's shy, if they say she don't like hard knocks, why, black the white of my eye. When we thumped it into the *Bellone*, there wasn't a single foremast jack that did not do his duty like a lion. So we'll run into Chaulieu, I say, and we'll hammer Bonaparte. That's the right way to bring the war to an end – that's the right way, not listening to a set of galley-rangers and clever chaps – and the sooner it's over and you can go home, the better I'll be pleased. I know it's not a bed of roses, looking after our country the way we have to. Now I tell you this, and mark what I do say. There is going to be no punishment over this business: it will not even be logged, and there's my word upon it. There is going to be no punishment. But every man and boy must attend to his duty tonight, he must mind it very carefully, because Chaulieu is a tough nut to crack – an awkward set of shoals – an awkward tide – and we must be every hand to his rope, and haul with a will, d'ye hear? Quick's the word and sharp's the action. Now I am going to pick some men for the barge, and then we shall crowd all the sail she can bear.' He walked into the tight crowd of men, into the low buzz of talk, the whispers, and silence went before him. Smiling, confident faces, worried faces or blank, some apprehensive, some brute-terrified and savage. 'Davis,' he said, 'go along into the barge.' The man's eyes were frightened as a wild beast's: he darted looks left and right. 'Come on, now, come along, you heard what I said,' said Jack quietly, and Davis lumbered aft, bowed and unnatural. The silence was general now, the atmosphere quite different. But he was not going to leave these men to have dinner with their messmates and try some desperate foolery. He was in a state of exceedingly acute awareness; he had no shadow of a doubt of the men he chose. 'Wilcocks, into the barge. Anderson.' He was far in among them. He had no weapons. 'Johnson. Look alive.' The tension was heightening very fast; it must go no higher. 'Bonden, into the barge,' he said, looking over his coxswain's head. 'Me, sir?' cried Bonden piteously. 'Cut along,' said Jack. 'Bantock, Lakey, Screech.' The low excited talk had begun again on the periphery. Men who could not be suspected were being sent into the barge: they were going aft, down the sternladder and into the boat towing behind: this was no punishment, nor no threat of punishment. He flemished down the offending slab-line in a seamanlike manner and walked back to the quarterdeck.

'Now, Polychrests,' he said, 'now we are going to crack on until she groans again. Stuns'ls aloft and alow, royals, and, damn me, royal stuns'ls and skys'ls if she'll bear 'em. The sooner we're there, the sooner we're home. Topmen, upperyardmen, are you ready?'

'Ready, aye ready, sir.' A comfortable, good body of sound – relief, thankfulness?

'Then at the word, up you go. Lay aloft!'

The *Polychrest* bloomed like a white rose. Her rarely-used studdingsails stretched out brilliant white one after another, her brand-new royals shone high, and above them all, her hitherto unseen skysails twinkled in the sun. The ship groaned and groaned again as they were sheeted home; she plunged her forefoot deep while behind her the barge raced along in her wake, the water almost to its gunwales.

*   *   *

If the *Polychrest* could be said to have a good point of sailing, it was with the wind three points abaft the beam; and here the wind stayed all day, scarcely varying from west-north-west by north, and blowing with a gentle urgency that kept all eyes aloft for the safety of her royals and skysails. She was cracking on indeed, racing down the Channel as though their lives depended upon it, making so much water that Mr Gray the carpenter, coming up from the well, officially registered his protest. She did carry away a skysail, and at one point a large unidentified object tore from her bottom, but the leagues raced away in her wake, and Jack, perpetually on the quarterdeck, could almost have loved her.

On the forecastle the watch below were at their make and mend; the watch on duty were kept busy, necessarily busy, trimming sail; and everybody seemed to be enjoying the speed, the racing tension to get the last ounce out of her. His orders about starting were being punctually obeyed; and so far no man or boy seemed to move any slower for it. The men in the barge had been brought aboard, lest it should tow under, and they had had their dinner in the galley: he was not afraid of them now – their influence was gone, their shipmates avoided them. Davis, the really dangerous brute for a sudden reckless explosion, seemed wholly amazed; and Wilcocks, the eloquent attorney's clerk turned pickpocket, could find no one to listen to him. The seamen, for the most part, had turned with their usual calm volatility from one disaster to the interval before the next. For the moment he had the situation in hand.

His only anxiety was the wind. As the afternoon wore on it grew fainter and more irregular, giving every sign of falling away altogether with the setting of the sun: as the damp evening settled from the sky, with the dew tightening the rigging, it revived a little, still breathing from the longed-for north-west; but there was no trusting to it.

By six o'clock they had run off their distance, standing in to raise the unmistakable tower and headland of Point Noir, with a cross-bearing on Camaret; but now, as they steered east-south-east to make the coast a little north of Chaulieu, the haze thickened, thickened, until at the very entrance to Chaulieu bay itself, they found themselves in a fog, their royals faint blurs high over the deck – a fog that lay a little above the smoothly swelling surface of the sea, and that was torn in long wafts of thick and clear, faintly luminous from the rising moon.

They were no more than a little late for their tide, and they stood in steadily with the master at the con and two leads going without a pause – 'By the deep eight, by the deep eight, by the mark ten, a quarter less ten, by the deep nine, and a half seven, by the mark five, a quarter less five, and a half four.' The bottom was shelving fast. 'We are on the edge of the outer bank, sir,' said the master, looking at the sample of shelly ooze from the lead. 'All well. Tops'ls alone, I believe.'

'She is yours, Mr Goodridge,' said Jack, and he stood back a step, while the ship whispered through the water and the master took her in. She had been cleared for action long before; the hands were silent and attentive; the ship answered her helm promptly as she worked through the channels, sheets and braces tightening at the word. 'That will be the Galloper,' said the master, nodding towards a stretch of pale water on the starboard bow. 'Starboard a point. Two points. Steady – easy, now. As she goes. Port your helm. Hard over.' Silence. Dead silence in the fog.

'Morgan's Knock to larboard, sir,' he said, coming aft. Jack was glad to hear it. Their last sure cross-bearing seemed a terribly long time ago; and this was blindman's buff: it was water he did not know. With Morgan's Knock astern, they would have to bear westward round the tail of Old Paul Hill's bank, and then head a little south of east and so into the outer road, crossing the Ile Saint-Jacques. 'Starboard three points,' said the master, and the ship swung to the west. It was wonderful how these old Channel pilots knew their sea: by the smell and feel of it, no doubt. 'Mind your bowline, for'ard there,' called the master in a low voice. A long, long pause, with the *Polychrest* close-hauled to the now freshening breeze. 'Down with your helm, now. Steady, steady. As she goes. Look, sir, on the larboard bow – that's St Jacques.' A tear in the fog, and there, about a mile away, rose a tall white mass with a fortification on its top and half-way down its side.

'Well done, Mr Goodridge, well done indeed.'

'On deck, there,' hailed the look-out. 'Sail on the larboard beam. Oh, a mort of craft,' he added conversationally. 'Eight, nine – a proper old crowd of 'em.'

'They'll be at the far end of the outer road, sir,' said the master. 'We are in it now.'

The breeze was tearing great windows in the fog, and gazing over to port Jack had a sudden vision of an assembly of fair-sized vessels, ship- and brig-rigged, bright in the moonlight. These were his prey, the transports and cannonières for the invasion.

'You are happy that they are in the outer road, Mr Goodridge?' he asked.

'Oh, yes, sir. We just had St Jacques bearing south-south-east. There's nothing but open water between you and them.'

'Down with your helm,' said Jack. With the wind on her larboard quarter the *Polychrest* ran through the sea, going fast in with the tide, straight for the gun-vessels.

'Out tompions,' he said. 'Stand to your guns.' He meant to run right in among them, firing both sides, to get the very most out of the surprise and the first discharge, for a moment after it all hell would break loose from the batteries, and the men would never be so steady again. The mist had drifted across again, but it was clearing – he could see them dimly, coming closer and closer.

'Not a gun till . . . ' he called, and a shock threw him flat on the deck. The *Polychrest* was brought up all standing. She had run full tilt on to the West Anvil.

This was plain as he got to his feet and the clearing of the fog showed one fort right astern and another almost exactly alike on the starboard bow, forts that woke to instant life with a shattering roar, a blast of flame that lit the sky. They had mistaken Convention for St Jacques, the inner road for the outer: they had come in by a different channel, and the vessels were separated from him by an impassable spit of sand. Those ships were in the inner, not the outer road. By some miracle the *Polychrest* had all her masts still standing: she lifted on the swell and ground a little farther on to the bank.

'Up sheets,' he shouted, full voice – no call for silence now. 'Up sheets.' The strain on the masts eased. 'Parker, Pullings, Babbington, Rossall, get the guns aft.' If she were only hanging by her forefoot this might bring her off. On the far side of the bank a great flurry of canvas – ships getting under way in every direction – and amidst this confusion two distinct well-ordered shapes steering to cross his bows. Gun-brigs, which marked their presence by two double jets of fire, meaning to rake him from stern to stern. 'Leave the fo'c'sle guns,' he cried. 'Mr Rossall, Adams, keep up a steady fire on those brigs.'

Now the moon shone out with surprising brilliance, and as the wind blew away the smoke, it showed the batteries as clear as day. It showed the whole inner road, crowded with shipping – a corvette moored right up against Convention, under its guns; certainly the ship *Thetis* and *Andromeda* had chased in, his quarry. 'A damned-fool place to moor her' – one thought among countless others racing through his head. It showed the deck of the *Polychrest*, most of the men well disciplined, over their amazement, working fast at the guns, trundling them aft, not much concerned by the thunder of the forts. St Jacques was firing wide, afraid of hitting its own people ahead of the *Polychrest*. Convention had not yet got the range: the iron hail was still high overhead. The gun-brigs were more dangerous.

He clapped on to a rope, helped run a gun aft, called for coigns to wedge them until they could make fast.

'All the people aft. All hands, all hands aft. We'll jounce her off. All jump together at the word. One, two. One, two.' They jumped, a hundred men together: would their weight and the weight of the guns slide her off into deep water? 'One, two. One, two.' It would not. ''Vast jumping.' He ran forward, looking hard and quick right round the port; glanced at his watch. A quarter past nine – not much left of the flood. 'Get all the boats over the side. Mr Parker,' he said, 'carronade into the barge.'

She had to be got off. A bower anchor carried out, dropped in deep water and heaved upon would bring her off: but even the barge could not bear the weight of such an anchor. A larger vessel must be cut out. A ball passed within a few feet of him, and its wind made him stagger. A cheer from forward, as the starboard carronade hit one of the gun-brigs square on the figurehead. Something had to be cut out. The transports were all crowding sail for the Ras du Point; they could not be caught in time. There were some small luggers in the harbour mouth; the corvette alone under Convention's guns. Absurdly close under Convention's guns, moored fore and aft, fifty yards from the shore, broad-side and headed towards St Jacques. Why not the corvette herself? He dismissed the question as absurd. But why not? The risk would be enormous, but no greater than lying here under the cross-fire, once the batteries had the range. It was very near to wild mad recklessness; but it was not quite there. And with the corvette in his possession there would be no need to carry out an anchor – a time-consuming job.

'Mr Rossall,' he said, 'take the barge. Draw off the fire of those brigs. Plenty of cartridge, a dozen muskets. Make all the noise you can – shout – sing out.' The barge-crew dropped over the side. Drawing a deep breath he shouted above the guns, 'Volunteers, volunteers to come along with me and cut out that corvette. Richards, serve out cutlasses, pistols, axes. Mr Parker, you will stay in the ship.' – The men would not follow Parker: how many would follow *him*? 'Mr Smithers, the red cutter: you and your Marines board over her starboard bow. Mr Pullings, blue cutter to her larboard quarter, and the moment you are aboard cut her cables. Take axes. Then lay aloft and let fall her tops'ls. Attend to nothing else at all. Pick your men: quick. The rest come along with me and look alive, now. There's not a moment to be lost.' Killick handed him his pistols and he dropped into his gig, never looking behind him. The Polychrests poured over the side, thump thump thump down into the boats. The clash of arms, a voice bawling in his ear 'Squeeze up, George. Make room, can't you?' How many men in the boats? Seventy? Eighty? Even more. A magnificent rise in his heart, all the blackness falling clear away.

'Give way,' he said. 'Silence, all boats. Bonden, right over the bank. Go straight for her.' A crash behind him as a salvo from Convention took away the *Polychrest's* foretopmast.

'No great loss,' he said, settling in the stern-sheets with his sword between his knees. They touched once, a bare scrape, on the top of the sand-bank, then they were beyond it, in the inner road, going straight for the corvette half a mile away. The risk was enormous – she might have two hundred men aboard – but here again there was the chance of surprise. They would scarcely expect to be boarded from a grounded ship, not right under their own guns. Too far under their own guns – what a simple place to moor – for the Convention battery was high-perched up on the headland: its guns could never be depressed so far as to sweep the sea two or three hundred yards in front of the fort. Only five hundred yards to go. The men were pulling like maniacs, grunt, grunt, grunt, but the boat was crammed, heavy and encumbered – no room to stretch to their oars. Bonden wedged next to him, little Parslow – that child should never have come – the purser, deathly pale in the moonlight, the villainous face of Davis; Lakey, Plaice, all the Sophies . . .

Four hundred yards, and at last the corvette had woken to her danger. A hail. An uneven broadside, musketry. And now musketry crackling all along the shore. A deluge of water from Convention's great guns, no longer firing at the *Polychrest* but at her boats, and missing only by a very little. And all the time the barge, banging away behind them at the gun-brigs with its little six-pounder carronade, roaring, firing muskets, wonderfully diverting attention from this silent rush across the inner road. Convention again, at extreme depression, but firing over them.

Two hundred yards, one. The other boats drawing ahead, Smithers to the right, Pullings turning left-handed to go round her stern.

'Mizen chains, Bonden,' he said, loosening his sword in its scabbard.

A shattering burst of fire, a great roaring – the Marines were boarding her over the bows.

'Mizen chains it is, sir,' said Bonden, heaving on the tiller. A last broadside overhead, and the boat came kissing against the side.

Up. He leapt on the high roll, his hands catching the dead-eyes. Up. No boarding-netting, by God! Men thrusting, grasping all round him, one holding his hair. Up and over the rail, through the thin fringe of defenders – a few pikes, swabs, a musket banging in his ear – on to the quarterdeck, his sharp sword out, pistol in his left hand. Straight for the group of officers, shouting 'Polychrest! Polychrest!' a swarm of men behind him, a swirling scuffle by the mizenmast, an open maul, men grappling silently, open extreme brutal violence. Fired his pistol, flinging it straight at the next man's face. Babbington on his left running full into the flash and smoke of a musket – he was down. Jack checked his rush and stood over him; lunging hard he deflected the plunging bayonet into the deck. His heavy sword carried on, and now with all his weight and strength he whipped it up in a wicked backhanded stroke that took the soldier's head half off his body.

A little officer in the clear space in front of him, sword-point darting at his breast. Swerve and parry, and there they were dancing towards the taffrail, their swords flashing in the moonlight. A burning stab in his shoulder, and before the officer could recover his point Jack had closed, crashing the pommel into his chest and kicking his legs from under him. 'Rendez-vous,' he said.

'Jé mé rendre,' said the officer on the deck, dropping his sword. 'Parola.'

Firing, crashing, shouting in the bows, in the waist. And now Pullings was over the side, hacking at the cables. Red coats, dark in the moonlight, clearing the starboard gangway, and everywhere, everywhere the shout of Polychrest. Jack raced forward at the tight group by the mainmast, mostly officers; they were backing, firing their pistols, pointing swords and pikes, and behind them, on the landward side, their men were dropping into the boats and into the water by the score. Haines ran past him, dodging through the fight, and hurled himself aloft, followed by a string of other men.

Here was Smithers, shouting, sweating, a dozen other Marines – they had reached the quarterdeck from the bows. Now Pullings, with a bloody axe in his hand, and the top-sails were letting fall, mizen main and fore – men already at the sheets.

'Capitaine,' cried Jack, 'Capitaine, cessez effusion sang. Rendez-vous. Hommes desertés. Rendez-vous.'

'Jamais, monsieur,' said the Frenchman, and came for him with a furious lunge.

'Bonden, trip up his heels,' said Jack, parrying the thrust and cutting high. The French captain's sword flashed up. Bonden ran beneath it, collared him, and it was over.

Goodridge was at the wheel – where had he come

from? – calling like thunder for the foretopsail to be sheeted home; already the land was gently receding, gliding, sliding backwards and away.

'Capitaine, en bas, dessous, s'il vous plait. Toutes officiers dessous.' Officers giving up their swords; Jack taking them, passing them to Bonden. Incomprehensible words – Italian? 'Mr Smithers, put 'em in the cable-tier.'

An isolated scuffle and a single shot on the forecastle, to join the firing from the shore. Bodies on deck: the wounded crawling.

She was heading westward, and the blessed wind was just before her beam. She must go round the tail of the West Anvil before she could tack to reach the *Polychrest*, and all the way she would be sailing straight into the fire of St Jacques: half a mile's creep, always closer to that deadly raking battery.

'Foresail and driver,' cried Jack. The quicker the better, and above all she must not miss stays. She seemed to be handling beautifully, but if she missed stays she would be cut to pieces.

Convention was firing behind them: wildly at present, though one great ball passed through all three topsails. He hurried forward to help sort out the foresail tack. The deck was swarming with Polychrests – they called out to him: tearing high spirits, some quite beside themselves. 'Wilkins,' he said, putting his hand on the man's shoulder, 'you and Shaddock start getting the corpses over the side.'

She was a trim little vessel. Eighteen, no, twenty guns. Broader than the *Polychrest*. *Fanciulla* was her name – she was indeed the *Fanciulla*. Why did St Jacques not fire? 'Mr Malloch, clear away the small bower and get a cable out of a stern-port.' Why did they not fire? A triple crash abaft the mainmast – Convention hulling the corvette – but nothing from St Jacques. St Jacques had not yet realized that the *Fanciulla* had been carried – they thought she was standing out to attack the grounded *Polychrest*. 'Long may it last,' he said. The tack was hard down, the corvette moving faster through the water – slack water now. He looked at his watch, holding it up to the moon: and a flash from St Jacques showed him just eleven. They had smoked him at last. But the tail of the sandbank was no great way off.

'I killed one, sir,' cried Parslow, running across the deck to tell him. 'I shot him into the body just as he was going for Barker with a half-pike.'

'Very good, Mr Parslow. Now cut along to the cable-tier and give Mr Malloch a hand, will you? Mr Goodridge, I believe we may go about very soon.'

'Another hundred yards, sir,' said the master, his eyes fixed on St Jacques. 'I must just get those two turrets in a line.'

Nearer, nearer. The towers were converging. 'All hands, all hands,' shouted Jack. 'Ready about ship. Mr Pullings, are you ready, there?' The towers blazed out, vanished in their own smoke, the corvette's mizen topmast went by the board, sheets of spray flew over the quarterdeck. 'Ready oh! Helm's a-lee. Up tacks and sheets. Haul mains'l, haul.' Round she came, paying off all the faster for the loss of her after sails. 'Haul of all, haul with a will.' She was round, had spun like a cutter, and now with the wind three points free she was running for the *Polychrest* – the *Polychrest* with no foremast, no maintopgallant and only the stump of her bowsprit, but still firing her forward carronades and cheering thinly as the *Fanciulla* ran alongside, came up into the wind on the far side of the channel and dropped anchor.

'All well, Mr Parker?' hailed Jack.

'All's well, sir. We are a little knocked about, and the barge sank alongside; but all's well.'

'Rig the capstan, Mr Parker, and make a lane for the cable.' The roar of guns, the din of shot hitting both ships, tearing up the water, and passing overhead, drowned his voice. He repeated the order and went on, 'Mr Pullings, veer the cutter under the stern to take the line.'

'Red cutter was stove by that old topmast, sir, and I'm afraid the Marine's painter came adrift like, somehow. Only your gig left, sir. The Frenchmen went ashore in all theirn.'

'The gig, then. Mr Goodridge, as soon as the cable is to, start heaving ahead. Pullings, come with me.' He dropped into the gig, took the line in his hand – their life-line – and said, 'We shall need at least twenty more men for the capstan. Ply to and from as quick as ever you can, Pullings.'

The *Polychrest* again, and hands reaching eagerly from the stern-port for the line. A mortar-shell burst, brilliant orange, closer to the gun-brigs than to its target.

'Hot work, sir,' said Parker. 'I wish you joy of your prize.' He spoke with an odd hesitation, forcing the words: in the light of the flashes he looked an old, old man, bent and old.

'Thankee, Parker. Pretty warm. Clap on to the line, there. Heave hearty.' The line came in hand over hand, followed briskly by a small hawser, and then far more slowly by a great heavy snake of cable. Pullings' men kept coming aboard, and at last the cable was to the capstan. While the bars were being swifted, Jack looked at his watch again: just past midnight: the tide had been ebbing for half an hour.

'Heave away,' he called to the *Fanciulla*. 'Now, Polychrests, step out. Heave hearty. Heave and rally.' The capstan span, the pawls going click-click-click; the cable began to rise from the sea, to tighten, squirting water.

And now, with the gun-brigs sheering off, frightened by the shell, St Jacques let fly – heavy mortars, all the guns they possessed. A shot killed four men at the bars; the maintopmast toppled over the forecastle; the gig was knocked to pieces alongside just as its last man left it. 'Heave. Heave and rally,' cried Jack, slipping in the blood and kicking a body out of his way as he forced the bar round. 'Heave. Heave.' The cable rose right from the sea, almost straight. The men saved from the gig flung themselves on the bars. 'Heave, heave. She moves!' Clear through the roar of guns they could hear, or rather feel, the grind of the ship's bottom shifting over the sand. A kind of gasping cheer: the pawls clicked once more, twice, and then they were flat on their faces, no resistance in the bars at all, the capstan turning free. A ball had cut the cable.

Jack fell with the rest. He was trampled upon. Clearing himself from the limbs and bodies he leapt to the rail. 'Goodridge! Goodridge ahoy! Can you bring her alongside?'

'I dare not, sir. Not on the ebb. I've only got a couple of fathoms here. No boat?'

'No boat. Heave in quick and bend on another line. D'ye hear me, now?' He could scarcely hear himself. The gun-brigs had worked round and were firing over the bank from near the harbour. He stripped off his coat, laid down his sword and went straight in; and as he dived a jagged piece of iron caught him on the head, sending him deep under. But dazed or not his body swam on, and he found his hands scrabbling at the *Fanciulla*'s side. 'Haul me aboard,' he cried.

He sat, gasping and streaming, on deck. 'Is there anyone here can swim?' Not a word, no answer. 'I'll try on a grating,' said an anxious voice.

'Give me the line,' he said, walking to the stern-ladder.

'Won't you sit down, sir, and take a dram? You're all bloody, sir,' said Goodridge, with a beseeching look into his face. Jack shook his head impatiently, and the blood spattered the deck. Every second counted, on the ebb. Even now there was six inches less of water round the *Polychrest*. He went down the ladder, let himself into the water and pushed off, swimming on his back. The sky was in a state of almost continual coruscation: between the flashes the moon shone out, her face bent like a shield. Abruptly he realized that there were two moons, floating apart, turning; and Cassiopeia was the wrong way about.

Water filled his throat. 'By God, I'm tiring. Wits going,' he said, and slid round in the water, straining his head up and taking his bearings. The *Polychrest* was far over on his left: not ahead. And hailing; yes, they were hailing. He took a turn with the line round his shoulder and concentrated his whole spirit on swimming, fixing the ship, plunging with every stroke, fixing it again: but such feeble strokes. Of course, it was against the tide: and how the line dragged.

'Thus, very well thus,' he said, changing his direction to allow for the current. In the last twenty yards his strength seemed to revive, but he could only cling there under her stern – no force in his arms to get aboard. They were fussing about, trying to haul him in. 'Take the line, God damn you all,' he cried in a voice that he heard from a distance. 'Carry it for'ard and heave, heave . . .'

At the foot of the stern-ladder Bonden lifted him out of the water, guided him up, and he sat on a match-tub while the capstan turned fast, then slower, slower, slower. And all the time they heaved the slow steady swell lifted the *Polychrest*'s stern and set it down with a thump on the hard sand; and all the French artillery played upon her. The carpenter hurried past with still another wad to stop a shot-hole; they had hulled the *Polychrest* perhaps a dozen times since he had been back aboard, but now he was utterly indifferent to their fire – a mere background, a nuisance, a hindrance to the one thing that really mattered. 'Heave and rally, heave and rally,' he cried. The full strain was on: not a click from the capstan-pawls. He staggered to an empty place on a bar and threw his weight forward, slipping in blood, finding his feet again. Click: and the whole capstan was groaning. Click. 'She moves,' whispered the man next to him. A slow, hesitant grind, and then as the swell came along from aft she lifted clear. 'She swims! She swims!' Wild cheering, and an answering cheer from over the water.

'Heave, heave,' he said. She must be pulled full clear. Now the capstan turned, now it fairly span, faster than the cable could be passed forward, and the *Polychrest* surged heavily right into the deep channel. "Vast heaving. All hands to make sail. Mr Parker, everything that can be set.'

'What? I beg pardon, sir? I did not – ' It did not matter. The seamen who had heard were aloft: the tattered mainsail dropped, the mainstaysail almost whole, and the *Polychrest* had steering-way. She was alive under him, and the life rose into his heart, quite filling him again. 'Mr Goodridge!' he shouted with new strength, 'cut your cables and lead me out by the Ras du Point. Veer out a towline as soon as you are under way.'

'Aye, aye, sir.'

He took the wheel, moving her over to the windward side of the channel, so that her leeway should not run her aground again. Lord, how heavy she was, and how she wallowed on the swell! How low in the water, too. A little more sail appeared – mizen topmast staysail, a piece of driver, odd scraps; but they gave her two knots, and with the run of the tide, setting straight down the channel, he should carry her out of range in ten minutes. 'Mr Rolfe.'

'Mr Rolfe's dead, sir.'

'His mate, then: the guns back into their places.' It was no good asking Parker; the man was only just holding himself upright. 'Mr Pullings, take some lively hands forward and see if you can pick up the towline. What is it, Mr Gray?'

'Six foot of water below, sir, if you please. And the Doctor says may he put the wounded into your cabin? He moved 'em from the cockpit to the gun-room, but now it's all awash.'

'Yes. Certainly. Can you come at any more of the holes? We'll have the pumps going directly.'

'I'll do my best, sir; but I fear it's not the shot-holes. She's opening like a flower.'

A fury of shot drowned his words, some of it glowing red, for now they had the furnaces at work: mostly wide and astern, but three went home, jarring the water-logged ship from stem to stern and cutting the last of her starboard mizen shrouds. Babbington came staggering aft, one sleeve hanging empty, to report the towline aboard and made fast to the knight-heads.

'Very good, Mr Babbington. Allen, take some hands below and help Dr Maturin move the wounded into the cabin.' He realized that he was shouting with great force, and that there was no need to be shouting. Everywhere, apart from one wicked long gun in the Convention battery, there was silence: silence and dimness, for the moon was dipping low. He felt the towline tighten, plucking at the *Polychrest*; and she gave a little spurt. The corvette just ahead had set her courses as well as main and fore topsails, and they were busy clearing the wreck of her mizen topmast. What a pretty thing she was, taut and trim: great strength in her pull – she would be a fast one.

They were running along the landward edge of the East Anvil – the bank was above the surface now, with a gentle surf breaking over it – and ahead of them was the opening of the Ras du Point, full of the transports. They too seemed unaware of the *Fanciulla*'s changed character – sitting ducks – the chance of a lifetime.

'Mr Goodridge, there. How are your guns?'

'Prime, sir, prime. Brass twelve-pounders: and four eights. Plenty of cartridge filled.'

'Then lead right through those transports, will you?'

'Aye aye, sir.'

'Jenkins, how is our powder?'

'Drowned, sir. The magazine is drowned. But we got three rounds a gun, and shot a-plenty.'

'Then double-shot 'em, Jenkins, and we'll give them a salute as we pass by.'

It would be no stylish broadside; there were scarcely enough men even to fire both sides, let alone run the guns in and out, loading fast; but it would mark the point. And it was in his orders. He laughed aloud; and he laughed too to find that he was holding himself up by the wheel.

The moonlight faded; the Ras du Point glided very slowly nearer. Pullings had set up some kind of a jury-rig forward, and another sail was drawing. Parslow was fast asleep under the shattered fife-rail.

Now there was movement, agitation, among the transports. He heard a hail, and a muffled response from the *Fanciulla*, followed by low laughter. Sails appeared, and with them confusion.

The *Fanciulla* was a hundred yards ahead. 'Mr Goodridge,' called Jack, 'back your maintops'l a trifle.' The *Polychrest* ploughed heavily on, closing the distance. The transports were moving in several directions: at least three had fallen foul of one another in the narrow channel. The moments passed in dreamlike procession, and then suddenly there it was, the immediate vivid action, vivid even after all this saturation of noise and violence. One transport on the port bow, two hundred yards away; three locked together, aground, to starboard. 'Fire as they bear,' said Jack, putting down the helm two points. At the same moment the *Fanciulla* burst into flame and smoke – a much shriller crash. Now they were in the middle of them, firing both sides. The grounded vessels waved lanterns, shouting something that could not be heard. Another, having missed stays, drifted down the *Polychrest*'s side after the last carronade had shot its final charge. Her yards caught in the *Polychrest*'s remaining shrouds; some bright spirit lashed her mainyard fast; and standing there right under the mouth of her empty guns her commander said he had struck.

'Take possession, Mr Pullings,' said Jack. 'Keep close under my lee. You can only have five men. Mr Goodridge, Mr Goodridge! Stand on.'

In half an hour the channel was clear of floating transports. Three had grounded. Two had run themselves ashore. One had sunk – the twenty-four pound smashers at close range – and the rest had doubled into the outer road or back to Chaulieu, where one was set ablaze by red-hot shot from St Jacques. And in half an hour, the time to run the length of the channel and to wreak all this havoc, the *Polychrest* was moving so heavily, keeping such a strain on the towline, that Jack hailed the *Fanciulla* and the transport to come alongside.

He went below, Bonden holding him by the arm, confirmed the carpenter's desperate report, gave orders for the wounded to be moved into the corvette, the prisoners to be secured, his papers brought, and sat there as the three vessels rocked on the gentle swell of slack water, watching the tired men carry their shipmates, their belongings, all the necessaries out of the *Polychrest*.

'It is time to go, sir,' said Parker, with Pullings and Rossall standing by him, ready to lift their captain over.

'Go,' said Jack. 'I shall follow you.' They hesitated, caught the earnestness of his tone and look, crossed and stood hovering on the rail of the corvette. Now the veering breeze blew off the land; the eastern sky was lightening; they were out of the Ras du Point, beyond the shoals; and the water in the offing was a fine deep blue. He stood up, walked as straight as he could to a ruined gun-port, made a feeble spring that just carried him to the *Fanciulla*, staggered, and turned to look at his ship. She did not sink for a good ten minutes, and by then the blood – what little he had left – had made a pool at his feet. She went very gently, with a sigh of air rushing through the hatches, and settled on the bottom, the tips of her broken masts showing a foot above the surface.

'Come, brother,' said Stephen in his ear, very like a dream. 'Come below. You must come below – here is too much blood altogether. Below, below. Here, Bonden, carry him with me.'

CHAPTER TWELVE

Fanciulla
The Downs
20 September 04

My dear Sir,

By desire of your son William, my brave and respectable midshipman, I write a hasty line to inform you of our brush with the French last week. The claim of distinction which has been bestowed on the ship I commanded, I must entirely, after God, attribute to the zeal and fidelity of my officers, amongst whom your son stands conspicuous. He is very well, and I hope will continue so. He had the misfortune of being wounded a few minutes after boarding the *Fanciulla*, and his arm is so badly broken, that I fear it must suffer amputation. But as it is his left arm, and likely to do well under the great skill of Dr Maturin, I hope you will think it an honourable mark instead of a misfortune.

We ran into Chaulieu road on the 14th instant and had the annoyance of grounding in a fog under the cross-fire of their batteries, when it became necessary to cut out a vessel to heave us off. We chose a ship moored under one of the batteries and proceeded with all dispatch in the boats. It was in taking her that your son received his wound: and she proved to be the Ligurian corvetto *Fanciulla* of 20 guns, with some French officers. We then proceeded to attack the transports, your son exerting himself all this time with the utmost gallantry, of which we took one, sank one, and drove five ashore. At this point the *Polychrest* unfortunately sank, having been hulled by upwards of 200 shot and having beaten five hours on the bank. We therefore proceeded in the prizes to the Downs, where the court-martial, sitting yesterday afternoon in the *Monarch*, most honourably acquitted the *Polychrest*'s officers for the loss of their ship, not without some very obliging remarks. You will find a fuller account of this little action in my Gazette letter, which appears in tomorrow's newspaper, and in which I have the pleasure of naming your son; and since I am this moment bound for the Admiralty, I shall have the pleasure of mentioning him to the First Lord.

My best compliments wait on Mrs Babbington, and I am, my dear Sir,

With great truth, sincerely yours,

Jno. Aubrey

PS. Dr Maturin desires his compliments, and wishes me to say, that the arm may very well be saved. But, I may add, he is the best hand in the Fleet with a saw, if it comes to that; which I am sure will be a comfort to you and Mrs Babbington.

'Killick,' he cried, folding and sealing it. 'That's for the post. Is the Doctor ready?'

'Ready and waiting these fourteen minutes,' said Stephen in a loud, sour voice. 'What a wretched tedious slow hand you are with a pen, upon my soul. Scratch-scratch, gasp-gasp. You might have written the Iliad in half the time, and a commentary upon it, too.'

'I am truly sorry, my dear fellow – I hate writing letters: it don't seem to come natural, somehow.'

'Non omnia possumus omnes,' said Stephen, 'but at least we can step into a boat at a stated time, can we not? Now here is your physic, and here is your bolus; and remember, a quart of porter with your breakfast, a quart at midday . . . '

They reached the deck, a scene of very great activity: swabs, squeegees, holystones, prayer-books, bears grinding in all directions; her twenty brass guns hot with polishing; the smell of paint; for the Fanciullas, late Polychrests, had heard that their prize was to be bought into the service, and they felt that a pretty ship would fetch a higher price than a slattern – a price that concerned them intimately, since three-eighths of it would be theirs.

'You will bear my recommendations in mind, Mr Parker,' said Jack, preparing to go down the side.

'Oh yes, sir,' cried Parker. 'All this is voluntary.' He looked at Jack with great earnestness; apart from any other reason, the lieutenant's entire future hung on what his captain would say of him at the Admiralty that evening.

Jack nodded, took the side-ropes with a careful grasp and lowered himself slowly into the boat: a ragged, good-natured, but very brief cheer as it pushed off, and the Fanciullas hurried back to their scouring, currying and polishing; the surveyor was due at nine o'clock.

'A little to the left – to the *larboard*,' said Stephen. 'Where was I? A quart of porter with your dinner: no wine, though you may take a glass or two of cold negus before retiring; no beef or mutton – fish, I say, chicken, a pair of rabbits; and, of course, Venerem omitte.'

'Eh? Oh, her. Yes. Certainly. Quite so. Very proper. Rowed of all – run her up.' The boat ground through the shingle. They ploughed across the beach, crossed the road into the dunes. 'Here?' asked Jack.

'Just past the gibbet – a little dell, a place I know, convenient in every way. Here we are.' They turned a dune and there was a dark-green post-chaise and its postillion eating his breakfast out of a cloth bag.

'I wish we could have worked the hearse,' muttered Jack.

'Stuff. Your own father would not recognize you in that bandage and in this dirty-yellow come-kiss-me-death exsanguine state: though indeed you look fitter for a hearse

387

than many a subject I have cut up. Come, come, there is not a moment to lose. Get in. Mind the step. Preserved Killick, take good care of the Captain: his physic, well shaken, twice a day; the bolus thrice. He may offer to forget his bolus, Killick.'

'He'll take his nice bolus, sir, or my name's not Preserved.'

'Clap to the door. Give way, now; give way all together. Step out! Lay aloft! Tally! And belay!'

They stood watching the dust of the post-chaise; and Bonden said, 'Oh, I do wish as we'd worked the hearse-and-coffin lark, sir: if they was to nab him now, it would break my heart.'

'How can you be so simple, Bonden? Do but think of a hearse and four cracking on regardless all the way up the Dover Road. It would be bound to excite comment. And you are to consider, that a recumbent posture is bad for the Captain at present.'

'Well, sir. But, a hearse is sure: no bum ever arrested a corpse, as I know of. Howsoever, it's too late now. Shall you pull back along of us, sir, or shall we come for you again?'

'I am obliged to you, Bonden, but I believe I shall walk into Dover and take a boat back from there.'

The post-chaise whirled through Kent, saying little. Ever since Chaulieu Jack had been haunted by the dread of tipstaffs. His return to the Downs, with no ship and a couple of prizes, had made a good deal of noise – very favourable noise, but still noise – and he had not set foot on shore until this morning, refusing invitations even from the Lord Warden himself. He was moderately well-to-do; the *Fanciulla* might bring him close on a thousand pounds and the transport a hundred or two; but would the Admiralty pay head-money according to the *Fanciulla*'s muster-roll when so many of her people had escaped on shore? And would his claim for gun-money for the destroyed transports be allowed? His new prize-agent had shaken his head, saying he could promise nothing but delay; he had advanced a fair sum, however, and Jack's bosom had the pleasant crinkle of Bank of England notes. Yet he was nowhere near being solvent, and passing through Canterbury, Rochester and Dartford he cowered deep in his corner. Stephen's assurances had little force with him: he knew he was Jack Aubrey, and it seemed inevitable that others too should see him as Jack Aubrey, debtor to Grobian, Slendrian and Co. for £11,012 6s 8d. With better reason it seemed to him inevitable that those interested should know that he must necessarily be summoned to the Admiralty, and take their steps accordingly. He did not get out when they changed horses; he passed most of the journey keeping out of sight and dozing – he was perpetually tired these days – and he was asleep when Killick roused him with a respectful but firm 'Time for your bolus, sir.'

Jack eyed it: this was perhaps the most nauseating dose that Stephen had ever yet compounded, so vile that health itself was scarcely worth the price of swallowing it. 'I can't get it down without a drink,' he said.

'Hold hard,' cried Killick, putting his head and shoulders out of the window. 'Post-boy, ahoy. Pull in at the next public, d'ye hear me, there? Now, sir,' – as the carriage came to a stop – I'll just step in and see if the coast is clear.' Killick had spent little of his life ashore, and most of that little in an amphibious village in the Essex mud; but he was fly; he knew a great deal about landsmen, most of whom were crimps, pickpockets, whores, or officials of the Sick and Hurt Office, and he could tell a gum a mile off. He saw them everywhere. He was the worst possible companion for a weak, reduced, anxious debtor that could well be found, the more so in that his absolute copper-bottomed certainty of being a right deep file, no sort or kind of a flat, carried a certain conviction. By way of a ruse de guerre he had somehow acquired a clergyman's hat, and this, combined with his earrings, his yard of pigtail, his watchet-blue jacket with brass buttons, his white trousers and low silver-buckled shoes, succeeded so well that several customers followed him from the tap-room to gaze while he leaned in and said to Jack, 'It's no go, sir. I seen some slang coves in the tap. You'll have to drink it in the shay. What'll it be, sir? Dog's nose? Flip? Come, sir,' he said, with the authority of the well over the sick in their care, or even out of it, 'What'll it be? For down it must go, or it will miss the tide.' Jack thought he would like a little sherry. 'Oh no, sir. No wine. The Doctor said, *No wine*. Porter is more the mark.' He brought back sherry – had been obliged to call for wine, it being a shay – and a mug of porter; drank the sherry, gave back such change as he saw fit, and watched the bolus go gasping, retching down, helped by the porter. 'That's thundering good physic,' he said. 'Drive on, mate.'

The next time he woke Jack it was from a deeper sleep. 'Eh? What's amiss?' cried Jack.

'We'm alongside, sir. We'm there.'

'Ay. Ay. So we are,' said Jack, gazing at the familiar doorway, the familiar courtyard, and suddenly coming to life. 'Very well. Killick, stand off and on, and when you see my signal, drive smartly in and pick me up again.'

He was sure of a fairly kind reception at the Admiralty: the cutting-out of the *Fanciulla* had been well spoken of in the service and very well spoken of in the press – it had come at a time when there was little to fill the papers and when people were feeling nervous and low in their spirits about the invasion. The *Polychrest* could not have chosen a better moment for sinking; nothing could have earned her more praise. The journalists were delighted with the fact that both ships were nominally sloops and that the *Fanciulla* carried almost twice as many men; they did not point out that eighty of the Fanciullas were peaceable Italian conscripts, and they were good enough to number the little guns borne by the transports in the general argument. One gentleman in the *Post*, particularly dear to Jack's heart, had spoken of 'this gallant, nay, amazing feat, carried out by a raw crew, far below its complement and consisting largely of landsmen and boys. It must show the French Emperor the fate that necessarily awaits his invasion flotilla; for if our lion-hearted tars handle it so roughly when it is skulking behind impenetrable sand-banks under the cross-fire of imposing batteries, what may they not do should it ever put to sea?' There was a good deal more about hearts of oak and honest tars, which had pleased the Fanciullas – the more literate hearts perpetually read it to the rest from the thumbed copies that circulated through the ship – and Jack knew that it would please the Admiralty too: in spite of their lordly station they were as sensitive to loud public praise as common mortals. He knew that this approval would grow after the publication of his official letter, with its grim list of casualties – seventeen dead and twenty-three wounded – for civilians liked to have sailors' blood to deplore, and the more a victory cost the more it was esteemed. If only little Parslow could have contrived to get himself knocked on the head it would have been perfect. He also knew something that the papers did not know, but that the Admiralty did: the *Fanciulla*'s captain had not had the time or the wit to destroy his secret papers, and for the moment the French private signals were private no longer – their codes were broken.

But as he sat there in the waiting-room thoughts of past misdeeds filled his uneasy mind; anything that Admiral Harte's malignance could do would have been done; and in fact he had not behaved irreproachably in the Downs. Stephen's warning had fallen on a raw conscience: and it could only have come through Dundas – Dundas, who was so well placed to know what they thought of his conduct here. If his logs and order-books were sent for, there would be some things he would find hard to explain away. Those strokes of profound cunning, those little stratagems that had seemed individually so impenetrable, now in the mass took on a sadly imbecile appearance. And how did the *Polychrest* come to be on the sand-bank in the first place? Explain that, you infernal lubber. So he was more than usually pleased when Lord Melville rose from behind his desk, shook him warmly by the hand, and cried, 'Captain Aubrey, I am delighted to see you. I said you would be sure to distinguish yourself, do you recall? I said so in this very room. And now you have done so, sir: the Board is content, pleased, eminently satisfied with its choice of you as commander of the *Polychrest*, and with your conduct at Chaulieu. I wish you could have done so with less cost: I am afraid you suffered terribly both in your ship's company and in your person. Tell me,' he said, looking at Jack's head, 'what is the nature of your wounds? Do they . . . do they hurt?'

'Why, no, my lord, I cannot say they do.'

'How were they inflicted?'

'Well, my lord, the one was something that dropped on my head – a piece of mortar-shell, I imagine; but luckily I was in the water at the time, so it did little damage, only tearing off a handsbreadth of scalp. The other was a sword-thrust I did not notice at the moment, but it seems it nicked some vessel, and most of my blood ran out before I was aware. Dr Maturin said he did not suppose there was more than three ounces left, and that mostly in my toes.'

'You are in good hands, I find.'

'Oh yes, my lord. He clapped a red-hot iron to the place, brought up the bleeding with a round turn, and set me up directly.'

'Pray what did he prescribe?' asked Lord Melville, who was intensely interested in his own body, and so in bodies in general.

'Soup, my lord. Enormous quantities of soup, and barley-water, and fish. Physic, of course – a green physic. And porter.'

'Porter? Is porter good for the blood? I shall try some today. Dr Maturin is a remarkable man.'

'He is indeed, my lord. Our butcher's bill would have been far, far longer but for his devotion. The men think the world of him: they have subscribed to present him with a gold-headed cane.'

'Good. Good. Very good. Now I have your official letter here, and I see that you mention all your officers with great approval, particularly Pullings, Babbington and Goodridge, the master. By the bye, I hope young Babbington's wound is not too grave? His father voted with us in the last two divisions, out of compliment to the service.'

'His arm was broken by a musket-shot as we boarded, my lord, but he tucked it into his jacket and fought on in a most desperate fashion; and afterwards, as soon as it was dressed, he came on deck again and behaved extremely well.'

'So you are truly satisfied with all your officers? With Mr Parker?'

'More than satisfied with them all, my lord.'

Lord Melville felt the hint of evasion, and said, 'Is he fit to command?' looking straight into Jack's eye.

'Yes, my lord.'

Turmoil of conscience: immediate loyalty and fellow-feeling overcoming good sense, responsibility, love of truth, love of the service, all other considerations.

'I am glad to hear it. Prince William has been pressing us for some time on the subject of his old shipmate.' He touched his bell, and a clerk came in with an envelope; at the sight of it Jack's heart began to beat wildly, his thin sparse blood to race about his body; yet his face turned extremely pale. 'This is an interesting occasion, Captain Aubrey: you must allow me the pleasure of being the first to congratulate you on your promotion. I have stretched a point, and you are made post with seniority from May 23rd.'

'Thank you, my lord, thank you very much indeed,'

cried Jack, flushing scarlet now. 'It gives me – it gives me very great pleasure to receive it from your hands – even greater pleasure from the handsome way in which it is given. I am very deeply obliged to you, my lord.'

'Weel, weel, there we are,' said Lord Melville, quite touched. 'Sit down, sit down, Captain Aubrey. You are looking far from well. What are your plans? I dare say your health requires you to take some months of sick-leave?'

'Oh no, my lord! Oh, very far from it. It was only a passing weakness – quite gone now – and Dr Maturin assures me that my particular constitution calls for sea air, nothing but sea air, as far from land as possible.'

'Well, you cannot have the *Fanciulla*, of course, since she will not be rated a post-ship – what the gods give with one hand they take away with the other. And seeing that you cannot have her, then in compliment to you, it seems but just that she should be given to your first lieutenant.'

'Thank you, my lord,' said Jack, with a face so dashed and glum that the other looked at him with surprise.

'However,' he said, 'I think we may hold out some hope of a frigate. The *Blackwater*: she is on the stocks, and all being well she may be launched in six months. That will give you time to recover your strength, to see your friends, and to watch over her fitting-out from the very beginning.'

'My lord,' cried Jack, 'I do not know how to thank you for your goodness to me, and indeed I am ashamed to ask for more, having had so much. But to be quite frank with you, my affairs were thrown into such a state of confusion by the breaking of my prize-agent, that something is quite necessary to me. A temporary command, or anything.'

'You were with that villain Jackson?' asked Lord Melville, looking at him from under his bushy eyebrows. 'So was poor Robert. He lost better than two thousand pound, a ca'hoopit sum. Weel, weel. So you would accept an acting-command, however short?'

'Most willingly, my lord. However short or however inconvenient. With both hands.'

'There may be some slight fleeting remote possibility – I do not commit myself, mind. The *Ethalion*'s commander is sick. There is Captain Hamond's *Lively*, and Lord Carlow's *Immortalité*; they both wish to attend parliament, I know. There are other service members too, but I have not the details in my head. I will desire Mr Bainton to look into it when he has a moment. There is no certainty in these matters, you understand. Where are you staying, since you will not be rejoining the *Fanciulla*?'

'At the Grapes, in the Savoy, my lord.'

'In the Savoy?' said Lord Melville, writing it down. 'Och aye. Just so. Now have we any more official business?'

'If I might be permitted an observation, my lord. The *Polychrest*'s people behaved exceedingly well; they could not have done better. But if they were left together in a body, there might be unpleasant consequences. It seems to me they would be far better drafted in small parties to ships of the line.'

'Is this a general impression, Captain Aubrey, or can you bring forward any names, however tentatively?'

'A general impression, my lord.'

'It shall be attended to. So much for business. If you are not bespoke, it would give Lady Melville and me great pleasure if you would dine with us on Sunday. Robert will be there, and Heneage.'

'Thank you, my lord; I shall be very happy indeed to wait upon Lady Melville.'

'Then let me wish you joy once more, and bid you a very good day.'

Joy. As he walked heavily, solemnly down the stairs, it mounted in him, a great calm flood-tide of joy. His momentary disappointment about the *Fanciulla* (he had counted on her – such a quick, stiff, sweet-handling, weatherly pet) entirely vanished by the third step – forgotten, overwhelmed – and by the landing he had realized his happiness almost to the full. He had been made post. He was a post-captain; and he would die an admiral at last.

He gazed with quiet benevolence at the hall-porter in his red waistcoat, smiling and bobbing at the foot of the stairs.

'Give you joy, sir,' said Tom. 'But oh dear me, sir, you're improperly dressed.'

'Thankee, Tom,' said Jack, rising a little way out of his beatitude. 'Eh?' He cast a quick glance down his front.

'No, no, sir,' said Tom, guiding him into the shelter of the hooded leather porter's chair and unfastening the epaulette on his left shoulder to transfer it to his right. 'There. You had your swab shipped like a mere commander. There: that's better. Why, bless you, I did that for Lord Viscount Nelson, when he come down them stairs, made post.'

'Did you indeed, Tom?' said Jack, intensely pleased. The thing was materially impossible, but it delighted him and he emitted a stream of gold – a moderate stream, but enough to make Tom very affable, affectionate, and brisk in hailing the chaise and bringing it into the court.

He woke slowly, in a state of wholly relaxed comfort, blinking with ease; he had gone to bed at nine, as soon as he had swallowed his bolus and his tankard of porter, and he had slept the clock round, a sleep full of diffused happiness and a longing to impart it – a longing too oppressed by languor to have any effect. Some exquisite dreams: the Magdalene in Queenie's picture saying, 'Why do not you tune your fiddle to orange-tawny, yellow, green and this blue, instead of those old common notes?' It was so obvious: he and Stephen set to their tuning, the 'cello brown and full crimson, and they dashed away in colour alone – such colour! But he could not seize it again; it

396

was fading into no more than words; it no longer made evident, luminous good sense. His bandaged head, mulling about dreams, how they sometimes made sense and how sometimes they did not, suddenly shot from the pillow, all the pink happiness wiped off it. His coat, which had slipped from the back of the chair, looked exactly like the coat of yesterday. But there, exactly squared and trimmed on the chimney-piece, stood that material sail-cloth envelope, that valuable envelope or wrapper. He sprang out of bed, fetched it, returned, poised it on his chest above the sheets, and went to sleep again.

Killick was moving about the room, making an unnecessary noise, kicking things not altogether by accident, cursing steadily. He was in a vile temper: he could be smelt from the pillow. Jack had given him a guinea to drink to his swab, and he had done so conscientiously, down to the last penny, being brought home on a shutter. 'Now sir,' he said, coughing artificially. 'Time for this ere bolus.' Jack slept on. 'It's no good coming it the Abraham, sir. I seen you twitch. Down it must go. Post-captain or no post-captain,' he added, possibly to himself, 'you'll post it down, my lord, or I'll know the reason why. And your nice porter, too.'

About twelve Jack got up, stared at the back of his head with his shaving-mirror and the looking-glass – it seemed to be healing well, but as Stephen had shaved the whole crown, leaving the long hair at the back, he had an oddly criminal look of alopecia or the common mange – dressed in civilian clothes, and walked out to see the light of day, for none ever reached the Grapes, at any time of the year. Before leaving he asked at the bar for an exact description of the Savoy, the boundaries of the sanctuary; he was particularly interested in these old survivals, he said.

'You may go as far as Falconer's Rents, and then cut through to Essex Street and go along as far as the fourth house from the corner, then right back to the City side of Cecil Street; but don't ever you cross it, nor don't ever you pass the posts in Sweating-house Lane, your honour, or all is up. You pee, up,' said the Grapes, who heard this piece about interesting old survivals a hundred times a year.

He walked up and down the streets of the Duchy, stepped into a coffee-house, and idly picked up the paper. His own Gazette letter leapt straight out of the open page at him, with its absurdly familiar phrasing, and his signature, quite transmogrified by print. On the same page there was a piece about the action: it said that our gallant tars were never happier than when they were fighting against odds of twelve and an eighth to one, which was news to Jack. How had the man arrived at that figure? Presumably by adding up all the guns and mortars in the batteries and all the vessels afloat in the bay and dividing by the *Polychrest*. But apart from this odd notion of happiness, the man obviously had sense, and he obviously knew something about the Navy: Captain Aubrey, said he, was known as an officer who was very careful of his men's lives – 'That's right,' said Jack – and he asked how it came about that the *Polychrest*, with all her notorious defects, was sent on a mission for which she was so entirely unsuited, when there were other vessels – naming them – lying idle in the Downs. A casualty-list of a third of the ship's company called for explanation: the *Sophie*, under the same commander, had taken the *Cacafuego* with a loss of no more than three men killed.

'Parse that, you old – ,' said Jack inwardly, to Admiral Harte.

Wandering out, he came to the back of the chapel: an organ was playing inside, a sweet, light-footed organ hunting a fugue through its charming complexities. He circled the railings to come to the door, but he had scarcely found it, opened it and settled himself in a pew before the whole elaborate structure collapsed in a dying wheeze and a thick boy crept from a hole under the loft and clashed down the aisle, whistling. It was a strong disappointment, the sudden breaking of a delightful tension, like being dismasted under full sail.

'What a disappointment, sir,' he said to the organist, who had emerged into the dim light. 'I had so hoped you would bring it to a close.'

'Alas, I have no wind,' said the organist, an elderly parson. 'That chuff lad has blown his hour, and no power on earth will keep him in. But I am glad you liked the organ – it is a Father Smith. A musician, sir?'

'Oh, the merest dilettante, sir; but I should be happy to blow for you, if you choose to go on. It would be a sad shame to leave Handel up in the air, for want of wind.'

'Should you, indeed? You are very good, sir. Let me show you the handle – you understand these things, I am sure. I must hurry to the loft, or these young people will be here. I have a marriage very soon.'

So Jack pumped and the music wound away and away, the separate strands following one another in baroque flights and twirls until at last they came together and ran to the final magnificence, astonishing the young couple who had come silently in, and who were sitting furtive, embarrassed, nervous and intensely clean in the shadows, with their landlady and a midwife; for they had not paid for music – only the simplest ceremony. They were absurdly young, pretty creatures, with little more than a gasp between them; and they had anticipated the rites by a hairsbreadth under full term. But the parson joined them very gravely, telling them that the purpose of their union was the getting of children, and that it was better to marry than to burn.

When it was over they came to life again, regained their colour, smiled, seemed very pleased with being married, amazed at themselves. Jack kissed the pink bride, shook the other child by the hand, wishing him all possible good fortune, and walked out into the air, smiling with pleasure. 'How happy they will be, poor young things – mutual support – no loneliness – no God-damned solitude – tell happiness and sorrows quite openly – sweet child, not the least trace of the shrew – trusting, confident – marriage a very capital thing, quite different from – by God, I am on the wrong side of Cecil Street.'

He turned to cross back, and as he turned he collided with a sharp youth who had darted after him through the traffic with a paper in his hand. 'Captain Aubrey, sir?' asked the youth. Escape to the other side was impossible. He shot a glance behind him – surely they could not hope to make the arrest with just this younker? 'They told me at the Grapes I should find you walking about the Duchy, your honour.' There was no menace in his voice, only a modest satisfaction. 'I should have hollered out, but for manners.'

'Who are you?' asked Jack, still poised to deal with him.

'Tom's nevvy, your honour, if you please, the duty-porter. Which I was to give you this,' – handing the letter.

'Thankee, boy,' said Jack, unpoising himself. 'You are a sharp lad. Tell your uncle I am obliged to him: and this is for your errand.'

A gap appeared in the traffic and he darted back into Lancaster, back to the Grapes, called for a glass of brandy, and sat down in greater flutter of spirits than he had ever known.

'No brandy, sir,' said Killick, cutting the pot-boy off at the head of the stairs and confiscating the little glass. 'No spirits of wine, the Doctor said. Swab-face, you jump to the bar and draw the Captain a quart of porter: and none of your guardo-moves with the froth.'

'Killick,' said Jack, 'God damn your eyes. Cut along to the kitchen and desire Mrs Broad to step up. Mrs Broad, what have you for dinner? I am amazing sharp-set.'

'No beef or mutton, Mr Killick says,' said Mrs Broad, 'but I have a nice loin of weal, and a nice piece of wenison, as plump as you could wish; a tender young doe, sir.'

'The wenison, if you please, Mrs Broad; and perhaps

you would send me up some pens and a pot of ink. Ah dear God,' he said to the empty room, 'a tender young doe.'

The Grapes
Saturday

My dear Stephen, he wrote

Oh wish me joy – I am made post! I never thought it would be, though he received me in the kindest way; but then suddenly he popped it out, signed, sealed and delivered, with seniority from May 23rd. It was like a prodigious unexpected vast great broadside from a three-decker, but of happiness: I could not get it all aboard directly, I was so taken aback, but by the time I had smuggled myself back to the Grapes I was swelling like a rose – so happy. How I wish you had been there! I celebrated with a quart of your vile porter and a bolus, and turned in at once, quite fagged out.

This morning I was very much better, however, and in the Savoy chapel I said the finest thing in my life. The parson was playing a Handel fugue, the organ-boy deserted his post, and I said 'it would be a pity to leave Handel up in the air, *for want of wind*,' and blew for him. It was the wittiest thing! I did not smoke it entirely all at once, however, only after I had been pumping for some time; and then I could hardly keep from laughing aloud. It may be that post captains are a very witty set of men, and that I am coming to it.

But then you very nearly lost your patient. Like a fool I strayed out of bounds: a little chap heaves in sight, sings out, 'Captain A!' and I say, 'This claps a stopper over all: Jack, you are brought by the lee.' But, however, it was orders to join the *Lively*.

She is only a temporary command, and of course as acting-captain I do not take my friends with me; but I do beg you, my dear Stephen, to sail with me as my guest. The Polychrests will be paid off – Parker is to have the *Fanciulla*, in compliment to me, which is as cruel a kindness as the world has seen since that fellow in the play, but I have looked after the *Polychrest*'s people – so there will be no difficulty of any kind. Pray come. I cannot tell you what pleasure it would give me. And to be even more egotistical in what I am afraid is a sadly egotistical letter, let me say, that having had your care, I should never trust my frame to a common sawbones again – my health is far from good, Stephen.

She is a crack frigate, with a good reputation, and I believe we shall have orders for the West Indies – think of the bonitoes, the bosun birds, the turtles, the palm-trees!

I am sending Killick with this – heartily glad I am to be shot of him too, such a pragmatical brute he has grown, with his physic-spoon – and he will see our dunnage round to the Nore. I am dining with Lord Melville on Sunday; Robert will run me down in his curricle, and I shall sneak aboard that night, without touching at an inn. Then, I swear to God, I shall not set foot ashore until I can do so without this wretched fear of being taken to a sponging-house and then to a debtor's prison.

Yours most affectionately

'Killick!' he shouted.

'Sir?'

'Are you sober?'

'As a judge, sir.'

'Then pack my shore-going trunk all but my uniform and number one scraper, take it down to the Nore, aboard the *Lively*, and give the first lieutenant this chit: we join her on Sunday night, temporary command. Then proceed to the Downs: give this letter to the Doctor and this to Mr Parker – it has good news for him, so give it into his hands yourself. If the Doctor chooses to join the *Lively*, take his sea-chest and anything else he wants, no matter what – a stuffed whale or a double-headed ape got with child by the bosun. My sea-chest, of course, and what we saved from the *Polychrest*. Repeat your instructions. Good. Here is what you will need for the journey, and here is five shillings for a decent glazed hat: you may skim the other into the Thames. I will not have you go aboard the *Lively* without a Christian covering to your head. And get yourself a new jacket, while you are about it. She is a crack frigate.'

She was a crack frigate, she was indeed; and seeing that a wheel came off Robert's curricle in a remote and midnight ditch Jack was obliged to go aboard her in the glare of the risen sun, passing through the crowded streets of Chatham – a considerable trial to him after an already trying night. But this was nothing to the trial of meeting Dr Maturin on the water; for Stephen had been inspired to put off from the shore at about the same time, though from a different place, and their courses converged some three furlongs from the frigate's side. Stephen's conveyance was one of the *Lively*'s cutters, which saluted Jack by tossing oars, and which fell under his wherry's lee, so that they pulled in close company, Stephen calling out pleasantly all the way. Jack caught a frightened glance from Killick, noticed the wooden composure of the midshipman and the cutter's crew, saw the grinning face of Matthew Paris, an old Polychrest, Stephen's servant, once a framework knitter and still no kind of seaman – no notion of common propriety in his myopic, friendly gaze. And as Stephen rose to wave and hoot, Jack saw that he was dressed from head to foot in a single tight dull-brown garment; it clung to him, and his pale, delighted face emerged from a woollen roll at the top, looking unnaturally large. His general appearance was something between that of an attenuated ape and a meagre heart; and he was carrying his narwhal horn. Captain Aubrey's back and shoulders went perfectly rigid: he adopted the features of one who is smiling; he even called out, 'Good morning to you – yes – no – ha, ha.' And as he recomposed them to a look of immovable gravity and unconcern, the thought darted through his mind, 'I believe the wicked old creature is drunk.'

Up and up the side – a long haul after the *Polychrest* – the wailing of the calls, the stamp and clash of the Marines presenting arms, and he was aboard.

Mathematical precision, rigorous exactitude fore and aft: he had rarely seen a more splendid array of blue and gold on the quarterdeck: even the midshipmen were in cocked hats and snowy breeches. The officers stood motionless, bare-headed. The naval lieutenants, the Marine lieutenants; then the master, the surgeon, the purser, and a couple of black coats, chaplain and schoolmaster, no doubt; and then the flock of young gentlemen, one of whom, three feet tall and five years of age, had his thumb in his mouth, a comfortably jarring note in all this perfection of gold lace, ivory deck, ebony seams.

Jack moved his hat to the quarterdeck, tilting it no more than an inch or so, because of his bandage. 'We got a rogue,' whispered the captain of the foretop. 'A proud son of wrath, mate,' replied the yeoman of the sheets. The first lieutenant stepped forward, a grave, severe, tall thin man. 'Welcome aboard, sir,' said he. 'My name is Simmons.'

'Thank you, Mr Simmons. Gentlemen, good morning to you. Mr Simmons, pray be so good as to name the officers.' Bows, civil mutterings. They were youngish men, except for the purser and the chaplain; a pleasant-looking set, but reserved and politely distant. 'Very well,' said Jack to the first lieutenant, 'we will muster the ship's company at six bells, if you please, and I shall read myself in then.' Leaning over the side he called, 'Dr Maturin, will you not come aboard?' Stephen was no more of a mariner now than he had been at the outset of his naval career, and it took him a long moment to clamber snorting up the frigate's side, propped by the agonized Killick, a moment that increased the attentive quarterdeck's sense of expectation. 'Mr Simmons,' said Jack, fixing him with a hard, savage eye, 'this is my friend Dr Maturin, who will be accompanying me. Dr Maturin, Mr Simmons, the first lieutenant of the *Lively*.'

'Your servant, sir,' said Stephen, making a leg: and this, thought Jack, was perhaps the most hideous action that a person in so subhuman a garment could perform. Hitherto the *Lively*'s quarterdeck had taken the apparition nobly, with a vexing, remote perfection; but now, as Mr Simmons bowed stiffly, saying, 'Servant, sir,' and as Stephen, by way of being amiable, said, 'What a splendid vessel, to be sure – vast spacious decks: one might almost imagine oneself aboard an Indiaman,' there was a wild shriek of childish laughter – a quickly smothered shriek, followed by a howl that vanished sobbing down the companion-ladder.

'Perhaps you would like to come into the cabin,' said Jack, taking Stephen's elbow in an iron grip. 'Your things will be brought aboard directly, never trouble yourself' – Stephen cast a look into the boat and seemed about to break away.

'I shall see to it myself at once, sir,' said the first lieutenant.

'Oh, Mr Simmons,' cried Stephen, 'pray bid them be very tender of my bees.'

'Certainly, sir,' said the first lieutenant, with a civil inclination of his head.

Jack got him into the after-cabin at last, a finely-proportioned, bare, spacious cabin with a great gun on either side and little else but the splendid curving breadth of the stern-windows: Hamond was clearly no Sybarite. Here he sat on a locker and gazed at Stephen's garment. It had been horrible at a distance; it was worse near to – far worse. 'Stephen,' he said, 'I say, Stephen . . . Come in!'

It was Paris, with a rectangular sail-cloth parcel. Stephen ran to him, took it from his arms with infinite precaution and set it on the table, pressing his ear to its side. 'Listen, Jack,' he said, smiling. 'Put your ear firmly to the top and listen while I tap.' The parcel gave a sudden momentary hum. 'Did you hear? That shows they are queen-right – that no harm has come to their queen. But we must open it at once; they must have air. There! A glass hive. Is it not ingenious, charming? I have always wanted to keep bees.'

'But how in God's name do you expect to keep bees in a man-of-war?' cried Jack. 'Where in God's name do you expect them to find flowers, at sea? How will they eat?'

'You can see their every motion,' said Stephen, close against the glass, entranced. 'Oh, as for their feeding, never fret your anxious mind; they will feed with us upon a saucer of sugar, at stated intervals. If the ingenious Monsieur Huber can keep bees, and he blind, the poor man, surely we can manage in a great spacious xebec?'

'This is a frigate.'

'Let us never split hairs, for all love. There is the queen! Come, look at the queen!'

'How many of those reptiles might there be?' asked Jack, holding pretty much aloof.

'Oh, sixty thousand or so, I dare say,' said Stephen carelessly. 'And when it comes on to blow, we will ship gimbals for the hive. This will preserve them from undue lateral motion.'

'You think of almost everything,' said Jack. 'Well, I will wear the bees, like Damon and Pythagoras – ho, a mere sixty thousand bees in the cabin don't signify, much. But I tell you what it is, Stephen: you don't always think of quite everything.'

'You refer to the queen's being a virgin?' said Stephen.

'Not really. No. What I really meant was, that this is a crack frigate.'

'I am delighted to hear it. There she goes – she lays an egg! You need not fear for her virginity, Jack.'

'And in this frigate they are very particular. Did not

you remark the show of uniforms as you came aboard –
an admiral's inspection – a royal review.'

'No. I cannot truthfully say that I did. Tell me, brother,
is there some uneasiness on your mind?'

'Stephen, will you for the love of God take off that
thing?'

'My wool garment? You have noticed it, have you? I
had forgot, or I should have pointed it out. Have you ever
seen anything so deeply rational? See, I can withdraw my
head entirely: the same applies to the feet and the hands.
Warm, yet uncumbering; light; and above all healthy – no
constriction anywhere! Paris, who was once a framework
knitter, made it to my design; he is working on one for
you at present.'

'Stephen, you would favour me deeply by taking it right
off. It is unphilosophical of me, I know, but this is only an
acting-command, and I cannot afford to be laughed at.'

'But you have often told me that it does not matter
what one wears at sea. You yourself appear in nankeen
trousers, a thing that I should never, never countenance.
And this' – plucking at his bosom with a disappointed air
– 'partakes of the nature both of the Guernsey frock and
of the free and easy pantaloon.'

The *Lively* had remained in commission throughout the
peace; her people had been together many years, with few
changes among the officers, and they had their own way
of doing things. All ships were to some degree separate
kingdoms, with different customs and a different atmosphere: this was particularly true of those that were on
detached service or much by themselves, far from their
admirals and the rest of the fleet, and the *Lively* had
been in the East Indies for years on end – it was on her
return during the first days of the renewed war that she
had had her luck, two French Indiamen in the same day
off Finisterre. When she was paid off, Captain Hamond

had no difficulty in manning her again, for most of his people re-entered, and he even had the luxury of turning volunteers away. Jack had met him once or twice – a quiet, thoughtful, unhumorous, unimaginative man in his forties, prematurely grey, devoted to hydrography and the physics of sailing, somewhat old for a frigate-captain – and as he had met him in the company of Lord Cochrane, he had seemed rather to want colour, in comparison with that ebullient nobleman. His first impression of the *Lively* did not alter during the ceremonies of mustering and quarters: she was obviously a most competent ship with a highly efficient crew of right man-of-war's men; probably a happy ship in her quiet way, judging from the men's demeanour and those countless very small signs that a searching, professional eye could see – happy, yet taut; a great distance between officers and men. But as he and Stephen were sitting in the dining-cabin, waiting for their supper, he wondered how she had come by her reputation as a crack frigate. It was certainly not from her appearance, for although everything aboard was unexceptionally ship-shape and man-of-war fashion, there was no extraordinary show of perfection, indeed nothing extraordinary at all, apart from her huge yards and her white manilla cordage: her hull and portlids were painted dull grey, with an ochre streak for the gun-tier, her thirty-eight guns were chocolate-coloured, and the only obvious piece of brass was her bell, which shone like burnished gold. Nor was it from her fighting qualities, since from no fault of her own she had seen no action with anything approaching a match for her long eighteen-pounders. Perhaps it was from her remarkable state of readiness. She was permanently cleared for action, or very nearly so: when the drum beat for quarters she might almost have gone straight into battle, apart from a few bulkheads and a minimum of furniture; the two quarterdeck goats walked straight down the ladder by themselves, the hen-coops vanished on an ingenious slide, and the guns in his own cabins were cast loose, something he had never seen before in an exercise. She had a Spartan air: but that in itself was not enough to explain anything, although it did not arise from poverty – the *Lively* was well-to-do; her captain had recently bought himself a seat in Parliament, her officers were men of private means even before their fortunate stroke, and Hamond insisted upon a handsome allowance from the parents of his midshipmen.

'Stephen,' he said, 'how are your bees?'

'They are very well, I thank you; they show great activity, even enthusiasm. But,' he added, with a slight hesitation, 'I seem to detect a certain reluctance to return to their hive.'

'Do you mean to say you let them out?' cried Jack. 'Do you mean that there are sixty thousand bees howling for blood in the cabin?'

'No, no. Oh no. Not above half that number; perhaps even less. And if you do not provoke them, I am persuaded you may go to and fro without the least concern; they are not froward bees. They will have gone home by morning, sure; I shall creep in during the middle watch and close their little wicket. But perhaps it might be as well, were we to sit together in this room tonight, just to let them get used to their surroundings. A certain initial agitation is understandable after all, and should not be discountenanced.'

Jack was not a bee, however, and his initial agitation was something else again. It was clear to him that the *Lively* was a closed, self-sufficing community, an entity to which he was an outsider. He had served under acting-captains himself, and he knew that they could be regarded as intruders – that they could excite resentment if they took too much upon themselves. They had great powers, certainly, but they were wise not to use them. Yet on the other hand, he might have to fight this ship; the ultimate responsibility, the loss of reputation or its gain was his, and although he was here only for the time, and although he was not the real owner, he was not going to play King Log. He must move with care, and at the same time with decision . . . a difficult passage. An awkward first lieutenant could prove the very devil. By the grace of God he had a little money in hand: he would be able to entertain them decently for the present, although he could not keep Hamond's table, with half a dozen to dinner every day. He must hope for another advance from his agent soon, but for the moment he would not look poverty-stricken. There was a Latin tag about poverty and ridicule – elusive: no hand at Latin. He must not be ridiculous; no captain could afford to be ridiculous. 'Stephen, oh my dear fellow,' he said to the tell-tale compass over his cot (for he was in his sleeping-cabin), 'what induced you to put on that vile thing? What a singular genius you have for hiding your talent under a bushel – a bushel that no one could possibly have foreseen.'

In the gun-room, however, another sound of things was heard. 'No, gentlemen,' said Mr Floris, the surgeon. 'I do assure you he is a great man. I have read his book until it is dog-eared – a most luminous exposition, full of pregnant reflections, a mine of nervous expressions. When the Physician of the Fleet came to inspect us, he asked me whether I had read it, and I was happy to show him my copy, interleaved and annotated, and to tell him that I required my assistants to get whole passages by heart. I tell you, I long to be introduced to him. I long for his opinion on poor Wallace.'

The gun-room was impressed; it had a deep respect for learning, and but for that unfortunate remark about East Indiamen it would have been ready to accept the wool garment as a philosopher's vagary, a knitted Diogenes' tub.

'Yet if he has been in the service,' said Mr Simmons, 'what are we to make of his remark about the East Indiaman? It was very like a direct affront, and it was delivered with a strangely knowing leer.'

Mr Floris looked at his plate, but found no justification

410

there. The chaplain coughed, and said that perhaps they should not judge by appearances – perhaps the gentleman had had a momentary absence – perhaps he meant that the Indiaman was the very type of sea-going luxury, which indeed it was; a well-appointed Indiaman was to be preferred, in point of comfort, to a first-rate.

'That makes it worse,' observed the third lieutenant, an ascetic young man so tall and thin that it was difficult to see where he could sleep at length, if not in the cable-tier.

'Well, for my part,' said the senior Marine, the caterer to the mess, 'I shall drink to his health and eternal happiness in a glass of this excellent Margaux, as sound as a nut, whatever the parson may say. Such an example of courage as coming aboard like Badger-Bag, with a narwhal-horn in one hand and a green umbrella in the other, has never come under my observation. Bless him.'

The gun-room blessed him, but without much conviction, except for Mr Floris; and they went on to discuss the health of Cassandra, the last of the *Lively*'s gibbons, the last of that numerous menagerie which she had borne away from Java and the remoter islands of the eastern seas. They did not discuss their acting-captain at all: he had come with the reputation of a seaman and a fighter; of a rake and of a protégé of Lord Melville. Captain Hamond was a supporter of Lord St Vincent; and he had gone to Parliament to vote with St Vincent's friends; and Lord St Vincent, who hated Pitt and his administration, was working to impeach Lord Melville for malversation of the secret funds and to get him out of the Admiralty. The *Lively*'s officers all shared their captain's views – strong Whigs to a man.

Breakfast was something of a disappointment. Captain Hamond had always drunk cocoa, originally to encourage the crew to do the same and then because he liked it, whereas Jack and Stephen were neither of them human until the first pot of coffee was down, hot and strong.

'Killick,' said Jack, 'toss this hog's wash over the side and bring coffee at once.'

'Ax pardon, sir,' said Killick, seriously alarmed. 'I forgot the beans, and the cook's got none.'

'Then jump to the purser's steward, the gun-room cook, the sick-bay, anywhere, and get some, or your name will not be Preserved much longer, I can tell you. Cut along. God-damned lubber, to forget our coffee,' he said to Stephen, with warm indignation.

'A little pause will make it all the more welcome when it comes, sure,' said Stephen, and to divert his friend's mind he took up a bee and said, 'Be so good as to watch my honey-bee.' He put it down on the edge of a saucer in which he had made a syrup of cocoa and sugar; the bee tasted to the syrup, pumped a reasonable quantity, took to the air, hovered before the saucer, and returned to the hive. 'Now, sir,' said Stephen, noting the time on his watch, 'now you will behold a prodigy.'

In twenty-five seconds two bees appeared, questing over the saucer with a particular high shrill buzz. They pitched, pumped syrup, and went home. After the same interval four bees came, then sixteen, then two hundred and fifty-six; but when four minutes had elapsed this simple progression was obscured by earlier bees who knew the way and who no longer had to fix either their hive or the syrup.

'Now,' cried Stephen, from out of the cloud, 'have you any doubt of their power to communicate a locus? How do they do it? What is their signal? Is it a compass-bearing? Jack, do not offer to molest that bee, I beg. For shame. It is only resting.'

'Beg pardon, sir, but there ain't a drop of coffee in the barky. Oh God almighty,' said Killick.

'Stephen, I am going to take a turn,' said Jack, withdrawing from the table in a sly undulatory motion and darting through the door with hunched shoulders.

'Why they call this a crack frigate,' he said, swilling

412

down a glass of water in his sleeping-cabin, 'I cannot for the life of me imagine: not a drop of coffee among two hundred and sixty men.'

The reason became apparent to him some two hours later, when the port-admiral signalled *Lively proceed to sea*. 'Acknowledge,' said Jack, this news being brought to him. 'Mr Simmons, we will unmoor, if you please.'

The unmooring was a pleasure to watch. At the pipe of All hands to unmoor ship the men flowed rather than ran to their stations; there was no stampede along the gangways, no stream of men blundering into one another in their haste to escape the rope's end; as far as he could see there was no starting, and there was certainly very little noise. The capstan-bars were pinned and swifted, the Marines and afterguard manned them, the piercing fife struck up Drops of Brandy, and one cable came in while the other went out. A midshipman from the fore-castle reported the best bower catted; the first lieutenant relayed this to Jack, who said, 'Carry on, Mr Simmons.'

Now the *Lively* was at single anchor, and as the cap-stan turned again so she crept across the sea until she was immediately over it. 'Up and down, sir,' called the bosun.

'Up and down, sir,' said the first lieutenant to Jack.

'Carry on, Mr Simmons,' said Jack. This was the crucial moment: the crew had both to clap on fresh nippers – the bands that attached the great cable to the messenger, the rope that actually turned on the capstan – for a firmer hold, and to loose the topsails so as to sail the anchor out of the ground. In even the best-managed ships there was a good deal of hullabaloo at such a time, and in this case, with the tide running across the wind – an awkward cast in which split-second timing was called for – he expected a rapid volley, a broadside of orders.

Mr Simmons advanced to the break of the quarterdeck, glancing quickly up and down, said, 'Thick and dry for weighing,' and then, before the rush of feet had died away,

413

'Make sail.' No more. Instantly the shrouds were dark with men racing aloft. Her topsails, her deep, very well cut topsails were let fall in silence, sheeted home, the yards hoisted up, and the *Lively*, surging forward, weighed her anchor without a word. But this was not all: even before the small bower was fished, the jib, forestaysail and foretopgallant had appeared and the frigate was moving faster and faster through the water, heading almost straight for the Nore light. All this without a word, without a cry except for an unearthly hooting of Woe, woe, woe high in the upper rigging. Jack had never seen anything like it. In his astonishment he looked up at the main topgallant yard, and there he saw a small form hanging by one arm; it swung itself forward on the roll of the ship and fell in a sickening curve towards the maintopmaststay. Almost unbelievably it caught this rope, and then, altogether unbelievably, shot up from one piece of rigging to another to the fore-royal and sat there.

'That is Cassandra, sir,' said Mr Simmons, seeing Jack's face of horror. 'A sort of Java ape.'

'God help us,' said Jack, recovering himself. 'I thought it was a ship's boy gone mad. I have never seen anything like it – this manoeuvre, I mean. Do your people usually make sail according to their own notions?'

'Yes, sir,' said the first lieutenant, in civil triumph.

'Well. Very well. The *Lively* has her own way of doing things, I see. I have never seen . . . ' The frigate was heeling to the breeze, marvellously alive, and he stepped to the taffrail, where Stephen, dressed in a sad-coloured coat and drab small-clothes, stood conversing with Mr Randall, bending to hear his tiny pipe. Jack looked at the dark water slipping fast by her side, curving deep under the chains; she was making seven knots already, seven and a half. He looked at her wake, fixing an anchored seventy-four and a church tower – hardly a trace of leeway. He leant over the larboard quarter, and there, one point on the larboard bow, was the Nore light. The wind was two points free on the starboard tack, and any ship he had sailed in would be aground in the next five minutes.

'You are happy about your course, Mr Simmons?' he said.

'Quite happy, sir,' said the first lieutenant.

Simmons knew his ship, that was obvious: he most certainly knew her capabilities. Jack repeated this – he was convinced of it; it must be so. But the next five minutes were as unhappy as any he had ever spent – this beautiful, beautiful ship a mere hulk, dismasted, bilged . . . During the moments when the Lively was racing through the turbid shoaling water at the edge of the bank and where a trifle of leeway would wreck her hopelessly, he did not breathe at all. Then the bank was astern.

With as much impassivity as he could summon he drew in the good sparkling air and desired Mr Simmons to set course for the Downs, where he was to pick up some supernumeraries and, if Bonden had not vanished, his own coxswain, seeing that Captain Hamond had taken his with him to London. He set to pacing the windward side of the quarterdeck, keenly watching the behaviour of the Lively and her crew.

No wonder they called her a crack frigate: her sailing qualities were quite out of the ordinary, and the smooth quiet discipline of her people was beyond anything he had seen: her speed in getting under way and making sail had something unnatural about it, as eerie as the cry of the gibbon in the rigging.

The familiar low, grey, muddy shores glided by; the sea was a hard metallic grey, the horizon in the offing ruled sharply from the mottled sky, and the frigate ran on, the wind now one point free, as though a precise, undeviating rail were guiding her. Merchantmen were coming in for the London river, four sail of Guineamen, and a brig of war for Chatham, apart from the usual hovellers and

415

peterboats: how flabby and loose they looked, by comparison.

The fact of the matter was that Captain Hamond, a gentleman of a scientific turn of mind, had chosen his officers with great care and he had spent years training his crew; even the waisters could hand, reef and steer; and for the first years he had raced them mast against mast in furling and loosing sail, putting them through every manoeuvre and combination of manoeuvres until they reached equality at a speed that could not be improved upon. And today, jealous for the honour of their ship, they had excelled themselves; they knew it very well, and as they passed near their acting-captain they glanced at him with discreet complacency, as who should say, 'We showed you a thing or two, cock; we made you stretch your eyes.'

What a ship to fight, he reflected: if he met one of the big French frigates, he could make rings round her, beautifully built though they were. Yes. But what of the Livelies themselves? They were seamen, to be sure, quite remarkable seamen; but were they not a little elderly, on the whole, oddly quiet? Even the ship's boys were stout hairy fellows, rather heavy for lying out on the royal yards; and most of them talked gruff. Then there were a good many brown and yellow men aboard. Low Bum, who was now at the wheel, steering wonderfully small, had had no need to grow a pigtail when he entered at Macao; nor had John Satisfaction, Horatio Jelly-Belly or half a dozen of his shipmates. Were they fighting men? The Livelies had had none of the incessant cutting-out expeditions that made danger an everyday affair and so disarmed it: circumstances had been entirely different – he should have read her log to see exactly what she had done. His eye fell on one of the quarterdeck carronades. It was painted brown, and some of the dull, scrubbed paint overlapped the touch-hole. It had not been fired for a long while. Certainly he should look at the log to see how the Livelies spent their day.

416

On the leeward side Mr Randall told Stephen that his mother was dead, and that they had a tortoise at home; he hoped the tortoise did not miss him. Was it really true that the Chinese never ate bread and butter? Never, at any time whatsoever? He and old Smith messed with the gunner, and Mrs Armstrong was very kind to them. Plucking at Stephen's hand to draw his attention, he said in his clear pipe, 'Do you think the new captain will flog George Rogers, sir?'

'I cannot tell, my dear. I hope not, I am sure.'

'Oh, I hope he does,' cried the child, with a skip. 'I have never seen a man flogged. Have you ever seen a man flogged, sir?'

'Yes,' said Stephen.

'Was there a great deal of blood, sir?'

'Indeed there was,' said Stephen. 'Several buckets full.'

Mr Randall skipped again, and asked whether it would be long to six bells. 'George Rogers was in a horrid passion, sir,' he added. 'He called Joe Brown a Dutch galliot-built bugger, and damned his eyes twice: I heard him. Should you like to hear me recite the points of the compass without a pause, sir? There is my Papa beckoning. Goodbye, sir.'

'Sir,' said the first lieutenant, stepping across to Jack, 'I must beg your pardon, but there are two things I forgot to mention. Captain Hamond indulged the young gentlemen with the use of his fore-cabin in the mornings, for their lessons with the schoolmaster. Should you wish to continue the custom?'

'Certainly, Mr Simmons. A capital notion.'

'Thank you, sir. And the other thing was that we usually punish on Mondays in the *Lively*.'

'On Mondays? How curious.'

'Yes, sir. Captain Hamond thought it was well to let defaulters have Sunday for quiet reflection.'

'Well, well. Let it be so, then. I had meant to ask you what the ship's general policy is, with regard to punishment. I do not like to make any sudden changes, but I must warn you, I am no great friend to the cat.'

Simmons smiled. 'Nor is Captain Hamond, sir. Our usual punishment is pumping: we open a sea-cock, let clean water in to mix with what is in the bilges, and pump it out again – it keeps the ship sweet. We rarely flog. In the Indian Ocean we were nearly two years without bringing the cat out of its bag; and since then, not above once in two or three months. But I am afraid that today you may think it necessary: an unpleasant case.'

'Not article thirty-nine?'

'No, sir. Theft.'

Theft it was said to be. Authority, speaking hoarse and official through the mouth of the master-at-arms, said it was theft, riotous conduct, and resisting arrest. With the ship's company assembled aft, the Marines drawn up, and all the officers present, he led his victim before the captain and said, 'Did steal one ape's head . . . '

'It's all lies,' cried George Rogers, still clearly in a horrid passion.

' . . . the property of Evan Evans, quarter-gunner . . . '

'It's all lies.'

'And being desired to step aft . . . '

'It's all lies, lies!' cried Rogers.

'Silence, there,' said Jack. 'You shall have your turn, Rogers. Carry on, Brown.'

'And on being told I had information that led me to believe he was in possession of this head, and on being desired, civil, to step aft and verify the statements of Evan Evans, quarter-gunner, larboard watch,' said the master-at-arms, swivelling his eyes alone in the direction of Rogers, 'did call out expressions of contempt: was in liquor; and endeavoured to conceal hisself in the sail-room.'

'All lies.'

'And when roused out, did offer violence to Button, Menhasset and Mutton, able seamen.'

'It's all lies,' cried Rogers, beside himself with indignation. 'All lies.'

'Well, what did happen?' said Jack. 'Tell me in your own words.'

'I will, your honour,' said Rogers, glaring round, pale and trembling with fury. 'In my own Gospel words. Master-at-arms comes for'ard – which I was taking a caulk, my watch below – tips me a shove on the arse, begging your pardon, and says, "Get your skates on, George; you're fucked." And I up and says, "I don't care for you, Joe Brown, nor for that fucking little cunt Evans." No offence, your honour; but that's the Gospel truth, to show your honour the lies he tells, with his "verify the statements". It's all lies.'

There seemed to be a more familiar ring about this version; but it was followed by a rambling account of who pushed whom, in what part of the ship, with contradictory evidence from Button, Menhasset and Mutton, and remarks on character; and it seemed that the main issue might be lost in a discussion of who lent someone two dollars off of Banda, and was never repaid, in grog, tobacco, or any other form.

'What about this ape's head?' said Jack.

'Here, sir,' said the master-at-arms, producing a hairy thing from his bosom.

'You say it is yours, Evans; and you say it is yours, Rogers? Your own property?'

'She's my Andrew Masher, your honour,' said Evans.

'He's my poor old Ajax, sir, been in my ditty-bag ever since he took sick off the Cape.'

'How can you identify it, Evans?'

'Anan, sir?'

'How do you know it is your Andrew Masher?'

'By her loving expressions, sir, your honour. By her expressions. Griffi Jones, stuffed animals, Dover, is giving me a guinea for her tomorning, yis, yis.'

'What have you to say, Rogers?'

'It's all lies, sir!' cried Rogers. 'He's my Ajax. Which I fed him from Kampong – shared my grog, ate biscuit like a Christian.'

'Any distinguishing marks?'

'Why, the cut of his jib, sir: I know him anywheres, though shrivelled.'

Jack studied the ape's face, which was set in an expression of deep, melancholy contempt. Who was telling the truth? Both thought they were, no doubt. There had been two ape's heads in the ship, and now there was only one. Though how anyone could pretend to recognize the features of this wizened red coconut heavy in his hand he could not tell. 'Andrew Masher was a female, I take it, and Ajax a male?' he said.

'That's right, your honour.'

'Beg Dr Maturin to come on deck, if he is not engaged,' said Jack. 'Dr Maturin, is it possible to tell the sex of an ape by its teeth, or that kind of thing?'

'It depends on the ape,' said Stephen, looking eagerly at the object in Jack's hands. 'This, for example,' he said, taking it and turning it about, 'is an excellent specimen of the male simia satyrus, Buffon's wild man of the woods: see the lateral expansion of the cheeks, mentioned by Hunter, and the remains of that particular throat-sac, so characteristic of the male.'

'Well, there you are,' said Jack. 'Ajax it is. Thank you very much, Doctor. The charge of theft is dismissed. But you must not knock people about, Rogers. Has anyone something to say in his favour?'

The second lieutenant stepped forward, said that Rogers was in his division – attentive to his duty, generally sober, a good character, but apt to fly into a passion. Jack told Rogers that he must not fly into a passion; that flying into a passion was a very bad thing – it would certainly lead him to the gallows, if indulged in. He was to command his temper, and do without grog for the next week. The head was confiscated temporarily, for further examination

– indeed, it had already vanished into the cabin, leaving Rogers looking somewhat blank. 'I dare say you will get it back in time,' said Jack, with more conviction than he felt. The other defaulters, all guilty of uncomplicated drunkenness, were all dealt with in the same way; the grating was unrigged; the cat, still in its bag, returned to its resting-place; and shortly after the hands were piped to dinner. Jack invited the first lieutenant, the officer and midshipman of the watch, and the chaplain to dine with him, and resumed his pacing.

His thoughts ran on gunnery. There were ships, and plenty of them, that hardly ever exercised the great guns, hardly fired them except in action or for saluting, and if this was the case with the *Lively*, he would change it. Even at close quarters it was as well to hit where it hurt most; and in a typical frigate-action accuracy and speed were everything. Yet this was not the *Sophie*, with her pop-guns: a single broadside from the *Lively* would burn well over a hundredweight of powder – a consideration. Dear *Sophie*, how she blazed away . . .

He identified the music that was running so insistently through his head. It was the piece of Hummel's that he and Stephen had played so often at Melbury Lodge, the adagio. And almost at once he had the clearest visual image of Sophia standing tall and willowy by the piano, looking confused, hanging her head.

He turned short in his stride and brought his mind to bear strongly on the question in hand. But it was no use; the music wove in among his calculations of powder and shot; he grew more agitated and unhappy, and clapping his hands together with a sudden report he said to himself, 'I shall run through the log and see what their practice really is – tell Killick to uncork the claret – he did not forget *that*, at all events.'

He went below, noticed the smell of midshipmen in the fore-cabin, walked through into the after-cabin, and found himself in total darkness.

'Close the door,' cried Stephen, swarming past him and clapping it to.

'What's amiss?' asked Jack, whose mind had moved so deep into naval life that he had forgotten the bees, as he might have forgotten even a vivid nightmare.

'They are remarkably adaptable – perhaps the most adaptable of all social insects,' said Stephen, from another part of the cabin. 'We find them from Norway to the burning wastes of the Sahara; but they have not grown quite used to their surroundings yet.'

'Oh God,' said Jack, scrabbling for the handle. 'Are they all out?'

'Not all,' said Stephen. 'And learning from Killick that you expected guests, I conceived you might prefer them away. There is so much ignorant prejudice against bees in a dining-room.' Something was crawling on Jack's neck; the door had completely vanished; he began to sweat heavily. 'So I thought to create an artificial night, when, in the course of nature, they return to their hive. I also made three fires for the sake of the smoke: these did not have the desired effect, however. It may be that the darkness is too complete. Let us compromise with a twilight – dark, but not too dark.' He raised a corner of sailcloth, and a beam of sun showed an incalculable number of bees on every vertical surface and on most of those that were flat; bees flying in a jerky, meaningless fashion from point to point; fifty or so sitting on his coat and breeches. 'There,' said Stephen, 'that is far, far better is it not? Urge them to mount on your finger, Jack, and carry them back to their hive. Gently, gently, and on no account exhibit, or even feel, the least uneasiness: fear is wholly fatal, as I dare say you know.'

Jack had the door-handle; he opened it a crack and glided swiftly through. 'Killick!' he shouted, beating at his clothes.

'Sir?'

'Go and help the Doctor. Bear a hand, now.'

'I dursn't,' said Killick.

'You don't mean to tell me you are afraid, a man-of-war's man?'

'Yes I am, sir,' said Killick.

'Well, clear the fore-cabin and lay the cloth there. And uncork a dozen of claret.' He plunged into his sleeping-cabin and tore off his stock – there was something creeping beneath it. 'What is there for dinner?' he called.

'Wenison, sir. I found a prime saddle at Chators', the same as the ladies sent us from Mapes.'

'Gentlemen,' said Jack, as the last stroke of six bells in the afternoon watch was struck and his guests arrived, 'you are very welcome. I am afraid we may have to sit a little close, but for the moment my friend is engaged in a philosophical experiment aft. Killick, tell the Doctor we hope to see him when he is at leisure. Go on,' he muttered, clenching his fist secretly and vibrating his head at the steward. 'Go on, I say: you can call through the door.'

Dinner ran very well. The *Lively* might be Spartan in her appearance and cabin furniture, but Jack had inherited an excellent cook, accustomed to sea-borne appetites, and his guests were well-bred men, easy within the strict limits of naval etiquette – even the midshipman of the watch, though mute, was mute gracefully. But the sense of rank, of deference to the captain, was very strong, and as Stephen's mind was clearly far away, Jack was pleased to find in the chaplain a lively, conversible man, with little notion of the solemnities of dining in the cabin. Mr Lydgate, the Perpetual Curate of Wool, was a cousin of Captain Hamond's, and he was taking this voyage for the sake of his health, leaving his living not for a new career but for a temporary change of air and scenery. The air of Lisbon and Madeira was particularly recommended; that of Bermuda even more so; and this, he understood, was their destination?

'It may well be,' said Jack. 'I hope so, indeed; but with the changing face of the war there is no certainty about these things. I have known captains lay in stores for the Cape, only to find themselves ordered to the Baltic at the last moment. Everything must depend on the good of the service,' he added piously; and then feeling that remarks of this kind might have a damping effect, he cried, 'Mr Dashwood, the wine stands by you: the good of the service requires that it should circulate. Mr Simmons, pray tell me about the ape that so astonished me this morning. The living ape.'

'Cassandra, sir? She is one of half a dozen that came aboard at Tungoo; the surgeon says she is a Tenasserim gibbon. All hands are very fond of her, but we are afraid she is pining. We rigged her out in a flannel jacket when we came into the chops of the Channel, but she will not wear it; and she will not eat English food.'

'Do you hear, Stephen?' said Jack. 'There is a gibbon aboard, that is not well.'

'Yes, yes,' said Stephen, returning to the present. 'I had the pleasure of meeting her this morning, walking hand in hand with the very young gentleman: it was impossible to tell which was supporting which. A fetching, attractive creature, in spite of its deplorable state. I look forward eagerly to dissecting it. Monsieur de Buffon hints that the naked callosities on the buttocks of the hylobates may conceal scent glands, but he does not go so far as to assert it.'

A chill fell on the conversation, and after a slight pause Jack said, 'I think, my dear fellow, that the ship's company would be infinitely more obliged to you, was you to cure it, than for putting Monsieur de Buffon right – for putting Cassandra in order, rather than a Frenchman, eh, eh?'

'Yet it is the ship's company that is killing her. That ape is a confirmed alcoholic; and from what little I know of your foremast jack, no earthly consideration will prevent him from giving rum to anything he loves. Our monk-seal in the Mediterranean, for example: it drowned in a state of besotted inebriation, with a fixed smile upon its face; and when fished up and dissected, its kidneys and liver were found to be ruined, very much like those of Mr Blanckley of the Carcass bomb-ketch, an unpromoted master's mate of sixty-three whom I had the pleasure of opening at Port Mahon, a gentleman who had not been sober for five and thirty years. I met this gibbon a little after the serving out of the grog – it had plunged from an upper pinnacle at the first notes of Nancy Dawson – and the animal was hopelessly fuddled. It was conscious of its state, endeavoured to conceal it, and put its black hand in mine with an embarrassed air. Who is that very young gentleman, by the way?'

He was Josiah Randall, they told him, the son of the second lieutenant, who had come home to find his wife dead, and this child unprovided for – no near family at all. 'So he brought him aboard,' said Mr Dashwood, 'and the Captain rated him bosun's servant.'

'How very, very painful,' said Jack. 'I hope we have some action soon; there is nothing like it for changing the current of a man's mind. A French frigate, or a Spaniard, if they come in; there is nothing like your Spaniard for dogged fighting.'

'I dare say you have seen a great deal of action, sir?' said the parson, nodding towards Jack's bandage.

'Not more than most, sir,' said Jack. 'Many officers have been far more fortunate.'

'Pray what would you consider a reasonable number of actions?' asked the parson. 'I was astonished, on joining the ship, to find that none of the gentlemen could tell me what a pitched battle was like.'

'It is so much a question of luck, or perhaps I should say of Providence,' said Jack, with a bow to the cloth. 'Where one is stationed, and so on. After all,' he said, pausing, for on the verge of his mind there was a witticism, if he could but grasp it. 'After all, it takes two to make a quarrel, and if the French don't come out, why, you cannot very well have a battle all by yourself. Indeed, there is so much routine work, blockading and convoy-duty and carrying troops, you know, that I dare say half the lieutenants of the Navy List have never seen action at all, in the sense of a meeting of ships of equal force, or of fleets. More than half, perhaps.'

'I never have, I am sure,' said Dashwood.

'I *saw* an action when I was in the *Culloden* in ninety-eight,' said Simmons. 'A very great action; but we ran aground, and never could come up. It nearly broke our hearts.'

'It must have been a sad trial,' said Jack. 'I remember how you carried out warps, pulling like heroes.'

'You were at the Nile, sir?'

'Yes, yes. I was in the *Leander*. I remember coming on deck just as the *Mutine* rounded to under your stern, to try to heave you off.'

'So you were in a great battle, Captain Aubrey,' said the chaplain eagerly. 'Pray, can you tell me what it was like? Can you give me some impression of it?'

'Why, sir, I doubt that I could, really, any more than I could give you much impression of let us say a symphony or a splendid dinner. There is a great deal of noise, more noise than you would believe possible; and time does not seem to have the same meaning, if you follow me; and you get very tired. And afterwards you have to clear up the mess.'

'Ah, that is what I wanted to know. And is the din so very great?'

'It is enormous. At the Nile, for example, we had the *Orion* blow up near us, and we all conversed in shouts for ten days after. But St Vincent was noisier. In what we call the slaughter-house, where I was stationed at St Vincent – that is the part of the gun-deck in the middle of the ship, sir – you have sixteen thirty-two pounders in a row, all roaring away as fast as they can load and fire, recoiling and jumping up with a great crash when they are hot, and running out again to fire; and then just overhead you have another row of guns thundering on the deck above. And then the smashing blow as the enemy's shot hits you, and maybe the crash of falling spars above, and the screams of the wounded. And all this in such a smoke you can hardly see or breathe, and the men cheering like mad, and sweating and gulping down water when there is a second's pause. At St Vincent we fought both sides, which doubled the row. No: that is what you remember – the huge noise everywhere, the flashes in the darkness. And,' he added, 'the importance of gunnery – speed and accuracy and discipline. We were firing a broadside every two minutes, and they took three and a half or four – that's what wins the day.'

'So you were at St Vincent too,' said the parson. 'And at what other actions, if I am not too indiscreet – I mean, apart from this last most daring capture, of which we have all read?'

'Only small affairs – skirmishing in the Mediterranean and the West Indies in the last war – that kind of thing,' said Jack.

'There was the *Cacafuego*, sir, I believe,' said Mr Simmons, with a smile.

'It must have been wonderful, when you were young, sir,' said the midshipman, sick with envy. 'Nothing ever happens now.'

'I am sure you will forgive me if I seem personal,' said the chaplain, 'but I should like to form an image of the officer who has seen, as you say, a moderate amount of fighting. In addition to your fleet actions, about how many others have you taken part in?'

'Why, upon my word, I forget,' said Jack, feeling that the others had an unfair advantage of him, and feeling too that parsons were out of place in a man-of-war. He signalled to Killick for fresh decanter and the roast; and as he set to carving the flow of his mind changed as thoroughly as if an eighteen-pound shot had hulled the frigate. He felt a rising oppression in his bosom and choked, standing

427

bowed there, carving the venison. The first lieutenant had long ago seen that Mr Lydgate's persistence was disagreeable to Captain Aubrey, and he turned the conversation back to animals aboard. Dogs in ships he had known: the Newfoundland that so lovingly brought a smoking grenade; the *Culloden*'s pet crocodile; cats . . . '

'Dogs,' said the chaplain, who was not one to leave his corner of the table silent long. 'That reminds me of a question I had meant to put to you gentlemen. This short watch that is about to come, or rather these two short watches – why are they called *dog* watches? Where, heu, heu, is the *canine* connection?'

'Why,' said Stephen, 'it is because they are curtailed, of course.'

A total blank. Stephen gave a faint inward sigh; but he was used to this. 'Mr Butler, the bottle stands by you,' said Jack. 'Mr Lydgate, allow me to help you to a little of the undercut.'

It was the midshipman who first reacted. He whispered to his neighbour Dashwood, 'He said, cur-tailed: the *dog*-watch is *cur*-tailed. Do you twig?'

It was the sort of wretched clench perfectly suited to the company. The spreading merriment, the relish, the thunderous mirth, reached the forecastle, causing amazement and conjecture: Jack leaned back in his chair, wiping the tears from his scarlet face, and cried, 'Oh, it is the best thing – the best thing. Bless you, Stephen – a glass of wine with you. Mr Simmons, if we dine with the admiral, you must ask me, and I will say, "Why, it is because *they have been docked*, of course." No, no. I am out. *Cur-tailed* – cur-tailed. But I doubt I should ever be able to get it out gravely enough.'

They did not dine with the admiral, however; no loving messages answered their salute to the flagship; but the moment they dropped anchor in the crowded Downs Parker came aboard from the *Fanciulla* with his brand-new epaulette, to congratulate and to be congratulated.

Jack felt a certain pang when the boat answered the *Lively*'s hail with '*Fanciulla*', meaning that her captain was aboard; but the sight of Parker's face as it came level with the deck and the affection that beamed from it, did away with all repining. Parker looked ten, fifteen years younger; he came up the side like a boy; he was wholly and absolutely delighted. He most bitterly regretted that he was under orders to sail within the hour, but he solemnly engaged Jack and Stephen to dine with him at the very next meeting; he thought *curtailed* by far the best thing he had ever heard in his life – should certainly repeat it – but he had always known that Dr Maturin was a towering intellect – was still taking his pill, morning and evening, and should continue to do so until the end of his life; and on leaving he took Jack's hesitant 'Captain Parker would not be offended if he suggested a relaxation – a *curtailing* of the cat, as he might say' very well indeed. He said he should pay the utmost attention to advice from such a – such an esteemed quarter, such a very, very highly esteemed quarter. On saying good-bye he took both Jack's hands in his and, with tears in his small, close-set eyes, he said, 'You don't know what it means, sir, success at fifty-six – success at last. It changes a man's whole, eh *heart*. Why I could kiss the ship's boys.'

Jack's eyebrows shot into his bandage but he returned Parker's fervent grip and saw him to the gangway. He, was profoundly touched and he stood there looking after the boat as it pulled over to the beautiful little sloop until the first lieutenant came up to him and said, 'Mr Dashwood has a request to make, sir, if you please. He would like to take his sister down to Portsmouth: she is married to a Marine officer there.'

'Oh, certainly, Mr Simmons. She will be very welcome. She may have the after-cabin. But stay, the after-cabin is filled with . . . '

'No, no, sir. He would not hear of putting you out – it is only his sister. He will sling a hammock in the gun-room, and she shall have his cabin. That is how we always did these things when Captain Hamond was aboard. Shall you be going ashore, sir?'

'No. Killick will go to pick up my coxswain and some stores and salve against bee-stings; but I shall stay aboard. Keep a boat for Dr Maturin, however: I believe he will wish to go. Good day to you, ma'am,' he said, moving aside and taking off his hat as Mrs Armstrong, the gunner's wife, shook the gangway with her bulk. 'Take care – hold on to the side-ropes with both hands.'

'Bless you sir,' said Mrs Armstrong with a jolly wheeze, 'I been in and out of ships since I was a little maid.' She took one basket between her teeth, two more under her left arm, and dropped into the boat like a midshipman.

'That is an excellent woman, sir,' said the first lieutenant, looking down into the hoveller. 'She nursed me through a fever in Java when Mr Floris and the Dutch surgeons had given me up.'

'Well,' said Jack, 'there were women in the Ark, so I suppose there must be some good in 'em; but generally speaking I have never known anything but trouble come of shipping them on a voyage – quarrels, discussions, not enough to go round, jealousies. I do not even care for them in port – drunkenness, and a sick-list as long as your arm. Not that this has the least bearing on Mrs Gunner of course, or the other warrant officers' wives – still less to Mr Dashwood's sister. Ah, Stephen, there you are – ' Simmons withdrew – 'I was just telling the first lieutenant that you would probably be going ashore. You will take the barge, will you not? Two of the supernumeraries are not to report aboard until the morning, so you will have all the time in the world.'

Stephen looked at him with his strange pale unblinking eyes. Had that old constraint returned, that curious misery? Jack was looking conscious – unnaturally, inappropriately gay: a wretched actor. 'Shall you not go, Jack?' he said.

'No, sir,' said Jack. 'I shall stay aboard. Between ourselves,' he added in a much lower tone, 'I do not believe I shall ever willingly set foot on shore again: indeed, I have sworn an oath never to risk arrest. But,' he cried, with that painful, jarring, artificial assumption of levity that Stephen knew so well, 'I must beg you to get some decent coffee when you go. Killick is no judge. He can tell good wine from bad, as you would expect in a smuggler; but he is no judge of coffee.'

Stephen nodded. 'I must also buy some issue-peas,' he said. 'I shall call at New Place, and I shall look into the hospital. Have you any messages?'

'Compliments, of course, best compliments: and my very kindest wishes to Babbington and the other wounded Polychrests – this is for their comforts, if you please. Macdonald, too. Please tell Babbington I am particularly sorry not to be able to visit him – it is quite impossible.'

CHAPTER THIRTEEN

It was drawing towards evening when Stephen left the hospital: his patients were doing well – one shocking belly-wound had astonished him by living – and Babbington's arm was safe; his professional mind was easy and content as he walked up through the town towards New Place. His professional mind: but the whole of the rest of his spirit, feeling out with un-logical antennae, sensing the immaterial, was in such a state of preparedness that he was not in any way surprised to see the house boarded and shut up.

It seemed that the mad gentleman had been driven away in a coach and four 'weeks and weeks ago' or 'some time last month, maybe' or 'before we got in the apples', bowing from the window and laughing fit to burst his sides; and that the coachman wore a black cockade. The servants followed in the waggon the next day, a week after, some time later, going to a little place in Sussex, to Brighton, to London town. His informants had not noticed the lady these last weeks. Mr Pope, the butler at New Place, was a proud, touch-me-not gentleman; all the servants were a stiff London lot, and kept themselves to themselves.

Less downright in his approach than Jack, Stephen opened the simple lock of the garden gate with a piece of wire, and the kitchen door with a Morton's retractor. He walked composedly up the stairs, through the green-baize door and into the hall. A tall thirty-day clock was still going, its weight nearly touching the ground; a solemn tock-tock that echoed through the hall and followed him up into the drawing-room. Silence; a perfection of dust-sheets, rolled carpets, ranged furniture; rays of light that came through the shutters, motes turning in them; moths;

the first delicate cobwebs in unexpected places, such as the carved mantelpiece in the library, where Mr Lowndes had written some lines of Sappho large on the wall in chalk.

'An elegant hand,' said Stephen, as he stood to consider it. *'The moon has set, and the Pleiades; midnight is gone; the hours wear by, and here I lie alone: alone. Perhaps and here I, Sappho, lie alone,* to give the sex. No. The sex is immaterial. It is the same for both.'

Silence; anonymous perfection; unstirring air – never a waft or a movement; silence. The smell of bare boards. A tallboy with its face turned to the wall.

In her room the same trim bare sterility; even the looking-glass was shrouded. It was not so much severe, for the grey light was too soft, as meaningless. There was no waiting in this silence, no tension of any kind: the creaking of the boards under his feet contained no threat, no sort of passion: he could have leapt or shrieked without affecting the inhuman vacuum of sense. It was as meaningless as total death, a skull in a dim thicket, the future gone, its past wiped out. He had the strongest feeling of the déjà-vu that he had ever experienced, and yet it was familiar enough to him, that certain knowledge of the turn of a dream, the sequence of words that would be said by a stranger in a coach and of his reply, the disposition of a room he had never seen, even to the pattern of the paper on its walls.

In the waste-paper-basket there were some balled-up sheets, the only imperfection, apart from the living clock, in this desert of negation, and the only exception to the completeness of his déjà-vu. 'What indeed am I looking for?' he said, and the sound of his voice ran through the open rooms. 'An out-of-date announcement of my death?' But they were lists in a servant's hand, quite meaningless, and one paper where a pen had been tried – spluttering lines of ink that might have had a meaning once, but none that could be understood. He tossed them back, stood for a long moment listening to his heart, and walked straight into her dressing-room. Here he found what he had known he should find: the stark bareness, the pretty satinwood furniture huddled against the wall was of no importance, did not signify; but here, coming from no particular shelf or cupboard, there was the ghost of her scent, now a little stronger, now so tenuous that his most extreme attention could hardly catch it.

'At least,' he said, 'this is not the horror of the last.'

He closed the door with the greatest caution, walked down into the hall; stopped the clock, setting his mark upon the house, and let himself out into the garden. He turned the lock behind him, walked along the leaf-strewn, already neglected paths, out by the green door and so to the road along the coast. With his hands behind his back and his eyes on this road as it streamed evenly beneath him, watching its flow while there was still any day to see, he followed it until he reached the lights of Deal. Then, remembering that he had left his boat at Dover, he turned and paced the smooth miles back again. 'It is very well,' he said. 'I should have sat in the parlour of an inn, in any case, until I could return and go to bed without any conversation or civilities. This is better by far. I rejoice in this even, sandy road, stretching on and on for ever.'

The morning was rich in such events as the introduction of Mr Floris, the surgeon, his invitation to view the sick-bay, equipped with his personally-invented wind-sail to bring fresh air below, and his flattering eagerness, his flattering *deferential* eagerness for Dr Maturin's opinion on Wallace – as clear a case for instant suprapubic cystotomy as Stephen had ever seen; and the appearance of Mrs Miller and her child, bright and early, for the *Lively* was at single anchor, with the blue peter flying.

She was a pretty young woman with a decided air, and with a hint not of boldness but rather of that freedom which a wedding-ring and the protection of a child provides. Not that any of this was visible when Jack greeted her on the quarterdeck, however; all was demure gratitude and apologies for the intrusion. Little Brydges would be no trouble, she assured him – he was thoroughly accustomed to ships – had been to Gibraltar and back – was never sick, and never cried.

'Why, ma'am,' said Jack, 'we are delighted to have the honour of your company, and wish it were for farther than Portsmouth. If a man cannot give a brother-officer's wife and sister a lift, things are in a sad way. Though I believe we may look forward to the pleasure of having you with us for quite a while; the wind is getting round into that God – that bothersome southerly quarter.'

'Uncle John,' said young Brydges, 'why are you nodding and winking at Mama? She has not talked to the Captain too much, yet; and I dare say she will stop directly. And I have said nothing at all.'

'Stephen,' said Jack, 'may I come in? I hope I have not woken you – was you asleep?'

'No,' said Stephen. 'Not at all.'

'Well, the gun-room is in rather a taking. It seems that a round million of your reptiles got into their cocoa-pot this morning – immolated themselves by the hundred, crawling in at the spout. They say that the wear and anxiety of such another breakfast would make them give up the service.'

'Did they note down the exact time?'

'Oh, I am sure they did. I am sure that in the intervals of avoiding attack, eating their breakfast, and navigating the ship, they hurried off to check the precise moment by the master's twin chronometers. Ha, ha.'

'You speak ironically, no doubt. But this is a striking instance of sagacity in bees. I feed them with a syrup of cocoa and sugar. They connect the scent of cocoa with their nourishment. They discover a new source of cocoa-scent; they busily communicate this discovery to their fellows, together with its location, and there you have the whole situation – as satisfactory a proof as you could wish to see. Tomorrow I hope the gun-room will note down the time of their first appearance. I bet you a considerable sum of money that it will be within ten minutes either side of seven bells, the moment at which they were first fed.'

'Do you mean that they will rush in again?'

'So long as the gun-room continues to drink heavily-sugared cocoa, I see no reason why they should ever stop. It will be interesting to see whether this knowledge is passed on to all the subsequent generations of bees. I thank you, Jack, for telling me this: no discovery has given me so much satisfaction for years. Once it has been thoroughly tested – a sequence of some weeks or months – I shall communicate it to Monsieur Huber.'

His waxy, tormented face had such a glow of pleasure that Jack could not find it in his heart to fulfil his promise to the gun-room. They might caulk their bulkheads, key-holes, skylights, drink tea or coffee, shroud themselves in mosquito netting for a day or so – what was a little discomfort, on active service? He said, 'I have a treat for you today, Stephen – a pretty young woman for dinner! Dashwood's sister came aboard this morning, a very fine young woman indeed. A pleasure to look at, and very well behaved – went straight below and has never been seen since.'

'Alas, I must beg to be excused. I am only waiting for my opiates to have their effect, and then I shall operate. Mr Floris is waiting for me, and his mates are sharpening the bistouries at this very moment. I should have preferred to wait until we reached Haslar, but with this wind I presume it will take a couple of days or so; and the patient cannot wait. They are eager to see the operation; I am equally eager to gratify them. That is why I am resting my limbs at present; it would never do to make a blunder in such a demonstration. Besides, we must consider our patient. Oh, certainly. He must feel assured of a steady hand, when we are groping in his vitals with our instrument, for it will be some little while before we tally and belay.'

The patient, the unhappy Wallace, might feel assured of a steady hand as he was led, or rather propelled, to the bench, stupefied with opium, dazed with rum, and buoyed up with accounts of the eminence of the hand that was going to deal with him; but he was assured of little else, to judge by his staring pallor. His messmates led him to his place and made him fast in a seamanlike manner: one seized his pigtail to a ring-bolt, another gave him a bullet to bite upon, and a third told him he was saving at least a hundred guineas by being there – no physical gent with a gold-headed stick would think of opening him for less.

'Gentlemen,' said Stephen, turning back his cuffs, 'you will observe that I take my point of departure from the iliac crest; I traverse thus, and so find my point of incision.'

So, in the fore-cabin, Jack held the point of his carver over a dimple in the venison pasty and said, 'Allow me to cut you a little of this pasty, ma'am. It is one of the few things I can carve. When we have a joint, I usually call upon my friend Dr Maturin, whom I hope to introduce to you this afternoon. He is such a hand at carving.'

'If you please, sir,' said Mrs Miller. 'It looks so very good. But I cannot quite believe what you say about carving. You cut out the *Fanciulla* only the other day, and surely that was a very pretty piece of carving.'

While these delights were going forward, the *Lively* stood across the Channel, close-hauled to the freshening south-west breeze with her starboard tacks aboard, under topgallants and a fine spread of staysails.

'Now, Mr Simmons,' said Jack, appearing upon deck, 'this is very capital, is it not? How she does love to sail upon a bowline.' It was a warm, bright afternoon, with patches of cloud moving across the sky, and her brilliant canvas, her white rigging, shone splendid against them as she heeled to the wind. There was nothing of the yacht about her; her paintwork was strictly utilitarian and even

437

ugly; but this one point of snowy cordage, the rare manilla she had brought back from the Philippines, raised her to an uncommon height of beauty – that, and of course, her lovely, supple command of the sea. There was a long, even swell from the south and a surface ripple that came lipping along her weather bow, sometimes sending a little shower of spray aft across the waist, with momentary rainbows in it. This would be a perfect afternoon and evening for gunnery.

'Tell me, Mr Simmons,' he said, 'what has been your practice in exercising the great guns?'

'Well, sir,' said the first lieutenant, 'we used to fire once a week at the beginning of the commission, but Captain Hamond was so checked by the Navy Board for expenditure of powder and ball that he grew discouraged.' Jack nodded: he too had received those querulous, righteous, indignant letters that ended so strangely with 'your affectionate friends'. 'So now we only fire by divisions once a month. Though of course we run them in and out at least once a week at quarters.'

Jack paced the windward side of the quarterdeck. Rattling the guns in and out was very well, but it was not the same thing as firing them. Nothing like it at all. Yet a broadside from the *Lively* would cost ten guineas. He considered, turning it over in his mind; stepped into the master's cabin to look at the charts, and sent for the gunner, who gave him a statement of cartridge filled, powder at hand, and an appreciation of each gun. The four long nine-pounders were his darlings, and they did most of the firing in the *Lively*, worked by him, his mates and the quarter-gunners.

The horizon beyond the larboard bow was broken now by the irregular line of the French coast, and the *Lively* heaved about on the other tack. How beautifully she handled! She came smoothly up into the wind, paid off and filled in a cable's length, hardly losing any way at all. In spite of her spread of canvas, with all the staysail sheets to be passed over, scarcely a quarter of an hour passed between the pipe of All hands about ship and the moment when the mastmen began flemishing their ropes and making pretty, while France dropped out of sight astern.

What a ship to handle – no noise, no fuss, no shadow of a doubt as to whether she would stay. And she was making eight knots already: he could eat the wind out of any square-rigged craft afloat. But what was the good of that, if he could not hit his enemy when he came up with him?

'We will make a short board, Mr Norrey,' he said to the master, who now had the watch. 'And then you will be so good as to lay her in half a mile from Balbec, under topsails.'

'Stephen,' he said, some minutes later, 'how did your operation go?'

'Very prettily, I thank you,' said Stephen. 'It was as charming a demonstration of my method as you could wish: a perfect case for immediate intervention, good light, plenty of elbow-room. And the patient survived.'

'Well done, well done! Tell me, Stephen, would you do me a kindness?'

'I might,' said Stephen, looking shrewish.

'It is just to shift your brutes into the quarter-gallery. The guns are to fire in the cabin, and perhaps the bang might be bad for them. Besides, I do not want another mutiny on my hands.'

'Oh, certainly. I shall carry the hive and you shall fix the gimbals. Let us do it at once.'

When Jack returned, still trembling and with the sweat running down the hollow of his spine, it was time for quarters. The drum beat and the Livelies hurried to their stations in the usual way; but they knew very well that this was no ordinary ritual, not only from the gunner's uncommon activity and knowing looks, but also because Mrs Miller had been desired to step down into the hold, with a midshipman bearing an armful of cushions to show her the way: asked if she minded a bang, had replied, 'Oh no, I love it.'

The frigate was gliding along half a mile from the shore under topsails alone, so close in that the members of a flock of sheep could be seen on the green grass, surrounding their shepherd as he stared out to sea; and the Livelies were not surprised, after they had been reported present and sober, sir, to hear the order 'Out tompions.'

Some of the tompions needed a furious heave to get them out, they having sat in the muzzles of their guns for so long, but as the frigate approached the battery guarding the little port of Balbec all the guns were staring at it with their iron eyes wide open. This was a little battery of three twenty-four pounders on an islet outside the creek, and it vanished in its own smoke at extreme range, so that only its immense tri-colour could be seen floating over the cloud.

'We will fire the guns in succession, Mr Simmons,' said Jack, 'with a half-minute interval between each. I will give the word. Mr Fanning, note down the fall of each shot with the number of the gun.'

The French gunners were accurate but slow – short-handed, no doubt. They knocked away the *Lively*'s stern lantern with their third salvo, but they did not do more than make a hole in her maintopsail before the frigate was within the range that Jack had chosen – before he gave the word to fire. The *Lively* was slow and inaccurate – little notion of independent fire, almost none of elevation. Only one shot from her starboard guns hit the battery at all, and her last gun was followed by a derisive cheer from the land.

The frigate was coming abreast of the battery, a little over a quarter of a mile away. 'Are those after guns run out, Mr Simmons?' asked Jack. 'Then we will give them a broadside.' As he waited for the long roll, one twenty-four pounder hulled the *Lively* in the mizen-chains and another passed over the quarterdeck with a deep howl. He noticed that two of the midshipmen bobbed to the ball and then looked anxiously to see whether he had noticed: they had not been under fire before. 'Fire!' said Jack, and the whole ship erupted in a vast roaring crash, trembling to her keelson. For a moment the smoke blotted out the sun, then raced away to leeward. Jack stretched eagerly over the rail: this was a little better – stones knocked sideways, the flag leaning drunkenly. The Livelies were cheering; but they were not running up their guns with anything like the speed they furled their topsails. The minutes dragged by. The battery sent a ball into the *Lively*'s stern. 'Perhaps that was the quarter-gallery,' he thought, with a spurt of hope through his boiling impatience. 'Shiver the maintops'l. Hard a-starboard. Will you get those guns run up, Mr Simmons?' The range was lengthening, drawing out and out. A ball hit the boats on the booms, scattering planks and splinters. 'Port your helm. Thus, thus. Fire. Ready about, ready oh!'

Only two of her shots had gone home, but one of them had silenced a gun, hitting the embrasure fair and square. The *Lively* came about, fired her larboard guns in succession – the men had their shirts off now – and then a broadside. As she came abreast of the battery for the second time, gliding smoothly up much nearer to and with her carronades ready to join in, the little garrison was seen to be pulling furiously for the shore, all crammed into one small boat, for the other had gone adrift, its painter cut. 'Fire,' said Jack, and the battery leapt in a cloud of dust and chips of stone.

'How are our boats?' he asked a quarterdeck midshipman.

'Your gig has been hit, sir. The others are all right.'

'Cutter away. Mr Dashwood, be so good as to take the cutter, spike up any serviceable guns and carry what is left of the colours to Mrs Miller with the *Lively*'s compliments. And just secure that boat of theirs, will you? Then we shall be all square.'

The frigate lay gently pitching on the swell while the

cutter hurried across the sea and back. There was nothing in the little port except fishing craft: nothing to be done there. 'However,' he said, when the boats were hoisted in, 'the good of the service requires us to batter the battery a little more. Up jib. We really must see if we can do better than four and a half minutes between broadsides, Mr Simmons.'

To and fro she went, shattering and pulverizing the heap of rubble, the gun-crews very pleased with themselves and plying their pieces with great zeal if not much accuracy.

By the time she sailed away her practice was a little better, the co-ordination was a trifle nearer what he could wish, and the men were more accustomed to the crash and leap of their deadly charges; but of course it was still pitifully slow.

'Well, Mr Simmons,' he said to the first lieutenant, who was looking at him with a certain uneasiness, 'that was not bad at all. Number four and seven fired very well. But if we can manage three accurate broadsides in five minutes, then there will be nothing that can stand against us. We must salute every French battery we pass like this – so much more fun than firing at a mark – and our affectionate friends cannot handsomely object. I hope we shall have a little more Channel duty before they send us foreign.'

He would not have formed this wish if he had known how surprisingly soon it was to be fulfilled. The *Lively* had not anchored in Spithead before orders came off desiring and directing him to proceed immediately to Plymouth to take charge of a north-bound convoy – Bermuda was off for the next few weeks, perhaps for good. The port admiral's boat also brought a young man from Jack's new agent, bearing a cheque for a hundred and thirty pounds more than Jack had dared hope for, and a letter from General Aubrey announcing his return from St Muryan, the rottenest

442

of all the rotten Cornish boroughs, the property of his friend Mr Polwhele, on the simple platform of Death to the Whigs. 'I have composed my maiden speech,' wrote the General, 'and am to deliver it on Monday. It will dish them completely – such corruption you would not credit, hardly. And I shall deliver another, worse, after the recess, if they do not do something for us. We have bled for our country, and may I be damned if our country shall not bleed for us, moderately.' The *moderately* was scratched out, and the letter concluded by desiring Jack to enter his little brother's name on the ship's books, 'as it might come in useful, some day.' Jack's face took on a very thoughtful cast; it was not that he disliked the sentiment about bleeding – he was all for it; but he knew his father's notions of discretion, alas. They bundled Mrs Miller ashore, as proud as Pontius Pilate with her piece of flag, and carried on their zigzag course down the Channel against the west and south-west winds, pausing only to celebrate Jack's wealth and General Aubrey's election by beating a battery on the headland of Barfleur into the ground and destroying the semaphore-station at Cap Levi. The frigate spent barrel after barrel of powder and scattered some tons of iron over the French landscape; her gunnery improved remarkably. Next to the pleasure of shooting at a fellow man, the Livelies loved destroying his works; no shooting at the mark at sea could possibly have given them such delight or have increased their zeal a tenth part as much as shooting at the windows of the semaphore-station, with their guns at their utmost elevation. And when at last they hit them, when the glass and frames vanished with a crash, they cheered as though they had sunk a ship of the line; and the whole quarterdeck, including the chaplain, laughed and simpered like a holiday.

He would not have formed the wish, if he had known that it would mean depriving Stephen of the tropical delights he had promised, to say nothing of the pleasure of walking about on land himself, unhunted, with never an anxious glance behind, in Madeira, Bermuda or the West Indies, unharassed by any but the French, and perhaps the Spaniards and the yellow fever.

Yet there it was, formed and fulfilled; and here he was, under the lee of Drake's Island, with Plymouth Hoe on his larboard bow, waiting for the 92nd Foot to get into their transports in Hamoaze: and a long business it would be, judging from their present state of total unpreparedness.

'Jack,' said Stephen, 'shall you call on Admiral Haddock?'

'No,' said Jack. 'I shall not. I have sworn not to go ashore, you know.'

'Sophie and Cecilia are still there,' observed Stephen.

'Oh,' cried Jack, and took a turn up and down the cabin. 'Stephen,' he said, 'I shall not go. What in God's name have I to offer her? I have thought about it a great deal. It was wrong and selfish in me to pursue her to Bath – I should never have done it; but I was hurried along by my feelings, you know – I did not reflect. What sort of a match am I? Post, if you like, but up to the ears in debt, and with nothing much in the way of prospects if Melville goes. A chap that goes sneaking and skulking about on land like a pickpocket with the thieftakers on his line. No. I am not going to pester her as once I did. And I am not going to tear my heart to pieces again: besides, what can she care for me, after all this?'

CHAPTER FOURTEEN

'Beg pardon, ma'am, but can you tell me where Miss Williams is?' asked the Admiral's butler. 'There is a gentleman to see her.'

'She will be down presently,' said Cecilia. 'Who is it?'

'Dr Maturin, ma'am. He particularly told me to say, Dr Maturin.'

'Oh, show him in to me, Rowley,' cried Cecilia. 'I'll entertain him. Dear Dr Maturin, how do you do? How come you are here? Oh, I am amazed, I declare! What a splendid thing about Captain Aubrey, the dear man, and the *Fanciulla*: but to think of the poor *Polychrest*, all sunk beneath the wave – but you saved your clothes, however, I dare say? Oh, we were so pleased to read the Gazette! Sophie and I held hands and skipped about like lambs in the pink room, roaring out Huzzay, huzzay! Though we were in such a taking – Lord, Dr Maturin, such a taking! We wept and wept, and I was all swollen and horrid for the port admiral's ball, and Sophie would not even go at all, not that she missed much – a very stupid ball, with all the young men stuck in the door and only the old codgers dancing – call that dancing! – by order of rank. I only stood up once. Oh, how we wept – handkerchiefs all sopping, I do assure you – and of course it is very sad. But she might have thought of us. We shall never be able to hold up our heads again! I think it was very wrong of her – she might have waited until we were married. I think she is a – but I must not say that to you, because I believe you were quite smitten once, ages and ages ago, were you not?'

'What upset you so?'

'Why, Diana, of course. Didn't you know? Oh, Lord.'

'Pray tell me now.'

'Mama said I was never to mention it. And I never will. But if you promise not to tell, I will whisper it. Di has gone into keeping with that Mr Canning. I thought that would surprise you. Who ever would have guessed it? Mama did not, although she is so amazing wise. She was in a horrid rage – she still is. She says it has quite ruined our chances of a decent marriage, which is such a shame. Not that I mind so much about a *decent* marriage; but I should not like to be an old maid. That is quite my aversion. Hush, I hear her door closing: she is coming down. I will leave you together, and not play gooseberry. I may not be six foot tall, but at least no one can say I am a gooseberry. You won't tell, will you? Remember, you promised.'

'Sophie, my dear,' he said, kissing her, 'how do you do? I will answer your questions at once. Jack is made post. We came in that frigate by the little small island. He has an acting command.'

'Which frigate? Where? Where?'

'Come,' said Stephen, swivelling the admiral's great brass telescope on its stand. 'There you have him, walking on the quarterdeck in his old nankeen trousers.'

There in the bright round paced Jack, from the hances to the aftermost carronade and back again.

'Oh,' she cried, 'he has a bandage on his head. Not – not his poor ears again?' she murmured, focusing the glass.

'No, no, a mere scalp-wound. Not above a dozen stitches.'

'Will he not come ashore?' she asked.

'He will not. What, set foot on land to be arrested for debt? No friend of his but would stop him by force – no woman with any heart of friendship in her would ask it.'

'No, no. Of course. I was forgetting . . .'

Each time he turned he glanced up to Mount Edgcumb, to Admiral Haddock's official residence. Their eyes seemed to meet, and she started back.

'Is it out of focus?' asked Stephen.

'No, no. It is so prying to look like this – indecent.

How is he? I am so very glad that – I am quite confused – everything is so sudden – I had no idea. How is he? And how are you? Dear Stephen, how are you?'

'I am very well, I thank you.'

'No, no, you are not. Come, come and sit down at once. Stephen, has Cissy been prattling?'

'Never mind,' said Stephen, looking aside. 'Tell me, is it true?'

She could not reply, but sat by him and took his hand.

'Now listen, honey,' he said, returning the kindness of her clasp.

'Oh, I beg your pardon,' cried Admiral Haddock, putting his head in at the door and instantly withdrawing.

'Now listen, honey. The *Lively*, the frigate, is ordered up-Channel, to the Nore, with these foolish soldiers. She will sail the minute they are ready. You must go aboard this afternoon and ask him to give you a lift to the Downs.'

'Oh, I could never, never do such a thing. It would be very, very improper. Forward, pushing, bold, improper.'

'Not at all. With your sister, perfectly proper, the most usual thing in the world. Come now, my dear, start packing your things. It is now or never. He may be in the West Indies next month.'

'Never. I know you mean so very kindly – you are a darling, Stephen – but a young woman cannot, *cannot* do such things.'

'Now I have no time at all, none, acushla,' said Stephen, rising. 'So listen now. Do what I say. Pack your bonnet: go aboard. Now is the time. Now, or there will be three thousand miles of salt unhappy sea between you, and a waste of years.'

'I am so confused. But I cannot. No, I never will. I cannot. He might not want me.' The tears overflowed: she wrung her handkerchief desperately, shaking her head and murmuring, 'No, no, never.'

'Good day to you, now, Sophie,' he said. 'How can

you be so simple. So missish? Fie Sophie. Where's your courage, girl? Sure, it is the one thing in the world he admires.'

In his diary he wrote, 'So much wretchedness, misery and squalor I do not believe I have ever seen collected together in one place, as in this town of Plymouth. All the naval ports I have visited have been cold smelly blackguardly places, but for pox-upon-pox this Plymouth bears the bell. Yet the suburb or parasite they call Dock goes even beyond Plymouth, as Sodom outran Gomorrah: I wandered about its dirty lanes, solicited, importuned by its barbarous inhabitants, male, female and epicene, and I came to the poor-house, where the old are kept until they can be buried with some show of decency. The impression of meaningless absolute unhappiness is with me yet. Medicine has brought me acquainted with misery in many forms; I am not squeamish; but for complications of filth, cruelty, and bestial ignorance, that place, with its infirmary, exceeded any thing I have ever seen or imagined. An old man, his wits quite gone, chained in the dark, squatting in his excrement, naked but for a blanket; the idiot children; the whipping. I knew it all; it is nothing new; but in this concentration it overcame me so that I could no longer feel indignation but only a hopeless nausea. It was the merest chance that I kept my appointment with the chaplain to listen to a concert – my feet, more civil than my mind, led me to the place. Curious music, well played, particularly the trumpet: a German composer, one Molter. The music, I believe, had nothing to say, but it provided a pleasant background of 'cellos and woodwinds and allowed the trumpet to make exquisite sounds – pure colour tearing through this formal elegance. I grope to define a connection that is half clear to me – I once thought that this was music, much as I thought that physical grace and style was virtue; or replaced virtue; or was virtue on

448

another plane. But although the music shifted the current of my thoughts for a while, they are back again today, and I have not the spiritual energy to clarify this or any other position. At home there is a Roman stone I know (I often lay there to listen to my nightjars) with *fui non sum non curo* carved on it; and there I have felt such a peace, such a *tranquillitas animi et indolentia corporis. Home* I say, which is singular: yet indeed there is still a glow of hatred for the Spaniards under these indulgent, unmanly ashes – a living attachment to Catalan independence.' He looked out of the cabin window at the water of the Sound, oily, with the nameless filth of Plymouth floating on it, a bloated puppy, and dipped his pen. 'Yet on the other hand, will this glow ever blaze up again, when I think of what they will do with independence? When I let my mind dwell on the vast potentiality for happiness, and our present state? Such potentiality, and so much misery? Hatred the only moving force, a petulant unhappy striving – childhood the only happiness, and that unknowing; then the continual battle that cannot ever possibly be won; a losing fight against ill-health – poverty for nearly all. Life is a long disease with only one termination and its last years are appalling: weak, racked by the stone, rheumatismal pains, senses going, friends, family, occupation gone, a man must pray for imbecility or a heart of stone. All under sentence of death, often ignominious, frequently agonizing: and then the unspeakable levity with which the faint chance of happiness is thrown away for some jealousy, tiff, sullenness, private vanity, mistaken sense of honour, that deadly, weak and silly notion. I am not acute in my perceptions – my whole conduct with Diana proves it – but I would have sworn that Sophie had more bottom; was more straightforward, direct, courageous. Though to be sure, I know the depth of Jack's feeling for her, and perhaps she does not.' He looked up from his page again, straight into her face. It was outside the window, a few feet below him, moving from left to right as the boat pulled

449

round the frigate's stern; she was looking up beyond the cabin window towards the taffrail, with her mouth slightly open and her lip caught behind her upper teeth, with an expression of contained alarm in her immense upturned eyes. Admiral Haddock sat beside her, and Cecilia.

When Stephen reached the quarterdeck the admiral was uttering his thoughts on manilla cordage, and Jack and Sophie were standing some distance apart, looking extraordinary conscious. 'His appearance,' reflected Stephen, 'is not so much that of concern as of consternation. His wits are overset: how very much at random he answers the admiral.'

'And all that, my dears, has to be tarred, in the case we are rigged with common hemp,' said the admiral.

'Tarred, sir?' cried Sophie. 'Oh, indeed. With – with a tar-brush, I dare say?' Her voice died away, and she blushed again.

'So I entrust the girls to you, Aubrey,' said the admiral. 'I shift the responsibility on to your shoulders – two great girls is a very shocking responsibility – and send 'em aboard on Thursday.'

'Upon my word, sir, you are very good – but not fit for a lady. That is to say, very fit for a lady; but cramped. Should be very happy, more than happy, to show Miss Williams any attention in my power.'

'Oh, never mind them. They are only girls, you know – they can rough it – don't put yourself out. Think what you will save them in pin-money. Stow them anywhere. Berth them with the Doctor, ha, ha! There you are, Dr Maturin. I am happy to see you. You would not mind it, eh? Eh? Ha, ha, ha. I saw you, you sly dog. Take care of him, Aubrey; he is a sly one.' The scattered officers on the quarterdeck frowned: the Admiral belonged to an older, coarser Navy; and he had been dining with his carnal colleague, the port admiral. 'So that is settled, Aubrey? Capital, capital. Come, Sophie; come, Cecilia: into the chair – hang on to your petticoats; mind the wind. Oh,' he added in what passed for a whisper, as the girls were lowered away in the ignominy of a bosun's chair, 'a word in your ear, Aubrey. Have you read your father's speech? I thought not. "And now let us turn to the Navy," said he to the House. "Here too we find that the former administration allowed, nay, *encouraged* the grossest laxity and unheard-of corruption. My son, a serving officer, tells me that things were very bad – the wrong officers promoted through mere influence, the ropes and sails not at all the thing; and to crown all, Mr Speaker, sir, women, *women* allowed on board! Scenes of unspeakable debauchery, fitter, oh far fitter, for the French." Now if you will take an old man's advice, you will clap a stopper over all by express. It will do you no good in the service. Let him stick to the army. A word to the wise, eh, eh? You get my meaning?'

With a look of infinite cunning, the Admiral went over the side, attended by the honours due to his splendid rank; and having stood watching respectfully for the proper length of time, Jack turned to a messenger. 'Pass the word for the carpenter,' he said. 'Mr Simmons, be so good as to select our very best hands with holystone and swab and send them aft. And tell me, who of the officers is the most remarkable for taste?'

'For taste, sir?' cried Simmons.

'Yes, yes, artistic taste. You know, a sense of the sublime.'

'Why, sir, I don't know that any of us is much gifted in that line. I do not remember the sublime ever having been mentioned in the gun-room. But there is Mallet, sir, carpenter's crew, who understands these things. He was a receiver of stolen property, specializing in pretty sublime pieces, as I understand it – old masters and so on. He is rather old himself, and not strong, so he helps Mr Charnock with the joinery and fine-work; but I am sure he understands things in the sublime way as well as anyone in the ship.'

'We will have a word with him. I need some ornaments for the cabin. He can be trusted ashore, I suppose?'

'Oh dear me, no, sir. He has run twice, and at Lisbon he tried to get ashore in a barrel, from the wrong side of the bar. And once he stole Mrs Armstrong's gown and tried to slip past the master-at-arms, saying he was a woman.'

'Then he shall go with Bonden and a file of Marines. Mr Charnock,' he said to the waiting carpenter, 'come along with me and let us see what we can do to the cabin to make it fit for a lady. Mr Simmons, while we are settling this, pray let the sailmaker start making a sailcloth carpet: black and white squares, exactly like the *Victory*. There is not a moment to be lost. Stephen, my hero,' he said, in the comparative privacy of the fore-cabin, putting one arm round him in a bear-like hug, 'ain't you amazed, delighted and amazed? Lord, what luck I have some money! Come and give me your ideas on improving the cabin.'

'The cabin is very well as it is. Perfectly adequate. All that is needed is another hanging bed, a simple cot, with the proper blankets and pillows. A water-carafe, and a tumbler.'

'We can shift the bulkhead a good eighteen inches for'ard,' said Jack. 'By the bye, you will not object to the bees going ashore, just for a while?'

'They did not go ashore for Mrs Miller. There were none of these tyrannical caprices for Mrs Miller, I believe. They are just growing used to their surroundings – they have started a queen-cell!'

'Brother, I insist. I should send my bees ashore for you, upon my sacred honour. Now there is a great favour I must ask you. I believe I have told you how I dined with Lord Nelson?'

'Not above two or three hundred times.'

'And I dare say I described those elegant silver plates he has? They were made here. Please would you go ashore and order me four, if it can be done with this?

If not, two. They must have a hawser-laid rope-border. You will remember that? The border, the rim, must be in the form of a hawser-laid rope. Mallet,' he said, turning to a very elderly young man with lank sparse curls who stood bowing and undulating beside the first lieutenant, 'Mr Simmons tell me you are a man of taste.'

'Oh, sir,' cried Mallet, bridling, 'I protest he is too sweetly kind. But I had some slight pretensions in former days. I contributed my mite to the Pavilion, sir.'

'Very good. Now I want some ornaments for the cabin, do you understand? A looking-glass, a vast great looking-glass. Curtains. Delicate little chairs. Perhaps a – what do you call the thing? – a pouffe. Everything suitable for a young lady.'

'Yes, sir. I understand perfectly. In what style, sir? Chinoiserie, classical, directoire?'

'In the *best* style, Mallet. And if you can pick up some pictures, so much the better. Bonden will go with you, to see there are no purser's tricks, no Raphaelos passed off for Rembrandts. He will carry the purse.'

The last days of Stephen's stay in the *Lively* were tedious and wearing to the spirit. The cabin was scrubbed and scrubbed again; it reeked of paint, beeswax and turpentine, sailcloth; its two cots were slung in different positions several times a day, with stork flowers in match-tubs arranged about them; the whole was shut up, forbidden ground, except for a space where he had to lie in disagreeable proximity to Jack, who tossed and snorted through the night. And whereas the general atmosphere in the frigate grew more and more like that of the *Polychrest* on the verge of mutiny, with sullen looks and murmuring, her captain was in a wearisome flow of spirits, laughing, snapping his fingers, skipping heavily about the deck. The married officers looked at him with malignant satisfaction; the rest with disapproval.

Stephen walked up to Admiral Haddock's house, where he sat with Sophie in the summerhouse overlooking the

Sound. 'You will find him very much changed,' he observed. 'You might not think so at the present moment, but he has in fact lost much of his gaiety of heart. In comparison of what he was, he is sombre, and less inclined to make friends. I have noticed it particularly in this ship – distinctly more remote from his officers and the crew. Then again, he suffers frustration with more patience than he used; he cares less passionately about many things. Indeed, I should say that the boy has quite vanished now – certainly the piratical youth of my first acquaintance is no longer to be seen. But when a man puts on maturity and invulnerability, it seems that he necessarily becomes indifferent to many things that gave him joy. I do not, of course, refer to the pleasure of your company,' he added, seeing her look of alarm. 'Upon my word, Sophie, you are in prodigious fine looks today,' he said, narrowing his eyes and peering at her. 'Your hair – I dare say you have been brushing it? No: what it comes to is this, that he is a better officer, and a duller man.'

'Dull? Oh, Stephen.'

'But his future worries me, I must confess. From what I understand thère may be changes in Whitehall from one day to the next. His influence is small; and good, capable officer though he undoubtedly is, he may never get another ship. There are some hundreds of post captains unemployed. I passed several of them on that sparse barren dismal grass-plat they call the Hoe, looking hungrily at the shipping in the Sound. This acting-command will soon be over, and then he will be on the shore. At present there are just eighty-three sea-going ships of the line in commission, a hundred and one frigates, and maybe a score of other post-ships. And Jack is 587th in a list of 639. It would have been simpler if he had remained a commander, or even a lieutenant: there are so many more opportunities for employment.'

'But surely, General Aubrey being in Parliament must be a very good thing?'

'Sure, if he could be induced to keep his mouth shut, it might be. But just now he is on his hind legs in the House, busily stamping Jack as a double-dyed Tory. And St Vincent and his friends, you know, are rabid Whigs – the general feeling of the service is whiggish to a degree.'

'Oh dear. Oh dear. Perhaps he will take a splendid prize. He does deserve it so. The Admiral says the *Lively* is one of the best sailers that ever was; he is full of admiration for her.'

'So she is. She runs along with a most surprising smooth velocity, a pleasure to behold, and her hands are most attentive to their duty. But, my dear, the day of splendid prizes is gone. At the beginning of the war there were French and Dutch Indiamen: there is not one left on the seas at present. And he would have to cut out a dozen *Fanciullas* to pay off his debts, so that he could set foot on shore without danger – by the bye, he is coming to see you on Sunday. How happy we shall be to be rid of him for a while – pray keep him as long as ever you can, or the men will break out in open rebellion. Not only are they compelled to scrub the ship below the water-line, but now they are required to comb the lambs.'

'How very happy we shall be to see you both. Pray, are lambs a part of the ship? I have read the Marine Dictionary until the pages have begun to come out, to understand the actions; but I do not remember any lambs.'

'They may well be. There are horses, fishes, cats, dogs and mice in their barbarous jargon; and bears; so I dare say there are lambs, rams, ewes, wethers and tegs. But these particular animals are for your nourishment: they are literally lambs. He has laid in stores that would be excessive for a pair of ogresses – a cask of petits-fours (they will be damnably stale), four Stilton cheeses, a tub of scented soap, forsooth, handtowels – and now, I say, these lambs are required to be washed and combed twice a day. Keep him to dinner – let him sup with you – and perhaps we may have a little peace.'

'What would he like to eat? A pudding, of course; and perhaps souse. And what would you like, Stephen? Something with mushrooms in it, I know.'

'Alas, I shall be a hundred miles away. I have one commission to perform for Captain Aubrey, and then I hoist myself into this evening's coach. I do not expect to be gone for long. Here is my direction in London: I have written it on a card for you. Pray send me word how you liked your voyage.'

'Shall you not be coming, Stephen?' cried Sophia, clasping his arm. 'What will happen to me?'

'No, my dear. I cast you adrift. Sink or swim, Sophie; sink or swim. Where is my hat? Come, give me a buss, and I must away.'

'Jack,' said he, walking into the cabin, 'what are you at?'

'I am trying to get this God-damned plant to stand upright. Do what I may, they keep wilting. I water them before breakfast and again in the last dog-watch, and still they wilt. Upon my word, it is too bad.'

'What do you water them with?'

'The best water, straight from the scuttle-butt.'

'If you anoint them with the vile decoction we drink and wash in, of course they wilt. You must send ashore for some rain-water; and at that rate of watering, some aquatic plants.'

'What an admirable notion, Stephen. I shall do so at once. Thank you. But apart from these poxed vegetables, don't you think it looks tolerably well? Comfortable? Homelike? The gunner's wife said she had never seen the like: all she could suggest was somewhere to hang their clothes, and a pincushion.'

The cabin resembled a cross between a brothel and an undertaker's parlour, but Stephen only said that he agreed with Mrs Armstrong and suggested that it might be a little less like a state funeral if the tubs were not quite so rigidly arranged about each cot. 'I have your plates,' he said, holding out a green-baize parcel.

'Oh, thank you, thank you, Stephen. What a good fellow you are. Here's elegance, damn my eyes. How they shine! Oh, oh,' his face fell. 'Stephen, I do not like to seem ungrateful, but I did say hawser-laid, you know. The border was to be hawser-laid.'

'Well, and did I not say, "Let there be a hawser about the periphery" and did he not say, the shopman, God's curse upon him, the thief, "Here, sir, is as pretty a hawser as Lord Viscount Nelson himself could desire"?'

'And so it is. A capital hawser. But surely my dear Stephen, you must be aware, after all this time at sea, that a hawser is *cable-laid*, not hawser-laid?'

'I am not. And I absolutely decline to hear more of the matter. A hawser not hawser-laid – what stuff. I badger the silversmith early and late, and we are to be told that hawsers are not hawser-laid. No, no. The wine is drawn, it must be drunk. The frog has neither feathers nor wool, and yet she sings. You will have to sail up to the Downs, eating the bread of affliction off your cable-laid baubles, and wetting it with the tears of misery; and I may tell you, sir, that you will eat it without me. Essential business calls me away. I shall put up at the Grapes, when I am in London: I hope to be there well before Michaelmas. Pray send me a line. Good day to you, now: God bless.'

The grapes were home in Catalonia when Dr Maturin left the Abbot of Montserrat. All through the country as he rode his swift-trotting mule westwards, the vineyards had their familiar shattered, raped appearance; in the villages the streets ran purple-red with lees and the hot air was heavy with fermentation – an early year, an auspicious year. Melons everywhere, ten for a realillo, figs drying all round Lérida, oranges bronze on the trees. Then a more decided autumn in Aragon; and throughout the green Basque country rain, solid rain day after day, pursuing him even to the dark lonely beach where he stood waiting

457

for the boat, the drops running off his sodden cloak and vanishing into the shingle underfoot.

The surge and grind of waves withdrawing, then at last the sound of careful oars and a low call through the rain: 'Abraham and his seed for ever.'

'Wilkes and liberty,' said Stephen.

'Let go the kedge, Tom.' Splashes, a thump; and then, very close to him, 'Are you there? Let me give you a back, sir. Why, you are all wet.'

'It is on account of the rain.'

Rain pouring off the deck of the lugger; rain flattening the waves the whole length of the Channel; rain pelting down in the streets of London, overflowing from the Admiralty's gutter.

'How it rains,' said the young gentleman in a flowered dressing-gown and nightcap who received him. 'May I take your cloak, sir, and spread it by the fire?'

'You are very good, sir, but since Sir Joseph is not in the way, I believe I shall go straight to my inn. I have been travelling hard.'

'I am infinitely concerned, sir, that both the First Lord and Sir Joseph should be at Windsor, but I will send a messenger at once, if you are quite sure that Admiral Knowles will not do.'

'This is essentially a political decision, as I take it. It would be better to wait until tomorrow, though by God the matter presses.'

'They should have started back tonight, I know: and from the orders Sir Joseph left with me, I am sure I should not do wrong to invite you to breakfast with him – to come to his official apartment as early as you think fit.'

The Grapes were fast asleep, shuttered, dark, and so unwilling to reply that they might all have died of the plague. He had a despairing vision of never being fed again, of passing the night in the hackney-coach or a bagnio. 'Perhaps we had better try the Hummums,' he said wearily.

'I'll just give 'em one more knock,' said the coachman, 'the stiff-necked bloody set of dormice.' He rattled his whip against the shutters with righteous venom, and at last life spoke in the dripping void, asking 'who it was?'

'It's a gent as wants to come in out of the rain,' said the coachman. 'He ain't no bleeding mermaid, he says.'

'Why, it's you, Dr Maturin,' cried Mrs Broad, opening the door with many a creak and gasp. 'Come in. There's been a fire in your room since Tuesday. God preserve you, sir, how wet you are. Let me take your cloak – it weighs a ton.'

'Mrs Broad,' said Stephen, yielding it with a sigh, 'pray be so kind as to give me an egg and a glass of wine. I am faint with hunger.'

Enveloped in a flannel garment, the property of the late Mr Broad, he gazed at his skin: it was thick, pale, sodden, lifeless; where it had had his shirt or drawers about it, as upon his belly, it showed a greyish-blue tinge, elsewhere the indigo of his stockings and the snuff-coloured dye of his coat had soaked so deep that his penknife reached blood before the end of it.

'Here's your egg, sir,' said Mrs Broad, 'with a nice piece of gammon. And here are some letters come for you.'

He sat by the fire, devouring his food, with the letters balanced on his knee. Jack's strong hand, remarkably neat. Sophie's round, disconnected script: yet the down-strokes had determination in them.

'This will be all blotted with tears,' ran Sophie's, 'for although I shall try to make them fall to one side of my writing-desk, I am afraid some will drop on the paper, there are so many of them.' They had, indeed; the surface of the letter was mottled and uneven. 'Most of them are tears of pure undiluted happiness, for Captain Aubrey and I have come to an understanding – we are never to marry anyone else, ever! It is *not* a secret engagement, which would be very wrong; but it is so like one, that I fear my conscience must have grown sadly elastic. I am sure you can see the difference, even if no one else can. How happy I am! And how very, very kind you have been to me . . . ' 'Yes yes, my dear,' said Stephen, skipping some prettily-detailed expressions of gratitude, some particularly obliging remarks, and a highly-detailed account of the interesting occasion when, becalmed off the Isle of Wight on a Saturday evening 'so warm and balmy, with the dear sailors singing on the forecastle and dancing to the squeaky fiddle, and Cecilia being shown the stars by Mr Dredge of the Marines', they came to their understanding in the cabin, 'yes, yes. Come to the point, I beg. Let us hear about these other tears.'

The point came on the back of page three. Mrs Williams had flown into a horrid passion on their return – had wondered what Admiral Haddock could possibly have been thinking about – was amazed that her daughter could so have exposed herself with a man known to be in difficulties – a fortune-hunter, no doubt – had Sophia no conception of her sacred duty to her mother – to a mother who had made such endless sacrifices? – Had she no idea of religion? Mrs Williams insisted upon an instant cessation of intercourse; and if that man had the impudence to call, he should be shown the door – not that Mrs Williams imagined he dared show his face on land. It was very well to go and capture this little French ship and get his name in the newspapers, but a man's first duty was to his creditors and his bank-account. Mrs Williams's head was not to be turned by these tales: none of *her* family had ever had their names in the newspapers, she thanked God, except for the announcement of their marriage in *The Times*. What kind of a husband would such a man make, always wandering off into foreign parts whenever the whim took him, and attacking people in that rash way? Some folk might cry up her precious Lord Nelson, but did Sophie wish to share poor Lady Nelson's fate? Did she know what a mistress meant? In any case, what did they know of Captain Aubrey? He might very well have liaisons in every port, and a large quantity of natural children. Mrs Williams was very far from well.

The tears had fallen thicker here by far: spelling and syntax had gone astray: two lines were blotted out. 'But I shall wait for ever, if need be,' was legible, and so was 'and I am sure, quite sure, that he will too.' Stephen sniffed, glanced at the lines that said 'she must hurry now, to catch the post,' smiled at the 'yours, *very* affectionately, Sophie,' and picked up Jack's letter. With an overwhelming yawn he opened it, lay down on the bed with the candle near the pillow, and focused his drooping eyes on the paper, 'Lively, at sea. September 12, '04. My dear Stephen . . . ' September 12: the day Mendoza was in El Ferrol. He forced his eyes wide open. The lines seemed to crackle with life and happiness, but still they swam. 'Wish me joy!' Well, so I do, too. 'You will never guess the news I have to tell you!' Oh yes I shall, brother: pray do not use so many points of admiration. 'I have the best part of a wife!! viz, her heart!! Stephen sniffed again. An intolerably tedious description of Miss Williams, whom Stephen knew a good deal better than Captain Aubrey – her appearance, virtues. 'So direct – straightforward – nothing hole in the corner, if you understand me – no damned purser's tricks – must not swear, however, – like a 32 lber.' Could he really have likened Sophie to a thirty-two pounder? It was quite possible. How the lines did swim. 'He must not speak disrespectfully of his putative mother-in-law, but . . . ' What did Jack imagine putative to mean? 'Would be perfectly happy if only . . . ship . . . join me at Falmouth . . . Portsmouth . . . convoy . . . Madeira, the Cape Verdes! Coconut-trees! . . . must hurry not to miss the post.' Coconut-trees, immeasurably tall palms waving, waving . . . Deus ex machina.

He awoke in daylight from a deep uninterrupted sleep, feeling happy, called for coffee, buns and a dram of whisky, read their letters again, smiling and nodding his head, as he breakfasted, drank to their happiness,

461

and took his papers from their oiled-silk roll. He sat at the table, decoding, drawing up his summary. In his diary he wrote, 'All happiness is a good: but if theirs is to be bought by years of waiting and perhaps disgrace, then even this may come too dear. JA is older than he was by far, perhaps as mature as it is in his nature to be; but he is only a man, and celibacy will never do for him. Ld Nelson said, Once past Gibraltar, every man is a bachelor. What will tropical warmth, unscrupulous young women, a fixed habit of eating too much, and high animal spirits accomplish? What a renewed fire, a renewed challenge from Diana? No, no. If no deus ex machina appears at this interesting juncture, the whole turns into a sad, sad, long-drawn-out, ultimately squalid tragedy. I have seen a long engagement, the dear knows. Yet as I understand it, Ld Melville is nearly down: in this trade there are facts he cannot reveal – he cannot defend himself, nor, consequently, his friends. NB I slept upwards of nine hours this night, *without a single drop*. This morning I saw my bottle on the chimneypiece, untouched: this is unparalleled.'

He closed his book, rang the bell, and said, 'Young gentlewoman, be so good as to call me a hackney-coach.' And to the coachman. 'The Horseguards' Parade.'

Here he paid the man, watched him drive off, and after a turn or two he walked quickly to a small green door that led to the back of the Admiralty.

There was lather still on Sir Joseph's pink jowls as he hurried in and begged Stephen to sit by the fire, to look at the paper, to make himself comfortable – victuals would be up directly – he would not be a moment. 'We have been most anxious for you, Dr Maturin,' he said, coming back, neat and trim. 'Mendoza was taken at Hendaye.'

'He had nothing on him,' said Stephen, 'and the only knowledge he could betray is already useless. Spain is coming into the war.'

'Ah,' said Sir Joseph, putting down his cup and looking at him very hard. 'It is a firm commitment?'

'It is. They are wholly engaged. That is why I ventured to call so late last night.'

'How I wish I had been here! How I cursed Windsor when the messenger met us just this side of Staines. I knew it must be something of the very first importance: the First Lord said the same.'

Stephen took his short statement from his pocket and said, 'An armament is fitting out in Ferrol, the ships of the San Ildefonso treaty: here is a list of the vessels. Those marked with a cross are ready for sea with six months' stores aboard. These are the Spanish regiments stationed in and about the port, with an appreciation of their commanding officers: I do not place great reliance upon the remarks in the case of those names that are followed by a mark of interrogation. These are the French regiments actually upon the march.' He passed the sheet.

'Perfectly, perfectly,' said Sir Joseph, looking at it greedily – he loved a tabulated list, numbers, factual intelligence, rather than the usual vague impressions and hearsay. 'Perfect. This corresponds very closely to what we have from Admiral Cochrane.'

'Yes,' said Stephen. 'A little too perfect, maybe. Mendoza was an intelligent agent, but he was a paid agent, a professional. I do not vouch for it personally, although I think it highly probable. But what I do vouch for, and what induced me to reach you at the earliest possible moment, is the programme that has been settled between Paris and Madrid. Madrid has been under increasing pressure since July, as you know: now Godoy has yielded, but he refuses to declare until the treasure-ships reach Cadiz from Monte Video. Without this vast amount of specie Spain is very nearly bankrupt. The ships in question are frigates of the Spanish navy: the *Medea*, of forty guns, and the *Fama, Clara*, and *Mercedes*, all of 34. The *Fama* is said to be an uncommon swift sailer; the others are well spoken of. The squadron is commanded by Rear-Admiral don José Bustamente, a capable and determined officer. The total value of the specie embarked at Monte Video was five million, eight hundred and ten thousand pieces of eight. These ships are expected in Cadiz early in October, and once the news that the treasure is landed has reached Madrid, we are to expect a declaration of war, the Sarastro incident being the casus belli. Without this treasure Madrid will be so embarrassed that a rising in Catalonia, supported by the vessels now off Toulon, would have every likelihood of success.'

'Dr Maturin,' cried Sir Joseph, shaking his hand, 'we are infinitely obliged to you. It had to come, sooner or later, as we all knew – but to have the very moment, or something close to it . . . ! There is still time to act. I must tell Lord Melville at once: he will certainly wish to see you. Mr Pitt must know immediately – oh, how I curse that Windsor visit – forgive me a moment.' He ran out of the room. Stephen at once took Sir Joseph's untasted coffee and poured it into his own cup.

He was drinking it still when Sir Joseph came back, discouraged. 'He is at that wretched inquiry: he will not be free for some hours, and every minute counts. However, I have sent a note . . . we must act at once. It is a cabinet decision, of course; but I have no doubt that we must act at once. God send the wind stays fair: the time is very short.'

'You intend a decisive action, I take it?'

'Certainly. I cannot answer for the cabinet, but if my advice is attended to, the bold stroke is the only one. Is it the morality of the thing that you refer to?' he asked with a smile.

'The morality of the thing is not my concern,' said Stephen. 'I present the state of fact, with the observation that action would greatly increase the chance of Catalan success. Tell me, how does the inquiry go?'

'Badly, very badly. You and I know that Lord M's hands are tied: he cannot in honour account for the secret funds, and his enemies, some of whom know this as well as we do, are taking full advantage of the situation. I must not say more, because I am an official.' He was indeed an official, a permanent official, one of the most powerful in the Admiralty; and every First Lord except St Vincent had followed his advice. He was also something of an entomologist, and when, after a pause, he said, 'What news from the other world, Dr Maturin?' Stephen recollected himself, felt in his bosom, and replied, 'Great news, sir. Bless me, I was so hurried I had almost forgot. The ingenious priest of Sant Martí found her, or him, or them, this summer. A little crushed, a little spoilt by the rain, but still recognizable.' Between the pages of his opened pocket-book lay a depressed Clouded Yellow, a genetic freak with both its starboard wings bright green, the others gold.

'A true gynandromorph!' cried Sir Joseph, bending over the creature. 'I have never see one in my life before. Perfectly male the one side, perfectly female the other. I am amazed, sir, amazed. This is almost as astonishing as your news.'

Butterflies, moths, the dubious privilege of having two sexes at once, and an aged clerk came in, whispered in Sir Joseph's ear, and tiptoed out.

'We shall know in half an hour or so. Dr Maturin, let me ring for some more coffee; it has gone down strangely.'

'If you please. Now, Sir Joseph, may I speak to you in an unofficial or at the most a semi-official way, about a naval friend of mine, in whom I am particularly interested?'

'By all means. Pray do.'

'I refer to Captain Aubrey. Captain John Aubrey.'

'Lucky Jack Aubrey? Yes, yes: he cut out the *Fanciulla* – a very creditable little action. But you know that perfectly well, of course – you were there!'

'What I should like to ask is, whether he has good prospects of employment.'

'Well,' said Sir Joseph, leaning back and considering. 'Well. I do not have a great deal to do with patronage or appointments: that is not my department. But I do know that Lord Melville has a regard for him, and that he intended to advance his interests in time; possibly in the command of a vessel now on the stocks. His recent promotion, however, was intended as a full reward for his past services; and perhaps he would be well advised to expect nothing but the occasional acting, temporary command for some considerable period. The pressure on patronage is very great, as you know. Then again, I am afraid it is all too likely that Lord M may have left us before the proposed command can, shall I say, *eventuate*; his successor may have other views; and if this is so, your friend's chances are – well . . . ' He waved his hand. 'There are, I believe, a certain number of objections to set against his brilliant services: and he is unfortunate in his choice of a father. Are you acquainted with General Aubrey, my dear sir?'

'I have met the gentleman. He did not strike me as being very wise.'

'Every speech of his is said to be worth five votes to the other side; and he makes a surprising number of them. He has a tendency to address the House on subjects he does not quite understand.'

'It would be difficult for him to do otherwise, unless the Commons were to discuss the strategy of a fox-chase.'

'Exactly so. And naval affairs are his chief delight, alas. If there should be even a partial change of administration, his son is likely to be looked upon with a jaundiced eye.'

'You confirm all that I had supposed, Sir Joseph. I am obliged to you.'

They returned to their butterflies, to beetles – Sir Joseph had not attended to beetles as much as he could have wished – to a discussion of Cimarosa – an excellent performance of *Le Astuzie Feminili* at Covent Garden – Sir Joseph adjured Dr Maturin to hear it – he himself had heard it twice and would be going a third time tonight – charming, charming – but his eye kept wandering to a severe, accurate clock, and his defence of Cimarosa, though earnest, occupied no more than a quarter of his mind.

The aged clerk returned, ten years younger, skipping with excitement, handed a note, and darted out.

'We act!' cried Sir Joseph, ringing a number of bells. 'Now I must find the ships. Mr Akers, files A12 and 27 and the current dockets. Mr Roberts, copying-clerks and messengers to stand by. Dr Maturin, Lord Melville's compliments, his very particular compliments, and he begs the favour of a word with you at twenty minutes past eleven precisely. Now, my dear sir, will you accompany the squadron? A negotiation might prove possible; it would be better by far than the *main forte*.'

'I will. But I must not appear. It would destroy my value as an agent. Give me a gentleman who speaks Spanish, and I will speak through him. And may I say this? To deal with Bustamente you must send a powerful squadron – ships of the line – to allow him to yield with honour. An overwhelming force, or he will fight like a lion. These are frigates in high training, and, for Spain, high discipline: ships to be reckoned with.'

'I will attend to what you say, Dr Maturin. With the disposition of our fleets I promise nothing. Have you any further counsels or observations – one moment, Mr Robinson – or remarks?'

'Yes, sir. I have a request to make – I have a favour to beg. As you are aware, I have accepted nothing, at any time, for what services I may have been able to perform, in spite of the Admiralty's very obliging insistence.'

Sir Joseph looked grave, but said he was sure that any request from Dr Maturin would receive the most sympathetic attention.

'My request is, that Captain Aubrey, in the *Lively*, should form part of the squadron.'

Sir Joseph's face cleared wonderfully. 'Certainly: I think

I may promise that on my own responsibility,' he said. 'I believe Lord Melville would wish it: it may be the last thing he can do for his young friend. But is that all, sir? Surely, that cannot be all?'

'That is all, sir. You oblige me most extremely: I am deeply obliged to you, Sir Joseph.'

'Lord, Lord,' cried Sir Joseph, waving away the obligation with a file. 'Let me see: she has a surgeon, of course. I cannot in decency supersede him – besides, that would not answer. You must have a temporary rank – you shall go in her with a temporary rank, and join early in the morning. The full instructions will take some time to draw up – the Board must sit – but they will be ready by this evening, and you can go down with the Admiralty messenger. You will not object to travelling in the darkness?'

The rain was no more than a drizzle by the time Stephen came out into the park, but it was enough to prevent him from wandering among the bookstalls of Wych Street as he had intended, and he returned to the Grapes. There he sat in a high leather chair, staring at the fire, his mind ranging in many, many directions or sometimes merely turning on itself in a comfortable lethargy, until the grey daylight faded into a dim, unemphatic night, foggy and suffused with orange from the lamps outside. The coming of an Admiralty messenger aroused him from his delicious sense of inhabiting a body with indefinite, woollen bounds, and he realized that he had not eaten since his biscuit and madeira with Lord Melville.

He called for tea and crumpets, a large number of crumpets, and with candles lit on the table by his side, he read what the messenger had brought: a friendly note from Sir Joseph, confirming that the *Lively* should be sent and observing 'that in compliment to Dr Maturin he had given orders that the temporary commission should be modelled as closely as possible upon that granted to Sir J.

Banks, of the Royal Society', which he hoped might give pleasure; the commission itself, an imposing document, entirely handwritten because of the rarity of its form, with Melville's signature smudged with haste; an official letter requesting and directing him to proceed to the Nore to join his ship forthwith; a later note from Sir Joseph to say that the instructions could not be ready until after midnight, begging his pardon for the delay, and enclosing a ticket for *Le Astuzie Feminili* – it might help Dr Maturin to pass the hours agreeably, and persuade him to do justice to Cimarosa, 'that amiable phoenix'.

Sir Joseph was a wealthy man, a bachelor; he liked to do himself well; and the ticket was for a box, a small box high on the left-hand side of the house. It gave a better view of the audience and the band than the stage, but Stephen settled into it with a certain complacency; he leant his hands, still greasy from the crumpets, upon the padded edge and looked down at the groundlings – his fellows on almost every other occasion – with some degree of spiritual as well as physical loftiness. The house was filling rapidly, for the opera was much talked of, much in fashion; and although the royal box away on his right was empty, nearly all the others had people in them, moving about, arranging chairs, staring at the audience, waving to friends; and immediately opposite him there was a group of naval officers, two of whom he knew. Beneath him, in the pit, he recognized Macdonald with his empty sleeve pinned across his coat, sitting next to a man who must surely be his twin brother, they were so alike. There were other faces he knew: all London that attended to music seemed to be there, and some thousands that did not – an animated scene, a fine buzz of conversation, the sparkle of jewels; and now that most of the audience was thoroughly settled, the waving of fans.

The house darkened and the first notes of the overture quelled the greater part of the talk, muting the rest. Stephen turned his eyes and his attention to the band.

469

Poor thin pompous overblown stuff, he thought; not unpleasant, but quite trivial. What was Sir Joseph thinking of, to compare this man with Mozart? He admired the red-faced 'cellist's bowing, however – agile, determined, brisk. To his right a flash of brightness drew his eye: a party of latecomers walking into their box and letting in the light from the door at the back. Goths: Moorish barbarity. Not, indeed, that the music had much to say: not that his attention had been wrenched painfully from something that required close concentration. Though it would have been all one to those grass-combing Huns, had it been Orpheus in person.

A charming harp came up through the strings, two harps running up and down, an amiable warbling. Signifying nothing, sure; but how pleasant to hear them. Pleasant, oh certainly it was pleasant, just as it had been pleasant to hear Molter's trumpet; so why was his heart oppressed, filled with an anxious foreboding, a dread of something imminent that he could not define? That arch girl posturing upon the stage had a sweet, true little voice; she was as pretty as God and art could make her; and he took no pleasure in it. His hands were sweating.

A foolish German had said that man thought in words. It was totally false; a pernicious doctrine; the thought flashed into being in a hundred simultaneous forms, with a thousand associations, and the speaking mind selected one, forming it grossly into the inadequate symbols of words, inadequate because common to disparate situations – admitted to be inadequate for vast regions of expression, since for them there were the parallel languages of music and painting. Words were not called for in many or indeed most forms of thought: Mozart certainly thought in terms of music. He himself at this moment was thinking in terms of scent.

The orchestra and the people on the stage pumped busily up to the obvious climax: it blared out – the house burst into a roar of applause, and in the latecomers' box

470

he saw Diana Villiers, clapping politely but with no great enthusiasm, not looking at the stage with its smirking bowing actors but at someone deeper in the box behind her. Her head was turned in a curve he would have recognized in an even greater crowd: her long white gloves, pointing upwards, beat steadily together as she talked over the general din, her expression and the movements of her head pushing her meaning through the noise.

There was another woman beside her – Lady Jersey, he thought – and four men behind. Canning; two officers in scarlet and gold; a civilian with the high colour and oyster eye of Hanover and the ribbon of the Garter across his breast – a minor royal. This was the man to whom she was speaking: he looked stupid, uncomprehending; but pleased, almost lively.

Stephen watched with no particular emotion but with extreme accuracy. He had noted the great leap of his heart at the first moment and the disorder in his breathing, and he noted too that this had no effect upon his powers of observation. He must in fact have been aware of her presence from the first: it was her scent that was running in his mind before the curtain fell; it was in connection with her that he had reflected upon these harps.

Now the applause had stopped, but Diana's hands were still raised, and leaning forward he watched with an even greater intensity. She was moving her right hand as she talked to the man behind her and by Christ she was moving it with a *conscious* grace. The door at the back of the box opened. Another broad blue ribbon, and the women stood up, bobbed. He could not see the face for the tall standing men, but he could see, he did see this essential change confirmed – her whole movement, from the carriage of her head to the pretty flirt of her ostrich-fan was subtly altered. Bows, more bobs, laughter, the door closed, the outward-facing group reformed: the figure reappeared in another box. Stephen took no notice of him, did not care if he were the Duke of Hell, but concentrated his utmost attention upon Diana to prove what he knew to be the fact. It was so: everything showed it, and he extracted the last dreg of pain from the knowledge, the spectacle. She was on display. The purity of wild grace was gone, and the thought that from now on he must associate vulgarity with his idea of her was so painful that for a while he could not think clearly. Not that it was in the least obvious to anyone who knew her less well, or who valued that purity less highly, and not that it detracted in any way from the admiration of the men in the audience or of her companions, for it was done with great instinctive art; but the woman in the box over there was not one to whom he would have paid any attention, at any time.

She was uneasy. She felt the intensity of his gaze and from time to time she looked round the house; and each time she did so he dropped his eyes, as he would have done, stalking a doe: there were plenty of people looking at her from the pit and the other boxes – indeed, she was perhaps the finest woman there, in her low sky-blue dress and the diamonds in her black, high-piled hair. In spite of his precaution their eyes crossed at last: she stopped talking. He meant to rise and bow, but there was no power whatsoever in his legs. He was astonished, and before he could grip the pad in front of him to raise himself the curtain had gone up and the harps were racing through glissando after glissando.

That my body should be affected to this point, he said, is something beyond my experience. I have felt the great nausea before, God knows, but this want of control . . . Did the Diana I last saw at New Place ever exist in fact? A creation of my own? Can you create a unicorn by longing?

Through the music and the caterwauling on the stage the insistent knocking at the locked door of his box disturbed the course of his reflection. He did not reply, and presently it went away. Had he had a hand in her death? He shook his head to deny it.

At last the curtain came sweeping down and the light increased. The box over there was empty, a pair of long white gloves drooped over the plush in front; and the band was playing God save the King. He sat on, and in time the standing slowly-moving crowd below shuffled out, a few people darting back for forgotten hats, and the place was empty, an enormous shell. The people of the house walked about the emptiness with an everyday step, picking up rubbish, putting out the lights.

Two said, 'There's a gent still there, up in the box.'

'Is he drunk?'

'Perhaps he thinks there is another act; but there ain't no more, thank God.'

'Come, sir,' they said, opening the door with their little key, 'it's all over now. This is the end of the piece.'

Long before dawn the *Lively*'s warm, smelly, close-packed gun-deck awoke to violent and unexpected life, the strong-voiced bosun's mates roaring 'All hands! All hands unmoor ship. Rise and shine! Show a leg there! Tumble up, tumble up, tumble up!' The Livelies – the male Livelies, for there were about a hundred women aboard – tore themselves from their pink companions or their more prosaic wives, tumbled up into the wet darkness and unmoored the ship, as they were desired. The capstan turned, the fiddle squeaked, the temporary ladies hurried ashore, and the Nore light faded astern: the frigate stood for the North Foreland with a favourable tide and a quartering wind.

The officer of the watch checked the noise of speculation, but it continued under the cover of the rumbling holystones while the people washed the decks. What was up? Had Boney started his invasion? Something was up, or they would never have been ordered to sea with only half their water filled. Port admiral's barge had come alongside, a civilian and an officer: one gent was with the captain yet.

473

No news so far, but that there Killick or Bonden would know before breakfast-time was over.

In the gun-room the wonder was quite as great, and quite as uninformed; but it had a depth of apprehension and uneasiness that was lacking before the mast. Word had gone about that Dr Maturin was aboard again, and although they liked him well enough, they dreaded what he might bring with him.

'Are you quite sure?' they asked Dashwood, who had had the morning watch.

'I would not positively take my oath,' he said, 'because he was muffled against the rain, and it was dark. But I have never seen anyone else on earth come up the side like a left-handed bear: you would never believe it could be done, without you see it. I should be certain, if the boat had not answered "aye aye".'

'That decides it,' said Mr Simmons. 'The Admiral's coxswain could never have made such a mistake. It must have been some commissioned officer that the Captain knew well enough to call him his dear fellow; an old shipmate, no doubt. It cannot be Dr Maturin.'

'Certainly not,' said Mr Randall.

'Never in life,' said the master.

The purser, whose cabin had been out of reach of the bees, was more concerned with the political aspects of their sudden move, and with the wretched state of his stores. 'I have not above fifty fathoms of duck aboard,' he said, 'and not a scrap of sennit. What will become of us when we cross the line? What will become of us at Madeira, even: to say nothing of Fernando Poo? And Fernando Poo is our destination, I am very sure, for reasons of high strategy.'

Some time before this, Jack, having given directions to put to sea, came back in his nightshirt and watch-coat to his cabin, where his immediate orders lay, next to the sheaf of detailed instructions and a fat sealed envelope marked Not to be opened until latitude 43° N. He looked somewhat ecclesiastical, but also deeply concerned. 'Dear

Stephen,' he said, 'thank you a thousand times for coming down so quick; I hardly hoped to see you before Falmouth. But I find I have lured you aboard on false pretences – Madeira and the West Indies are quite exploded. I am ordered to proceed to sea with the utmost possible dispatch – rendezvous off the Dodman.' He held the paper close to the light. 'Rendezvous with *Indefatigable, Medusa* and *Amphion*. Strange. And sealed orders not to be opened until so and so. What can they mean by that, Stephen?'

'I have no idea,' said Stephen.

'God damn and blast the Admiralty and all its lords,' cried Jack. 'Utmost dispatch – muck up all one's plans – I do apologize most humbly, Stephen.' He read on. 'Hey, hey, Stephen? I thought you had no idea: I thought you had just chanced to come down with the messenger. But in case of separation of one or more . . . certain eventualities and all that, I am requested and directed to avail myself of the counsels and advice of S. Maturin, esquire, MD etc., etc., appointed pro hac vice a captain in the Royal Navy . . . his knowledge and discretion.'

'It is possible that you may be required to undertake some negotiations, and that I may be of use in them.'

'Well, I must be discreet myself, I find,' said Jack, sitting down and looking wonderingly at Stephen. 'But you did say . . . '

'Now listen, Jack, will you? I am somewhat given to lying: my occasions require it from time to time. But I do not choose to have any man alive tell me of it.'

'Oh no, no, no,' cried Jack. 'I should never dream of doing such a thing. Not,' he added, recollecting himself and blushing, 'not when I am in my right mind. Quite apart from my love for you, it is far, far too dangerous. Hush: mum's the word. Tace is the Latin for a candle. I quite understand – am amazed I did not smoke it before: what a deep old file you are. But I twig it now.'

'Do you, my dear? Bless you.'

'But what takes my breath away, what flabbergasts me to this high pitch,' said Jack, 'is, that they should have given you a temporary commission. The Navy, you know, is uncommon jealous of rank, very sparing of such compliments. I hardly remember ever to have heard of it, except once. They must think the world of you in Whitehall.'

'I wonder at it too, this insistence upon a commission. It struck me at the time. I am sensible of the compliment, but puzzled. Why should I not have been your guest?'

'I have it,' cried Jack. 'Stephen, may I ask without indiscretion whether this could be a – what shall I say? – a *profitable* expedition?'

'It might be, too.'

'Then they mean to cut you in on the prize-money. Depend upon it, they mean you to share as a captain. These are Admiralty orders, so no flag gets a share: if it comes to anything, your cut should be pretty handsome.'

'What a pretty thought in Sir Joseph; remarkably delicate in him. I do not regret sending him my gynandromorph by the messenger now: the fellow seemed amazed, as well he might – a princely gift. Tell me, what would be a captain's share of – I name a hypothetical sum – a million pounds?'

'Taken by a squadron with four, no, five, captains in it? Let me see, fives into ten is two, and eights into two hundred, five and twenty – seventy-five thousand pounds. But there are no prizes like that afloat these days, my poor Stephen, more's the pity.'

'Seventy-five thousand pounds? How absurd. What could Sir Joseph imagine I should do with such a sum? What could any reasonable man do with such a sum?'

'I can tell you what I should do,' cried Jack, his eyes ablaze. He darted out of the cabin in spite of the cry of 'Stay!' to see whether the inner jibs were drawing, and every bowline harp-string taut. Having harassed the watch

476

for some minutes he returned, leaving tart, unfavourable comments behind him.

'I hope this skipper is not going to turn into a jib and stays'l jack,' said the captain of the foretop.

'I don't like the look of it at all,' said the yeoman of the sheets. 'This giving of himself such airs is something new.'

'Perhaps he has a rendezvous with his Miss,' said Blue Edward, the Malay. 'God damn my eye, I should crack on, if I had such a Miss to see, Sophie by name.'

'No disrespectful words, Blue Edward,' cried George Allen. 'For I won't abide it.'

'A man might, of course, make a circumambulation of Lapland, or emulate Banks in the Great South Sea,' observed Stephen. 'But tell me, Jack, how did your journey go? How did Sophie withstand the motion of the vessel? Did she take her porter with her meals?'

'Oh, admirably, admirably!' It had been the most perfect series of warm, gentle days, scarcely a fleck of white water – Simmons had made a magnificent show with royals and skysails, and studdingsails aloft and alow; she had never seen anything more beautiful, she said – the *Lively* had left the *Amethyst* standing: red faces on her quarterdeck – and then there had been some charming dead calms, the whole day long – they had often talked of Stephen – how they had missed him! – and she had been so kind to that youngster Randall, who wept when poor Cassandra died – Randall senior loved her to distraction; so did the whole gun-room – they had dined twice with the officers – Cecilia seemed very well with Dredge, of the Marines – Jack was grateful to him for drawing her off – certainly Sophie had drunk her porter, and a glass of bosun's grog – had eaten splendidly: Jack loved a girl that tucked in hearty – and as for the future, they were full of hope, but . . . could do with very little . . . no horses . . . cottage . . . potatoes. 'Stephen,' he said, 'you are asleep.'

'I am not,' said Stephen. 'You just mentioned the last

477

syllable of recorded time with evident approval. But I am weary, I confess. I travelled all night, and yesterday was something of a trial. I will turn in, if I may. Where must I sleep?'

'There's a question,' said Jack. 'Where should you berth, in fact? Of course you shall sleep in my cot; but officially where should you be? That would puzzle Solomon. What seniority did they give you?'

'I have no idea. I did not read the document, apart from the phrase. *We, reposing especial trust and confidence in S.M.*, which pleased me.'

'Well, I suppose you are junior to me; so you shall have the leeward side of the cabin and I the windward, and every time we go about, we shall change sides, ha, ha, ha. Ain't I a rattle? But seriously, I suppose you should be read in to the ship's company – an amazing situation.'

'If there is any doubt, pray do no such thing. It would be far better for me to remain unobserved. And Jack, in all this that has passed between us, all that you may have guessed, I rely wholly upon your discretion, eh? There are moments when my life might turn upon it.'

He had every reason to rely upon Jack, who could keep close counsel; but not all captains were so discreet, and when the *Medusa* came tearing out of Plymouth with a dark gentleman aboard, known to speak Spanish – a gentleman who remained closeted with the captains of the *Lively*, the *Amphion* and the *Medusa*, and Dr Maturin while they were lying to off the Dodman, waiting for the *Indefatigable* to join – the general opinion of the ship was that they were bound for Cadiz, that Spain had come in or was just about to come in; and this gave a great deal of simple pleasure, for hitherto Spanish merchantmen had been immune from capture. In a sea swept almost clear of prizes, they ploughed steadily along past cruisers, through blockading squadrons, laughing and kissing their hands, their holds so full of wealth that a foremast jack might make five years' pay in one pleasant Saturday afternoon.

At last the *Indefatigable* hove in sight, a heavy forty-gun frigate, making heavy weather of it too, close-hauled on the westerly gale with green seas keeping her beak-head clean and the signal flying *Form in line astern: make all suitable sail.*

Now, as the four frigates, in a perfect line, each two cables from the next, stretched away to the south-south-west, came a tedious, frustrating time for the Livelies: the topmen were rarely on deck, but it was not to make sail. In order to keep rigidly to her station in the *Amphion*'s wake, the *Lively* was perpetually reefing, clewing up, hauling down jibs, staysails, spanker, starting sheets. And when the sealed orders were opened – when, after the captains' last conference aboard the *Indefatigable*, it became certain knowledge that they were to intercept a Spanish squadron from the River Plate to Cadiz, this impatience grew to such a height that they welcomed the dirty look of Sunday evening. A vast unformed blackness filled the south and western sky, an enormous swell was running, so great that men who had scarcely set foot on shore for years were sick; the wind boxed the compass, blowing now hot, now cold, and the sun went down in an ill-looking bank of livid purple with green lights showing through. Cape Finisterre was not far under their lee, and they doubled their preventer-stays and rolling-tackle, roused up storm-canvas, secured the boats on the booms, double-breeched their guns, struck the topgallants down on deck, and made all snug.

At two bells in the middle watch the wind, which had been blowing fitfully from the south-west, backed suddenly into the north, hurling itself against the mountainous swell with tripled force – thunder just overhead, lightning, and such a deluge of rain that a storm-lantern on the forecastle could not be seen from the quarterdeck. The maintopmast staysail blew out of its boltrope, vanishing ghostly to leeward in pale strips of cloth. Jack sent more hands to the wheel, rigged relieving-tackles, and came into the cabin, where Stephen lay swinging in his cot, to tell him that it was coming on to blow.

'How you do exaggerate, brother,' said Stephen. 'And how you drip! The best part of a quart of water has run off your person in this short space of time – see how it sweeps to and fro, defying gravity.'

'I love a good blow,' said Jack, 'and this is one of your genuine charmers; for, do you see, it must hold the Spaniards back, and the dear knows we are very short of time. Was they to slip into Cadiz before us, what flats we should look.'

'Jack, do you see that piece of string hanging down? Would you have the goodness to tie it to the hook over there, to reattach it? It came undone. Thank you. I pull upon it to moderate the motion of the cot, which exacerbates all my symptoms.'

'Are you unwell? Queasy? Sick?'

'No, no. Not at all. What a foolish suggestion. No. This may be the onset of a very serious malady. I was bitten by a tame bat a little while ago, and I have reasons to doubt its sanity: it was a horseshoe bat, a female. It seems to me that I detect a likeness between my symptoms and the Ludolphus' description of his disease.'

'Should you like a glass of grog?' asked Jack. 'Or a ham sandwich, with luscious white fat?' he added, with a grin.

'No, no, no,' cried Stephen. 'Nothing of the kind. I tell you, this is a serious matter, calling for . . . there it goes again. Oh, this is a vile ship: the *Sophie* never behaved so – wild, unmeaning lurches. Would it be too much to ask you to turn down the lamp and to go away? Surely this is a situation that requires all your vigilance? Surely this is no time to stand idly smirking?'

'Are you sure there is nothing I can fetch you? A basin?'

'No, no, no.' Stephen's face assumed a pinched, mean expression: his beard showed black against the nacreous green. 'Does this sort of tempest last long?'

'Oh, three or four days, no more,' said Jack, staggering with the lee-lurch. 'I will send Killick with a basin.'

'Jesus, Mary, Joseph,' said Stephen. 'There she goes again.' In the trough of the enormous waves the frigate lay becalmed, but as she rose, so the gale took her and laid her down, down and down, in a never-ending roll, while her forefoot heaved up until her bowsprit pointed at the racing clouds. 'Three days of this,' he thought. 'No human frame can withstand it.'

Happily it was only the tail of the notorious September blow that the *Lively* had to deal with. The sky cleared in the morning watch; the glass rose, and although she could show no more than close-reefed topsails it was plain that she would spread more by noon. Dawn showed a sea white from horizon to horizon, a sea with nothing on it but the waterlogged wreck of a Portuguese bean-cod, and far to windward the *Medusa*, apparently intact. Jack was now senior captain, and he signalled her to make more sail – to make for their next rendezvous off Cape Santa Maria, the landfall for Cadiz.

Towards noon he altered course due south, which brought the wind on the *Lively*'s quarter, easing her motion greatly. Stephen appeared on deck, still very grave, but more humane. He and Mr Floris and Mr Floris's assistants had spent the morning dosing one another; they had all suffered more or less from the onset of diseases (orchitis, scurvy, the fell Ludolphus' palsy), but in Dr Maturin's case at least the attack had been averted by a judicious mixture of Lucatellus' balsam and powder of Algaroth.

After dinner the *Lively* exercised the great guns, swell or no, rattling them in and out, but also firing broadside after broadside, so that the frigate was preceded by a cloud of her own making as she ran southwards at eleven knots, some twenty leagues off the coast of Portugal. The recent training had had effect, and although the fire was still painfully slow – three minutes and ten seconds between broadsides was the best they could do – it was more accurate by far, in spite of the roll and pitch. A palm-tree trunk, drifting by on the starboard bow three hundred yards away, was blown clear of the water on the first discharge; and they hit it again, with cheers that reached the *Medusa*, before it went astern. The *Medusa* also put in an hour's strenuous practice; and aboard the *Medusa* too, a good many hands were employed carefully picking over the round-shot, choosing the most spherical and chipping off flakes of rust. But most of the Medusa's time was taken up with trying to overhaul the *Lively*; she set topgallants before the *Lively* had shaken out the last reef in her topsails, and she tried studdingsails and royals as the breeze moderated, only to lose two of her booms, without the gain of half a mile. The *Lively*'s officers and her sailmaker watched with intense satisfaction; but underlying their pleasure there was a haunting anxiety – were they going to be in time to cut the Spanish squadron off from Cadiz? And even if they were, would the *Indefatigable* and *Amphion* reach the rendezvous before the clash? The Spanish reputation for courage, if not for seamanship, stood high; and the odds were very great – a forty-gun frigate and three thirty-fours against a thirty-eight and a thirty-two; for Jack had explained the tactical situation to his officers as soon as he had opened his sealed orders – as soon as there was no danger of communication with the shore. The same anxiety, that they might be too late, was general throughout the ship: there was scarcely a man aboard who did not know what came from the River Plate, and those few – a person from Borneo and two Javanese – were told. 'It's gold, mate. That's what they ship from the River Plate: gold and silver, in chests and leather bags.'

All through the day the wind declined, and all through the night; and whereas the log had once taken the line straight off the reel, tearing it away to show twelve and even thirteen knots, heave after heave, at dawn on the last day of September it had to be helped gently off and veered away, so that the midshipman of the watch could announce a dismal 'Two and a fathom, sir, if you please.'

A day of light variable airs, mostly in their teeth – whistling fore and aft, and prayers that were answered by a fair breeze on Thursday, October 2. They passed Cape St Vincent later that day, under royals, with the *Medusa* in company, and they had been exercising the guns for some time – a very particular salute for that great headland, just visible from the masthead on the larboard beam when the bosun came aft and spoke to the first lieutenant. Mr Simmons pursed his lips, looked doubtful, hesitated, and then stepped across to Jack. 'Sir,' he said, 'the bosun represents to me, that the men, with the utmost respect, would wish you to consider whether it might be advisable not to fire the bow guns.'

'They do, do they?' cried Jack, who had caught some odd, reproachful glances before this. 'Do they also think it advisable to double the ration of grog?'

'Oh no, sir,' said the sweating crew of the gun nearest at hand.

'Silence, there,' cried Mr Simmons. 'No, sir: what they mean is – that is to say, there is a general belief that firing the bow guns checks her way; and time being so short . . . '

'Well, there may be something in what they say. The philosophers don't believe it, but we will not run the risk. Let the bow guns be run in and out, and fired in dumb show.'

A pleased smile spread along the deck. The men wiped their faces – it was 80° in the shade of the sails – tightened the handkerchiefs round their foreheads, spat on their hands, and prepared to whip their iron monsters in and out in under two minutes and a half. After a couple of broadsides – in for a penny, in for a pound – and some independent firing, the tension, strongly present throughout the ship since Finisterre, suddenly rose to the highest pitch. *Medusa* was signalling a sail one point on the larboard quarter.

'Up you go, Mr Harvey,' said Jack to a tall, light midshipman. 'Take the best glass in the ship. Mr Simmons may lend you his.'

Up he went, up and up with the glass slung over his shoulder, up to the royal pole and the tie; poor Cassandra could hardly have outstripped him. Presently his voice came floating down. 'On deck, there, *Amphion*, sir. I believe she has sent up a jury foretopmast.'

The *Amphion* she was, and bringing up the breeze she joined company before the fall of night. Now they were three, and the next morning found them at their last rendezvous, with Cape Santa Maria bearing north-east, thirty miles away, visible from the fighting-tops in the brilliant light.

The three frigates, with Sutton of the *Amphion* now senior captain, stood off and on all day, their mastheads thick with telescopes, perpetually sweeping the western sea, a vast blue rolling sea, with nothing between them and America except, perhaps, the Spanish squadron. In the evening the *Indefatigable* joined, and on the fourth day of October the frigates spread wide to cover as great an area as possible, still remaining within signalling distance: silently they beat up and down – gunnery had been laid aside since Cape St Vincent, for fear of giving the alarm. Aboard the *Lively* almost the only sound was the squeaking of the grindstone on the forecastle as the men sharpened their cutlasses and pikes, and the chip-chip-chip of the gunner's party scaling the shot.

To and fro, to and fro, wearing every half hour at the first stroke of the ship's bell, men at every masthead watching the other frigates for a signal, a dozen glasses scanning the remote horizon.

'Do you remember Anson, Stephen?' said Jack, as they paced the quarterdeck. 'He did this for weeks and weeks off Paita. Did you ever read his book?'

'I did. How that man wasted his opportunities.'

'He went round the world, and worried the Spaniards

out of their wits, and took the Manilla galleon – what more could you ask?'

'Some slight attention to the nature of the world round which he sailed so thoughtlessly. Apart from some very superficial remarks about the sea-elephant, there is barely a curious observation in the book. He should certainly have taken a naturalist.'

'If he had had you aboard, he might be godfather to half a dozen birds with curious beaks; but on the other hand, you would now be ninety-six. How he and his people ever stood this standing off and on, I do not know. However, it all ended happy.'

'Not a bird, not a plant, not a smell of geology . . . Shall we have some music after tea? I have written a piece I should like you to hear. It is a lament for the Tir nan Og.'

'What is the Tir nan Og?'

'The only bearable part of my country: it vanished long ago.'

'Let us wait until the darkness falls, may we? Then I am your man: we will lament to your heart's content.'

Darkness; a long, long night in the stifling gun-deck and the cabins, little sleep, and many a man, and officer too, taking a caulk on deck or in the tops. Before dawn on the fifth the decks were being cleaned – no trouble in getting the hands to tumble up – and the smoke from the galley fire was streaming away on the steady north-east wind, when the forward look-out, the blessed Michael Scanlon, hailed the deck with a voice that might have been heard in Cadiz – the *Medusa*, the last ship in the line of frigates as they stood to the north, was signalling four large sail bearing west by south.

The eastern sky lightened, high wisps of cloud catching the golden light from below the horizon; the milky sea grew brilliant, and there they were, right aft, beating up for Cadiz, four white flecks on the rim of the world.

'Are they Spaniards?' asked Stephen, creeping into the maintop.

'Of course they are,' said Jack. 'Look at their stumpy topmasts. Here, take my glass. On deck, there. All hands stand by to wear ship.'

At the same moment the signal to wear and chase broke out aboard the *Indefatigable*, and Stephen began his laborious descent, propped by Jack, Bonden, and a bosun's mate, clinging to his tail until tears came into the poor man's eyes. He had prepared his lines of argument for Mr Osborne, but he wished to pass them over in his mind before he conferred with him aboard the *Indefatigable*, whose captain was in command of the squadron as commodore. He went below, his heart beating at an unusual pace. The Spaniards were gathering together, signals passing between them: negotiations would be delicate; oh, very delicate indeed.

Breakfast, a scrappy meal. The Commodore signalling for Dr Maturin: Stephen upon deck with a cup of coffee in one hand and a piece of bread and butter in the other as the cutter was lowered away. How very much closer they were, so suddenly! The Spaniards had already formed their battle-line, standing on the starboard tack with the wind one point free, and they were so near that he could see their gun-ports – every one of them open, yawning wide.

The British frigates, obeying the signal to chase, had broken their line, and the *Medusa*, the southernmost ship and therefore the foremost once they had worn, was running straight before the wind for the leading Spanish ship; a few hundred yards behind her there was the *Indefatigable*, steering for the second Spaniard, the *Medea*, with Bustamente's flag at the mizen; then came the *Amphion*; and bringing up the rear, the *Lively*. She was closing the gap fast, and as soon as Stephen had been

486

bundled into the cutter she spread her foretopgallant, crossed the *Amphion*'s wake, and steered for the *Clara*, the last ship in the Spanish line.

The *Indefatigable* yawed a trifle, backed her topsails, hoisted Stephen aboard, and plunged on. The Commodore, a dark, red-faced, choleric man, very much on edge, hurried him below, paid very little attention to his words as he ran over the heads of the argument that was to persuade the Spanish admiral to yield, but sat there drumming his fingers on the table, breathing fast with angry excitement. Mr Osborne, a quick, intelligent man, nodded, staring into Stephen's eyes: he nodded, taking each point, and nodded again, his mouth tight shut. ' . . . and lastly,' said Stephen, 'induce him by all possible means to come across, so that we may concert our answer to unforeseen objections.'

'Come, gentlemen, come,' cried the Commodore, running on deck. Closer, closer: they were well within range, all colours abroad; within musket-shot, the Spanish decks crowded with faces; within pistol-shot.

'Hard over,' said the Commodore. The wheel spun and the big frigate turned with a roar of orders to round to and lie on the admiral's starboard beam, twenty yards to windward. The Commodore took his speaking-trumpet. 'Shorten sail,' he cried, aiming it at the *Medea*'s quarter-deck. The Spanish officers spoke slightly to one another; one of them shrugged his shoulders. There was dead silence all along the line: wind in the rigging, the lapping of the sea.

'Shorten sail,' he repeated, louder still. No reply: no sign. The Spaniard held his course for Cadiz, two hours away. The two squadrons ran in parallel lines, gliding silently along at five knots, so close that the low sun sent the shadow of the Spanish topgallantmasts across the English decks.

'Fire across his bows,' said the Commodore. The shot struck the water a yard before the *Medea*'s forefoot, the spray sweeping aft. And as though the crash had broken the spell of silence and immobility there was a quick swirl of movement aboard the *Medea*, a shout of orders, and her topsails were clewed up.

'Do your best, Mr Osborne,' said the Commodore. 'But by God he shall make up his mind in five minutes.'

'Bring him if you possibly can,' said Stephen. 'And above all, remember Godoy has betrayed the kingdom to the French.'

The boat pulled across and hooked on. Osborne climbed aboard the Spanish frigate, took off his hat and bowed to the crucifix, the admiral and the captain, each in turn. They saw him go below with Bustamente.

And now the time dragged slow. Stephen stood by the mainmast, his hands tight clasped behind his back: he hated Graham, the commodore: he hated what was going to happen. He tried with all his force to follow and to influence the argument that was carrying on half a pistol shot away. If only Osborne could bring Bustamente aboard there might be a fair chance of an arrangement.

Mechanically he glanced up and down the line. Ahead of the *Indefatigable* the *Medusa* lay rocking gently beside the *Fama*; astern of the *Medea* the *Amphion* had now slipped round under the *Mercedes*'s lee, and in the rear lay the *Lively*, close to windward of the *Clara*. Even to Stephen's unprofessional eye, the Spaniards were in a remarkable state of readiness; there was none of that hurried flight of barrels, coops, livestock, tossed into the sea to clear the decks, that he had seen often enough in the Mediterranean. At each gun, its waiting, motionless crew; and the smoke from the slow-match in every tub wafted in a thin blue haze along the long range of cannon.

Graham was pacing up and down with a quick uneven step. 'Is he going to be all night?' he said aloud, looking at the watch in his hand. 'All night? All night?'

A quarter of an endless hour, and all the time the sharp smell of burning match in their nostrils. Another dozen turns and the Commodore could bear it no longer.

'A gun for the boat,' he cried, and again a shot whipped across the *Medea*'s bows.

Osborne appeared on the Spanish deck, clambered down into the boat, came aboard the *Indefatigable*, shaking his head. His face was pale and tense. 'Admiral Bustamente's compliments, sir,' he said to the Commodore, 'but he cannot entertain your proposals. He cannot consent to being detained. He nearly yielded when I spoke of Godoy,' he said to Stephen, aside. 'He hates him.'

'Let me go across, sir,' cried Stephen. 'There is still time.'

'No, sir,' cried the Commodore, a wild, furious glare in his face. 'He has had his time. Mr Carrol, lay me across her bows.'

'Lee braces – ' The cry was drowned by the *Mercedes*'s crashing broadside as she fired straight into the *Amphion*.

'Signal close engagement,' said the Commodore, and the vast bay roared and echoed with a hundred guns. A great pall of smoke formed at once, rising and drifting away south-west, and within the pall the flashes of the guns followed one another in a continuous blaze of lightning. An enormous din, trembling heart and spine: Stephen stood there near the mainmast, with his hands behind his back, looking up and down; there was the cruel taste of powder in his mouth, and in his bosom he felt the rising fierce emotion of a bull-fight – the furious cheering of the gun-crews was invading him. Then the cheering was cut off, drowned, annihilated by a blast so huge that it wiped out thought and almost consciousness: the *Mercedes* blew up in a fountain of brilliant orange light that pierced the sky.

Spars, great shapeless timbers rained down out of the pillar of smoke, a severed head, and now through their fall there was the roar of guns again. The *Amphion* had moved up to the leeward side of the *Medea*, and the Spaniard was between two fires.

489

Cheer upon cheer, a rolling fire, and the powder-boys ran by in an unbroken stream. Cheers, and then one greater than the rest, quite different, a great exultant cry 'She's struck! The admiral has struck!'

The fire was slackening all along the line. Only the *Lively* was still hammering the *Clara*, while the *Medusa* was sending a few shots after the distant *Fama*, who, having struck, had nevertheless borne up: she was flying, uninjured, under a press of sail to leeward.

A few minutes later the *Clara*'s colours came down. The *Lively* shot ahead alongside the *Indefatigable* and Jack hailed the Commodore. 'Give you joy, sir. May I go in chase?'

'Thankee, Aubrey,' called the Commodore. 'Chase for all you are worth – she has the treasure aboard. Crack on: we are all chewed up.'

'May I have Dr Maturin, sir? My surgeon is aboard the prize.'

'Yes, yes. Bear a hand, there. Don't let her get away, Aubrey, do you hear me?'

'Aye aye, sir. Briskly the cutter, now.'

The *Lively* wore clear of the crippled *Amphion*, just shaving her bowsprit, sheeted home her topgallants and headed south-west. The *Fama*, untouched in her masts and rigging, was already three miles off, stretching away for a band of deeper blue, a stronger wind that might carry her to the Canaries, or allow her to double back by night for Algeciras.

'Well, old Stephen,' cried Jack, hauling him inboard by main force, 'that was a hearty brush, eh? No bones broke, I trust? All sober and correct? Why, your face is black with powder-smoke. Go below – the gun-room will lend you a basin until the cabin is set to rights – wash, and we will go on with our breakfast as soon as the galley fire is lit again. I will be with you once we have knotted and spliced the worst of the danger.'

Stephen looked at him curiously. He was bolt upright,

larger than life, and he seemed fairly to glow with light. 'It was a necessary stroke,' said Stephen.

'Indeed it was,' said Jack. 'I do not know much about politics, but it was a damned necessary stroke for me. No, I don't mean that,' he cried, seeing Stephen jut out his lower lip and look away. 'I mean she let fly at us, and if we had not replied, why truly, we should have been in a pretty mess. She dismounted two guns with her first broadside. Though to be sure,' he added with a delighted chuckle, 'it was necessary in the other meaning too. Come, go below, and I will join you presently. We shall not be up with her –' nodding towards the distant *Fama* ' – much before noon, if that.'

Stephen went down into the cockpit. He had been in several actions, but this was the first time he had ever heard laughter coming from the place where men paid for what went on on deck. Mr Floris's two assistants and three patients were sitting on chests round the midshipmen's table, where the fourth patient, a simple fracture of the femur, had just been splinted and bandaged: he was telling them how in his haste he had left the rammer in his gun; it had been fired straight into the *Clara*'s side, and Mr Dashwood, seeing it sticking there, had spoken quite sharp and sarcastic – 'It shall be stopped from your pay, Bolt,' says he, 'you wicked dog.'

'Good morning, gentlemen,' said Stephen. 'Since Mr Floris is not aboard, I have come to see whether I may be of any assistance.'

The surgeon's mates leapt up; they became extremely grave, endeavoured to hide their bottle, assured him of their great obligation, but these men represented the whole of the butcher's bill – two splinter wounds, superficial, one musket-ball, and this femur.

'Apart from John Andrews and Bill Owen, who lost the number of their mess, in consequence of the figure-head of that old *Mercedes* cutting 'em in two,' observed the femur.

'Which she fired very wild, though willing,' said another seaman. 'And mostly at our rigging. Do you know, sir, we thumbed in seventeen broadsides in eight and twenty minutes, by Mr Dashwood's watch. Seventeen broadsides in just short of a glass!'

The *Lively*, knotting and splicing, fetched the *Fama*'s wake and settled down to a serious, a grave and concentrated stern-chase. They were a little short-handed, for want of the prize-crew and Mr Simmons aboard the *Clara*, and when Stephen walked into the cabin he found it still cleared for action, the guns still warm, the smell of battle, a Spanish eighteen-pound ball rolling among the splinters, under the gaping hole it had made in the *Lively*'s side; the place bare and deserted, a clean sweep fore and aft apart from half the forward bulkhead and a single chair, upon which there sat the Spanish captain, staring at the pommel of his sword.

He rose and made a distant bow. Stephen stepped up and introduced himself, speaking French; he said that he was sure Captain Aubrey would wish don Ignacio to take a little refreshment – what might he offer? Chocolate, coffee, wine?

'Damn it, I had clean forgot him,' said Jack, appearing in the gutted cabin. 'Stephen, this is the captain of the *Clara*. Monsieur, j'ai l'honneur de introduire une amie, le Dr Maturin: Dr Maturin, l'espagnol capitaine, don Garcio. Please explain that I beg he will take a little something – vino, chocolato, aguardiente?'

With immovable gravity the Spaniard bowed and bowed again; he was extremely grateful, but he would take nothing for the moment. A stilted conversation followed, ragging on until Jack had the idea of begging don Ignacio to rest in the first lieutenant's cabin until dinner time.

'I had clean forgot him,' he said again, returning. 'Poor devil: I know what it feels like. Life scarcely worth living, for a while. I made him keep his sword; it takes away a little of the sting, and he fought as well as he could.

But dear Lord, it makes you feel low. Killick, how much mutton is there left?'

'Two legs, sir; and the best part of the scrag end. There's a nice piece of sirloin, sir; plenty for three.'

'The mutton, then: and Killick, lay for four – the silver plates.'

'Four, sir? Aye aye, sir: four it is.'

'Let us take our coffee on to the quarterdeck: that poor don Garcio haunts me. By the way, Stephen, you have not congratulated me. The *Clara* struck to us, you know.'

'I wish you joy, my dear. I do indeed. I wish you may not have bought it too high. Come, give me the tray.'

The squadron and the prizes were far astern; the *Medusa* too had been detached to chase the *Fama*, but she was a great way off, hull down. The Spaniard seemed to be about the same distance ahead as when they began, or even a little more, but the Livelies looked quite unconcerned as they hurried about with fresh cordage, blocks, and bales of sailcloth, casting a casual eye at the chase from time to time. The ease and freedom of battle were still about the decks; there was a good deal of talk, particularly from the topmen re-reaving the rigging high above, and laughter. Quite unbidden a carpenter's mate, padding by with a rough-pole on his shoulder, said to Jack, 'It won't be long now, sir.'

'They smashed most of our stuns'l booms,' observed Jack, 'and we never touched one of theirs. Just wait till we rig 'em out.'

'She seems to be running extremely fast,' said Stephen.

'Yes. She is a flyer, certainly: they say she cleaned her bottom at the Grand Canary, and she has the sweetest lines. There! See, she's heaving her guns overboard. You see the splash? And another. She will be starting her water over the side presently. You remember how we pumped and pulled in the *Sophie*? Ha, ha. You heaved on your sweep like a hero, Stephen. *She* cannot sweep, however; no, no, *she* cannot sweep. There goes the last of her starboard guns. See how she draws away now – a charming sailer; one of the best they have.'

'Yet you mean to catch her? The *Medusa* is falling far behind.'

'I do not like to show away, Stephen, but I will bet you a dozen of any claret you choose to name against a can of ale that we lay her aboard before dinner. You may not think it, but her only chance of escape is a ship of the line heaving up ahead, or our carrying a mast away. Though she may wing us, too, if she keeps her chasers.'

'Will you not touch on wood when you say that? I take your wager, mind.'

Jack looked secretly at him. The dear creature's spirits were recovering a little: he must have been sadly shocked by that explosion. 'No,' he said. 'This time I shall defy fate: I did so, in any case, when I desired Killick to lay four places. The fourth is for the captain of the *Fama*. I shall invite him. I shall not give him back his sword, however, it was a shabby thing to do, to strike and then run.'

'All ready, sir,' said Mr Dashwood.

'Capital. capital: that was brisk work. Rig 'em out, Mr Dashwood, if you please.'

On either side of the *Lively*'s topgallants, topsails and courses there appeared her studdingsails, broadening her great spread of canvas with a speed, a perfect efficiency that made the *Fama*'s heart sink and die.

'There goes her water,' said the master, who had her scuppers fixed in his glass.

'I believe you may set water-sails,' said Jack, 'and clew up the mizen tops'l.'

Now the *Lively* began to lean forward, throwing up the water with her forefoot so that it raced creaming right down her side to join her wake. Now she was really showing her paces; now she was eating the wind out of the *Fama*; and the distance narrowed. Never a sail that was not drawing perfectly, attended every moment by

494

the crew – the now silent crew. A smooth, steady, urgent progression, the very height of sailing.

The *Fama* had almost everything abroad already, but now she tried her driver too, boomed far out. Jack and all the officers on the quarterdeck shook their heads simultaneously: it would never answer – it would not set well with the wind so far aft. She began to steer wild, and simultaneously they all nodded. A yaw that lost her two hundred yards – her wake was no longer a straight line.

'Mr Dashwood,' said Jack, 'the gunner may try the bow gun. I should like to win my bet.' He looked at his watch. 'It is a quarter to one.'

The starboard bow-gun spoke out, ringing faint after the din of battle: a plume of water astern of the *Fama*, white against the blue. The next, a very deliberate shot, was well pitched up, some thirty yards to one side of her. Another, and this must have passed low over her deck, for she yawed again, and now the *Lively* was coming up hand over hand.

The interval before the next gun was reaching its close: their ears were ready for the crash. But while they hung up there waiting for it there was an immense tumultuous cheering forward. It spread aft in a flash: the lieutenant came running through the crowd of men, pushing through them as they shook hands and clapped one another on the back. He took off his hat, and said, 'She has struck, sir, if you please.'

'Very good, Mr Dashwood. Be so kind as to take possession and send her captain back at once. I expect him to dinner.'

The *Lively* raced up, turned into the wind, folded her wings like a bird and lay athwart the *Fama*'s hawse. The boat splashed down, crossed, and returned. The Spanish captain came up the side, saluted, presented his sword with a bow: Jack passed it to Bonden, just behind him, and said, 'Do you speak English, sir?'

'A little, sir,' said the Spaniard.

495

'Then I should be very happy to have your company at dinner, sir. It is waiting in the cabin.'

They sat at the elegant table in the transformed cabin. The Spaniards behaved extremely well; they ate well, too, having been down to biscuit and chick-peas these last ten days; and as the courses followed one another their perfect dignity relaxed into something far more human. The bottles came and went: the tension wore away and away – talk flowed free in Spanish, English and a sort of French. There was even laughter and interruption, and when at last the noble pudding gave way to comfits, nuts and port, Jack sent the decanter round, desiring them to fill up to the brim; and raising his glass he said, 'Gentlemen, I give you a toast. I beg you will drink Sophia.'

'Sophia!' cried the Spanish captains, holding up their glasses.

'Sophie,' said Stephen. 'God bless her.'